Dear Joyce,

I hope you enjoy reading this book as much as I love writing it!

THE RIPPLE OF STONES

Kathryn Rankin Covington

♡ Katy

Birch Tree Press

BIRCH
TREE
PRESS

This book is dedicated to my children, my loved ones, the women who walked before me, and my husband, who looked at me with his blue eyes and told me to write it. Most of all, this work is dedicated to every person who dares to create.

PROLOGUE

The water is irresistible. Twinkling, blinking, it consumes her attention. Leaning over the edge of the dock, she can see the bottom. The little sailboat creaks in its mooring, and voices drift from the circle of adults on the dock. All a reassuring lull.

She dips her tiny palm into the lake. Light traces countless connections along its surface, a million paths in its depths. The soft reflection brings blessings to her little face. Birches and pines line the distant shore and the sky seems to rise endlessly. Sparkles pulse across the water and she reaches out, hoping to catch brilliance in her hand. She tips, she tumbles.

Brigid is subsumed in a watery world.

Blood blooms in the water. The old wooden dock has torn at her between her shoulders. Miniature sunbursts appear at the surface of the water, each spreading gold tendrils outward. It is quiet, peaceful. Warm. She floats downward, until the silty bottom wraps her in its embrace. Little blue eyes open in wonder.

The sunbursts above merge into a circle, gathering all the colors of the water. Eternity reaches out to her and she smiles, closing her eyes.

A dark streak slashes through the water, scattering the light. Noises echo from above as the object plunges toward her. She sees the eyes first, twin pools of terror. Limbs rip through the water with fierce animal love. Strong arms scoop her from her sandy cradle. Up, up, up, she rises in a torrent of bubbles. The sparkles shatter as they erupt through the surface. Her ears sting and her chest bursts with agony. She is laid onto the hard, splintery dock. Coughing, crying, the water spills from her body. They rub her with a towel, shrieking as they see the gash between her shoulders. She is lifted up, held close, another towel pressing the blood.

"How could you?"

The air vibrated with a mother's scream.

"But you knew! You saved her. Love always saves."

CHAPTER 1

Brigid sighed and closed her classroom door. The wheeled crate filled with crayon drawings, books, and supplies refused to glide gracefully down the hallway. Brigid gave it a kick.

"Have a great weekend!" She flashed a polite smile to the bespeckled lady whose stern expression fooled no one.

"You too, honey. Get some rest." Mrs. Dunlap paused her march down the hallway to give Brigid a once over. She had seen many teachers simply burn out and shook her head at this young one. Brigid Firth was an excellent teacher; clearly at home in the classroom. It was the expression on her face every time she closed that door that left the principal concerned.

Brigid heaved the crate into the old sedan and collapsed into the driver's seat. Teaching first grade was exhilarating but exhausting. Twenty-four squirming bodies; their tiny minds expanding every minute. Part of Brigid's job was to constantly observe not only their academic process, but the myriad of social threads webbing their way across tables. Some of her little friends ate breakfast every morning before school; some could only rely on the free-and-reduced lunch they received at noon. Brigid kept a drawer full of cheese crackers for children whose parents "forgot" to pack a morning snack.

It was a hard life on the Peninsula. Scenery was profound, but jobs were scarce. Many parents in her district relied on the weather to make the crops grow and the finicky tourism season to provide enough to sustain through the winter. For years, the sun did not shine enough to bring the bounty.

Brigid smiled, thinking of little tousle-headed Riley, tongue sticking out of his mouth as he diligently practiced his writing. These little ones knew hard work and patience. They understood discipline. She knew that her crate contained stories of birds in the field and the velvet muzzle of the cattle. In fact, the school year ended in May so that the students could help on the farms. Math came easily to the Peninsula kids; measurement was second nature. Most of the students had chores at home: feeding animals every morning, doling out seed. Many overheard parents bicker over the budget.

These kids adored their enthusiastic Miss Firth, especially her stories. Brigid adored them in turn, and praised their honesty and tenacity. In her classroom, kindness counted for everything. She loved them all, and they loved her.

The car coasted down the hill. Brigid drove with the windows open and the breeze pulled wavy strands from her ponytail. The fields of cherry trees sent a sweetness in the air that was almost palpable. Pink and white blooms took their final bows, giving way to the tart berry that was a pillar of the Peninsula economy. Forests of maple, birch, and pine curved over the county road in gentle, steadfast embrace. Everything that was emerging from the ground burst verdant, the last buried flowers dreamed their dreams.

A rainbow emerged at afternoon recess, making her students dance with the glory of it all.

Rosie had learned to read today. The hours spent curled up in Brigid's lap with a book had finally paid off. Rosie was the last student in class to learn to read. The words and letters finally met their connections as she pulled her dark blonde locks. Her tiny wrists were dotted with bruises, and she winced moving her finger over the words, holding down the paper. She was too little to have hunched shoulders, Brigid thought.

Brigid had already met with the principal and the social worker. Rosie's father had finally agreed to come in after the police intervened. Raising children is frustrating, didn't she know? He would do better, he said. Rosie came in with a new dress and sparkly shoes that fell apart after a week on the playground. Brigid wondered if Rosie would get punished for that too.

Big Omann Lake burst into Brigid's view. Its indigo waters would still be icy cold in June. She ached for a respite on the beach, gazing at the horizon or searching for jewel-toned rocks under her feet. But tonight, duty called. She steered the car out of the countryside and into the town of Domhnall Hills. Family dinner loomed.

CHAPTER 2

In her dressing room, Lynn Firth placed a manicured hand on her trim waist. Even after all these years, she felt the familiar ache of an unfilled womb. Lynn and her husband Kelsey had wanted a big family. They had built this house, overlooking the city, with its amenities and wonderful school system, planning to fill it with children. Brigid was their first and they were thrilled to tuck her into the neatly appointed nursery. Twenty-four years later, the extra bedrooms in the "children's hallway" remained empty.

After Brigid's fall at the dock, Lynn had gone into very early labor. The baby was lost. A second girl.

There would be no more.

Lynn dabbed the tears from her eyes, furious that the old pain could still feel so scalding. She looked at herself in the mirror, seeing the high cheekbones brushed with golden highlighter and the frown lines at her lips. She adjusted the simple gold necklace with the inlaid pearl and pushed the matching teardrop earrings into her ears. Brushing imaginary dust from the tabletop, she straightened her shoulders and descended the stairs.

The massive entryway seemed to dwarf Brigid as she stood at the bottom of the stairs. Lynn looked at her daughter, her only child, seeing the buoyant auburn curls escaping from a messy ponytail. She looked past her daughter and saw through the two-story windows Brigid's old car parked partway on the lawn. That damn jalopy, thought Lynn. She and Kelsey had intended to buy her a practical, safe new car when she graduated college. Brigid, in a rare display of stubbornness, had insisted on buying the rusted sedan with 200,000 miles on it from her measly savings from her teaching job.

Brigid felt her mother's eyes assessing her and self-consciously tucked a stray curl behind her ear. Eyes turned down, she stepped toward Lynn and submitted to her mother's featherlight hug. Lynn patted Brigid's back with her soft, manicured hand precisely twice, paused as if to say something, and pulled away.

"Well. Brigid, how was school?"

"Good." Brigid forced herself to concentrate. The announcement she planned for tonight was nerve-racking and making her more scatterbrained than usual. What had happened at school that day? Recalling the big moment at last, she smiled. "My little Rosie learned to read today."

"That's excellent," Lynn said. "All children should read. Is this the girl with the abusive father?"

"Yes." Brigid shuddered, thinking of the man's red-veined face and overstuffed arms. The memory of him towering over her, yelling in the school conference room made her swallow hard. "Have you spoken to the police?" Lynn asked.

"Twice."

"And the child still lives with him?"

"Apparently." Brigid's shoulders sank and tears threatened behind her eyes. "I wish I could bring her home."

At the sight of her daughter's tears, Lynn's lips drew into a thin line. "The students are only your responsibility at school, Brigid."

Brigid stared at her mother. Always a lecture. Always a pronouncement. She was so tired of being lectured. Every movement she made in her life, it seemed, Lynn was looming like a peak of grandeur, ready to pronounce judgment. Brigid met her mother's eyes with a steely gaze. "I'm aware of that."

"The rest of their lives are not your problem," Lynn continued.

"It becomes my problem if it affects their ability to learn."

"It is <u>not</u> your problem," Lynn asserted, leaning forward toward her daughter. Lynn's eyes began to widen, she felt the familiar anger rising. Lynn took a deep breath through her nostrils, making her shoulder blades lower and soften. With a nearly imperceptible shake of her head, she gained control of herself. She forced her lips into a smile. "You've spoken to the police and to the social worker, I assume. You've done your job. Now let them do theirs. And please come help me with the dinner. I haven't had time to make a salad; there are carrots in the fridge."

Brigid swallowed, backing down yet again. It wasn't worth it to fight with Lynn. No one ever won.

She crossed the threshold into the kitchen, padding along in her mother's crisp footsteps and walked over to the double-door, stainless steel monster. Every item inside the refrigerator was itemized and labeled in clear Pyrex containers. Not a trace of original packaging remained. Lynn preferred her belongings encased in glass. Ignoring the carrots, Brigid found a bottle of chardonnay in the door and pulled it out.

"Bridge!" Kelsey burst through the door.

"Hey Dad!" An enormous grin spread across Brigid's chastened face.

"The angel of education has arrived! Good God, that smile! Brigid, if the sun retired, your smile could light up the world." Kelsey scooped his daughter up into a giant bear hug, and she leaned in, happily absorbing his effortless affection. "How was your week? How are the kiddos?" Before she could answer his question, Kelsey threw an arm around his wife who was efficiently chopping lettuce, landing a kiss on her coiffed hair. Brigid swallowed her answer as she watched her parents. Half of Lynn's mouth begrudgingly rose into a smile as she kept her eyes firmly on her task.

"Alright, Kelsey. That's enough. Is the grill going? How long until the chicken is ready?"

"Whenever you want, my love. You say the word and I will make your dreams come true." Kelsey released his daughter, dipped his wife and planted another kiss on her lips. "That is, if you're dreaming of grilled chicken." Kelsey let out a loud guffaw at his own joke. Brigid could feel her father's buried desperation for levity, for an audience, for something. So she laughed too. "Dad, I will throw up if you two keep up the PDA. And this is Mom's good wine I'm drinking, so please stop."

"Hey honey, no whining while you're wine-ing!" Kelsey laughed heartily again and pointed to her glass. Brigid shook her head, exhausted already from participating in this vaudeville act of Family Harmony. She was almost relieved when her mother shattered the frivolity.

"Kelsey, please! Go and start the grill."

"Yes ma'am!" Kelsey said. "If mama ain't happy, ain't nobody happy, isn't that right?" Kelsey clapped his big hands together and grabbed the platter of chicken, whistling tunelessly as he made his way out to the grill.

Lynn turned and arched an eyebrow at her daughter's glass. "And Brigid, if teaching is driving you to drink, there are many other career options."

Brigid set down her glass and gazed out into the great room.

Observation Pointe. The subdivision sprawled over the biggest hill in Domhnall Hills. Every pristine home overlooked the city center. There were several styles of homes on display, all McMansion in breed. Roof lines were as prevalent as the polished woodwork; many homes had multiple gables capping gray wooden siding. Kitchens were glaciers of marble, beveled cupboards were immaculate white or rich earthy stains. Multiple rooms for sitting ensured that no member of any family would need to share time and space with another human. Plantation shutters veiled the heart of each home from the peering eyes of nature. That is, what little nature was allowed to stay. The forested hill had been completely clear-cut when the neighborhood was built, and only measly little new trees and sliced boxwoods remained in the front gardens of the homes. The absence of breeze rustling the leaves made Brigid feel like she could not breathe.

Lynn sighed pointedly and snapped Brigid out of her reverie. "Brigid? What is going on with the salad?"

"What?" answered Brigid, peeling her gaze away from the enormous picture window.

"Never mind," answered Lynn, taking the carrots from under Brigid's limp hand and efficiently chopping them into equal slices. She brushed them from the cutting board into the bowl and reached for the chardonnay bottle, pouring herself a full glass.

"Sorry, Mom," said Brigid, taking the cutting board and knife. "I'll wash these."

"Mmm." Lynn answered. She took a long sip from her glass, trying to calm her nerves. She would present her plan to Brigid over dinner. Calmly, she had promised Kelsey. It would be their daughter's choice, as he had insisted. But what other choice could a rational person make than to accept a little help and move out of that dirty little rental.

"Lynn!" Kelsey opened the sliding glass door and popped his head in. "You got a platter for this?"

"I got it, Dad!" Happy for an escape, Brigid took one of the neatly displayed white China platters from the cupboard and handed it over to her father. He tugged on her ponytail in thanks.

Brigid returned to the kitchen and scooped the rice pilaf resting on the stove into a serving dish. Lynn stood next to her silently and followed suit with the pan of green beans almondine. Brigid shrank in her mother's silence. This was not a comfortable silence. Always, she was waiting for the next shoe to drop. She tapped her pocket reflexively. The letter was still poking out, though the envelope had grown soft from her clammy hands.

"Whatcha got there, kiddo? Did you bring your paycheck home to your old parents like a good child?" Kelsey burst into the room, sucking the silence away. "Here's the chicken, ladies!" With a flourish, he plopped the platter on the table. Brigid and Lynn carried the serving dishes over to join him.

Wine was poured and the sound of clinking silverware and polite chewing filled the room. Finally, Lynn set her glass down decidedly.

"Brigid," she began. "Your father and I have a proposal for you." Brigid's shoulders immediately tensed. Whenever her mother was about to inform her of a decision, she took a formal tone. Brigid checked her pocket again, grasping the letter.

Kelsey saw the move and remembered that his question had gone unanswered. He put an apologetic hand out to his wife. "Why don't we wait a minute, Lynn?" he asked. "What is that, Brigid? What do you keep fiddling with?"

Brigid found that her voice was gone. Almost without thought, she drew out the envelope and placed it on the table.

Lynn's eyes widened as she saw the handwriting. Her own father's handwriting. The father she had held at a distance, the father whose letters and Christmas cards went into the bin unread.

Brigid's grandfather.

CHAPTER 3

"It's from Grandpa," Brigid said.

Lynn's hand shook imperceptibly on her wine glass. Brigid's breath came short and shallow as she waited for her mother's inevitable reprimand.

Lynn kept her lips pursed together.

Brigid forged on. "He wants me to come live with him for the summer. He says he misses me. I could stay at Cairn Cottage — spend the summer at the lake. Swimming, sailing..."

"You don't know how to sail," spat Lynn. Brigid sat back in her chair, feeling as if she'd been slapped. Kelsey took his wife's hand, hearing the fear behind her harsh tone.

"Let's just let Brigid tell us what Morgan has to say," he said gently.

"Mom, I sail every year when we visit for..." Brigid hesitated, not wanting to mention why they returned to Cairn Cottage each July. Every year, cruelly set in the fully bloomed warmth of summer, they returned to honor the death of her Grandmother. Her mother's mother. Brigid couldn't bring herself to see the old pain flash across her mother's face, covered quickly, as always, by anger. Brigid cleared her throat and willed herself to speak calmly.

"Grandpa has been teaching me to sail since I was a little girl. I know what I'm doing. Besides, it's only a Sunfish; practically a paddle board with a sail." She smiled at the thought of coasting across the surface of the waves, soft breeze in her hair, the main sheet twisted around her palm as she adjusted the sail, dancing with the wind.

Lynn saw the familiar faraway look pass across her daughter's face and it made her panic rise. She had seen that look so often before in her own aunt's beautiful, lively face, and in her late mother's eyes when she plucked the stones from the lake shore and meditated on them with gentle reverence. No — thought Lynn, as the panic rose through her. That life was full of foolishness. She had worked too hard to remove herself from it, to prevent her only daughter from falling prey to it, from even knowing it. She had convinced Kelsey to move to the city, to make a life that was orderly, sensible. And they had been happy here. Brigid had been happy. At least, Lynn thought, she had been happy to follow the careful path Lynn had set out for her. The only rebellion she had dared to make was to choose teaching rather than law or education administration as Lynn had wanted. And then there was that business with Matt...

"Let's see the letter." Kelsey's voice cut through Lynn's thoughts. She stared at him, eyes wide with betrayal as he reached for the envelope. "Do you mind if I read it?" He asked Brigid. She nodded, unable to keep her eyes off her mother.

Kelsey reached for the glasses in his shirt pocket and carefully drew the letter from the envelope. "Such beautiful penmanship," he said, smiling warmly. "They don't teach that anymore, do they?"

"Kelsey." Harsh warning dripped from Lynn's tone. Kelsey only gazed at her calmly.

"Let's just read it," he said.

Brigid took a strong gulp of her wine.

My Dearest Brigid,

I would like to invite you to live at Cairn Cottage for the summer.

I feel that I have not been able to get to know you as a loving Grandfather should throughout these long years. I apologize for that, and take the blame completely upon myself.

But I do love you, Brigid, more than you might know. There are things I would like to tell you. Stories about the family, your dear late Grandmother, and the lake. These stories, if I do not share them, may pass with me as I go. I would rest easier in my old age if you would be kind enough to listen to an old man's stories and carry them with you in your heart.

I have taken the liberty of fixing up the old loft bedroom for you, and you would have use of your own bathroom as well. (If I am truly honest, as all good men strive to be, I have had much help from my good friend Graham's wife Emma, herself a great friend as well.) I know you must remember them both, and David, who you often see on your annual visit.

I know a cottage isolated on the Peninsula may not seem like an exciting prospect for a young woman. However, I have observed a unique tranquility about you which leads me to believe you may enjoy a summer here. My wish, of course, is that you treat Cairn Cottage as your home, entertaining friends and family whenever you wish.

I look forward to hearing from you, Brigid, and if I am lucky enough, seeing your sweet face.

With all my love,

Grandpa Morgan

Kelsey set the letter down and glanced at his wife. Her teeth were grinding with fear and frustration. "No," she said.

Brigid only saw the glare in her mother's eyes. "What do you mean, 'no'?" she asked.

Lynn met her daughter's eyes with passion. "I mean no. It's a ridiculous idea. Unnecessary."

"Why?" Brigid asked incredulously.

"Why?" Panic rose in Lynn, turning her tone knife-like as she scrambled for an answer she could actually say. "Why? Because you have an apartment? You have a lease?"

"You hate that apartment, Mom," Brigid answered. "You tell me all the time. You think it's seedy."

"It is seedy!" Lynn was practically shouting. Brigid raised her eyebrows. "Well," Lynn stammered, grasping for control. "Why don't you live here then? You have your own room here, nicer than that moldy old loft at Cairn Cottage. And all the amenities of the city. Domhnall Hills is a much more appropriate place to live."

"I need a break, Mom." Brigid sighed and looked down on her plate. She was ashamed of herself that at twenty-four years old, she still cowered in submission to her mother's demands. But this time she was resolved. "I need some peace and quiet. I need… nature."

"What you need," hissed Lynn, "Is not to break your lease. It's a foolish decision that will follow you forever."

Brigid looked at her father. "I'm month-to-month these days, actually." Kelsey straightened in his chair. His eyes glittered with pride as he grinned at his daughter. "Ever since you said it was seedy, Mom, I figured I should make a change. I was able to negotiate my terms."

Lynn stared at her daughter. Who taught her to negotiate a lease?

"And, actually, I gave notice to the landlord last month. I'm already packed." Brigid took a deep breath and reached across the table for the letter. She put it in her pocket and forced herself to meet her mother's eyes.

"I'm moving to Cairn Cottage tomorrow."

CHAPTER 4

Birch trees canopied the two-track driveway. Brigid navigated through the dappled sunlight and drove into the tiny round-a-bout. Tender summer air enveloped her as she stepped out of the sedan. Hand on the handle of the screen door, she paused, heart racing. The smell of old pine walls, bacon grease, and coffee beckoned. Taking a deep breath, she pulled and the door squeaked her arrival.

"Hello? Grandpa?"

No answer except the lapping of the waves against the shore. Stepping into the dark hallway, her eyes took in the bench with various shoes tossed underneath, the giant pewter key upon which hung jumbles of keys, the hat and jacket tossed haphazardly on the pegs. Brigid walked past the master bedroom and the steep, dark staircase and into the kitchen. Setting her purse down on the formica island, she scanned the great room. Mildewed vases of weedy blooms were scattered among the tables. Piles of stones were stacked on every surface. Peeking into the utility room, she shook her head at the bundle of sticks laid on the radiator.

Returning to the kitchen, Brigid lifted a plastic tumbler out of the cupboard and filled it with ice from the freezer. Tubs of ice cream were tucked into the freezer drawer. She found gallons of orange juice and milk, a loaf of rye bread, some ham and leftover bacon tossed in the fridge. Signs of life, surely, but there was one fireproof test to determine whether Grandpa Morgan was in residence. She opened the cupboard to the right of the sink and sure enough, a half-full bottle of scotch greeted her. Brigid smiled. She splashed some into her glass, and filled it to the top with tap water. She made a second drink, this time with a larger dollop of the amber liquid and a splash of water. Opening the old screen door with her hip, she carried both glasses outside. Grandpa must be on the dock.

Her footsteps made the wooden boards creak, startling the old man out of his reverie.

"Brigid!" He rose from his seat on the circular platform.

"Hello Grandpa." Brigid navigated the curved pathway, her face blossoming into a radiant smile as she reached the seating platform. Morgan wrapped his granddaughter in a gentle embrace. After several moments, he stepped back to face her. "Well. I don't think I've ever seen a more beautiful sight in all my life. Welcome home."

Brigid blushed.

"I'm so very glad you decided to come. It's time we spent some quality time together. Sit, sit!" Brigid lowered herself into one of the green plastic chairs and set the drinks down on the giant spool that served as a table.

"I have all the stuff I could carry in my car," she said. "My dad is coming over later with a few more things."

"Good, good." Morgan patted her knee and took a sip of his drink. "And your mother? Is she coming?"

Brigid raised an eyebrow and gazed out at the drop-off that lay a few feet beyond the round dock.

"Mmm." Morgan looked out at the lake and then over at his granddaughter. The resemblance tore at his heart. Clearing his throat, he said with a smile, "Drink it in, my dear. Soak in the healthy lake air!"

Brigid obeyed, taking a deep breath. Her back sank comfortably into the chair and she let the memories wash over her. The round dock was one of her favorite places in the world, and she had only been able to sneak out here once a year. One Saturday every August, her mother would begrudgingly pack several bottles of wine, a fresh salad, and the family into the car and drive to Cairn Cottage to celebrate the life of Shannon

Ayers. Lynn's late mother. The grandmother Brigid had never really known.

Each visit, Brigid would always take a moment to walk out to the very end of the dock, suspended over the drop-off. There was something about being alone, surrounded by the wind and the waves. She felt at peace. Connected to something greater than herself.

All the neighbors on Little Owrawn Lake had variations of spaces like this: a long dock extending over the deep drop-off, and a seating area with chairs, a wooden spool bolted to the dock boards, and an umbrella. The Ayers dock was unique in that its pathway was curved, and the seating area was circular. Harder to create, but inclusive.

The breeze made goosebumps rise on Brigid's arms; she shivered. Grandpa Morgan nodded.

"It's a north wind today. Chilly. Has been for about a week. But you'll bring the warmer weather, I know it." Morgan reached into his pocket for a handful of stones and shook them absentmindedly. "Yes, the warmth will come soon." He gazed at his granddaughter for a long moment. "Now. Tell me all about your classroom. I want to know about each of your students."

Brigid looked at her grandfather. His eyes were so kind as he leaned forward to hear her story. She lifted her drink and took a sip, feeling her shoulders fully relax. Leaning back, she told the story of her year. Grandpa Morgan listened, nodded, wiped his eyes with a handkerchief as he erupted into laughter at the shenanigans she described. When she got to Rosie, he listened intently. It was as if he was absorbing the pain, hers and the child's. When she got to the part about Rosie's bruises, Brigid broke off abruptly, looking at the horizon to control the onset of tears. Grandpa Morgan reached out a gnarled hand.

"You gave that child love, Brigid. Look at me." Tears escaped as she glanced into his indigo eyes – so like her mothers. "You gave love. And kindness. And light. And now she knows."

Brigid swiped a hand at her tears. "Knows?"

"She knows. About love."

"You're probably right." Brigid sniffed resolutely and straightened her shoulders, swallowing hard. Watching her, Morgan felt a sadness he hadn't felt in years. Changing the subject with a brisk nod, he slapped his knee and said, "Well then. Shall we unpack your car?"

"Grandpa, I can do it. You shouldn't be lifting all my heavy boxes."

"Nonsense! What kind of gentleman would I be if I didn't assist my lovely young granddaughter with her belongings? Let's get to it and then we can fix a lovely plate of cheese and crackers for your father when he arrives."

Picking up his cane, Grandpa hobbled off the dock with a wave of his hand. Brigid watched him carefully as he set off on the curvy, nonsensical pathway, but he navigated it perfectly, wavy white locks shining in the sun.

CHAPTER 5

The creak of the mast woke her. Stretching into the chilly morning air, Brigid smiled. She could smell the coffee wafting up through the floorboards. Through the window, Brigid could see the little Sunfish sailboat through the trees. The striped sail was loose against the wind, which looked southerly and promising. Pulling on a sweatshirt she grasped the thick rope that served as a stair-rail and headed downstairs.

"Good morning, Grandpa," Brigid called across the great room.

A white head looked up from the upholstered rocker and a hardback book gently closed. "Well good morning, lovely girl," Morgan said, smiling. "There's coffee in the pot."

"How long have you been up?" Brigid asked, with a wary glance at the clock. It was eight a.m.

"Oh, a few hours," Morgan answered, plucking his cane from the arm of the chair and heaving himself up. "Old bones don't rest easy and I like to see the sun rise."

"Have you eaten?" she asked as he shuffled into the kitchen.

"Not yet." Morgan pulled out the chair at the head of the table and settled heavily into the worn corduroy cushion.

"Can I make you an English muffin?" Brigid pulled out an ancient toaster oven.

"That would be lovely," Morgan said, beaming at her. "The jam is in the refrigerator."

Brigid gathered the breakfast items and lifted two old porcelain plates from the cupboard. She had spent her first few days at Cairn Cottage cleaning grime from every surface. The toaster oven had so many crumbs in the tray, it had become a fire hazard. She brought the pot to the long dining table and re-filled her grandfather's cup before pouring a steaming cup for herself. The look of gratitude he gave her made her look away.

They ate in silence for a few moments, enjoying the view and the fresh morning air blowing in through the windows. Morgan dabbed a cloth napkin to his lips before announcing, "The Websters are getting a new Sunfish today. I thought we might go over and visit."

Brigid swallowed the last of her coffee and gave him a wary look. "Are you sure they want us there?"

"Of course, my dear!" Morgan reached over and patted her hand. "They've been dying to see you. Usually, they only get to see my brilliant granddaughter once a year. Now you can spend the whole summer getting reacquainted." Brigid looked at the waves to avoid Morgan's glance. He caught the evasion and gently called her out. "Brigid, the Websters and David are my oldest friends. They are practically family, although your mother has refused to allow you to know them as well as you should." Morgan shook his head. "They love you. They've always looked out for you. And now that you're an adult, you can make your own choices. Shall we go?"

Brigid thought that she would rather hole up at Cairn Cot-tage, reading the dusty volumes of poetry, and sailing until her arms grew weary of the lines. But it was probably time to re-enter the real world. She was a bit wary of spending time with this purported "family," but she couldn't say no to her grand-father. She sensed there was something deep and desperate in her grandfather's need for her to truly know his friends. And the Websters had always been kind to her. How bad could it be? She smiled at him and nodded her assent.

"Lovely!" Morgan exclaimed. "We'll bring a bottle of wine to celebrate the new ship."

Brigid tossed her head back with a soft laugh.

"Ship, Grandpa? It's more like a dingy. About one and a half people can fit at best."

"Brigid, how dare you!" Grandpa Morgan put his hand to his chest in mock horror. "I don't see you complaining about our fine vessel when you're out conquering the waves every afternoon."

"I know, I know," she said, another genuine smile reaching across her face. "I'm just teasing. I love our Sunfish. Let me know when we plan to go over. I'll make a little plate of something to bring with the wine. An appetizer or something. What would you like?"

"A tub of bar cheese and crackers will suit me just fine," said Morgan, reveling in the company of his granddaughter.

"A tub of bar cheese and a plate of crackers suits my culinary skills just fine too."

"It's a deal," said Morgan. "My dear, you are a treasure," he said as she piled his dish on top of her own. "The boat is being delivered at eleven, so if you want to take a morning sail, young lady, leave those dishes to me and get out on the water!"

CHAPTER 6

The wind was ripe for sailing that morning. Brigid whipped across the lake, eyes peeled for wayward tourists on rented jet skis. When she steered the boat toward Cairn Cottage, the breeze blew her so fast that she jumped off of the hull and pushed back against the wind. Grasping the front of the sailboat, Brigid swam hard over the drop-off and waded through to the shallows to clip the sailboat to the anchor. Satisfied that the little boat was secure, Brigid quickly rubbed her legs with a towel and went into the house.

"Did you towel off?" she heard Morgan call from his armchair.

"Yes!" she called back over her shoulder as she dripped water up the stairs. From toddlerhood, she had been taught to scrub her legs off hard with a towel the minute she stepped out of Little Owrawn Lake. A bacterium existed in these waters, sprung from an unholy alliance between the chemicals from construction runoff and the snails who populated the lake bottom. If the water was left to air dry on the skin, the bacteria would penetrate and bloom into unsightly red bumps the size of a dime. The rash would itch for several days before fading away. It was nearly harmless, although young children and the elderly swimmers could become a bit lethargic if they contracted what was locally called Swimmer's Curse. Still, Brigid thought as she toweled off her thighs for a second time up in her room, it was a small price to pay for the freedom that swimming and sailing in the crystal-clear waters would bring.

Pulling a sundress over her head, she noticed the puddles of water she had dripped onto the old wood floor. She chastised herself for the mess before realizing that Grandpa Morgan would neither notice or care. She swiped at the wet spots before tossing the towel and her bathing suit over the footboard of the bed. Combing out her curly hair, Brigid glanced at herself in the spidered antique mirror. Tanned, flushed cheekbones and bright eyes looked back. She raised an eyebrow in surprise. Certainly she felt healthier and happier since arriving at Cairn Cottage, but she hadn't expected her regular pallor and bagged eyes to disappear so rapidly. She applied a bit of mascara and lipstick, then twisted in the mirror. Assured that her upper back was covered, she started to go down the stairs when a glint from the windowsill gave her pause.

Yesterday at dusk, her grandfather had set a long velvet box on the dining table and pushed it toward her. Brigid had opened it and saw a single, cushion-cut stone mounted in gold, hanging from a delicate gold chain.

"It's not a diamond," her grandfather had said quickly. "It's quartz. Less valuable to some, I suppose. But it was your grandmother's. And now I would like to give it to you." Brigid immediately demurred, but her grandfather had insisted. "This belongs to you." He had pressed the box into her hand with instructions that seemed strange to his granddaughter. Leave the box open at all times, store it within view of a window. Place it on the sill during a full moon. The light from the sun and reflection of the moon will make the stone seem brighter. Brigid had forced a smile, but when she brought the box to her room, she saw no real reason to close the lid.

Now, she took the box and turned back to the dresser and lifted the necklace out of its case, clipping it around her neck so the clear, sparkling stone nestled in the hollow of her throat. An anxious glance at her watch sitting on the dresser top sent her rushing down the stairs.

CHAPTER 7

Brigid grabbed the cheese and crackers from the kitchen, slipped her sandals on and rushed out onto the sandy wooden pathway between the cabins, the screen door slamming behind her.

"Hello David!" she called to the sinewy man on the slate blue porch.

"Well hello, Brigid! Where are you off to with that snack?"

"Heading to the Websters. Their new Sunfish is being delivered today." She walked up to the porch as her grandfather's oldest friend stood up to give her a hug.

"Tell your Grandpa hello for me. And tell him we need to go sailing." Winking at her, he snatched a handful of crackers from her bowl. "Or would you like to race with me? I've been watching you out there. You're a natural."

"Oh, I wouldn't dare." She smiled up at the tall older gentleman. "You'd leave me in the dust."

"You could do it. Would you like a cup of coffee?" David took a few more crackers out of the bowl.

"No, thank you," she said, discreetly placing the tub of cheese on top the crackers. "I'm already late."

His eyes crinkled as he smiled at her.

"Off you go, then."

Old men with kind eyes, volumes of poetry stacked next to the armchair, sailing twice a day, cheese and crackers for lunch. This was life at Little Owrawn Lake. Solitude was welcome after a year in the classroom, but she was beginning to feel isolated. Perhaps it was time to text some friends, and remember how to interact with people her own age.

The trees parted and the path opened up to reveal a steep stairway as tall as a man. Rustic stone steps led her to the Websters' sandy beach and the long, straight dock that extended over the water. Morgan was standing at the edge of the dock, ripe with anticipation. Graham Webster was chest-deep in the water, anchor held over his shoulders.

"Further east, Graham!" Grandpa Morgan called. "You sink it there, it'll blow right into the dock with a strong north wind."

Graham waded to the right another four feet. "There?" he shouted over the waves.

"Right there!" Morgan pointed to the east with his cane. "That's it."

Graham tossed the anchor over his shoulder and let it fly another short distance for good measure. White hair shimmering, he dove beneath the waves to ensure the anchor's proper placement. Following the line up the orange buoy, he resurfaced with a splash. "We're ready for her!" Graham beamed.

"Graham!" called a gentle voice from the sandy lawn. "The truck is pulling in! They're here!"

Graham swam briskly to the steps and heaved himself up. Seeing Brigid, he grinned. "Well hello, sweet girl! I see you arrived in time to see our new vessel."

"Wouldn't miss it," Brigid said, holding up the cheese and crackers.

"Ahh, and you've brought lunch! Well, let's go, let's go," Graham said, gesturing toward the staircase. Brigid bent down to set the food on the round table before glancing at her grandfather to see if he needed her arm.

"Go on, girl!" said Grandpa Morgan. "I can manage." Cane in one hand, a tree branch railing in the other, he followed Brigid up the stairs.

A white truck with SUNSET MARINA painted on the side expertly navigated the two-track driveway with the beautiful, cream-colored hull astride a gleaming silver trailer.

A sandy-haired, brawny young man hopped out of the passenger door and grinned at the assembled audience. "Hi folks! Oh wow, hey Brigid!"

Brigid barely recognized her colleague out of his usual uniform of khakis and a button down. "Chris? Hey! I didn't know you worked at the marina!" Her unaffected grin was infectious and he couldn't help but beam right back.

"Well some of us have to take a summer gig after the school year is over." He walked over and wrapped her in a big bear hug. "What have you been up to? Drinking margaritas and tanning on the dock?"

Brigid blushed, looking down at her feet. "Yeah, something like that. Recovering, you know?"

"God, we all need a break. What a year that was — those kids — wow. But hey, I thought you lived down in Domhnall Hills. What are you doing up on the Peninsula?" he asked. He seemed completely oblivious to Graham, who was shifting on his feet with impatience.

"I'm staying with my grandfather for the summer at his cabin." Brigid felt Graham's impatience and growing frustration from the moment Chris began to speak to her. "Grandpa, Emma, Graham, this is my friend Chris Mulligan. He teaches science and coaches basketball at my school. Chris, this is my grandpa, Morgan Ayers."

Before Morgan could hobble forward to shake the young man's hand, Graham stepped into the circle.

"And I am Graham Webster. The owner of that sailboat there." He pointed at the rig, chin high in the air.

"Mr. Webster. Mrs. Webster. Very nice to meet you." A deep voice made them all turn. The raven-haired man tucked his clipboard under his arm and shut the driver's side door of the truck, striding forward. He took Graham's hand and gave it a hearty shake. "I'm Gabe. I think you'll enjoy this Sunfish, sir," he said. Turning to Emma, he smiled and said, "Congratulations on the boat, ma'am. She's beautiful."

"She looks it," said Graham, striding over to run his hands

along the hull. Throwing an impish grin to Morgan, he said, "I can't wait to race this old man in his heavy old clodhopper. Play your cards right, Gabe, you could sell Morgan here a new fast boat too."

Gabe smiled and reached for Morgan's hand.

"Pleased to meet you, young man," Morgan said, leaning on his cane. "But I won't be buying a new rig anytime. Our Sunfish is just as fast as any on the water, even this beautiful, new-fangled thing. Isn't that right, Brigid?"

"Absolutely," Brigid said. Chris watched closely as his friend tried not to stare at Brigid. Was this the same shy girl who taught the crazy first graders? Hair always shoved into a ponytail, tired pallor on her face? The only time he'd seen this mixture of peace on her face and brightness in her eyes was when she would sit in the broken rocker and read stories to those little kids. And if he was being honest, that sundress did not hurt. For the first time, he noticed her curves which she apparently covered during the school year. And her tan skin — my God. He smirked at Gabe, delighted to watch his philandering friend struck dumb at the sight of sweet, reticent Miss Firth.

Chris coughed and shot a teasing glance at Brigid. "Gabe, this is my friend Brigid. She teaches first grade at the same school as me." Brigid could feel her heart racing and hoped against hope that blood was not rushing to her cheeks.

It was. The guilelessness of her scarlet cheeks struck something deep in Gabe's core. He reached out to shake her hand. "Nice to meet you, Brigid."

"You too," she said. When she raised her eyes to meet his own, a shiver ran through his body and he felt the world fall away. Brigid grasped his strong, calloused palm, in her own soft warm one, unable to move her gaze away from his hazel eyes. The leaves overhead rustled in chorus.

"Well boys, should we get her down to the lake?" Graham clapped his hands.

"Yes, Mr. Webster," Gabe said, releasing Brigid's hand quickly and clearing his throat. "Um, if you could just sign these final forms, we'll get her in the water."

Gabe handed his clipboard to Graham as Chris slapped him on the back. "If you don't mind, Mr. Webster, Gabe and I'll walk down to the beach and survey the best path to carry the boat to the water."

"Certainly, certainly," Graham said. "I'll go with you." He handed the clipboard to Emma.

"Can you get it down those stairs, young man, or would it be better to drive it to the public launch?" Grandpa Morgan called as he caned after the men.

Emma gave Brigid a studiously calm smile and said, "Shall we?" Brigid nodded, swallowing hard. The women arrived at the stairs just as Chris was clambering up from the beach.

"Oh, we can get it down there just fine, Mr. Webster. But it would be helpful if someone could push back and hold up these tree branches so we don't scratch the hull,"

"Brigid could do that, couldn't you, sweetheart?" asked Morgan with a twinkle in his eye.

"Sure, Grandpa," said Brigid, feeling Gabe's eyes on her. She found herself unable to look away from the shoreline. "Chris, just tell me when you're ready."

"Cool. If you all just stay here, Gabe and I will go unload."

Emma placed a tentative hand on Brigid's arm, snapping the younger woman out of her trance. "Brigid, I can't tell you how happy we are that you are staying at Cairn Cottage for the summer. It will be such a blessing to get to spend some real time with you." Brigid smiled politely. "You know," continued Emma, "Graham convinced me to get the new Sunfish in time for the visit from the grandbabies, although I'm sure Renee won't let Braylen or Avery near it." Brigid struggled to keep her polite smile plastered on her face at the mention of the Websters' haughty daughter. "Maybe you can come visit with her. Distract her so she can relax a bit."

"I'm sure that'd be great," Brigid lied. She watched Gabe and Chris walk down the path with the sail hoisted high above their heads. The sight of Gabe's determined look very nearly kept Brigid from remembering what an encounter with Renee Webster was like. Eight years older than Brigid, Renee was rearing her children on kale chips and anxiety. She and her banker husband had established rules for every conceivable circumstance.

Lynn, of course, loved her.

The ride home from the Firth's annual evening at Cairn Cottage would often be packed with praise for Renee's achievements and self-mastery, contrasted with Brigid's flightiness and humble teaching job. Brigid wished mightily that the other daughters of the lake people were closer to her age, or at the very least, her personality. But they were different generations; too far apart in age to be friends, and just a little too close in age to act as an extra set of aunts.

Graham advanced down the path with the rigging cradled in his arms. "They're bringing the hull!" he announced, jigging with excitement.

Brigid took her place on the stone steps, ready to lift the low-hanging pine branches out of the way. A giant grunt could be heard from the driveway, followed by a shout. "Yeah, man! We got this!" They all watched as Chris and Gabe carried the hull around the house and down the sandy path.

"Now, be careful there boys, those steps are narrow." Grandpa Morgan pointed with his cane, pacing as well as he could.

"We've got it, sir," Chris said, voice straining under the weight. "Brigid, lift those branches."

Standing on tiptoe in the sandy dirt, Brigid leaned against the saplings and spread her arms. She lifted as many pine branches as she could gather over her head. Both Chris and Gabe leaned their heads to the right as they picked their way down the steps, staring left to ensure that the spotless white hull incurred neither a scratch or drop of sap. A jewel-colored stone caught Gabe's right foot and he stumbled, catching the weight with his left arm. A muscular elbow slammed into Brigid's stomach. She flinched and sucked in. Gabe grimaced.

"I'm so sorry! Are you ok?" He looked at her, mortified.

"Oh, totally fine," Brigid said as brightly as she could. "No worries." She made dismissive gesture with her hand, dropping a branch in the process which whipped across Gabe's bare arm.

"Oh my God – sorry!" Brigid said, turning bright red.

Gabe grinned at her. "Guess you got me back."

"I didn't mean to," Brigid stuttered, staring at his arm. Gabe waited until she met his eyes. When her flushed face raised to his, he winked.

"Hello?" Chris turned around. "You guys ok up there? Can we please not drop this thing?"

"Got it, man," Gabe said, straightening up and taking more of the load that he was due. "Sorry."

The boat was delivered safely down the stone steps and lowered gently into the water. Mr. Webster skipped down the steps and into the lake to help with the rigging.

"Brigid, darling, did we bring the wine?" Brigid turned to her grandfather and climbed back up the curved stone steps.

"I brought the cheese and crackers," she said. "I thought you were bringing the wine."

"Blast it all, I forgot," said Morgan. "Would you run back to the cottage and get it?"

"Oh, don't put yourself out," said Emma. "We have plenty of bottles here. Brigid, would you mind running inside and getting the bottle of champagne from the fridge? The tumblers are on the counter."

"Oh no problem," said Brigid, her voice high and fast. She hustled into the Websters' cottage, not seeing the look exchanged between Morgan and Emma.

Standing in the Websters' gleaming kitchen, Brigid tried to calm her breath. She forced herself to move slowly, taking the bottle out, meticulously stacking the glasses. Looking out of the window for a glimpse of Gabe, she noticed several small rock towers arranged with deliberation on the sill. Much like her grandfather's, but these were polished and cut, almost like gemstones.

She could see that the men were done launching the sailboat, so with forced calm, she made her way back out to the dock.

"All done, Mrs. Webster." Gabe walked up out of the water, wavy dark hair shimmering in the sun. "The boat is beautiful, but you may not see your husband for awhile."

They all looked out at Morgan and Graham, inspecting the anchored boat in their bare chests and swim trunks, two old children with the best new toy.

Emma laughed. "Thank you, boys. Have a glass to celebrate. We appreciate your hard work. I know how heavy that is."

"Thank you so much, Mrs. Webster, but we can't," said Chris. "Against the rules. We can't be hauling around brandnew boats and driving under the influence, can we Gabe?"

"Probably not," Gabe said, eyes not moving from Brigid's face.

"Well, at least take a towel. You know to dry off your legs from these inland lakes," Emma said, handing towels to both men. These they accepted with thanks, duly rubbing off their legs and arms.

"Alright well, we gotta head out. Thank you again, Mrs. Webster. Very nice working with you and your husband." Chris smiled at Emma and slapped Gabe on the back, getting his attention.

"Thank you, ma'am." Gabe smiled at Emma, extending his hand once again. Turning his glance to Brigid, he said, "It was nice to meet you." Brigid caught her breath and gripped her glass.

"You too," was all she could manage. Suddenly, she could sense his nervousness, his apprehension. Her own nerves instinctively melted away. When she smiled up at him, the polite expression he had plastered on his face melted all the way into his eyes.

"We'll walk you out," said Emma, and the quartet walked in companionable silence back to the truck.

"Bye Bridge," said Chris, offering a high-five. "I'm sopping wet — no hug this time."

"Thanks," Brigid said laughing. "Good to see you."

Brigid stared at Gabe's wide shoulders and strong back, the water that dripped from his dark hair. She felt a warmth draining from her. A gust of wind blew the nape of Brigid's neck. Shivering, she slipped out of her reverie and turned back toward the Webster dock.

"Hey!" The truck backed up slip-shod through the tree-lined driveway as Brigid turned at the sound of Chris's voice. "SHIT – I'm gonna hit that birch!" Chris threw his head out of the driver's window as he slammed it into park. "Brigid! Come here!"

She jogged up the dirt two-track and peeked into the cab.

"Hey, I just thought," Chris said. "We're having a bonfire out at the rock beach tonight. You should come! You know where the rock beach is, right?"

Brigid grinned. "Off of the main road and then you take Barings Farm dirt road until it dead ends?"

"Yep!" said Chris, slapping the side of the cab. "The second two-track past the ice cream store."

"That sounds fun," said Brigid, tucking her wind-swept hair behind her ear. "Will I get to see Natalia? How is she? I haven't seen her since the school picnic."

Chris rolled his eyes. "Planning the wedding. Flowers, music, lace bullshit, something called a table runner, a bunch of stupid details – I dunno." Brigid tilted her head back and let loose a hearty laugh.

"Please," Chris said, in a mock pleading tone. "Please please come and talk to her so I don't have to hear about wedding planning for a few hours?"

"Oh stop," said Brigid, reaching in the cab and playfully smacking him on the arm. "Natalia's beautiful and brilliant. You picked the perfect woman."

"I know, I know. She's awesome and I'm very lucky. But hey — come, ok?"

"Sure, but text me or have Natalia text me– time and stuff – you know, all the details." Brigid winked at him.

"For sure!" Chris threw the car in drive and then slammed it back in park, saying absently, "Gabe, you're coming tonight, right?"

Gabe nodded. "If you don't kill us on the drive back to the marina."

"I'll try my best," said Chris, steering the truck onto the path. "Bye Bridge!" he called out the window. "See you tonight."

Brigid stood under the trees, smiling, heart racing. As the truck rounded the final turn of the driveway, Gabe stuck his head out of the window and beamed.

CHAPTER 8

Fires blazed along the beach, surrounded by local families and passels of teenagers. This secret shore was a respite from the tourists who descended upon the Peninsula every summer. A silent agreement among the locals ensured that this beach was never given an official name, or God forbid, official signage.

Brigid looked down the shoreline, straining to see Chris's tall form. She heard him first, his strong teacher's voice booming through the summer breeze. She strode southward, smiling at the squealing children who raced into the cold waters of Big Omann Lake.

"Brigid!" Natalia came racing over and enveloped Brigid in a woolen embrace. Brigid pulled back and grinned at her fitted cranberry sweater and pressed khaki shorts.

"You are so cute, even at the beach!" Brigid exclaimed. "How is wedding planning going?" she asked as Chris stepped over and wrapped Brigid in a hug.

Natalia laughed. "Oh, it's going, but this guy is no help at all," she said, punching her fiancée on his broad shoulder.

Brigid handed both of them a beer from the six-pack she carried before taking one for herself. They walked over to the campfire and Natalia introduced her around the circle. Natalia was a nurse at one of the local hospitals, and most of her friends worked there as well. Brigid sat in the sand and listened they compared stories of the day, her eyes widening at the blood and gore. Unable to stop herself, she kept stealing glances at the darkened pathway, hoping to catch a glimpse of him.

"Natalia, have you had any cases with that nasty rash?" Lucy asked, taking a swig from a tumbler.

"The one of the fever?" Natalia shuddered. "Yeah, I had one just today. It definitely presents like a bacterial infection." Natalia leaned forward and shook her head. "I had one little girl with a congenital heart defect and we had to pump her full of antibiotics. She's still in ICU. It's pretty scary. I heard there might be something in one of the inland lakes."

"I read something about that in the *Domhnall Hills Express*." Brigid said. "It said the DNR was investigating an imbalance of bacteria."

"They need to figure it out down there in the City." Brigid turned to see Lucas, one of Natalia's colleagues at the hospital. "I don't know what they're doing in those big McMansions or what they're dumping into the lake, but it needs to stop. It could poison the inland lakes and affect everyone in the area." He turned to Brigid and raised an eyebrow. "You live there?"

"My parents live there." Brigid raised her chin. "I was born on the Peninsula. My parents moved to Domhnall Hills when I was five."

Lucas looked at her with disdain. "You should tell Daddy that he needs to stop destroying the lake," He took a long pull from his drink.

"My father has nothing to do with it." Brigid felt the heat rising in her chest.

"Alright, alright, you two. Calm down." Chris moved deliberately next to Brigid. He threw a look at Lucas. "Dude."

Lucas reddened. "It's just that people like that..." He shook his head. "I'm sorry, but seriously. People with all that money buy up the best land in the city and on the Peninsula and they just don't get it. Or they don't care. I don't know which is worse."

"People 'like that' do a ton of work maintaining the waterways and researching how to keep the entire area safe," said Brigid, eyes bright in the moonlight.

Chris hopped up and clapped his hands together. "Hey! My man!" He waved the figure over to their campfire. Gabe emerged from the shadows of a woodland footpath, hands in the pockets of his jacket. "You showed!" Chris said, shaking his hand. "And just in time. Brigid and Lucas are about to get into a fist-fight." Gabe locked eyes with Brigid and raised his eyebrow in mock surprise. Without being able to stop herself, she beamed up at him.

"Fist-fighting?" Gabe asked. "At a bonfire? Come on, guys. We all know Chris wants to talk about the wedding." He slapped Chris on the back. "Right buddy? Tell us about the flowers. Did she say yes to the dress? Come on, Natalia, help him out." Natalia stood up from her sandy seat and threw her arms around Gabe's neck. Brigid felt a sharp stab of jealousy and looked down at her hands, trying valiantly to mask her emotions.

"Finally, a man who understands!" Natalia reached into the cooler. "Gabe, have a beer. You want a s'more? I will make you one."

"Aww, babe, can I get a s'more?" said Chris, nuzzling the top of her head.

"No Chris," chirped Natalia, wriggling out of his embrace. "You get nothing. Gabe understands the needs of a bride so he's getting a s'more."

The tension broke as the circle laughed at this little performance.

"I'm good, Natalia," Gabe said, popping the tab. "Don't make me anything. Thank you, though."

People stood to greet Gabe. Each time he accepted an embrace, he looked over the person's shoulder to meet Brigid's eyes. She found she couldn't hold the intensity of his smile and to her horror, had to keep blushing down into her hands like a teen. When she finally dared to look up, she saw tenderness in his eyes. She stood up as he stepped away from the last hug.

He wanted to touch that hair of hers, tuck the errant auburn curl behind her soft earlobe. But he kept still. "Hi Brigid," he said.

"Hi Gabe." He raised his eyebrows in question, but there was a twinkle in his eye. She stepped forward to accept his brief embrace, inhaling the scent of fresh summer air and cologne.

"Do you mind?" Gabe gestured to the patch of sand next to where Brigid had been sitting.

"Of course not." He waited until she sat down and then settled himself.

"So, how's the boat?" he asked.

"The boat?" Brigid shifted her posture so she faced him.

"Mr. Webster's sailboat."

"Oh, of course, yes" Brigid said, shifting again. "It's good. Great, actually. He's had it out three times since you guys brought it over." Her shoulders relaxed at the memory. "It is really fast. My grandpa's a little disgruntled."

Gabe chuckled. "Well, we need to sell one to your grandpa."

"Oh, he'll never trade ours in. He treats the Sunfish like an heirloom, although the rigging is so stiff and creaky it takes the force of God to get it to move."

"I could fix that," Gabe said.

"You could?" Brigid smiled up at him. "I could probably get Grandpa to spring for that. How much would it cost, do you think?"

"Cost? Nothing. I'd be happy to do it. It would just take a little grease and maybe some new lines."

"You don't need to fix our boat for free," Brigid said, blushing.

"I'd love to." He gave her elbow a playful nudge.

"Sticks! Marshmallows!" Natalia marched around the circle, breaking the air between them. "Everyone needs a s'more, come on." She passed a long branch to Brigid and another to Gabe, shaking the open marshmallow bag at them with eyebrows raised. They each took two.

Gabe noticed Brigid's trembling hands and reached for her roasting stick. "Here," he said. A smile played at his lips as he held his palm open. Brigid handed her marshmallows over.

When their hands brushed, Brigid felt an electric shock travel through her arm. The roasting stick Gabe was holding tumbled into the sand.

Gabe fumbled for a moment. He was usually much smoother than this. Brigid lifted his roasting stick from the sand and began gently blowing the effervescent particles off. They sparkled in the light of the fire as they flew on her breath into the air.

"Thanks," Gabe said, as she handed the stick back to him. He pushed all four marshmallows onto the tip. "Nothing like some sand sprinkles," he said with a shrug. Brigid laughed and the tension that had been roiling through her veins finally subsided. Gabe carefully suspended the marshmallows on the top of the flames, rotating them ever so slightly until they were the perfect golden brown. Pulling the mound of sweet spun sugar from the stick, Gabe offered it to Brigid. She parted her lips and he placed the marshmallow onto her tongue before taking one for himself. They bit into the crunchy outsides and the warm, gooey heart melted on their tongues. Smiling through her mouthful, Brigid wiped a trail of warm marshmallow from her lips. A gust of wind came up from the lake and tossed Brigid's curls across her face.

"I think you have some marshmallow in your hair." Gabe said. Reaching over, he gently touched the tendril that fell on Brigid's cheekbone. Pressing the hardening sugar between his thumb and forefinger, he tried to ease it out, but it was cemented to her cheek. His jaw clenched as he flinched "Sorry!" he said, dropping his hand. "I didn't mean to hurt you."

"It's my own fault," she said, laughter twinkling in the air. "What kind of person gets marshmallow all over her face?" She squeezed his hand. "Let's go down to the lake, I'll wash it out."

Squinting in the darkness, they brushed themselves off and made their way down to the water. The waves slowly lapped the shore, clouds shrouding the indigo night. Brigid dipped her hands in the brisk water. Gabe watched as she reached up and wet her forehead, drawing the water across her brow and into the curls of her hair. She took a deep breath, satiated by the warm summer air. The moon parted the clouds, casting eddies on the horizon. Gabe looked at her face, luminescent, gazing at the stars. He swallowed hard.

"Look," Brigid said softly, pointing skyward. "You can see the Big Dipper,"

"And the Little Dipper," said Gabe.

She looked up at him, eyes shining. "I can never find the Little Dipper."

Gabe stepped into the cold water where she stood, "You have to remember it's upside down. Find the two stars at the right corner of the bowl." He pointed and paused, making sure her eyes found his mark. "Merak at the bottom, and Dubhe at the top. Follow Dubhe." Gabe tentatively wrapped his hand under Brigid's wrist, fingers pressing lightly into the bottom of her palm, guiding her hand. "Dubhe will point you to Polaris."

"Polaris," she said, eyes on the sky. "The North Star."

The southernly wind swirled around them, pushing and pulling the clouds, lifting their veil. The Milky Way appeared, sparkling across the sky.

"Do you see the Little Dipper now?" Gabe found his throat was tight.

"I do." Brigid turned to look at him. "They fit into each other."

"They do." Gabe lowered her arm. He kept her hand. Brigid stood still, breathing in the scent of his skin, hearing her heartbeat and his. She leaned back into his broad chest, her cheek brushing against his soft t-shirt. A warm, liquid feeling subsumed her as she stared into the sky. Her heart pulsed in concert with the waves. The two of them seemed to be creating their own world.

A buzzing vibration crashed through their reverie as Brigid felt the startling movement at the small of her back. She shuddered, involuntarily freeing her hand.

"Shit," muttered Gabe. "I'm sorry." He reached in his pocket and pulled out his phone. "I'm really sorry. I have to take this."

Gabe grimaced, one hand on the phone, the other in a fist, he strode down the shore. Brigid's eyes followed him, her skin racing with shivers. She felt freezing cold. Rubbing her palms together, she walked back to the fire. She forced a smile onto her face and sat down next to Natalia, ignoring Lucas's hostile stare. Trying to warm her hands, warm her body, she crouched by the fire and held her hands over the flames.

"Yes, I know." Gabe's voice echoed across the dunes. "I understand. I'm leaving now – hang on." Gabe took two strides toward the fire and put his hand over his phone. "I'm so sorry, guys. I have to go." Everyone waved, shouted their goodbyes. Gabe looked desperately at Brigid as the voice in his phone became persistent. She tried to control her features, casually smile. Wave, like everyone else was doing. He stepped toward her and then suddenly turned back to his phone. "Ok, yes, hang ON," he said. "Please," he added, forcing his voice to be level. "I know. I'm on my way." Gabe turned, hurrying up the dunes. He threw a wave in her direction and she saw his wrinkled brow and clenched jaw before he was enveloped by the shadows of the forest path. Brigid felt a drip on her cheek. And another one. She brushed them away furiously. Surely she wasn't crying, not in front of all these people! Gabe owed her nothing — they had only met hours ago. But still, did he really not even say goodbye? Another droplet splashed her hand.

"Uh oh." Chris stood and looked out at the menacing horizon. Brigid swiped at her cheeks and followed his gaze. Clouds were rolling in fast, out of the north. Rain was beginning to fall.

"What is going on?" Natalia stood and brushed droplets from her sweater. "The sky was clear like two minutes ago!" Everyone leapt into action, packing empties into cardboard boxes, gathering sticks and wrappers. Those with nothing to carry knelt beside the fire and scooped sand onto the flames.

CHAPTER 9

Gabe had called the next morning.

A smile illuminated Brigid's face as she slid deeper under the covers, shivering at the memory of the night before. The crystal at her throat caught the light filtering through smudged window pane as she laid there.

Domhnall Symphony Orchestra was playing an outreach concert in Birch Glen, the little fishing village nearby. "The Pines of Rome." He had tickets and could pick her up at seven.

At five minutes to seven, she had raced down the stairs to find her purse, her shoes, her phone. Morgan stood at the kitchen island, a whiskey and water in his hand. He smiled at Brigid and waved her over before placing a folded handkerchief on the counter. Oblivious to his granddaughter's rush, he unfolded the cloth with reverence. Pulsing vermilion and silver sparkled in the light. "Your grandmother's," Morgan said. "It was a special bracelet. The most special one. Look." His gnarled finger tapped the stones. "Jasper. This Jasper was pulled from Big Omann Lake. Jasper will bring passion, but also steadfastness."

Brigid forced herself to stop, and give him her attention. Her fingers brushed a cinnamon-colored stone. "Ah," said Morgan. "That is Hessonite. Hessonite, so you remember your worth." He patted her hand. "You are worthy, Brigid." She covered the choke of emotion with a tight smile. Worthy? No one spoke to her like this. To push the embarrassment away, she pointed to the jagged black stones. They seemed out of place in this warm, resonant bracelet.

"What are these?" she asked.

"Those stones were birthed from volcanoes that once existed under these waters," Morgan said, proud with the knowledge. "The red stones represent the fire, but this stone... she is <u>made</u> from the fire."

Brigid subtly looked down at her watch. This supply of odd jewelry seemed to be bottomless. She could hear Gabe's truck rumbling down the driveway and she still hadn't located her shoes. "It's beautiful, Grandpa. I'd love to look at it in more detail later."

"Oh, you misunderstand me, sweet girl," said Morgan. "I brought it out to give to you." He pushed it across the countertop. "Wear it, Brigid." He clasped her hand again, searching her eyes.

"I couldn't," she said, with a tone she hoped was polite yet firm. The bracelet was certainly interesting, but it didn't quite go with her meticulously planned outfit.

"Take it." Morgan waved away her refusal, and, taking up her slim wrist, fixed the gold filigree clasp. "It is meant to be yours." She looked across the counter at her grandfather, feeling a shiver run up her arm as he clasped her hand in his own.

A knock on the back door turned the old man gregarious, and he bustled down to the hall to welcome Gabe. The men shook hands before Morgan took Brigid to him and kissed her forehead. "Have a lovely evening with your gentleman." Brigid couldn't suppress a grin and she hugged her grandfather back before turning to leave with Gabe. Morgan followed them to the back porch, waving them off.

The ride down the curvy roads was alive with laughter and the twenty-minute drive to Birch Glen passed in a flash. When they arrived at the renovated schoolhouse, Gabe ushered Brigid to their seats, his hand warm on the small of her back. The interior was cavernous; the simple clapboard walls adorned with landscapes created by local artists. The orchestra trilled and stretched waves of sound as they warmed up.

"I actually played the viola in middle school," Brigid whispered.

"Oh yeah?" Gabe grinned at her. "Which one is the viola?"

Brigid pointed discreetly at the orchestra. "The violists are in the middle. It's a slightly bigger instrument than the violin, with a richer timbre."

"Why the viola?" asked Gabe.

"Well, the violin is what everyone chooses." She gestured conspiratorially. "Then the cello — the cello is very popular; very intellectual. Sort of sexy," she said, meeting his eyes.

"Hmm, I see," he said. "In that case, I'm shocked that you're not the female Yo Yo Ma." Brigid blushed and rolled her eyes.

Gabe winked at her and looked out at the orchestra. "What about the double bass?" he asked. "No bass for you?"

"Oh please," Brigid said. "I don't have the stamina to carry the bass. It would've been great though, because it's different. My main goal was not to be ordinary. Anything is better than to be ordinary. So, the viola it was."

"I bet you were really good," Gabe said.

"Oh my God, I was terrible!" Brigid laughed. "My pinkie finger is abnormally short – look at this." She lifted her left hand to show him. "Every time I would play a scale, the first four notes would be perfect and the fifth would be so flat. My teacher would say, 'Tune that instrument, Brigid!' Use your ears!'"

"I don't believe you," said Gabe. "Let me see this rogue pinkie." He made a spectacle of measuring her pinkie and ring fingers, comparing them to his own, placing his hand palm to palm with hers. Suddenly the room erupted in applause. They both looked up to see the conductor ascending the podium and their hands separated to join in the ovation. The conductor bowed to the room, turned to the orchestra, and struck the air. As the woodwinds glittered through the air in Respighi's opening salvo, Gabe reached for her hand.

The intensity of the music barely registered in her racing body. Brigid peeked at Gabe. He was so confident, seeming to always know what to say, when to look, how to smile. She was smart enough to have reserve. Surely it was ridiculous to think she was falling for anyone so soon, and that he could possibly be falling for her. But he was kind. And the way he looked at her, for a fraction of a second longer than he should... Brigid forced herself to relax into the music, feeling his warm, calloused hand on her skin. Just as she surrendered in the rapture of the crescendo, the horns blasted their interruption. Gabe and Brigid startled together, involuntarily gripping hands. He looked down at her and their composure broke. His shoulders fell and his tightened bicep relaxed. Collapsing into stifled giggles, they leaned into their own elated reality.

After the concert, they walked hand in hand along the harbor, peeking into the fishing boats of the locals and the polished pleasure craft of the summer residents. Both unwilling for the evening to end, they landed at the Captain's Seat, a greasy-spoon restaurant with an outdoor patio overlooking the harbor. The bartender watched their laughter and non-stop banter, deciding not to push them out at closing time. Smiling at the besotted couple, he poured himself a nightcap and ignored the clock.

The moon was high by the time they drove back to Cairn Cottage. At ten minutes before midnight, he stopped the truck on the main road, on the edge of the long driveway. Her heart raced as she prepared herself for his kiss. Before she could decide how to react, he was out of the cab and opening her door, offering her a hand that already seemed like a part of her life. As he helped her down, she said, "Not escorting me to the door, sir?" A teasing smile played at her lips. "I thought you were a gentleman."

"Oh, I'm absolutely escorting you to the door. I just am not going to shine the headlights all the way down that driveway into the bedroom windows of your sleeping neighbors." He tucked her hand into the crook of his arm and smiled down at her as they walked down the moonlit driveway. Far too soon, the path ended at her late grandmother's garden. He looked at the tiny purple-bordered buds, indigo heart and sunshine soul reaching to the moon. "I thought those were violas," he said.

"They are." Brigid could feel her heart racing in her chest.

"But you played the viola... I'm so confused," he said, smiling. Brigid saw his feet shifting in the sandy dirt and smiled to herself. He was stalling.

She playfully punched his hard arm with her other hand. "You're just hilarious," she said.

Gabe turned toward her. He released their hands and slid his fingers to the small of her back. The other hand found her cheekbone and wove its way into her hair. Without thinking, she echoed his movement, brushing her hands up his broad chest and wrapping them around his neck. The undulating light of the moon passed through the veil of clouds and adorned her face.

Looking down at her, a feeling like lightening shot through him, and he had to root his feet to the earth to hold onto the embrace.

"Can I kiss you?" he whispered

Brigid answered by rising to her tiptoes and touching her lips to his.

All thought left her mind as she surrendered to his gentle kiss. Every worry, every question of being enough melted away in the softness of his lips. She felt his arms encircle her back, steady like the branches of the trees that bowed over the long country roads. His tongue opened her mouth, gently. She clung to him, specks of stardust sparking through her nerves, reaching, joining. Nothing in the world mattered except this moment, the taste of his mouth upon hers, her body cradled in his arms.

The low, mournful call of a loon burst through their reverie

Slowly, shaking, they drew themselves apart. Brigid gazed up at him.

"What now?"

CHAPTER 10

Morgan had spoken to Kelsey and invited Brigid's parents to come for Sunday supper. Lynn had apparently agreed, much to Brigid's shock. The next morning passed in a flurry as Brigid helped her grandfather get Cairn Cottage ready for the big dinner. There was barely time to think about the taste of Gabe's lips on hers, the way the moon sparkled on the still lake as she stood on the end of the dock after he drove away.

She had gotten used to the ease of living with her grandpa but Brigid knew that every unkempt particle in the cottage would draw wrath from her mother, so she spent the day in a tizzy, dusting and scrubbing and preparing food. Morgan came into the great room as afternoon turned into evening and gazed around the cottage. Kitchen cupboard doors were open, dirty mixing bowls lay pushed to the side. The vacuum stood sentry in the middle of the room, its cord stretched across the carpet. Brigid was setting the table, her forehead slick with sweat.

"Go get ready, my dear," said Morgan, sitting in his chair and sorting the silverware. "Or better yet, go jump in the lake. You look like you need a cool down."

"I can't," said Brigid, resolutely slapping the plates on the table. "They'll be here in less than an hour and we're not ready."

"We're ready enough," said Morgan, an unusual firmness in his tone. "This is our family coming to dinner, Brigid. Not the Queen."

Brigid arched her eyebrows at her grandfather. "Well," he said, patting her hand. He took a deep breath in. "Be that as it

may, you've been working much too hard. Let me finish this."
He waved her away. "Shoo."

* * *

The evening was a disaster. It began when Morgan called Brigid by her late grandmother's name — Shannon. Three separate times. Lynn began her lecture on the cost of Cairn Cottage over happy hour on the dock. Grandpa bowed his head, waved her concerns away, and yes dear-ed his daughter until she delivered her final blow:

"When you cannot take care of yourself without my daughter here to act as housemaid, you will have to move to an assisted living facility."

Sparks flew across his eyes at that. He gripped his cane and rose in a fury. "I will not have you telling me what to do. I am your father and this is my home. This is your home too. If you would remove that blasted veil of pretension, you could be the woman your mother raised you to be, instead of this modicum of control I see before me!"

Lynn leaned back into the green plastic chair and raised an eyebrow. Heavy, drooping clouds moved across the horizon.

"This is not about rocks and false healing," she said. Her eyes bored into Morgan's, her clenched jaw slicing into the suspended air around them. "This is about real life. Your safety, and the safety of my child. Not your child, not my mother's child, but my child."

"Your child has the Gift!" said Morgan, pointing a gnarled finger at Brigid.

Thunder roared in the distance.

Brigid began to speak, but before she could get a word out, Kelsey placed a quieting hand on her arm.

"Lynn. Morgan." Kelsey cleared his throat and looked hard at each of them. "We don't need to do this now. We are here to enjoy a dinner. Let's everybody take a breath." Droplets splashed on Lynn's sharp cheekbones and she raised a mani-cured hand as if to push the water away. Kelsey stood. He said firmly, "Brigid, why don't I help you carry these drinks inside. It's starting to rain."

Dinner passed in mannered vindictiveness. The rain pounded at the windows as the family ate, passing the salt and measurements of spite.

A full-blown thunderstorm had erupted by the time Brigid placed the dessert on the table. Piling an enormous helping of strawberries onto his angel food cake, Morgan calmly patted Brigid's hand. "You know, all the Ayers women have the Gift." Morgan waved his glass at Lynn. "Your mother is afraid of hers."

Lynn slammed her wine glass on the plastic tablecloth and glared at Morgan. "Dad, I will not have you passing this nonsense onto my family. I have made that clear more than enough times." Brigid looked down at her plate.

"Enough," Lynn said. "We are done." Lynn pushed back from the table. Her chair fell backwards, entangled in her legs. "Dammit!" she yelped as she tumbled to the ground. Kelsey and Brigid jumped to help her as she tumbled backwards, but her hands clawed outward, fending them off. Outside, a tree branch gave a mournful creak. "I do not need your help!" Lynn shrieked. The tree branch slammed to the ground.

Lynn scrambled up from the floor and straightened her linen shift. "Kelsey, I can't do this," she said, her whispered voice like iron. He gingerly placed one hand on Lynn's back. At his touch, she took a shuddering breath and forced herself to look at Brigid. "Please clear the dishes for your grandfather and get in the car. Immediately." Lynn retreated to the bathroom.

Kelsey bent over his father-in-law. "Morgan," he said gently. "We talked about this, remember? It does no good to upset Lynn." Morgan merely stared into the storm, absently rattling the stones he had pulled from his pocket. "You can believe whatever you want in your heart. I'm sure it helps you remem-ber Shannon. I know you miss her. We all do." Kelsey patted the older man on the shoulder. "Lynn especially."

Morgan was silent for several moments. When he spoke, his voice was hollow and cold. "Lynn betrayed her."

Heels clicked along the wooden floorboards and Kelsey turned to see his wife, tears wiped away, face as unmoving as granite.

"Brigid," she said. "Pack your things. You're coming home now. Your father will drive your car tonight. We can come pack the rest of your belongings tomorrow."

"Mom – " Brigid began. Lynn interrupted swiftly. "Are the dishes done?" Lynn asked. "Good. Go and pack a bag."

Brigid set a glass down and walked toward her mother. "I'm not coming to Domhnall Hills," she said, voice shaking.

"Brigid, don't do this now," Lynn said. "Let's go."

Brigid forced herself to meet her mother's gaze. "I'm staying here," she said with as much conviction as she could muster.

Lynn's eyes flamed as she leaned toward Brigid. "Young lady, I do not have the patience for this right now. Surely you can see that."

"Lynn." Kelsey stepped between the women. "There is no need for this." Lynn shifted her furious eyes to her husband. Brigid gained courage once her mother's gaze was off of her. She lifted her chin. "Mom, I am twenty-four years old. I'm sorry, but you really can't tell me what to do anymore." Brigid felt her grandfather's eyes and her voice became even clearer when she said, "I'm staying here. I enjoy helping Grandpa and..."

"And what? What?" Lynn's voice never rose in anger. It sank. When she was truly angry, her voice came from the depths of hell. "What on earth is there possibly to keep you here besides dirt and sand and piles of rocks?"

"I'm seeing someone." Bridget spat the truth out quickly.

"Oh wonderful – a boyfriend. From here. That's absolutely wonderful," she hissed.

"Mom, you don't know anything about him! You don't

know anything about my life here either. I actually feel like myself here. I feel..." Brigid fumbled for the right word. "I feel free."

Lynn froze. She held up a hand to stop the flow of her daughter's words. Cairn Cottage was silent as the eye of the storm hovered over the roof. Brigid had spent her life walking the path Lynn had set for her, bowing her shoulders for the verbal lashes that came when she stumbled. No one really knew what Brigid wanted. She seemed happy enough. Certainly, she was a listening ear for everyone she met. People liked quiet Brigid, she seemed to exude a peacefulness that comforted every hungry soul. But was she peaceful in her own soul?

When Lynn finally spoke, her voice was deathly calm and even. "You're right," she said. "I don't know the details about this man you're seeing, or your life here. I do, however, have all the information I need." Brigid braced herself for the cruel blow that always fell onto her shoulders after a statement like this. For the first time in her life, Brigid didn't lower her eyes in submission. She stared at her mother full on, daring her to continue. Lynn saw the defiance and it crystallized her anger. Slowly, she said, "Fine, Brigid. You win. You want to stay at Cairn Cottage, throw away your summer, date some moron from the Peninsula, ignore what I've worked so hard to give you, fine. I'm done."

Staring forward at the knots in the pine, Lynn strode down the hallway without a second glance at her only child. Brigid followed her mother, aching to say something, anything to make her turn back. The words caught in her throat.

Suddenly, Lynn whirled around in the narrow hallway. Stopping just inches from Brigid, her eyes had a wild look when she said, "Know this. This – gift – this <u>nonsense</u> that your grandfather may try to tell you.... That's all it is. Absolute nonsense. Actually, it's worse than nonsense – it's harmful. It's ruined..."

She broke off, her jaw working in circles to push back the

tears that threatened to fall. She looked down fiercely. "I've given you everything. I've given you <u>reality.</u> For god's sake, Brigid, come live in the real world."

CHAPTER 11

Plastic dock chairs lay prone in the shallows, backs submerged. Their legs stuck helplessly in the air. Brigid waded into the lake, eyes sharp for the drop-off. Sighing, she peeled them out of the silty bottom one by one. Dragging them to the edge of the beach, she slowly heaved them in and out of the waves, washing the sand from the crevices. When all eight chairs were rescued and cleaned, she leaned them against the round table on the end of the dock. Turning back to Cairn Cottage, she surveyed the sandy front yard as she toweled off her legs. The evening's storm had ripped an enormous tree branch from one of the old birch trees and flung it onto the slate pathway, shattering a mist-colored stone. She knew it would be impossible to clear on her own. She considered texting Gabe, but decided against it. Now was not the time.

Her grandfather had sunk into a catatonic mood after her family left. He refused to acknowledge Brigid, even look at her. She watched him drink scotch after scotch, and she was grateful he chose to stay seated at the head of the table rather than venturing out onto the rickety planks of the dock. As he drank, he obsessively balanced his pocketful of stones, making endless towers of stones, each cairn different. Smothered agitation rumbled in his clenched jaw; aching despair shook his forearms as he scooped up each cairn.

She bustled around like a mouse, willing the clock to move faster. Did she dare lock the door, risk a hidden wrath? What was worse, a barrier or a trap? A little after midnight, she bent to lift the bottle from the table.

"No." Morgan's voice echoed from the pine walls.

"I'm sorry," she whispered. As she scuttled away, she heard his voice crack, desolate.

"It won't work. It'll never work. Not again."

Turning back, she saw tears run down his wrinkled cheeks. Her throat caught and she lifted an old woolen blanket from the back of the couch. She folded it and placed it gently on the table. Not knowing what to do next, she sank into the only chair out of his eyeline. Realizing suddenly it was her late grandmother Shannon's chair, she jumped up and a horrid squeak rose forth, causing Morgan to turn slowing around.

"I'm – I'm sorry," Brigid said, looking at her feet.

"Sit." Morgan's eyes were slits as his gaze bored into hers. Brigid froze. It was her mother's gaze, the gaze that always prompted Kelsey to pad up to her, arms outstretched. Lead her out of the room, away. Instinct made her rise quickly and back away. Seeing the hurt and confusion in her eyes snapped something in Morgan's brain. He shuddered a sigh.

"Brigid, my darling," he said, eyes softening. "Please sit. That chair is just fine." Brigid pulled the chair near enough for politeness but out of arms reach. The gesture did not escape Morgan, who forced himself to make his tone as gentle as possible. "I'm sure you were confused tonight. About why your mother was so angry. You see, there is a gift. The Gift that all Ayers women do have that your grandmother..." Morgan stopped, unable to control the tears that fell from his eyes. Lifting a handkerchief from his pocket, he wiped his cheeks. "Well," he said, leaning back to pat Brigid's hand. "I'm sorry. It's late. And I believe I've had a bit too much to drink." His gaze slid to the cairn of stones on the table. "I really don't know what the point is anymore," he whispered. Brigid leaned forward and squeezed his wrinkled palm. He raised his eyes to hers. "You should know," he said. "You deserve to know." Morgan took a deep breath and looked out into the darkness. "Tomorrow. Tomorrow, we'll talk. When the storm has cleared."

CHAPTER 12

She didn't sleep until nearly dawn. The muscles in her back tensed, levitating her almost above the old mattress until she heard the click of his doorknob. When she arose a few fitful hours later, he was snoring heavily in the master bedroom.

She made the coffee quietly and gulped it down to clear her head. Her mind was too muddled to reach out to Gabe. The aftermath of the storm had left the lake stagnant and still; the perfect environment for the swimmer's curse bacteria to blossom. There would be no sailing today.

Pouring her third cup of coffee, she contemplated a walk down the old weed-covered two-track that led to Big Omann Lake. But as much as she ached to leave, she was pulled to stay. Who knew what condition Morgan would be in when he arose? And would he make good on his promise to tell her about her grandmother? What was this Gift?

The combination of caffeine and stress was making her thoughts scattered. She had to do something with this unnatural energy. Deciding that straightening up her room was better than sitting in worry, Brigid walked up the stairs to the loft and opened the double doors of the small attic closet.

Tucked under the eaves, the doors were swollen shut with decades of humid air. She gathered parcels, pictures, and hand-woven baskets of wooden toys up from the dusty plank floors. Slowly, years of detritus began to line the corners of the bedroom. Brigid sighed at the antique toys: China dolls, blocks, forgotten teddy bears. Her grandmother had saved everything, waiting to welcome the grandchildren who never came.

There were still a few more boxes in the gloom of the closet, so Brigid ducked under the doorway, smacking her head on a makeshift shelf, setting piles of rocks a-flutter. An old wooden chest was pushed against the back wall. Brigid grasped the metal handles and dragged it into the light.

The chest was more beautiful and intricate than anything she had ever seen.

Triple-pronged swirls were carved into the fragrant wood, forming a wide border. Myrtle and trillium bloomed in relief on the sides of the chest, showing the blood-red heart of the tree. The lid was carved into a variety of curved shapes, and Brigid could see the muted paint. Red, gray, coral, and deep green. Some shapes were meticulously speckled in a rainbow of colors. Several were milky beige, with an angry red gash down the middle. The rounded figures surrounded a carving of an enormous tree, branches spreading.

Brigid hovered her palms above the lid, afraid to touch the fragile paint but some deep instinct drew her fingers to the latch. When her fingertips touched the tarnished silver, her breath came quick and shallow. She lifted the latch and raised the lid.

A sea of silk and lace flooded her vision. She pulled out the piece of fabric and shook it, filling the air with cedar-scented memories. As the pearlescent shroud fluttered to the floor, Brigid peered into the darkness of the cavernous chest.

A single object remained. A small hand-hewn box with polished beach pebbles glued to its lid rested at the bottom of the chest. As Brigid lifted the box out, the north wind pushed through the open windows. She pulled the piece of fabric over her shoulders against the chill. Tucking her legs underneath her, Brigid turned to face the light.

With both hands, she opened the smaller box. Several of the smaller pebbles fell from the lid and scattered to the floor. Brigid gathered them up and placed them inside the lid, setting the whole mess on the floor.

Nine polished stones lay inside the box, encased in velvet

slots. Brigid recognized them as simple beach rocks, collected by nearly everyone who walked the shores of Big Omann Lake. She cradled a speckled stone in her palm and gasped to see what lay beneath.

The spidery handwriting of her late grandmother was scrawled across a tiny card.

"Granite — protection, abundance, strength. A stone of diplomacy. Use to envision the bigger picture. Will balance the relationship."

Brigid lifted another stone, a perfect oval with dots of indigo and plum.

"Feldspar – a cousin of Moonstone. Brings self-awareness, self-confidence, feminine strength. Eternal energy."

A lustrous oblong stone was next, with countless pearl bands encircling its core.

"Agate – calming, elevating, uplifting. Secures positive energy, protects from negative attacks. Empowerment."

A perfect circle lay in the fourth slot, with satin valleys and cotton-colored peaks.

"Quartz — Soul-cleansing. Master Healer. Energy holder. Clarity giver. Of the Earth."

Two stones lay in the sixth slot, the first like muted lapis with spots of gray; islands in a fathomless lake. The second was scorched mahogany, with a shimmering band of snow along the middle.

"Basalt – from the Fires. Helps to see negative attributes and banish them. Stone of strength and courage."

The penultimate stone was the color of rose and lemonade, fern and sage of rooted trees.

"Jasper – the Mother stone. Supreme nurturer. Gives us strength and guides us. One must find ones' own Jasper; the painting on the stone tells us where we need to go."

The stone seemed to pulse in Brigid's hand. She closed her fingers around it and breathed, feeling a light streak up her arm and through her body.

She was so absorbed that she failed to hear the footsteps on the stairs.

CHAPTER 13

Gabe stumbled on the landing, arrested by the vision of her in the sunlight. "I'm sorry to just — come up here," he said. "I wasn't sure if you remembered that we talked about getting lunch before my shift at the marina. I called..."

The ivory mantle shimmered around her shoulders as she stood. She seemed to belong to another world. For a moment, Gabe lost a sense of reality, and backed up from the light shining behind her. His foot caught on a stray box and he stumbled back into the steep, dark staircase. Brigid rushed forward and grabbed his forearm. They landed in a tumble on the hard wooden floor, tangled in the sheet that had been wrapped around Brigid's shoulders.

Laughing, Brigid rolled off, and bundled up the cloth, tossing it away.

"Are you ok?" He asked, glancing around at the chaos. "What's going on in here?"

"I was trying to unpack. I cleaned out this closet..." Brigid gestured to the cubby hole, and the surrounding mess of cloth and debris.

He looked at her for a long moment.

Who was this woman?

"Let me help you," he said, pushing himself up. He picked up the piece of fabric she had tossed in the corner and shook it before folding it into a perfect square.

Brigid smirked at him.

"What?" he said, with mock defensiveness. "A guy can't fold a sheet?" For an answer, he got her twinkling laugh.

"Where does this go?" Gabe asked, proffering the perfectly folded linen. Brigid led him to the closet doorway, lifting the lid of the trunk. Picking up the box containing the stones, she tucked it gently on top of the linen papers. Gabe reached into the chest to touch the box.

"My grandma had one of these. Before she died. I never knew what was in it; I was never allowed to touch it." The stones were smooth, catching the dim light that filtered into the closet. He stared at them for another moment then shrugged his shoulders. "Didn't everybody make a bunch of stuff out of stones back in those days?"

"I think they did," answered Brigid vaguely, wondering if everyone on the Peninsula had mysteriously labeled compartments of stones. As Gabe helped her lower the heavy wooden lid, he pulled back in shock. Staring at the carvings, he froze.

"Gabe?"

The air seemed to pulse.

"I – I swear I've seen this before. I can't really remember, but... I'm sorry – I don't know." He shook his head, tossing the cobwebs away. "I'm sorry. We should go to lunch. I mean, if you still want to." She beamed up at him; all the answer he needed. Reaching for her hand, he lifted her to her feet. The world suspended between them as they stood facing each other, hand in hand, misty wind blowing in the windows from three sides of the cabin. He looked down at her and it felt like the world was shaking, crashing around him. When she suddenly screeched and pulled back, he moved to grab her close. It wasn't until he saw the panic and confusion in her eyes that he realized that there had been a horrendous crash from below.

CHAPTER 14

Brigid snatched her hands from Gabe's shoulders and flew down the steep steps. She let out a choked gasp at what she saw.

Morgan lay prostrate on the ground. The only movement in the room was coffee that flowed from the broken pot onto Morgan's still hand.

"Grandpa!" Brigid cried, shaking the older man's shoulders. Silence echoed back. Gabe was suddenly in front of her, two fingers on her grandfather's neck.

"He's alive, Brigid."

She looked at Gabe, fighting the useless tears. "Should I..." but before the question was out of her mouth, she had risen and grabbed the rotary phone. While she spoke to the EMT, Gabe grabbed a dishtowel hanging from a peg beneath the sink. Folding it into a scanty pillow, he carefully turned Morgan onto his back and placed the towel under the old man's head.

"Fifteen minutes," Brigid said, frustration in her voice. "Dammit." Her eyes went to her grandfather's burnt right hand, which Gabe had folded onto the man's stomach. Letting out a cry, she stepped around the men to the sink and soaked a towel under the tap. Brigid gently pressed the cold, wet cloth onto her grandfather's hand. Panic rose in her when he didn't flinch to what should have been excruciating pain. Gabe quickly moved to check Morgan's pulse again.

"Still there. He's ok." Gabe scratched the back of his head with his free hand, feeling helpless. Useless. "Um, should you call anyone else? Your parents, maybe?"

"Shit." Brigid mumbled under her breath. She looked down at the wet cloth as if she didn't know her next move.

"I'll keep watch. Go make the call." Gabe said gently.

Brigid stepped over the broken glass, avoiding the view of her grandfather's prostrate form. The conversation with Lynn lasted less than five minutes. She turned back to Gabe, features tight, tears held back with the force of her will. Gabe reached out to her. "Was your mom very upset?" Still stinging from Lynn's terse reprimand, Brigid yanked her hand away. "She is just…" Brigid broke off in smothered fury and began violently gathering up the broken glass, slamming it into the plastic trash can. Gabe gazed at her, searching. "Your mom is hard on you, huh?"

"Yes," came the strangled reply. Gabe felt helpless, and the feeling made him angry. He wanted to scoop her up, brush the tears out of her eyes, and make this situation go away. But he was pinned to the ground, the old man's head in his lap. He could only look at her. As he did, he saw a scarlet river run down her arm. Gabe scrambled up, thrusting the folded pillow beneath Morgan's head. He took her bleeding hand and turned it over, revealing a deep gash. A piece of the broken coffee pot gripped tight in her hand. He stared at her for a split second and then swiftly removed the shard of glass. The bleeding needed to be stopped, and, finding no other towel in the kitchen, he stripped off his jacket. This was a new summer fleece, purchased with sacrifice and guilt. Around her hand it went, Gabe binding the wound with the shirtsleeves.

He helped her sit on the kitchen floor, her back against cupboard door. He raised her bleeding hand in the air and arranged the bulk of the jacket to make a pillow to support her arm.

"Just sit still," he said. Rummaging through the cupboards, he found a glass and poured water from the tap. "Breathe and drink this," he told her. "And keep that hand elevated. Ok?"

Finally, the tears that Brigid had so fiercely pushed back escaped. Gabe knelt before her and lifted her chin. With a calloused thumb, he stroked the tears away.

"I'm sorry," she said.

"Why are you sorry?"

"I don't know."

Gabe moved his hand up to her hair, brushing it back from her bent head. He leaned forward and kissed her forehead. There was something that pulled him to her. He could barely hold his gaze when he really looked into the watery depths of her eyes. In this woman, he had found something more. He was sure of it.

The EMS team called through the back screen door. Gabe lifted Brigid to a standing position as they made room for the bustling medical workers.

CHAPTER 15

The framed picture of a romantic landscape was meant to soothe the simmering torrent of emotions in the waiting room. The windows looked out into a soggy courtyard. It had started raining as soon as they had arrived. Brigid stared into the picture, attempting to decipher the species of tree in the forefront of the pink and gray water. Weeping willow. She rolled her eyes. Although City Hospital was one of the best in the state, the decorating firm had screwed up the symbolism.

"Yes, Brigid is here. I can see her," The familiar clipped voice brought her to attention. "I'll call you back when I know, Kelsey. Goodbye."

Brigid stood up to greet her mother, who did not offer an embrace.

"I'm sorry..." Brigid stammered.

Lynn waved her daughter's emotions away. "What did the doctor say?"

Brigid rubbed her forehead. "The men in the ambulance thought Grandpa probably had a stroke."

"Probably?" Lynn's eyebrows slammed together, the beginnings of a fury. "What is 'probably'?" Lynn drew in a deep breath, attempting to calm herself. "Brigid. What is the diagnosis?"

Brigid struggled to remember exactly what the nurse had said. She wished her father was here, wished this had never happened, wished she could crawl into a deep, safe, hole and avoid this whole mess. Seeing the struggle play across Brigid's face, Lynn let out an exasperated little sigh, as if to resign herself to the knowledge that her daughter was useless. Something snapped inside Brigid, who drew her shoulders back and glared at her mother.

"He is back for evaluation. No one has talked to me. I have not attempted to bother any doctors because I assume they are busy helping my grandfather."

Lynn clenched her hands and Brigid reflexively looked down, ready to absorb the backlash.

"Brigid, I swear to God I do not know," Lynn paused for effect before her voice tightened into a fierce hiss. "Why you cannot answer a simple question. Why it is that I have to do everything <u>myself</u>?"

"Ma'am." A firm tone of authority caused Lynn to neutralize her expression. Seeing the elder woman back down, the doctor turned to Brigid. "Is everything alright?"

"Yes," answered Brigid, embarrassed. "We're fine. Do you have any news on my grandpa?" Lynn thrust a gold-bangled arm out and stepped in front of her daughter.

"You are the doctor, I assume?" She did not bother to wait for a reply. "I am Lynn Firth, Morgan Ayers' daughter. Can you give us an update as to his condition?"

The doctor fixed a steady gaze at Lynn for several moments. Then, softening her gaze, she turned to Brigid.

"Are you Mr. Ayers' granddaughter?" Brigid nodded. "You did good work getting him in here. In fact, your quick response may have saved his life."

"Saved his life?" Lynn said, leaning forward.

"Ladies, please sit down." The doctor gestured to two seats in the empty waiting room. "My name is Dr. Hú. I treated Mr. Ayers this afternoon. Although his condition is improving, it seems Mr. Ayers has suffered a stroke. He is currently in the catheterization room where we have been assessing him for clots or bleeding in the brain. We have determined that he had a blood clot which lodged in his brain. We have also detected atrial fibrillation, or an irregular heartbeat." The smart of tears gathered behind Brigid's eyes. Lynn narrowed hers.

"We need to perform more tests over the next several days," the doctor continued. "There is a risk that Mr. Ayers has had a cerebral embolism. We believe a blood clot formed in his heart and traveled through the bloodstream until it reached his brain, where the vessels are too thin for the clot to pass through. This is when, as in your grandfather's case, the clot lodged and blocked the blood flow. Unfortunately, if Mr. Ayers has had a cerebral embolism, as is highly likely considering his irregular heartbeat, this means that he is a risk factor for future strokes and problems with the atrial musculature."

"The what?" Brigid whispered.

"The heart." Dr. Hú answered gently. "Now." She slapped her hands on her knees. "The good news. When a stroke occurs, the brain is deprived of oxygen. The cells begin to die within four minutes. Because his granddaughter was able to call an ambulance so quickly, Mr. Ayers will likely have much less permanent damage than he might have had." She turned to Brigid. "You were with him at the time of the stroke?"

"She lives with him," Lynn said.

Brigid flinched at her mother's tone. "I'm staying at Cairn Cottage – it was the family cottage..." She squeezed her hands together. "I'm sorry. I'm a teacher and I'm staying there for the summer. I was there when he fell."

"I see," Dr. Hú said. "What is your name?"

"Brigid."

"Brigid, it's a good thing you were there. You saved his life." She gave a steady look to Lynn, who stared resolutely out of the window. "Do you know if he was cooking something when he fell?"

"We think he was pouring coffee," Brigid answered quickly, "The pot had shattered and the coffee scalded his hands. I tried to put some cold water on the burns – I hope I didn't do anything to hurt him."

"On the contrary. Your quick thinking turned what might have been third degree burns into second degree burns. Much easier to heal and much less painful." Glancing at Brigid's bandaged hand, she added "You cleaned up the broken glass too, didn't you?" Brigid nodded. "We'll take a closer look at that shortly." Dr. Hú smiled. "Well, ladies, sit tight. I'll update you as soon as I know more." The doctor marched away to the tune of their thank yous.

For the first time, Lynn noticed the thick gauze wrapped around her daughter's hand. Wincing, she clutched her own hands together and bit back the tears that rose in her throat. Coughing to clear the emotion, she tried to meet her Brigid's eyes but her daughter was attempting to dig her buzzing phone out of her purse with her left hand.

"Let me." She reached over, found Brigid's phone and handed it across. She couldn't miss seeing the name in bold white at the top of the screen.

"Who is Gabe?" Lynn asked

Brigid was balancing the phone on her crossed leg, trying to compose a text with one finger of her good hand. "A guy," she muttered.

Lynn rolled her eyes. Why must it always be so hard with her daughter?

"Yes, I assumed. Is this the new romance?" She forced a smile, ducking her head low in an attempt to grab Brigid's attention, who was still bent over her phone. Brigid snapped up at this, frustration wrinkling her brow.

"What? Mom, I thought you didn't want to know." She softened a bit. "I do like him though." Biting her bottom lip, she looked away, hiding her vulnerability from her mother.

"Where did the two of you meet?" Lynn's tone was still harsh with worry.

Brigid swallowed. "He was helping my friend Chris – you remember Chris, from school?" Lynn nodded. "Anyway, he was helping Chris deliver the Websters' new sailboat."

"Chris works at the marina?" Lynn asked.

"In the summer, yes. Teachers don't make that much money, you know." She dared a smirk at her mother.

"Yes, Brigid. I know." Lynn raised her eyebrows and smirked

back. "So, this Gabe," Lynn continued. "He works at the marina in the summer too? Is he a teacher as well?" Lynn forced herself to sound enthusiastic. God forbid her daughter should get involved with another teacher. The plan had been to send her to college, have her pursue a well-respected profession like law or medicine. Lynn had always feared that Brigid's soft heart would lead her to service, but she tried so hard to push her daughter into something more impactful, more prestigious. If Brigid must serve others, law offered plenty of opportunity to help the less fortunate, to create real, measurable change for the problems of this world. Alternatively, why not be a politician, a community organizer, a lobbyist? At the very least, if Brigid insisted that teaching was her calling, she must continue her education and become a professor.

"Gabe works on his family's farm on the Peninsula." The words crashed into Lynn's brain. "He has a part-time job at the marina to earn extra money."

Brigid busied herself with her phone, not willing to witness her mother's reaction. She tried to block the sound of her mother's teeth grinding together – a sound she had heard her whole life. The horrid squeaking meant that Lynn was attempting to condense her temper, and that the person on the receiving end was about to receive a terse reprimand that would inform them, in no uncertain terms, what a foolish disappointment they were. The only thing to do was to wait, head bowed, until the blow came.

The teeth grinding went on for several excruciating minutes, then silence. Brigid glanced up, unable to stand the anticipation. Lynn sat with her head in her hands.

"Oh Brigid," Lynn muttered, disappointment dripping from the words.

A pit of indignation started to flame in Brigid's belly. This was ridiculous. She had done what they asked – go to college, earn good grades, attain a degree, get a salaried job with benefits that she happened to love. And now she had found a kind, hardworking, smart man. Gabe had been there with her during the accident, helping her grandfather. He had cradled Morgan's head in his lap for God's sake! Brigid's anger flared up into her eyes and she threw her shoulders back, ready for the first time in her life to fling the truth at her mother's disapproval.

But Lynn was ready. Gazing at her daughter steadily, she asked, "Why did you ever let Matthew go?"

Matt's name disarmed Brigid completely.

Matt Opher. A communications major headed for Business School. They had met at a party her junior year and she had fallen hard. When Matt looked at her, it seemed like she was the only person in the world who existed. He had held her at arm's length for months, taking her on dates, bringing her to parties, calling her, sending texts, but never committing. Of course she slept with him after the first few weeks. She couldn't help herself. He was her first real love. When he finally agreed to make a commitment, she blurted out that she loved him. In response, he gave her his beaming, extroverted smile. Me too, he had said.

She should have known.

Brigid remembered the parties in his dilapidated student bungalow, how she worked hard to connect with the women in his circle, vapid, status-seeking tigers with spiral curls and protruding collarbones. Conversation with these women always spiraled around money and marriage, grades and weight loss. Never dipping a toe below the surface, conversation was always insipid. She hardly spoke to Matt at these parties. As soon as the first friends arrived, he would always tell her she looked hot, grab her ass, and tell her to have fun. It was up to her to ingratiate herself into his circle. The implication was, she was lucky to be there, to be with him, at all.

Brigid would go up to his bedroom with him after these parties, exhausted. He would be drunk and happy, a pig in mud. Nothing made him more satisfied than a houseful of carousing, with plenty of alcohol to grease the brakes. And so, she would smile and pretend. Sometimes drinking heavily and joining in, just to spare herself the questioning; the analyzation of this vacuous society, and her place in it.

The truth was, she stayed partly because her parents loved Matt. The Ophers were a minorly prestigious family, having made their fortune in real estate. They owned a block of buildings in Matt's town, rented out to restaurants, bars, and shops. Both parents were lawyers, and actively involved in a vast lobbying effort at the State level to protect the shores of the lakes. And of course, Matt was affable, chatting with ease to her mother, grilling and drinking beer with her father like an old friend. When Matt visited her family, he smoothed the rough edges, made the hissing and intimidation disappear. When he was around, they could all pretend to be happy.

All of this cover came at a price. If Brigid didn't play the game: dress up, act cute, know exactly what to say to his parents, his friends, know when to back off and when to present herself as the girl who deserved to be with him, his disappointment would show. Conversations on dates would stagnate anytime she wanted to speak of something deeper than the latest football game. In fact, he had avoided dates, preferring parties or big groups, to which she was expected to accompany him, smiling and benevolent. He was smart, but applied it only to his studies. There was a clear definition of work and play. She tried valiantly to articulate her desires, her needs, her longing for something more. Brigid wanted nothing so much as to reach deep in and love him for who he truly was. But when she peered beneath the surface, there was nothing there.

Matt eventually tired of all the analyzation. He was annoyed by Brigid's longing for authenticity and her quiet but persistent dissatisfaction with his carefully curated presentation of self. They descended into arguments, drifted apart. He had tried to let her down gently. He wanted to 'allow her to have more time to herself.' When she questioned even that, he finally gave up. "You need to learn to have fun," he told her. "Why are you always frustrated? You are pretty and smart, why can't you enjoy it?" And finally, truth: "I don't know how to make you happy." She slept with him one final time, and he left in the morning. Standing up to greet the harsh morning light, she had touched the raspberry silk curtains that hung from her window. They were gift from her late grandmother. So unique, so untrendy. When her fingers brushed the watery fabric, she felt a wisp of freedom, but quickly succumbed to the heartbreak. Rejection, she found, was searing.

So much time was spent wondering how to expand the relationship, deepen it, discover what his want and desires really were, she had never explored what was good. For months, all Brigid wanted was to call him, text him, share her triumphs and her joys. She hadn't realized how enthusiastically he celebrated her happiness. How much his smiles had made her smile, his broad-armed embrace of pleasure lightened her heart. Throwing dignity to the side, she reached out to him a few times, but he had moved on. Kind, but firm, he emphasized that their foray into happiness was over. Now it was her turn to brutally interrogate herself. Why couldn't she just be happy, be simple? How could she possibly have driven him away? What was wrong with her? Not finding answers and unable to endure her misery any longer, she had returned home. When Lynn discovered the reason for her daughter's unexpected visit, the inquisition intensified. Brigid couldn't answer why she felt the need to make everything so deep, so complicated. And she certainly couldn't face her mother's dismayed cross-examination. So, she returned to college.

But the questions remained.

And today, sitting in the bleak hospital waiting room, Brigid still did not have the answers.

Brigid looked at her mother and shook her head. Words were futile. She glanced down at her phone to see if Gabe had texted back again and the bracelet Morgan had given her the night before twinkled against the harsh fluorescent light.

"You're wearing my mother's bracelet," Lynn said, in a whisper. Without thinking, Brigid clasped her hand over her wrist protectively.

"Grandpa gave it to me," Brigid started. The words tumbled

71

out. "I'm sorry. If you want it back – I mean, if you want it, I suppose it should be yours rather than mine. But you don't even wear gemstones and I really like it..."

"Stop." Lynn said. "I don't want it. I just remember it. She wore it every day. Just please... be careful."

"I won't break it or lose it, I promise," Brigid looked at her mother earnestly. She loosened her grip on her wrist, revealing red indentations where the stones pressed against her skin.

"I know you won't," Lynn began. "Your grandmother used it for..." Lynn trailed off, unable to articulate the memories that floated to the surface. She shook her head, physically erasing the thoughts that pierced her mind. "Never mind," she said firmly. "Be careful with the bracelet. That's all I wanted to say."

"Mom?" Brigid looked at her mother tentatively. "Could you tell me a little more about Grandma? If not, I totally understand, but I don't really remember her and everyone's always making comments..."

Lynn regarded her daughter. She was grown and on her own. It could be possible to unburden herself ever so slightly. She weighed the truth against what may be best for Brigid to know. But what was truth and what was merely fairy dust? Lynn glanced at the bracelet again. The foreboding stones, the self-satisfied carvings in the setting, the entire piece of jewelry seemed counterfeit to the truth. The sight of it turned her stomach and changed her mind. It was better that Brigid continue to be protected.

"Brigid, your grandmother was a silly woman." Lynn said firmly. "She was kind, yes, but very silly. My mother never stuck to one goal, to one purpose. Always floating around, concocting make-believe stories for you, leaving things everywhere, completely scatterbrained."

Brigid laughed, "I remember she let me paint her face completely blue one time – when she babysat me, remember?"

Lynn scowled. "Yes, I remember. I had a doctor's appointment in town." Lynn swallowed hard. "She let you have cookies for lunch and you threw up. I even left your father there to supervise and he fell asleep in the chair."

"Well, I don't remember that, but I remember the face painting. And then some delivery guy came with a package and she went out to greet him."

"There was never a stranger that your grandmother wouldn't love to chat with for an hour." Lynn shook her head at the memory. Brigid burst into a grin.

"I know!" She exclaimed. "She absolutely did! I remember she rushed onto the porch, face completely blue and she was oblivious. She talked to this poor guy for what must have been twenty minutes. Asked him about his family, his health. I was so embarrassed. I mean, she was completely cobalt blue! And then – I remember this, but it was so weird – she gave him several rocks. Pressed them into his hand and said something very serious."

"Always with those damned rocks. Nothing was more important to her." Lynn spoke through clenched teeth. "You have no idea how much time she had me spend combing the beach for them. I must have walked miles on every beach on the Peninsula. She even had me swim out into Big Omann Lake and dive for them!" Lynn remembered with an aching fury how she was forbidden from trying out for the tennis team she so dearly wanted to join. Her mother had forced her to be on the swimming team; become a diving expert. All so Lynn would be able to plunge into the freezing waters of Big Omann Lake, snatching stones from the murky depths.

"When she died," Lynn broke off, hardening her face. "When my mother died, she had a list – not a will, mind you, but a list. A list of the rocks she wanted to be buried with, how to arrange them around her body and in the coffin. Even where to place them on her body. My god." She coughed her emotion down, shaking her coiffed hair to chase away the vulnerability. "I didn't do it. It was enough that the whole county thought my mother considered herself a mystic, some sort of spiritual shyster. Out on that damned Peninsula, it's such a tiny cesspool of gossip. I wasn't about to let them see my mother bedecked in foolishness. No. I gathered up all the rocks in the house and threw them in the trash." Lynn snapped her head over to her own daughter. "Brigid, I want you to know that your father and I have a proper will. It includes end of life plans, funeral arrangements, everything. I'm sure there's a better time to tell you this, but we've named you as the Executor. I hope you'll take this responsibility seriously when the time comes."

Brigid was shocked. Did her parents really value her that much to trust her with the future? Tearing up would provide no assurance to her mother that this was a good choice. Sarcasm was the preferred response to emotion in their family. Brigid neutralized her expression. "I promise not to bury you with rocks, Mom."

The corner of Lynn's mouth turned up at her daughter's quick wit. Her daughter was smart. Lynn could not understand why Brigid always buried her intelligence; always acted cowed. She allowed herself to smile at her daughter. "Good," she said.

"Mom?" Brigid looked at her mother, hoping this crack in the armor might allow one more secret to escape. Choosing her words carefully, she asked, "What is with the rocks? You called her a mystic. Clearly, she thought the rocks had some significance. What was it?"

Lynn sighed. The rumors and stories had mostly subsided, dying with the generation that bore the heartache. Brigid didn't need to know the entire truth, and if she were honest with herself, Lynn wasn't sure she had the emotional bearing to tell it. But part of the truth, the surface, would surely suffice. It may finally convince her eldest daughter the mystery surrounding her grandparents was no ethereal enigma, but a dwindling story of foolishness.

"First of all," Lynn said, "eccentric is a much better designation than mystic. Brigid, I hope we've raised you well enough to know the difference between science and make-believe. Unfortunately, your grandmother did not. She was the first woman in her family to attend college, and she studied geology. Somewhere along the way, she lost focus on the scientific part of her degree and began to explore the metaphysical properties of stone. Eventually, she dropped out of college when her ideas about the meaning and purpose of stones contrasted sharply with the professors' idea of what she should be studying. She suddenly claimed to have come from a line of spiritual healers, although how she would know this, I cannot imagine. Her mother died young. Her grandmother in childbirth. And of course, her sister..." Lynn looked out the window, pushing away the memory. "In any case," she said, a determined firmness in her voice. "Your grandmother thought the rocks around the Peninsula had special properties. Properties of healing. She sold them to farmers to heal the land and sold them to other people as medicine or for love. It was absolutely ridiculous. And she was so impractical, never supervising me, certainly not supervising you when you were little. She believed that if we connected with the land, the land would take care of us." Lynn spit this last sentence out, contempt dripping from her lips. "And look at you, look at your back!" Brigid startled and flinched at the mention of her scar. "You almost drowned in the lake — almost bled out as a baby from scraping your back on some rotted dock piece. All while she was consulting her rocks." Lynn shook her head and glared, the fury and fear of the memory bleeding into her relationship with her only child. "What a fool."

Brigid lowered her eyes and swallowed hard. In a quiet voice, she said, "You know, I think Grandpa believes in it too. He's always making towers of rocks. They're everywhere in the cottage. And he stares at them, like he's expecting something to happen."

"Brigid, you have to ignore all of that," Lynn said. "God-willing, it's over now. Just don't even touch them. Or, even better, gather them up if they're in your way and simply throw them in the trash."

Brigid gazed at her mother. Had Lynn just given her blessing for Brigid to stay at Cairn Cottage?

"Ladies." Dr. Hú strode down the hallway. "Mr. Ayers will be under sedation for the remainder of the evening and we will run tests tomorrow morning as well. You both should return home and get some rest."

Lynn reached into her purse and flipped out a business card to hand to the doctor. "Thank you, doctor. Here is my personal number. I expect to be contacted if there are any changes."

Dr. Hú threw Lynn a sardonic look. "Your daughter gave all of your numbers when she filled out the paperwork." The doctor turned to Brigid. "I'll contact you both if you are needed. I promise."

"Shouldn't someone stay with him?" Brigid asked. "In case he wakes up – I don't want him to feel alone."

"Go home, honey," said the doctor, Brigid's unmasked love for the man peeling back Dr. Hu's professional demeanor. "He'll be unconscious the whole time. Check in with me tomorrow morning. My rounds are at 10:00 am."

"We certainly will," Lynn broke in. "Thank you, Doctor. Brigid?" It wasn't a question. Brigid nodded to the doctor and followed her mother down the hall.

CHAPTER 16

Between Gabe's double shifts at the marina and the time that Brigid was spending with Grandpa Morgan, first at the hospital and then at the nursing home, there was no time to see each other for days. Instead, they sent scrolls of texts and talked on the phone well into the night. Brigid told him all about her adventures on the ancient sailboat and the faded sail that was too torn to really work well. She asked him every conceivable question about life on the farm, and he described it to her with more pride that he ever knew he felt. They talked of everything and anything, except their families. Neither felt able to speak the deep truths of their family lives. Late into the week, Gabe realized he couldn't stand not seeing her another day. He asked if Brigid would like to come over for a glass of wine on the porch of his small home between his last shift and making dinner for his family. She agreed immediately. He picked her up as the late afternoon sun spread over the hills. Brigid and Gabe found themselves standing in the tall grass at the end of the driveway.

Gabe produced a wine key out of his pocket and lifted the bottle of Riesling from the bag in the back of the truck.

"I thought we could sit on the porch," he said.

"Could I see the orchard?" Brigid asked.

Gabe replied, "They're just trees."

"They're your trees." She smiled up at him.

"Well, if that's what you want." He planted a kiss on her head. "Let me grab a couple of glasses." As he stepped inside the house, Brigid surveyed the porch. There was no dusting of pollen on the table and chairs, no smattering of leaves on the floor.

It occurred to Brigid that he must have swept the porch before he came to pick her up. A warmth rushed up through her body.

"Ready?" Gabe shut the door and led her down the hillside. Dandelions and purple heather dotted the orchard ground. Tall grass that had missed the mower's blades waved in the afternoon breeze. Brigid took a deep breath, inhaling the sweet, herbal scent of an up north summer.

Gabe led them into an orchard row. The last of the cherry blossoms caught the afternoon light, tossing it with fairy-like abandon. Brigid ducked under a low-hanging branch, and laughed as the young leaves caught in her hair. Gabe grimaced, starting to apologize when Brigid whispered "It's beautiful."

Gabe looked at her face, illuminated by the soft afternoon light. All around her and beyond, he saw the gnarled trunks of the old cherry trees, branches overgrown and twisted. A better man could take care of this place properly, he thought to himself. What did she see that was beautiful? All he could see was his own failure.

He glanced back at her. She stood on her tiptoes and was gently pulling a branch to her nose.

"I can't get over how sweet it smells," she said. Gabe was surprised to see a single resilient cherry blossom hanging to the branch. It was much too late in the season for flowers. He had no idea how this last one remained. Impulsively, he plucked it from the branch and handed it to her.

"Gabe!" she admonished. "It needed to stay on the branch! You've robbed us of a cherry!"

A small smile lifted one side of his lips. "Worth it." He took her hand. "Let's go."

Brigid took a moment to gaze at the flower. From a distance, it looked white, but up close, she could see the deep ruby center spreading pink waves outward.

"Should we open this?" Gabe asked, proffering the wine bottle. Brigid smiled up at him.

"Sure." He took off his fleece jacket and laid it in the path between the trees, gesturing her to sit on it. "I'm fine," she said, shoving her hands in her pockets.

"Just sit," he said, smiling. "I should've brought a blanket."

Brigid's mind went immediately to the mysterious mantle she had found in the chest. When she returned from the hospital, she had hung it on the clothesline. By the end of the day, it had absorbed the soft air of the lake and the scent of pine resin.

Gabe saw the faraway look in her eyes. He sat down in the grass beside her. "Are you thinking about your Grandpa?" he asked gently. Brigid snapped out of her reverie.

"Kind of," she said, nervously brushing an invisible speck off of her arm.

"How's he doing?"

"About the same." Brigid swallowed hard. "They say he'll live, but they're hedging about recovery." The familiar lump rose in her throat. Out of instinct, she froze, not allowing the sadness to gain hold. If she showed sadness, weakness, it could only lead to hurt. She had learned that all too well before. She straightened her shoulders and cleared her throat. "Are you going to pour that, or what?" She elbowed him, forcing a smile.

Gabe gave her a long look. She cast her eyes away, not wanting to find pity on his face. Silently, he poured the wine and passed her a glass. She took a deep drink and forced her shoulders to relax.

"Thank you," she said, more formally than she meant. Gabe raised his eyebrows and made a little bow.

"You are most welcome."

She looked at him. He was grinning. Finally, she laughed. "I'm sorry," she said.

Gabe reached over and brushed a curl off of her face. "Why are you sorry? There's no reason for you to be sorry. I'm sorry I couldn't take you on a real date tonight, but I just... I don't know. I had to see you."

Color rose in Brigid's cheeks as she leaned into his arm. His skin smelled like the sweet grasses of the Peninsula and the oil from the sailboats. She inhaled his scent and placed a soft kiss on the side of his neck. She felt his strong hand tightened around her shoulder and the pressure of his lips in her hair.

They sat in the stillness as the sun made its way across the sky, sending glistening rays across the tops of the cherry trees. A horse whinnied in the distance, breaking their trance. Brigid looked at her watch. It was nearly 6:30 and Gabe had said he needed to get dinner for his family. "I should go" she said. "You have things you need to do." Gabe sighed ruefully. He looked at her. How did the sun always seem to illuminate her face like that?

"Don't you have to cook?" she was saying. "Come on, we should go."

Gabe stood up and offered her his hand. "I can pick up a pizza from Moe's," he said. "At least I get to drive you home."

Brigid covered up the hint of hurt in her eyes with a bright smile. She had been hoping she might be invited to stay. But, she thought, it was way too soon. Probably he didn't want to introduce her to his family yet. She hadn't proven herself worthy.

Gabe ran a hand through his hair before gathering the wine bottle and the glasses. He constantly had the responsibility of his mother and his brother. But God, he thought, why couldn't he be spared for just this one night? More than that, he wanted Brigid to be there. With him, beside him. He wanted that bright smile to light up the kitchen, feel the touch of her soft hand on his arm. Maybe he should just ask her if by any chance she wanted to stay.

Then he thought of the small, dark kitchen in the main house with its grimy cupboard handles and crumbs on the counter. His mother in the ratty armchair, worry lining her face and her harsh voice. Even Mikey, sweet as he was, would surely get in Brigid's face, pestering her with questions and the never-ending stories of a child. He couldn't bear for Brigid to see all that yet. Besides, who was he to ask her to stay for a drab family dinner? He had asked her on a date and the best he could do was sitting in an orchard.

"It really was beautiful," Brigid was saying. She looked up and saw the grim line of his mouth. Had she said the wrong thing? Maybe real farmers didn't think of their crops as beautiful.

"You're beautiful." Gabe's voice was tight. He turned to her suddenly, wrapping one strong arm around her waist while he wove his other hand through her hair, guiding her mouth to his. He kissed her deeply, tasting the fruit of the wine on her lips.

Pulling himself away, he looked at the horizon. The day was dying. He looked at Brigid, forcing all the things he wanted to say to her away from his mind. It was too soon. He couldn't risk losing her.

Instead, he said only, "Let's get you home."

CHAPTER 17

Early the next morning, the crunching of gravel underneath tires woke Brigid. She reached over the side table and picked up her phone. No text, no call. She sighed. Was she mistaken? The connection between them during all the calls and texts, the time at the beach, the farm had all seemed so real. So simple. So true. Yet maybe, once again, she was reading much more into a situation than was really there.

She plodded into the kitchen and began to fill the new coffee pot with water. She had winced at the price when she bought it at the little grocery store in Birch Glen, but there was part of her that didn't want to spend a dime in Domhnall Hills, even if she went almost every day to visit her grandpa.

The clock read 8:30. She laughed a little at herself as she rubbed the sleep from her eyes. Only a few weeks into summer and she already used to sleeping in. When the coffee was ready, she poured a splash of milk in her coffee and opened the heavy front door to let in the soft morning light.

She saw the flowers first. The bouquet was enormous, a wild bundle of snapdragons, zinnias, sunflower, dahlias, and lavender, with pink-petaled sweet pea vines trailing down the sides. It was tied with twine and set on a long, cylindrical canvas-wrapped bundle. Brigid gingerly lifted the package. It was heavy, and the sound of metal on metal rang muffled in the bag. Her breath caught as she squeezed the bag, feeling heavy cloth. She knew what this was and didn't dare believe who it might be from. Gently setting the flowers aside, she loosened the string that tied the package. She drew out a brilliantly-colored sail, bound perfectly to a lower and upper boom. She could see pure blue, sunshine yellow, bright orange, indigo, and a spark of fuchsia pink. A grin spread from ear-to-ear. It was the sail in the window of Sunset Marina, the one she looked at every time she went into Birch Glen, and coveted since she came to the Peninsula. How could he possibly know?! Tucked into the halyard line was a note. She reached down and unfolded it.

"You said this week that sailing makes you feel free, but you can't have freedom with a torn sail.

This one reminded me of you.

Give me a shout if you need help with the rigging. I hope you will let me take you to dinner tonight.

~Gabe"

Impulsively, she reached down and hugged the sail, planting a kiss on the brilliant blue stripe. What she felt, what she knew in her heart...

...Maybe it was truth.

CHAPTER 18

Gabe picked her up in the late evening. From the minute she caught sight of him striding down the driveway, she was subsumed. The walls she had so carefully constructed around her heart crumbled even more under the easy brilliance of his smile. As he approached, Brigid took a breath. Tried to settle down. Calm the riotous beating of the blood through her veins.

It was futile.

He took her to dinner at one of the lakeside restaurants in Birch Glen. They sat on the patio watching the sky flare into peaks of rouge and magenta, and slowly melt into muted cerulean that nestled over the horizon. The meal passed in a blur, neither of them eating much. They couldn't seem to stop talking. Laughter sparkled in the dusk. When the untouched lava cake had been boxed up, Brigid sipped whiskey, waiting. Gabe finished his beer and reached for her hand. "Want to leave?"

Brigid looked at him, eyes blazing.

"Yes."

Gabe drove them back toward Cairn Cottage, speeding a little. Brigid's heart quickened as he pulled into the driveway. She didn't want to bring him into the cottage – she had slept in that bedroom as a child. But she couldn't bear the thought of him leaving. "Do you want to go for a walk?" Surprise and disappointment flew across his face until he artfully rearranged it into a mask of amenable friendliness. "Sure. You do know it's dark, though?" She grinned at him. "We have the moon. Let me just run in and grab a blanket."

Inside, Brigid snatched an old quilt from the linen closet. She tucked it under her arm and ran back out, locking the door behind her.

The old, secret two-track road that led back to Big Omann Lake cut through the untouched forest. Birches, beech, and pines rose tall and bent in a canopy over their heads. Ancient ferns sprouted up from the rich earth, and owls called their mournful song unseen. Gabe reached for Brigid's hand as they walked up the long, gentle hill toward the lake. They were silent. Words seemed redundant on the moonlit path. The lake beckoned, the sound of the waves traveling through the trees as they drew closer to the beach. They reached the clearing, soil giving way to sand where tentacles of poison ivy wove through the wildflowers.

Brigid had walked this path every day this summer. The sight of the crystal blue lake bursting through the tall grass and stretching across the horizon never failed to steal her breath. She allowed herself to explore the length and breadth of the beach, climbing the gentle dunes, discovering groves free of undergrowth where she could curl up and read. She led Gabe to a cove nestled in a peninsula of pines. Brigid spread the blanket and sat down, hands resting behind her back, leaning forward toward the lake. The moon shone down, shimmering on the water. Gabe knelt beside her.

Calloused fingers brushed the warmth of her cheek as Gabe led her eyes to his. Her heartbeat was racing. He drew her body toward his. She lifted one trembling palm, then the next, across his hollow cheekbones. His lips guided her own, gently parting her mouth as the whisper of moonlight twinkled through the trees. Brigid leaned back ever so slightly, and pressed into the kiss.

"Do you want me?" he whispered as color rose to his confident cheeks.

Brigid smiled up at him, yearning for what could be. She held his gaze like a magnet.

"Yes."

His strong hands wove through her hair, penetrating her auburn waves. The eternal reaching and release of the water, back and forth, propelled them onward. Lips graced lips, fervent. Reverent.

The world fell away, there was nothing but this.

* * *

As the moon grew brighter in the sky, Brigid's eyes fluttered open. She loosened one hand from his grip and touched the brown stubble on his cheekbone. She breathed in the scent of moss growing on fallen tree trunks, the sweetness of the tall grass. Tenderly, she kissed the crown of his head.

"We should go home."

CHAPTER 19

Brigid rubbed her eyes and shimmied deep into the bed-covers like a cat. Sun had illuminated the room since the very early hours, sending Brigid and Gabe into each other's arms again. He had left a few hours later, refusing to let her rise to make them breakfast, fix coffee, or even walk him to the door. Instead, he showered her with kisses, waiting until the last possible moment to leave for work. Grinning sleepily at the memories, she raised her arms to the sky in a languid stretch. She was deliciously sore.

Brigid gazed around the room. It was a mess. Between her haste to dress for the date early yesterday evening, and the passionate undressing that ensued after their return from the beach path, she could barely see the floor. With a sigh, Brigid relented to the day. Swinging her legs over the side of the bed, she looked around to see where her phone had landed, jumping up painfully when her foot landed on a sharp corner sticking out from under the bed. Twisting her chestnut curls over her shoulder, Brigid leaned down and lifted up a box she had never noticed until now.

Like the chest in the closet, this box had polished lake stones glued onto a heavy wooden lid. The bottom of the box was carved with the same symbols she had found on the large chest. Unlike the first box, this one was longer and wider.

Brigid lifted the lid.

The late morning sunshine illuminated the fine handwriting scrawled across at thick stack of pages. Brigid recognized it as her grandmother's script.

*"Instructions for Healing: Heart, Soul, and Land
The Society of Stone Seekers*

*Founding Members: Shannon and Morgan Ayers, Emma and
Graham Webster, Nieve and David Lee*

*Based on tradition and practices passed down from Asa Mar-
lowe and ancestors"*

Gently lifting the faded pages, Brigid realized she was
looking at an unbound book. The sections were paper-clipped
together. Heartbreak, Loss of a Parent, Dejection, Rejection,
Cruelty in the Home, Nervous Thoughts, Loss of a Child.
Shuffling through the papers, she found sections that puzzled
her until she remembered the land reference in the title: Wee-
vils, Gypsy Moths, Lack of Rain, Heat Spell, Cold Snap, Bow
Arrow Storm. Wrinkling her brow, she lifted the last section.
Brigid had never heard of this strange term. Below the heading, her grandmother had recorded:

"Bow Arrow Storm:
*Extremely high winds move in a straight path, cutting down
trees, crops, and buildings. Very rare but has occurred. In the event
of a bow arrow storm, place cairns of smooth-faced stones in fields,
and at the base of structures and trees. If polished, glowing stones
are on hand, wear them to reflect any light that might be available
and shine that light to others. Make amends with all creatures you
have harmed, or who have harmed you to lessen the force of this
type of relentless, driving storm."*

A sudden, strong gust of wind blew through the window,
causing Brigid to drop the papers onto the floor. They scattered, fanning out as the paperclips clung to them.

"Shit," she muttered under her breath. Her mind was beginning to spin. The clutter of the room, the stickiness of her body
and the relentless worry about her grandfather's illness tore at

the filaments of her mind. She should put this back, shower, make a plan for the day. And yet she was overwhelmed with fascination.

This box held a new truth about the women who made her. There was something indefinably right about her chosen isolation at Cairn Cottage, her union with Gabe. She couldn't explain it, but she felt it in her bones. Her eyes burned brighter, her spine laced with determination. She gathered up the papers and placed them back into the box. When the chaos was put back in order, Brigid went to the small closet. She dragged the heavy chest out from its hiding place in the darkness and placed it at the foot of her bed. When she opened the lid, she saw there was room for the box of papers to fit perfectly on top of the folded linen. The cobwebs were clearing. All she wanted was to spread her thoughts and the contents of the box on the sandy wooden floor, but clarity beckoned. She would carry everything down to the long dining room table, not rising until she had discovered the truth. But first, a shower and caffeine. She wrapped Gabe's fleece around her chest and padded downstairs.

The dining room windows were open to the lake, breathing happy fresh air into Cairn Cottage. The deep scent of the pine board perfumed the room and Brigid took a full, grateful breath. It seemed like the old building embraced her, breeze sighing through all the open windows, sunlight glinting and sparkling through the huge picture windows, illuminating the old arm chairs.

In this moment, she was strong. Free. In this place, it was safe to acknowledge the truth about her feelings for Gabe. Although they'd known each other for less than a month, they had spent every available waking moment together. Most of the moments had been awake, she thought. It was a year since she thought she lost the love of her life, and yet time with Gabe was so different than time with Matt. When Gabe was with her, she could be herself; laugh fully, employ her wit and sarcasm, let her gentleness show. He bent down beside her when she knelt to cup a ladyslipper flower in the palm of her hand, smiled when she stopped to gaze at the deer loping through the woods. He didn't mind her scatterbrained occasions, accepting them simply as part of who she was.

And the way Gabe looked at her. Shivers ran through her body at the thought of it. She could be reading a book nestled in the crook of his arm, pouring drinks for them, or gazing out at a moonglade over the lake, she would feel his eyes on her.

Her heart had given in completely. Logic was the only thing holding her back. They lived very different lives; had different expectations of the future. She told herself this gentle lie to push down the sliver of pretension, of privilege that wouldn't fade away. She wasn't sure if she'd fit into a family of farmers. She knew her mother didn't think so. Brigid felt her throat tighten unpleasantly.

The ringing seemed to shake the walls of the cottage. Brigid looked at her phone.

Mom Cell

Brigid sighed. She needed a hit of something before she answered this call. She looked quickly at the liquor cabinet but decided it was too early. Caffeine. She needed caffeine. She poured a mug and answered the phone.

"Brigid!" Her mother's voice came fast and angry. There was something else that Brigid couldn't identify. Was it fear? Had the worst happened? Her stomach sank to the floor.

"Mom, is it Grandpa? Is he okay?"

"What?" asked Lynn. "He's fine — I don't know, I'm sure he's fine. Brigid, you did not tell me the full name of this man you're dating." Fury flew over the phone and Brigid was taken aback by her vehemence. "A Sherland? You are dating a Sherland?" Lynn screeched Gabe's last name.

"Yes, his last name is Sherland," Brigid said, confused. "Gabe Sherland. His family owns the big farm on the corner of Rahounas Road."

"I know where those people live," Lynn spat. "Listen to me, Brigid. Just listen."

"Mom, what is the problem?" Brigid broke in. Her own anger was rising. This was absurd. She was doing nothing wrong. In fact, she was doing things right for the first time in her life. She was leaning into everything that made her happy, made her calm. Lynn's ridiculous expectations would not rob her of this. "Gabe is a really great guy. He's kind, he's hardworking, he's a gentleman. You would know this if you met him."

"I don't need to meet him, Brigid. I know his type, and I know his family. You cannot date him. Brigid, listen to me: you just can't."

"This is ridiculous!" Indignation made Brigid bold. "I'm twenty-four years old, I have a job, I'm a financially independent woman."

"You are not financially independent!" Lynn shouted into the phone. "You live rent-free at your grandfather's home! You are dependent on him for your shelter, dependent on your father and I for your education and your upbringing – My God, Brigid, nearly everything you have is a result of someone else's hard work!"

Brigid began to shrink again, head hanging. Her mother spoke the harsh truth, as always. A privileged, flighty young woman. That's what she was in her mother's eyes. In Matt's. This was her identity in the hard gaze of the world. As she set the phone down to compose her response, the stone bracelet tinkled on her wrist.

There was something more here. Something more to her. She was made of more than just the rigid pragmatism of her mother's life. Maybe she was not accomplished in the ostentatious way her mother seemed to long for, but her life did have some meaning.

Brigid lifted the phone to her ear with resolve.

"Mom, thank you for everything you and dad have done for me. Thank you. Okay? I can't repay you. Believe me, I realize that. But right now I'm doing what I love. And I am taking care of Grandpa to make up for my rent-free living. Or I was, before he got sick."

"Brigid, I don't care about that," Lynn said. "Your gratitude is unnecessary. I'm calling about this man you're dating. You are not hearing me. You cannot date a Sherland." Lynn's voice rung with finality, but for once in her life, Brigid ignored the tone.

"You have no right to tell me who I can and cannot date!" Brigid's vision blurred as her voice rose. "Gabe is wonderful and educated and you haven't even met him. Just meet him before you judge him. And what is your problem with the Sherlands? It's just a name, they're farmers in the area – the name has nothing to do with anything."

"The name has everything to do with it, Brigid. The Sherlands..." Lynn broke off, her tone desperately insistent. "The Sherlands are — a bad family. Okay, Brigid? They're just bad stock."

"Mom, how do you even know anything about them? You have no idea!"

"Do you want me to say it, Brigid? Fine, I'll say it. The Sherlands are trash. They are trash. This Gabe may seem nice and smart and whatever else you'd like to say, but I guarantee you that behind that façade, he's a deadbeat. A degenerate, just like his father and just his grandfather."

"A deadbeat? My God, Mom, he went to college just like me – he works full-time at the marina and practically runs that entire farm! What else do you want? I'm sorry he's not your precious Matt – who didn't give a shit about me, by the way."

"Brigid! Language!"

"Oh screw my language, Mom," Brigid spit venom, more like her mother than she could ever conceive. "I am with Gabe."

There was a terrible silence on the other end of the line. Brigid's whole body shook with the weight of what she had just said.

"You're with him." Lynn repeated sarcastically. "If you involve yourself with that family, Brigid..." Lynn paused. "It's worthless."

Tears streamed down Brigid's face. The tears that she'd been holding back, kept walled off behind her heart, escaped.

Worthless. Finally, her mother admitted the bald-faced truth. Brigid was worthless to her. From the time she was a young child, her mother had held back. Broken embraces and cold-lipped kisses, as if Brigid were filthy. Stern lectures on a well-ordered life, those were Brigid's maternal comforts. And Brigid had tried, she had certainly tried. Directives were followed to the best of her ability: she handed her mother good grades, she displayed meek, polite manners, she enrolled in her mother's alma mater, and although she earned her degree in education under the shadow of her mother's disappointment, she walked across that stage with highest honors. Brigid had employed hidden determination to secure a rare teaching job near her parent's home and had succeeded enormously. Her students were learning, passing tests that made the official measure of success to the state. More importantly, her students were loved.

Her imagination, her curiosity, the part of Brigid's heart that forced her to stop engaging with cold reality and instead, to cup a flower in her palm, stand still in a breeze, or savor the light that filtered through the trees, her thoughtful self could not be suppressed forever. It had irritated her mother from the time she was a small child. Touch, Brigid always had to touch. It was as if she were embraced by an other-worldly peace. Brigid couldn't explain it, least of all to her mother, but she needed to lean into this ethereal embrace constantly. If she stayed in the monotonous, striving, tangible world too long, she began to itch. Trapped and twisted inside her own pile of bones. It was why she had decided to move out to Cairn Cottage. Lynn despised this part of her daughter, calling it distracted, flighty. She tried to freeze it out of her daughter the best she knew how. And it had almost worked.

The sunlight shimmered on the lake, reaching out its rays through the old kitchen window. Brigid turned her face to its glow. There was something here. A tender mystery in air, the water, the stones, in those piles of writings. And Gabe. The love that she knew she felt, against all reason, against all logic, that was pure. It was real. More real than anything that had come to her life before. And she would not give it up. Her mother tried to shape her daughter into a ladder-climbing automaton who forgot all traces of the enchantment inside of her. But Brigid couldn't fit the mold. She would no longer try. From this moment, Brigid would turn to the instincts that had been calling out to her since birth.

She wiped her tears with the back of her hand and turned to the phone. The timer marking the length of the call kept ticking. Her mother had not hung up.

"Mom?" Brigid began. Courage stirred inside her. "Mom, I love you. I'm sorry for all the times I've disappointed you. I've tried to be what you want. I've really, really tried. But now I'm going to try living my own life."

Brigid swallowed hard, waiting for the inevitable sting. She could hear her mother breathing. Breath and a terrible silence. A minute passed. Two. The anger that swirled in her heart clenched into hurt. She had laid herself bare for her mother, admitted her failure, apologized for the person she couldn't become. She had professed her love – how many times? Unanswered. Unanswered today. Unanswered always. Her mother could call her worthless, but couldn't bring herself to say "I love you" back.

Brigid hung up.

CHAPTER 20

Emma Webster rolled Brigid's agate in her palm. Such an unusual stone. Delicate, with pearlescent stripes banding the circumference. The stone would only lie flat on one of its surfaces. The edge that could be seen was a jagged crater with wounded edges. It looked like a flaw, but when Emma held it to the light, a perfectly formed amber heart could be seen in the deepest part of the crevice.

Emma held it gently, but confusion marred her face. Children who would grow to be women like Brigid usually chose the gentle pink and green jaspers, or the harmonious marbled quartz. Her own daughter Renee had immediately gripped a dark basalt, with the glowing quartz band encircling its middle. Emma chuckled at the memory. Renee had shouted "Mine," refusing to give up the stone, even to allow Brigid's grandmother Shannon to examine it. Renee didn't need any divining for Emma to know her daughter's true nature; like the volcanic rock she chose, Renee was ruthless, melting everything in her path. And like the truth-telling basalt, Renee had no trouble pointing out the negative attributes of everyone and everything. Emma hoped the thick quartz band would be a sign that peace would encircle her fiery daughter, but she didn't know anymore. These days, it was hard to believe that any of it was true.

She set the agate down and watched as it played with the light. Brigid's Ceremony seemed like yesterday. Emma's friend Shannon had hoped that her granddaughter would choose the feldspar, the goddess stone infused with feminine energy.

Shannon herself had chosen a shimmering feldspar stone at her own Ceremony. She wore it on a silver chain, a miniature moon the color of sand, with an infinity of markings. Two bands, inky like the winter sky, hugged the stone from behind. Emma remembered with a smile how her husband Graham had chosen the twin stone, dark granite with gorgeous lightening streaks, with a burst of gentle, sand-colored feldspar in the middle. As if her feminine, mystical self leaned into his strong, protective chest and he wrapped his arms around her, even in their spirit stones.

Emma's grandchildren would never have a Ceremony. Renee wouldn't allow it. Emma didn't dare conduct it in secret like Shannon Ayers had done for Brigid. The day Brigid's Ceremony was held, Lynn and Kelsey had dropped Brigid at Cairn Cottage in the morning. They were headed back into town for a prenatal appointment. Lynn was already hesitant to leave her only child with her mother. Emma shook her head, remembering Shannon's tirade about Lynn's new home in Domhnall Hills. Lynn and Kelsey had been so proud of that house. In front of a room full of people, Morgan had declared it to be a pile of cookie-cutter nonsense. Shannon had called the new development a "raped and ravaged hillside."

Still, Lynn had delivered Brigid to Cairn Cottage that day, putting her in Shannon's arms with a mouthful of instructions. Brigid was not to eat any sugar. She was not to crawl anywhere near the steep staircase. And most importantly, she was forbidden to touch the water. When Shannon had inquired about whether Brigid's baby bathing suit was in the massive bag Lynn had brought, she answered with pursed lips. "Brigid is not to go in the lake. It is too deep, and too murky, and God knows what parasites are in there this summer." Shannon had put a calming hand on Morgan's arm, whose temper flared at the insult to the lake. A true basalt, Morgan, explosive and red-hot. Thank goodness his stone had a slash of quartz, pointing to a streak of kindness, healing, and clarity, which mercifully distinguished most of Morgan's interactions.

The stone Lynn had chosen at her Ceremony seemed now like a mistake. A beautiful, gentle jasper, with green trails, dots of moss, and golden flecks racing across its currant-colored surface. Meticulous as a toddler, Lynn had wrinkled her nose at the gorgeous blue basalt with the milky streaks and stars of quartz. Shannon had been convinced that her mercurial daughter would follow Morgan's stone spirit into the volcanic basalt family, but Lynn had chosen mellow, soothing jasper. This stone was known as the Supreme Nurturer, which was a cruel joke when one observed how Lynn mothered Brigid. Jasper also signified organization, the setting of the sun, endings. Well, Emma mused, Lynn was certainly organized. Her life was metered and planned with military rigidity. And as for endings, it could be argued that Lynn's actions had ended the Stone Society.

Who knew where that jasper lay now? The day of Brigid's ceremony, Shannon had glanced at her daughter's arm, where she hoped the jasper pendant would lay nestled, ready to protect them during this crucial medical appointment. Instead, Lynn's wrist was bare. Vulnerable. Lynn noticed her mother's glance and rolled her eyes. "No, Mother, I'm not wearing the bracelet. I don't even really know where it is. But don't worry," she said, sarcasm dripping from her tone. "I have a college degree, health insurance, and great doctors. I'll be fine." With that, she had handed Brigid over the threshold into Shannon's arms, and turned on her heel to leave. Kelsey stayed for a moment longer, offering hugs and thanks, kissed his baby on the head, and followed his wife down the sandy driveway.

Shannon carried her granddaughter into the kitchen, handing her a freshly-baked chocolate chip cookie. Morgan grabbed his coffee cup from the long dining table and the neighbors rose from the couches and armchairs in the living room, smiling at this sweet baby with the enormous blue eyes.

Shannon had been a good mother, but she was born to be a grandmother. The love she felt for her daughter's daughter shone unabashedly on her face. She mediated her strong voice to a gentle sing-song without thinking about it, lulling her fragile, nervous granddaughter into happy contentment. Shannon bounced and swayed in the age-old soothing motion. She had loved Lynn, of course, but like all mothers, worry, planning, the need to discipline and shape a tiny human elbowed in on the outward affection. But grandmothers didn't need to bother with all of that. The love of a grandmother was unabashed, untethered, enormous. And Brigid had felt it, beaming at Shannon with the unmasked joy of children.

After Lynn had left, the cream lace mantle was folded in the middle of the living room floor, with polished stones scattered across its surface. Some stones were decades old, some had been gathered on the day of Brigid's birth from Big Omann Lake. The coffee table contained a silver dish of water and a second silver dish of sand. A silver candlestick held a single candle, whose flame flickered in the breeze. Finally, an old glass jam-jar was placed in front of the candle. The late-morning sunlight danced through the giant picture windows. Four panes for the four elements of the earth, each slanted at the top to fit in the A-frame front of the cabin. Morgan and Shannon had settled on the plaid couch with Brigid between them, facing the coffee table. Nieve Lee, David's sweet, mysterial wife knelt before the coffee table. She dipped her right palm into the bowl of sand and reached for Brigid's feet. Smiling at the baby, she gave the first blessing while letting the sand dribble over her tiny feet:

"Brigid Ayers Firth, may you walk in the prosperity and abundance of the Earth. May you look to the ground, to the trees, to the flowers for wisdom. May you nourish all beings as the Earth nourishes all beings. May you become a giver of Life, just as the Earth is the giver and sustainer of Life. Let this sand upon your feet help you on your journey, not slippery or shifting, but as the dust of mountains, the essence of the stones, which lay within your heart from this day forward. In the God through Earth may you be kept."

Everyone in the room answered: "In God through Earth

may you be kept." Brigid giggled as the sand tickled her toes. Nieve smiled as she unscrewed the jam jar and held it under Brigid's nose.

"Brigid Ayers Firth, may you be a lover of freedom, a dreamer of dreams. May this pure Air, gathered from the beaches of Big Omann Lake, give flight to knowledge, and elevate your joy. May your thoughts be clear, and may your wings be wide. In God through Air may you be kept."

"In God through Air may you be kept," echoed the room. Nieve lifted the candle and gently blew the flame so it flickered toward the baby, who stretched out her plump little hands. Everyone in the room laughed softly as Nieve quickly pulled the candle away. Taking a moment to compose herself, Nieve began the third blessing:

"Brigid Ayers Firth, may your love be a warm embrace for all creatures who stand in your light. May your ethereal energy intensify the world at your fingertips. May you burn with passion, goodness, and love, but may you never allow the heat to consume you. In God through Fire may you be kept."

Emma glanced at Shannon as she repeated the blessing. Shannon held her granddaughter, smiling and sure, but her eyes brimmed with tears. Emma knew the Fire blessing was brutal for Shannon. Nieve noticed as well. She tried to catch Shannon's eye with gentle, penetrating gaze, but her friend was transfixed by the flickering flame. Nieve quickly blew out the candle, interfering with the ritual, but succeeding in snapping Shannon out of her trance. Nieve met her eyes and gave an imperceptible shake of her head. Shannon swiped the tears away and gave a shudder, kissing the baby's downy curls and gave Nieve a nod to continue with the final blessing.

Nieve dipped two fingers into the dish of water. She touched a drop to the crown of Brigid's head, her throat, her heart, and her belly.

"Brigid Ayers Firth, may your dreams and your creations flow as freely as the Water. May your love for the world become a healing power that purifies the beings around you, just as Water cleanses and purifies all that she touches. May your mind be as fresh and clear as the lakes of the Peninsula. May your love flow truly, kindly, and passionately to all. In God through Water may you be kept."

"In God through Water may you be kept." Everyone in the room rose to dip fingers into the bowl and bless themselves. Each member of the Society kissed the baby's cheeks, her hands, and the crown of her head.

Graham clapped his hands, eager to get on to his favorite part of the Ceremony: the choosing of the stone. "Put her down, put her down," he admonished playfully. "Let this child find her spirit! If I were a betting man, I'd put her as a feldspar, like her grandmother Shannon. Eh, David?"

David grinned. If they'd let him, Graham would run a bet on every Ceremony. He looked over at Brigid, giggling and sweet in her grandmother's arms. "No," he said. "This child is too calm to be a feldspar. I would peg this child as a jasper. A nurturer, an interpreter. A gentle giver of strength."

"No, she can't possibly be a jasper!" Graham sputtered. "Jaspers can be flighty, always trying to interpret the imagery, and they so often get it wrong." Shannon's face was desolate. Nieve and Emma looked from her to the men, now standing and pointing fingers like this was a great game. "Who am I thinking of?" Graham asked. "Which of us is jasper?"

"Graham," Emma had said. "You should not wager on these things. It robs its significance." Graham was silenced by her tone. Clipped from his amusement, he glanced around the room until his eyes met Shannon's. "Ruby," she said with shaking lips. "Ruby was our jasper. My sister."

Brigid squirmed against grandmother's tight grip. Morgan patted her arm as he glanced up at Graham. "It's alright," Morgan said. "He meant no harm. Don't go there." Turning to his wife, Morgan lifted her chin to make her face him. He spoke quietly. "Shannon, today is about Brigid. Ruby would have wanted you to enjoy this day. Let's allow the child to choose her stone." A look passed between them as Shannon loosened her hold on her granddaughter and handed her to Morgan. Nieve took her place for this final blessing, standing against the enormous windows to allow the morning light to form an aura behind her.

"Sweet child of God," she began. "You have been named Brigid by your parents, and should strive to honor them all of your days, as you should honor all of your family, your teachers, your friends, and if this is your path, your partner and your children. May the people who you love strive to help you. May they do their best by you. But, we are only human. Those around you will influence you to go their way, see the world through their eyes, tie yourself to their anchor. You must remember who you truly are, every day, every second of your time on this earth. Your stone is the sister of your spirit, a sign from God. It will protect you, give you strength, help you to know the love and peace that lay beyond the desolations of this world." Nieve lifted her arms. "Morgan Ayers, bring the child to sit upon this mantle, which has wrapped the people of your blood as they entered the world, and been their last comfort as they left us. After each birth and each death, we have washed this holy mantle in the waters of the lake, stains of human existence scrubbed away by the sand from the earth and the ash from the flames. It has dried in the soft, fresh air of springtime, and it now sits, waiting for you."

Shannon set Brigid gently down in the middle of the cloth, stones scattered around her.

The little girl flapped her chubby arms against her legs. She let out a soft giggle as she reached out for the stones. Brigid grasped rose-colored feldspar with dark gray streaks like tree limbs. Shannon raised her eyebrows and grinned. The child picked up an inky basalt with her other hand and scowled at it, tossing it away. The adults watching laughed softly. "She certainly knows who she's not," Morgan stage-whispered playfully. Brigid began to crawl across the cloth. Still holding the feldspar, she picked up a flame-colored jasper. Her mother's stone. She tapped the jasper and feldspar together, laughing at the warm clicking sound they made. Her arms stretched further and further outward, banging the stones together. As she hammered the stones against each other, the light filtering in through the huge windows faded away. Clouds began to form over the lake. Finally, she set the feldspar down.

Everyone in the room jumped when Brigid suddenly threw both stones toward the huge bay window. Nieve and Emma locked eyes above the baby's head. Brigid determinedly crawled to the edge of the cloth and picked up the pale, milky agate. With the stone in her right hand, she crawled back toward the direction of her grandmother, reaching to Shannon.

"Up," she said, in her bubbly baby's voice. As she spoke, the cloud cover lifted and sunbeams filtered in, making the stones left on the cloth sparkle. Shannon gently uncurled the tiny fingers. She lifted to stone to examine it.

"Agate," she pronounced, trying to hide the hint of disappointment in her voice. Agate was the least-assuming of stones, not especially picturesque even when polished. No striking bands, trails, shapes, spots or patterns that could be interpreted or meditated upon. Only pockmarks, wrinkles in the soft stone that made it look aged, ruined. Nieve cleared her throat and stepped back in front of the window.

"Brigid, you are Agate. Your spirit is calming and kind. You elevate the world for those around you. Those who come into your life will be energized and empowered. And if the ill-luck befalls you or the ones you love, your spirit will protect all in need." This last line she delivered straight to Shannon, who nodded slowly in gratitude.

Emma had stepped forward then. She took the stone from Shannon and lightly touched it to the baby's crown, lips, throat, and heart. "You chose a beautiful stone, Brigid. Subtle, yes, but sweet and calm and beautiful. Just like you." Emma kissed Brigid's downy head and lifted her chin. "I will make this into a bracelet for you to wear always." Brigid smiled at her and Emma felt her heart swell. The child truly was a calming force.

"Well!" Morgan said, clapping his hands. "Shall we adjourn to the dock? Shannon made a lovely spread and I've got a pitcher of gin fizz waiting to toast this sweet little girl."

They had all piled plates high with quiche and strawberry-rhubarb pie, fresh cherries with whipped cream. Laughing and toasting on the circular dock over the deep crystal water, they let the bright summer sun caress their aging cheeks. Brigid sat on the end of the curved dock, the mantle folded and placed between her soft skin and the slivery wood. Why they ever thought this was safe was beyond Emma's comprehension. Shannon insisted that her calm agate nature, and the respect for the waters that must run through her veins would protect her. But like all toddlers, Brigid was curious. And mobile. She had reached for the shimmering sun spots on the azure water and tipped quietly in. If Lynn had not arrived, at that exact moment...

Emma rubbed her temples against the memory.

Lynn strode onto the dock, anxious eyes already roaming for her daughter. Emma and Lynn had seen the bubbles at the surface of the water at the same time. Shame filled Emma as she remembered how her body seemed glued to her chair as she watched her Lynn's heavily pregnant body dive into the water. Time moved in a blur, yet they were frozen. Normally affable Kelsey was shouting, asking, begging. Where was Brigid? Where was his daughter? None of them could give an answer. After what seemed an eternity of time, Lynn resurfaced with the baby, who was limp against her shoulder. She swam briskly over to the ladder that hung from the end of the dock and scrambled up with one arm. Kelsey tried to lift his daughter from Lynn's arms, but Lynn held fast. In horror, they all saw the bright crimson blood seeping from Brigid's upper back. Brigid coughed and sputtered, and began to cry weakly. Kelsey yanked the mantle up from the dock edge and wrapped it around his dripping wife and daughter.

Morgan stood first, words locked in his throat. He met his son-in-law's eyes, that kind, gregarious man who had married his prickly daughter. The man who brought Lynn back to them, insisted that she allow the baby to visit. Kelsey, who wrapped tense dinners and difficult holidays in lightness, humor. Morgan tried to communicate his own horror, his unthinkable regret at this mistake. He was sure of Kelsey's kindness, forgiveness. But for once, in Kelsey's eyes, Morgan found fury. Fury, and the pain of betrayal. Shannon stood next, ashen. She gathered herself and walked over to her daughter.

"How could you?" Lynn said, staring at her mother. Shannon was visibly shaken. She heard only pain, and terrible fear. She opened her mouth to respond, but Lynn cut her off. "She was in the lake, Mom. She was lying at the bottom of the lake."

"But you knew!" Shannon tried to smile and reach out for her daughter but she couldn't find the courage to touch. "You saved her. Love always saves."

"No!" Lynn screamed, startling the bleeding child in her arms, making her cry harder. "This is not love! This is death. My daughter nearly drowned, and look – look at her!" Lynn raised her hand to her mother, dripping with the baby's blood. "You pay more attention to this nonsense than you do to anyone around you! That is not love!" Lynn glanced at Brigid's back again and realized this was no surface wound. They needed to go to the hospital, quickly. She met Kelsey's eyes and began to run down the dock, clutching the mantle to the bleeding baby.

"It's not nonsense, Lynn, look at what happened!" Shannon called after them. "You knew to come back early. You knew! I'm so sorry – I took my eyes off of her only for a moment! We saw her fall the moment you did. I would have saved her!"

Lynn spun around. "My daughter nearly died. Under your watch. Just like Aunt Ruby."

Shannon froze, teetering on her feet. "This ends now. All of this," Lynn spread her arm in an arc, wrapping the lake, the sky, the cottage, the assembled adults with their penitent eyes and the stone charms sparkling at their wrists. "It ends today."

Emma forced herself to breathe slowly, her wrinkled hand grasping the coffee cup. She tried to pull herself back into reality, but the memory of that awful day gnawed. The guilt she felt for Brigid's fall into the lake penetrated her still. Someone should have been watching. She should have been watching. Shannon and Morgan were always too flighty, too absorbed in their own thoughts. And look where their negligence led. Lynn had been terrified. Brigid was never allowed to spend time alone with her grandparents again. Compulsory visits to and from Cairn Cottage for holidays, that was it.

A few years later, Shannon's heart failed her. Planning the funeral, there were ugly scenes between Lynn and her father as grief coated their words with anger and blame. Lynn was so like Morgan, volatile, protective. But they could never see how similar they were. They still couldn't.

Emma sighed. She had to stop thinking about this. The loss of her friend still made her stomach drop a decade and a half later. Pushing herself up from the table, Emma forced herself to stand. She set Brigid's polished agate down and walked through the half door into the kitchen. God-willing, Graham had left some coffee in the pot.

CHAPTER 21

Emma smiled at the sound of the screen door slamming. The new Sunfish had been gone when she awoke; Graham must've taken an early morning sail. At least the man had made coffee before he left. She busied herself collecting the ingredients for fried eggs on toast, fresh orange juice and a bowl of berries. He would be hungry. Bless him, he always was.

"Is this mine?" A warm, crystalline voice permeated the room. An egg cracked and splattered all over the counter as it fell from Emma's hand. Shannon, Emma thought deliriously. She turned, nerves fluttering.

"I'm sorry," Brigid said. "I didn't mean to startle you! It's just that I remember this stone." Brigid walked into the Websters' kitchen, the sun filtering in behind her head and illuminating the tiny dust particles that floated in the air. "I think it's mine."

Wordlessly, Emma stepped around the counter and wrapped Brigid in a tight embrace. Leaning back, Emma met the younger woman's eyes and saw something there she had never seen before. "Coffee?" Emma asked. Brigid nodded, and sat down at a barstool, placing the papers she brought on the counter. The screen door slammed a second time and Graham marched into the kitchen, dripping. Brigid grinned at him. "Good morning, Graham! I saw you from the dock; you looked great out there." Graham startled and then smiled widely at the pretty young lady sitting in his kitchen. "Well good morning, sweet girl! So glad to see you over here. I want to hear all about your grandfather." Graham rounded the corner, arms outstretched to embrace Brigid. He stopped short when he saw the book on the counter. He bent to touch the fragile pages but pulled back as the lake water dripped from his arms. "Where did you find this?" Graham asked in a low voice.

Brigid met his eyes. "It was in a cedar chest. In my room, at Cairn Cottage. Along with a box of polished stones, with notes and instructions. This is my grandmother's handwriting." She looked from Emma to Graham. "Isn't it?" Emma cleared her throat and set down the coffee pot. "Yes, that's Shannon's handwriting. Your grandmother."

"And your names are listed, here on the cover page." Brigid drew her finger across the faded paper, underlining the inscription. "As well as David. And Nieve." Emma and Graham were frozen in place. "My grandpa was going to tell me something, the night before he..." Brigid straightened her shoulders to shake the memory away. "The night before he had his stroke," she continued, her voice strong. "And now he can't speak. Or write. Or anything. And my mother refuses to tell me." Brigid's face twisted in anger. "I mean, she obviously hates Cairn Cottage and resents that I'm here. A few weeks ago, at the hospital, she was distracted and actually told me that Grandma was performing a ceremony – something – with stones. But of course she refused to elaborate, except to tell me it was ridiculous." Brigid shook her head. "And I just feel like, I need to know. This is something about my family, something about me, and I don't know anything about it."

Emma and Graham exchanged a look.

"My Grandpa gave me my grandmother's bracelet." Brigid held out her wrist. Emma gasped. Brigid continued, "He implied there was something special about it. Something more than it being special because it's an heirloom, you know?" Now that Brigid had started, she found that she couldn't stop. And for once, she didn't care. It was so freeing, not to care. "All of these secrets, all the pretending, I'm just so tired of it," she said. "My grandpa can't explain it to me. Obviously my grandma can't. And you know my mother won't. So I'm asking you. What is this?" She placed her hands on the pile of papers, the bracelet twinkling in the sunlight. "What were you doing with the stones, with the community? And why did you stop?"

Emma swallowed hard. She sent a long look to her husband, who was gazing at Brigid with a mix of admiration and shock. He'd known this girl since birth and had never heard her utter so strong a speech. Always cowed by Lynn, and shyly obedient with Morgan, she had been polite and sweet in every encounter. He had wondered if she could ever take Shannon's place at their gathering. She always proved too timid, to ordinary. But now... by God, at this moment, Brigid seemed like an apparition of her steely-nerved grandmother. Graham met his wife's eyes and with a flash of mutual understanding.

Brigid had to know. And they were the only ones to tell her.

Graham took a heavy breath. "You're right, Brigid," he said. "There is something here, and you deserve to be told about it. Your mother wouldn't thank me for it."

"I'm an adult," Brigid interrupted, ice in her tone. "I don't need permission. For anything."

"You *are* an adult," Graham said slowly. "And it's time. It's time you knew. But I'm standing here dripping wet, and I think we need to prepare ourselves. Also, I think David should be here."

"I agree," Emma said. "Everyone who can be here, should be here. We need to have David."

Graham glanced down at the papers again. "Brigid, why don't you leave the book here? It would be nice to read it again – review it, if you will, before we explain it to you." Brigid looked at him warily. She stared into his eyes, trying to discern if she should trust him. The life-long conditioning to obey, to please, to anticipate the desires and feelings of others and put them above her own gnawed at her. But something deeper told her to keep the book. This book, whoever it had once belonged to, was hers now.

"I'll bring it back," she said, more firmly than she felt. "When can we talk about all of this?"

"Tonight," Graham said. A quiver of excitement lit his eyes. "At dusk."

CHAPTER 22

Brigid stared at three wooden chests. The carved waves bordering the Ayers chest were familiar by now. The Websters' chest was decorated with trees, long winding roots, carousing down the sides. David's chest had birds and clouds interspersed in the carving. She sipped her pinot noir and waited for the explanation.

Emma's breath was shallow as she knelt before their chest.

"Darling," Graham said. "Give it to her. It's time."

Emma ran her palm over the soft polished stones glued to the lid of the chest, and lifted the rusty latch. A gold bracelet sat on a folded pile of pearly lace. In the center of the delicate setting was Brigid's agate, polished to a gleam. Lifting the whole pile of fabric, Emma walked over to Brigid and knelt before her. Emma lifted the bracelet reverently from its lacy bed and offered it to Brigid.

Observing the older woman's obeisance, Brigid looked around for guidance. David spoke first.

"Brigid, this is your Spirit Stone," he said, his deep voice resonating on the pine boards of the cabin. "It is an agate, signifying your elevating, positive, protective nature. You and your stone chose each other when you were a small child, during the Ceremony. Our Craftswoman, Emma Webster, has polished and set it into this bracelet for you."

At this, Emma looked up at Brigid, smiling encouragingly. Brigid took the bracelet and gazed at it. It was a simple thing really, pretty, but perhaps not worthy of all of this pomp and circumstance.

Graham squirmed in his seat. "Put it on!" he said.

"She has to choose it," David said. "Choose us. And she should take her time. It shows her calming nature that she takes her time now."

Brigid set the bracelet carefully on her lap and slowly rested her gaze on each of these friends of her grandparents, these people with whom she did not share blood but seemed more like family than any aunt or uncle ever had. And they knew. These people gathered in the Webster's living room knew what had been kept from her all of her life. Maybe there was a reason why a moonglade or a trillium or the whisper of the wind through the birch leaves stopped her in her tracks. Elevated her. Maybe this would explain the ache she felt to dive below the surface of the mundanities of life.

"Who is 'us?'"

Graham cleared his throat and threw his shoulders back proudly. "Brigid, we are members of the Society of Stone Seekers," he said. "Your grandfather is a member; he is our Gatherer, or was before he fell ill. Shannon was our Diviner. David's wife Nieve was our Priestess, and David carries on the sacred duties and blessings in her stead. I am only a lowly Bookkeeper, but my beautiful Emma is our Craftswoman." He beamed at his wife, who blushed under his smile. "She takes the Spirit Stones and polishes them, and crafts beautiful jewelry, like the piece in your lap." Graham gave Brigid a once-over, stopping meaningfully at her right wrist. "She also made the bracelet you already wear." Graham's expression turned studiously polite. "If I may ask, who gave that stunning bracelet to you?"

"My grandpa gave it to me," Brigid said, covering the bracelet with her hand. "The night before my first date with Gabe. He told me it was my grandmother's." The elder folks nodded. Brigid fiddled with the stones as she continued. "My mother seemed to be concerned when she saw me wearing it – she told me to be careful with it, but I don't think she meant not to lose it or break it. I feel like there was something more she was trying to say."

"It was your grandmother's divining bracelet," Graham

said. "Morgan shouldn't have given it to you. You haven't been chosen as Diviner – in fact you haven't even been accepted into the Society. But I suppose he was hoping." Graham shook his head.

Brigid's mind was reeling. The bracelet seemed to be hot around her wrist. She wanted to rip it off, but somehow it was hers. And it was only a bracelet, she told herself. Just a piece of jewelry. Graham was speaking again but she couldn't seem to make out his words. She felt like she was sinking, underneath the water, and he was calling from above.

"I said do you understand?" asked Graham, consternation furrowing his face.

"I don't understand anything," Brigid said, squirming in her chair. "What is a Diviner? Why shouldn't I have this bracelet? And what is this one for?" Brigid asked, yanking the agate cuff into the air.

"Graham, you're going too fast," Emma said. "This is a lot to take in."

"Well, she's read the Book," said Graham. He huffed as he turned his head away from his wife. "I assume she's read it, she's had it for days!"

"I did flip through it," said Brigid. Graham's impatient tone was so like her mother's anger and a spasm of fear ran through her. She turned slowly to her grandfather's friend. "But it wasn't mine to read."

David raised his eyebrows in approval. The wooden legs of his chair scraped across the floor as he moved closer to Brigid. "Brigid," he said kindly. "It shows great restraint and respect that you've brought the Book to us without reading it. That act in itself signifies that you belong in our Society." He set the Book in her hands and turned to a page in the middle.

"Diviner. This Person shall be the Head of the Society of Stone Seekers. The Diviner shall see the pictures in the stones. The Diviner shall interpret the stones collected by the Gatherer and blessed by the Priestess. The Diviner shall be the ultimate builder of Totem

Cairns. The Diviner must prove his or her ability to the Society be-fore the choosing."

Below rested a handwritten list of names Brigid had never heard of. At the bottom, written in spidery hand, was the name Shannon Ayers.

"These names mark the Diviners since the Society of Stone Seekers began to create and record our rituals. No one has been able to prove his or her ability to Divine since your grand-mother passed. Your grandfather tried, but..." David broke off.

"But what?" Brigid asked. A quick glance passed between the three older people.

"He didn't have the ability," David said quickly.

"Brigid." Emma said, her voice suddenly low and rich. Brigid turned to her. Emma seemed to be in a trance, staring at her with an otherworldly sheen behind her eyes. "I feel some-thing, so strongly. When you walked into our kitchen this morning, I felt Shannon here. You look so like her."

"Emma, please," Graham said. He scowled at his wife, shift-ing uncomfortably in his chair. "I'm sorry, but she's too meek. If you don't have the ability, if David doesn't— hell, if Morgan doesn't, I'm sure Brigid doesn't either."

"She does, Graham." Emma's eyes didn't leave Brigid. "I can feel it." Emma was still kneeling before the younger woman, and she began to rock herself.

"This is ridiculous," Graham sputtered. "If we test her and it fails..."

"If she fails, fear wins," David said with a subtle smile. "It's been so long. We don't practice now anyway, why not take a chance? Let her try."

"There's no one at the neighboring cottages today," Emma said. "And it's not dark yet; we have a little time." She raised her eyes to her fellow Stone Seekers.

David looked at Brigid. "Brigid, will you come? Join us on the dock?" he asked gently. She nodded. "Bring the bracelets," he said.

Emma led Brigid gently to the edge of their dock. The velvet loamy smell of a coming rain hung in the air. Emma slid the agate bracelet onto the younger woman's wrist with an encouraging smile.

"Dusk is the best time, Brigid," David said. "This is the time when the efforts of the day give way to the mysteries and freedom of the night. This is the time of transition, the time where the veil between the worlds is very thin. We lay down our dependence on the sun, the rain, the clouds, and are free to observe the stars. We can see the whole galaxy; no longer anchored to our small slice of the world. We are made of stardust, Brigid. Dusk is when our internal light is given the freedom to shine."

Emma continued. "The energies bloom at dusk, Brigid. Can't you feel it?"

Brigid did feel a restless static in her veins. She shook her head. These previously passive friends of her grandpa's just pulled her out onto the edge of a dock and slid a bracelet on her wrist with the reverence of a groom slipping a wedding ring onto the hand of his bride. David was apparently a priest, intoning of dusk and stardust. Yes, she could feel an out-of-body energy – it was called adrenaline. If she wasn't confident in her ability to push away and run faster than their frail bodies, she'd be assessing the level of danger. Brigid looked askance at her neighbors.

Behind her, Graham huffed in frustration. "She doesn't understand," he said. Emma patted his arm consolingly. Taking Brigid's hand, she gave it a friendly squeeze. "Honey, just do me a favor. Look out at those dark clouds and think of something that makes you happy." Emma's easy tone brought her back into her body. The kind older woman who looked out for her, left casseroles and pies on the porch, discreetly watched from her own dock as Brigid embarked on her daily solo sail. Emma never bothered, never pried, but always quietly protected. Brigid appreciated the grace and humility in Emma Webster. She was grateful for a female, grandmotherly figure to emulate.

Rubbing the bridge of her nose, Brigid glanced at Emma. What could be the harm in fulfilling this simple request? Afterwards, she could demand more explanation, or make an excuse and go back home to Cairn Cottage. She had the Book — it might tell her all she needed to know.

"Look at the clouds and think happy thoughts?" Brigid asked. "This is what you need me to do?" Emma's lip curved upward at Brigid's gentle sarcasm. Whatever the men thought, this girl was smart. Emma saw that Brigid was a chameleon, turning herself into the person anyone wanted, at any time. The young woman could see a person's desire before he knew it himself, observing quietly until she knew which actions to take. Some people used this skill to manipulate for power. A chill went through Emma's spine as a memory pierced through. God, it was so long ago, but the thought of that day could still double her over. She forced the image from her mind and concentrated on the task at hand. Knowing Lynn as she did, Emma surmised that Brigid used her perception only for survival, if she even knew she was using it at all.

"Just gaze at those clouds and look inside yourself," Emma said. "Put your most joyful memory in your mind, something that fills your whole heart." Immediately the feeling of Gabe's arms wrapped around her body leapt into Brigid's memory. She blushed deeply.

Emma chuckled softly. "Yep," she said. "Keep that little thought in your head. And stare into those rainy clouds on the horizon."

Emma was pointing northward. Brigid noticed the faint gray curtain dripping down from the lead-colored clouds. There would be no sailing tomorrow. In fact, if they had another half an hour on the dock before getting soaked, it would be a miracle. Whatever Emma thought was going on here, it would be over soon enough. Straightening her shoulders, Brigid stared at the clouds.

It was lovely, taking a moment to really look at the horizon.

No phones, no distractions. The undesirable weather seemed to have its own beauty. The fading sunlight gave an encore, beaming out from the uppermost cloud like a golden portal. The warmth extended downward, reaching for the lake but disappearing behind the wall of rain. Emma's voice interrupted her reverie.

"You're not thinking of your joyful memory." Brigid startled slightly. How did Emma possibly know what she was thinking? Well, she might as well go along with this. That gray, dripping curtain would reach them in a moment.

Gabe. What was she going to do about him? He had sent a wildflower bouquet to the cottage earlier that day. She grinned at the thought of them, fuchsia sweet-peas stretching languorously out from the mason jar, fuzzy-leaved cosmos and snapdragons with their bright salutes. It was the fern fillers though, that really touched her. The same type of ferns that carpeted their pathway to the lake last night, that rustled and brushed their ankles as they walked back, not needing to speak. He had wrapped his arm tightly around her and she tripped down the darkened path, nestled into his broad chest. Did he know when he chose them? Of course not, she told herself; no man would notice that detail or go out of his way to add them to a bouquet. Brigid had spent most of the day in mental flagellation. How could she be so sentimental so quickly? Had she not learned anything from the Matt disaster? It had taken her over a year and a half to get over that break up. The pangs of it still lingered. It would be the height of stupidity to allow herself to fall again. Her mother despised Gabe inexplicably, or, with classist prejudice which was almost as bad. The relationship might be worth pursuing for that reason alone. Her stomach dropped with agitation.

She heard Graham sigh impatiently and remembered she was supposed to be thinking happy thoughts.

The way Gabe's mouth cracked into a beaming smile, and how his eyes lingered on her a little too long. And his laugh, illuminating his cheekbones. Gabe was smart, witty – it was engrossing talking with him. His deep-throated chuckle mingled with the memory of her students, collectively collapsing into giggles at a particularly silly storybook. There had been many times this past year where her professional composure had cracked in these moments. She found she was unable to withhold her enjoyment at their unabashed happiness.

Gabe's face appeared in her mind again, this time the memory of him pointing out the constellations the night of the bonfire. The first touch of his hand on hers, how she had failed to be wary and unable to anticipate what he wanted to do next. She had been left with no choice but to lean into each breath, feeling the warmth from his body as he stood behind her, raising her eyes to where his searched. Forgetting to bury her intelligence to boost his confidence by allowing him to explain everything to her. That night, she too had named the stars.

A gasp brought Brigid back to the surface. Her eyes focused suddenly on the horizon before them. The gray tendrils of rain were shuddering, disappearing. Evaporating back into the atmosphere. A warm south wind caressed her shoulder. Streams of sunshine stretched forth from the rapidly expanding gaps in the clouds. The gray horizon was gilded with light.

"She can actually do it," said Graham breathlessly. A wild grin burst across his face. "I'm bowled over! We have a Diviner, we can begin again!" He burst into a little jig on the wooden planks of the dock.

David's face held a deep, abiding peace. "I knew it," he said. "I knew it when she chose that agate. But I never thought we would see this day." He brushed the tears from his eyes.

Something eternal pulsed within Brigid. An inexplicable longing to float away and become part of the horizon filled her. She recognized this as the way she felt when she was overwhelmed, when the disapproval of the world was too much, when the mask she had constructed became too painful to wear a moment longer. Brigid never spoke of this feeling to anyone. She simply indulged it when she could, taking long hikes through the county trails, pausing to warm her face in the sun, kneeling to study the whorl of a newborn leaf. It was easier at Cairn Cottage. People seemed to understand.

Brigid found she was suddenly exhausted. Wavering on her legs, she reached hastily for a chair. Collapsing into the plastic seat, she gazed at the group assembled in front of her, rapture spread across their faces.

"What do I do now?"

CHAPTER 23

Lynn's china coffee cup rattled on the marble countertop. "She cannot be involved with a Sherland! My God, Kelsey, that was one, ONE – of the myriad reasons I did not want her out there!"

Kelsey gently slid the cup away from his wife. "Lynn, honey, she's twenty-four years old. She's a big girl. She can take care of herself."

Lynn put her head in her hands. "She's never taken care of herself, Kelsey. I've always had to push her. Always. If I hadn't sat across from her at that table, and made her fill out her college applications, she'd still be wandering the beach somewhere, reading poetry."

Kelsey chuckled softly. It was true. His daughter always seemed to have her head in the clouds. In his opinion, it was one of her many charms. But daydreaming scraped Lynn's nerves. Kelsey picked up his wife's hand, stroking the back of it with the pad of his thumb.

"She got that job by herself, remember?" he said. "She didn't even tell us about it until the first day!" Lynn made a scoffing sound, snatching her hand back.

"That teaching job. What a disaster. Babysitting low-rent brats and barely making enough to feed herself."

"Lynn!" Kelsey said, wincing. He loved his wife's feisty nature, her ability to make things happen. When they had met, it had been a delicious challenge to calm her, settle her. Almost like taming a wild beast. Now, she ran everyone's life like clockwork, making it easy to sit back and relax. But God, she could be downright cruel. Her words these days made him cringe.

"Alright fine, too far," Lynn said, noticing her husband's hurt look. "But really, Kelsey — what's her biggest accomplishment going to be there? Tenure? They grant that to every teacher who doesn't hit a student!"

Kelsey shook his head. "She likes the job, Lynn. She enjoys it and she's finding validation in her work. Teaching young kids is no easy task. She's making a difference in her own small way. Besides, I thought you were losing your mind about the boyfriend."

At the word boyfriend, Lynn stared out of the big great room window and began breathing. Tight, small, audible breaths. Kelsey's forehead wrinkled as he observed his wife. Almost three decades of marriage, and he knew this was Lynn's tell. When she was truly in the depths of anxiety, when she couldn't cover it up with formidable efficiency, when even haughty armor failed her, she breathed like this. He wrapped a strong arm around her shoulders. "This young man is an entirely different person," he said softly. "He's not his great-uncle. He may not even know anything about what happened. About your Aunt Ruby." He paused to assess her reaction. She had hardened every muscle in her body, refusing to allow herself to melt against him, mindfully rejecting any comfort. But at least she was breathing normally again. He kissed the top of her head and walked away. Lynn's spurning didn't hurt him anymore, not like it did when they were first together and he would try to hold her, calm her rage against her parents and the way she was raised. He understood now that her anger was just a mask for desolation. He knew that in the dead of night, when no one could see her, she would curl into him, wrapping herself around him. The passion that fueled her anger was more intense when it fueled her love.

Lynn listened to his footsteps retreat down the hall. Rain drizzled, blocking her view of the bay. The windows were open to the cool air, and she could smell the metallic scent of chemicals rising off the water. Shaking her head, she turned to the Lake Association report tucked neatly in its folder. Lynn had called her daughter on the drive over, hoping to talk sense into her, try to get her to give up this listless summer and the low-life man and come back into town. But it didn't work. Once again, she'd pushed her daughter too hard.

She shook her head. The world was ruthless and cruel. If you didn't protect yourself, build your own success, create a fortress around your life, no one else would.

But Brigid. Brigid had always been cowed. Lynn had tried relentlessly to build her eldest's daughter's strength up. She needed a strong backbone and a thick skin, especially to counter her natural flightiness. The last thing Brigid needed was indulgence. But it didn't seem to matter how stern Lynn was with her expectation, how clearly and concisely she communicated with Brigid, the girl would always bow her head.

Until now.

Lynn shuddered to think of this Gabe and his miserable family. It had been years since the accident, but she could still hear her mother's anguished scream when she answered that phone call. Lynn had been only seven when her Aunt Ruby was pushed into the bonfire. Ruby had survived it, but left the hospital horribly disfigured. Her right side, all the way to her scalp, looked red and angry, like it would melt off. She came to Cairn Cottage to recuperate and as a child, Lynn could not keep herself from crying whenever she looked at her beloved aunt.

After the accident, Ruby stayed in her room. She had moved into the old loft, right above Shannon and Morgan's room, overlooking the lake. Shannon would bring meals to her sister, staying hours with her. Lynn was left to look after herself. She would hear sobs of her aunt and imagine that she was in great pain, and devastated over the ruin of her once beautiful face. Lynn didn't find out until years later, when she was cleaning out the old loft, that Ruby also wept for heartbreak.

Aunt Ruby seemed like just another adult to young Lynn, ageless and in charge. In fact, she was only twenty-three. Young, mercurial, and gorgeous, she upended their quiet life whenever she visited. There would always be a man with her, handsome and fawning. Shannon would roll her eyes, Morgan would flirt with her gently and tease the new beau mercilessly. Lynn basked in her presence and Ruby adored her niece. She was just the kind of aunt a young girl wanted; full of fun and attention, always ready to read a story, play a game no matter how silly, with open arms for hugs and kisses. Ruby would let Lynn try on her new jewelry and play with her hair, not caring if the young girl mussed the careful style. Lynn would hear Ruby admonish her elder sister for her inattentiveness as a mother. Ruby would nag Shannon when Lynn's hair was left unbrushed, her clothes mismatched or even dirty. Shannon would look surprised, set down her incessant piles of stones and note paper and actually see her daughter.

Ruby changed when she brought Teddy home to visit. She simpered to him, checking her bright voice to melt below the volume of his confidence. His hands never seemed to leave her body, always at the small of her back, maneuvering her pathway to match his own. At the family dinner, his huge veined hand pinned Ruby's to the table, stroking her wrist with his thumb while he regaled them with the latest story of the farm. It made Lynn nervous to see the way Teddy would entrap her aunt on the couch after dinner, one huge arm wrapped around her shoulder, the other resting improperly on her thigh. She felt uncomfortable crawling into Ruby's arms the way she usually did. Teddy would smile at her, jutting his chin to beckon her close. When no one was looking, his smile was sly.

So Lynn turned away.

"She's in love," Shannon had said when Lynn tried in her child-like way to ask about the change in her favorite aunt. "She's always been like this; impetuous since childhood. After all, what do you expect from a jasper spirit?" Shannon had thrown up her hands at her younger sister's antics, patted her young daughter on the head, and went back to staring at the arrangement of polished stones on the table.

Theodore Sherland. "My friends call me Teddy," he had said, leering down at Lynn. "And you're my friend, aren't you, you little cutie?" Lynn shuddered at the memory. As a child, she vaguely knew of the farming family, and understood that her father and Graham had been working with the Sherlands to reverse the streak of bad harvests that had plagued their land. The Stone Society offered to canvass the land, take samples of the crops, and consult the weather. Ruby was sent with David and Nieve to take notes and gather information. When this preliminary estimate was completed, Graham presented it to the head of the Sherland family. They accepted. Lynn remembered combing the beaches with her parents for hours, gathering innumerable buckets of stones. They even took the Sunfish out into Big Omann Lake, Morgan diving for larger rocks, heaving and gasping as he tossed them into the hull. They were polished by Emma and then Shannon gazed at them for days, carefully putting groups together and taking them apart, building and rebuilding cairns. When Lynn glanced at her mother's notes, she read of pictures in the rocks, spiritual significance, specific strengths to help the land.

That summer, they ate all of their meals on the dock because the long dining room table was covered with stones. Finally, Ruby brought the stones to the Sherland farm. She walked with the family to special corners of the field, saying blessings over the stones and over the land. Graham accompanied her to collect the fee.

Four months later, the crop failed.

Shannon was distraught, and all the adults were mortified. Lynn remembered Graham with his hands in the air, shouting about returning the fee. Of course he had done it, how could the Stone Society possibly doubt him? The Sherland family was unreasonable. Upset, understandably, but unreasonable.

The next morning, Shannon had received the call from the hospital. There had been a bonfire at a beach. It had gotten rowdy, lots of drinking. Ruby had fallen in the fire. The police questioned everyone in attendance, but nobody could agree on a story. It was clear that Teddy Sherland was angry. Any reasonable person could understand that; his family was on the brink of losing their farm. He was a handsy, passionate young man, people said. Of course, he was holding onto his girl. Maybe he was gripping her arm a little too tightly, but men get into such passions, the people had said. And she had been fighting with him, yelling and crying. And the next thing anyone knew, poor Ruby had fallen into the fire. It was tragic. Teddy was the one who reached in, pulling her out and rolling her in the sand to put out the flames. But it was too late. She was ruined.

Teddy could not be found for questioning. The county sheriff visited the Sherland farm, but no one had heard from him.

When Ruby heard that the police had closed the case, she finally stopped her sobbing. Her room was silent for days, she refused to talk to anyone, not even Shannon.

It was Lynn who saw the Sunfish floating in the water on the other side of the lake, the sail spinning wildly around the mast.

Exactly two weeks after the fire, Lynn watched from the dock as the Coast Guard dragged her Aunt Ruby's gray lifeless body up from the water. A little anchor was tied around her waist.

The memory crashed around Lynn's mind, buzzing through her ears and making her sweat. Her breathing became shallow again as she fought to push the image back down in the depths of her psyche. Where had Kelsey gone? For a fleeting moment, she wished she could tell her husband about that day, tell him about the blue tinge around her Aunt's lips, the freckles of black around her eyes. Furious with her inability to talk about it, she slammed a manicured hand against the cold marble of the countertop. No one else needed to hear about that awful day. The pain shouldn't burden another heart. She could carry it alone.

Lynn walked over to the balcony and opened the double doors. The stench of rot hit her even on the cool night air. She had to get Brigid away from this Sherland man. Whatever it cost.

CHAPTER 24

Brigid scooped some hot potato casserole onto her plate, inhaling the scent of cooked onions with pleasure.

"Oh, get lots of the chips!" Mikey said. He pointed a plump childish finger at the buttered potato-chip crust. "The chips are the best part!" Brigid smiled at him and angled the dented spoon to get good helping of the cheesy, crusty topping. She felt Gabe's gaze on her from across the table. She dropped the serving spoon and it clattered onto her plate.

Ann Sherland leaned back and crossed her fleshy arms. She observed her eldest son. He was clearly entranced by this young woman. She was the latest in a string of pretty young things her handsome son brought simpering home on his arm. Watching him tonight though, she sensed what he felt for her was different. Stronger. Bile rose in her mouth and she cleared her throat.

"Brigid honey, take some salad," she said. Gesturing to the Corningware bowl rimmed with blue cornflowers, she raised her eyebrows at the other woman. Brigid nodded politely and scooped some chopped iceberg lettuce with carrots from the dish. Before she could reach across the table for the bottle of ranch dressing, Ann passed her three glass jars. "We get the fancy salad things out when we have company," she said. Hesitating for a split second, Brigid opened each one in turn and forked green olives, banana peppers, and pickled cauliflower onto her plate. As Brigid gingerly poured the dressing over the plate, Ann narrowed her eyes. "I know you're from Domhnall Hills, so you're probably used to something fancier." Brigid waved the comment away. "Oh no, Mrs. Sherland! This is delicious," she said, her voice pitched unnaturally high. "Thank you so much for having me to your home." Gabe shot a warning look to his mother, who sighed in resignation and leaned back again in her chair. It gave a creak and she gestured to her younger son.

"Mikey honey, take some of that meatloaf. You're thin as a rail. And see – I got the ketchup out. Want me to squirt some on your plate?" Mikey nodded enthusiastically and wiped grease from his mouth with the back of his hand. Ann Sherland smiled broadly as she lifted a slice of the fragrant meatloaf onto her son's plate and poured a great lake of ketchup alongside it. "We may not have big houses and fancy food like those people up in town, but we make do with our simple life. And my boys enjoy it." Brigid felt the challenge. She kept her eyes on her plate.

Gabe saw Brigid's face set into a mask of politeness and set his fork down firmly. He looked between the two women. His mother could be impossible, and Brigid was getting uncomfortable; he could tell. Why did women do this? They said something that sounded so drippingly kind and somehow could pinch another woman right in the heart. And he could never figure out exactly where the insult lay. All the words were correct. His mother was an expert at this. Some of the girls he had dated were nearly as good. God, what a pain in the ass, he thought. But still, Gabe considered – this was his mom. He decided to smooth over whatever drama was brewing with facts.

"Mom, Brigid doesn't live in Domhnall Hills. She's staying at her grandfather's cabin. In Birch Glen; right down the road from us."

"Oh, in one of those huge houses on Big Omann Lake, I bet," said Ann triumphantly. Brigid dropped her polite façade and gazed levelly at Gabe's mother.

"Actually, it's a modest cabin on Little Owrann Lake. My great-grandfather and his friends bought three plots of land and built the cottages. By hand. They owned the land across the road too, going through the forest all the way back to Big Omann Lake. But the government forced that buy-out in the forties, and now it's all national lakeshore. I moved out there at the beginning of summer to help care for my grandfather. But he..." Brigid faltered, remembering that awful morning. "He suffered a bad stroke – a debilitating stroke. He's in assisted living care now in a facility in Domhnall Hills." Gabe's mother gave a clucking noise of sympathy. She watched her son place a gentle arm around Brigid's shoulders. Brigid took a breath and continued.

"Gabe was there that day, did he tell you? He was so helpful. He held my grandpa's head..." She stopped suddenly, realizing that tears were pooling behind her eyes. She forced them down with a cough and said too brightly, "He was wonderful. So helpful."

The story melted Ann's reserve. She reached across the table to pat Brigid's hand. "Oh honey. It's good that you both were there. I'm sure your grandpa was real appreciative of the fact that you lived with him and that. What is your grandpa's name?" Ann asked. "If he lives over in Birch Glen, I'm sure I know him."

"His name is Morgan. Morgan Ayers. My grandmother's name was Shannon."

Ann froze. She looked hard at Brigid, recognition flooding forward as she noticed again the auburn curls, the deep blue-green of the younger woman's eyes. "Honey," she began. "Do you have a great-aunt named Ruby?" Brigid's eyes flashed in surprise.

"How do you know my Aunt Ruby? She died way before I was born," Brigid said.

"I just know the family – I know pretty much all the families around here," Ann said hurriedly. "And I remember hearing about Ruby – she was real pretty, just like you." A false smile spread across her face. Attempting to smooth the tension that had gathered in the room again, Brigid returned the smile. Her stomach had tightened. Between the events on the dock last night and the anticipation of this dinner, her entire body was tense. She really did not want to eat another bite of the heavy meal but figured Ann would be offended if she didn't clean her plate.

"Mikey, chew with your mouth closed. Please," Gabe implored.

"Gabe, leave him alone," Ann said, leaning back in her chair. "We're not trying to impress anyone here tonight." She gave self-satisfied look to the table. Regardless of who this young lady thought she was, Ann would not bow and scrape.

Brigid instinctively cowered. Mrs. Sherland could not be more clear: she disapproved. But of what? Brigid had been nothing but polite. She had made nice conversation, brought flowers, pretended that this dinner was delicious. She glanced under her lashes at Gabe, who had clearly understood his mother's dig and was visibly squirming, not knowing what to say. Well, Brigid thought. She had been told all her life that she was not impressive enough.

Mike was squirming uncomfortably too. The poor kid looked as if he didn't know whether to take another bite of his dinner or not.

Brigid straightened her shoulders and decided in that moment to ignore the uncomfortable silence which seemed to suck all the air out of the room. She stared at Mikey, a smile playing at her lips. When he felt her eyes on him, he stopped wiggling and looked at her furtively. Without breaking her gaze, Brigid speared a giant piece of lettuce and shoved it into her mouth, crunching loudly. Mikey began to giggle. Brigid winked at him and continued chewing, openmouthed. Finally, she swallowed and took a sip of water.

"So, Mikey," she asked calmly. "What is going on in your life? What is the craziest thing that has happened to you in the last week?"

Mikey threw his head back and let out a cascade of giggles before wiping his mouth with the back of his hand. "Ummm..." He squinched up his face, thinking. "Oh! Mom, can I tell her about the allowance thing?"

Ann looked at her youngest son, unable to hold her guard up against the sound of his laughter. "If you want to, Mikey. But I don't know if Brigid wants to hear a story like that."

"I cannot wait to hear a story like that, Mikey." Brigid leaned forward and made a beckoning gesture. "The allowance story. Let's go." Mikey looked at Gabe for approval, but his older brother was staring at Brigid like she had invented the sun.

"Ok. Well." Mikey leaned forward too, elbows on the table. "I get one dollar a week for allowance if I do my chores, right?"

"Right," said Brigid, listening intently.

"So my mom took me into Birch Glen, because I really wanted an ice cream, but she said if I wanted one, I had to spend my own money." Ann made a gesture to interrupt, but Brigid was quicker.

"I love ice cream," she said. "What flavor did you get?"

"Superman!" said Mikey. "I always get Superman. I got two scoops in a waffle cone."

Brigid rested her chin on her hand. "Hmm. I like Superman, but I would've gotten Blue Moon, I think. But good choice on the waffle cone."

"No, but Brigid, Superman <u>has</u> Blue Moon in it!" said Mikey, throwing a hand in the air for emphasis.

"You're right, you're right," Brigid conceded. "Superman is the better choice. Especially if you want a lot of flavors. Good choice, spending your money on ice cream. I bet it was delicious."

"No, but that's not even the story!"

"It's not?" asked Brigid. "Well, tell me the story!"

"Ok," Mikey slapped his hand on the table. "So the ice cream is four dollars. Like, exactly four dollars! So I had one dollar left which won't really buy anything, but there's this one store? With the sign with the fish wearing sunglasses?"

"Oh, yeah, Dockside! The toy store," said Brigid.

"Yeah! So I beg my mom to go there and she says <u>yes</u>," He threw an accusatory look at Ann.

Brigid held her hand out. "Hold up," she said. "You cannot possibly be mad at your mom for taking you to a toy store." Despite herself, Ann laughed.

"Well, ok, that was cool, but what happened after was so dumb! Ok, so the toy store, they have these bouncy balls which are kinda stupid but kinda fun. And they're only one dollar. And I had one dollar! But when we got there, they had this whole table. Like, a surprise table. And there were bags on it and everything was one dollar!"

"Bags of what?" asked Brigid.

"You didn't know. They were stapled shut! Like little white lunch bags. So, I started lifting them up — the sign said you couldn't look in them or shake them, but I figured maybe I could tell what was in them if I could sort of feel them, you know? There was one, and it was like... super heavy! And I thought maybe it was gold or something really important. And the store people maybe didn't know. The heaviest one would be the best, right?"

Brigid smiled at him. Mikey grinned back and slapped his forehead. "So I picked the heaviest one. The guy at the counter said I couldn't open it until I left the store. So I gave him my dollar when I could have bought a <u>ball</u>, and we left. And do you know what was in the bag?"

"What?"

"Rocks!!"

Brigid widened her eyes. "Rocks?"

"Yes!" Mikey slammed his palms on the table. "Rocks! I bought a one dollar bag of rocks!"

"Well," said Brigid, "Sometimes rocks are cool. When they're polished or something. Or when you get a really big Petoskey stone."

"No, Brigid. These were not cool. These were like... from the ground."

"All rocks are from the ground, Mikey," said Gabe.

"You know what I mean," said Mikey, rolling his eyes. "Like junk rocks. Cement and stuff. That's why the stupid bag was so heavy."

Brigid leaned back and laughed. "It's ok, Mikey. You can come over to Cairn Cottage and I'll give you some better rocks. For free," she added, still laughing.

"Cairn Cottage," Ann said quietly.

"Yes," said Brigid, blushing. "It's sort of a nickname for my grandpa's cottage. It's on Little Owrawn Lake, right near here."

"I know where Little Owrawn Lake is," Ann said coldly.

Brigid swallowed hard. "I'm sorry. Of course you do. I'm staying there for the summer with my grandpa... well, I was until..." She trailed off. Inhaling quickly, she forced a smile and turned back to Mikey.

"Anyway, you're welcome to visit anytime. I'll give you all the rocks you want."

CHAPTER 25

It began to rain at dusk, sending them scrambling from the pasture into the shelter of the porch. Mikey had really wanted to show Brigid the farm, and secretly Gabe did too. Brigid was so sweet with his little brother, asking him all kinds of questions, sharing in his delight. She laughed when Gabe questioned whether the strappy nonsense she called shoes would be adequate for a hike in the field. Pulling his old galoshes out from under the grimy hall bench, she raised her eyebrows in a smirk and shoved her feet in. He had shaken his head and grinned when she tromped through the mud in the vastly oversized boots. Mikey nearly fell over guffawing. When the storm sent them into the house, Brigid's bright mood lost its sparkle. The small living room was dark except for the glow of the big television. Ann sat in the pilled Lazyboy watching the news.

"Can I get you anything, Brigid honey?" she had asked formally, twisting her head around the back of the chair. Brigid shook her head and thanked her yet again for dinner. "Oh you don't need to thank me," Ann had said. "I just hope everything was up to your standards." Ann had raised her eyebrows in disapproval at her elder son, waited a beat to ensure that Brigid had seen her. She turned heavily back to her show.

There hadn't been much point in staying after that. Brigid gave a big bear hug to Mikey and followed Gabe out to his truck.

He now drove carefully down the curvy country roads, eyeing Brigid. She had been unusually quiet since they left, answering his questions in short bursts. He ran his hand through his hair.

"I'm sorry about my mom," Gabe said. "I don't know why she says things like that. I think maybe she's intimated by you."

"By me?" Brigid looked at him, unwilling to conceal the incredulousness on her face. "Gabe, she's your mother. She obviously has the upper hand here. I'm intimidated by her," Brigid said.

"Why?" Gabe asked. "I like you, that's what matters. She's just being crazy."

"Gabe..." Brigid glanced at him before looking away quickly. She knew what she wanted to say, but couldn't decide on the tone. Serious, joking, flirty? The uneasiness had dissipated somewhat in the field, but she couldn't make it go away entirely.

"What?" Gabe asked softly, placing his hand over hers.

"You... you yelled really loud in there," Brigid finally said. "At dinner. To your mom. And when you punched the table..."

"I did not punch the table," Gabe said, a little more forcibly than he meant. Brigid withdrew her hand.

"Ok," she said, a measured calm in her voice. "You slammed your hand on the table. Sorry. Is that... I dunno, is that normal for you?"

Gabe sighed, turning into the driveway of Cairn Cottage. He put the truck into park. "I'm really sorry, Brigid. Sometimes, you know, I just get angry. My mom drives me crazy; she acts so helpless and yet she sits there all day and does nothing. She upsets my brother..." He stopped, running his hand over his face. "I hate to see him looking like that. The way he did when she mentions my dad." Brigid looked warily at his churning jaw and was shocked to see tears welling in the corners of his eyes. Her defenses softened.

"I'm sorry," she said. "I'm sorry you have to deal with that. It must be so hard. It seems like you have to hold up the whole family."

"It's fine," Gabe said quickly, rubbing the bridge of his nose. Feigning a headache was better than wiping the tears that betrayed him. "It's fine – it's my job. My duty."

Brigid didn't know how to respond to that, so she decided to simply say what she wanted to say. "Well, I just want you to know, I don't take well to getting yelled at. My mom has a raging temper and I just... it scares me more than it maybe should." Gabe turned to her and took both her hands in his. His eyes were pleading.

"I won't yell at you, Brigid. Ok? I promise."

The pit in her stomach began to melt away and she kissed him, tasting his scruffy jaw. "Maybe don't yell that much in front of Mikey either. Or to your mom. She is still your mom." Gabe swallowed hard and pulled her awkwardly over the center console into a big bear hug. Brigid could smell the sharp sweet tang of the fields on his skin. She didn't want to leave his arms.

"Want to come in for a bit?" she asked, her breath on the nape of his neck. He nodded.

Inside Cairn Cottage, the aroma of pine beams mingled with the sanctifying scent of rain. Brigid mixed two whiskey and waters and led them through the kitchen. Behind the long dining table, the windows were open to the storm.

"Want me to close those?" asked Gabe.

"No, it's fine," said Brigid, casually dismissing the droplets of wet on the wooden sill. "The wind is good for the cottage. It blows the ghosts away." She smiled at him and sat on the couch facing the huge picture windows. Gabe lingered a minute, wanting to do something, anything, to make up for the night. His eyes caught sight of the birch logs stacked neatly next to the stone fireplace.

"Can I build you a fire?" he asked.

"No thank you," she said. Brigid's eyes were twinkling. She patted the cushion beside her. Gabe sat down and wrapped an arm around her shoulders, drawing her close. Brigid nestled her cheek into warm softness of his fleece jacket.

Together, they watched the storm flash across the lake. The giant picture windows were like a stage for the flashes of lightening which exploded in bursts of light the moment they touched the still, silken waters. Each meeting of fire and water was heralded by a fervent roar as the thunder bounced across the bowl of the lake. The sounds echoed so loudly that the whiskey in their glasses rippled.

Brigid saw this and laughed softly under her breath. She reached forward to cup her glass and take a drink. Gabe placed a hand on her bare leg, grazing the goosebumps that rose in the chilly air.

"You're cold."

Brigid drained the glass and set it down, tasting nutmeg and leather as the spicy spirit flowed through her veins. Gabe reached behind her and lifted the lace mantle that was folded neatly on the back of the couch. A vague surprise registered in Brigid's mind. She didn't remember taking the mantle out of the wooden chest. She certainly wouldn't have placed it on the couch. Before she could puzzle it out, Gabe was wrapping the mantle around her shoulders and drawing her close. The taste of mint cut through the warm spice of the whiskey as he brought his mouth to hers and gently urged her lips open. A swell of feeling rushed upward from her chest as she realized he must have chewed and discarded gum sometime in the evening, freshening his kiss in anticipation of her own. It made her smile.

"What?" he asked playfully. Brigid merely shook her head. Her next words were obliterated by a current that shot from the nape of her neck all the way down her body. Gabe's lips traveled from the back of her ear down to her collarbone. She leaned back onto the couch, pulling him down to cover her body.

Gabe reached his hand up her body urgently as he gripped the back of her hair with his other hand. Feeling his fist tighten, he suddenly was afraid to be too rough, to scare her again. Loosening his hand, he pulled his weight off of her. As he did, he realized his fingers were tangled in the lacy mantle he had wrapped around her shoulders. He fumbled around. His fingers would not come out from the web-like blanket. Willing himself not to curse, he laid a quick kiss on her forehead and leaned back farther. His long leg shot out and make contact with his untouched whiskey glass, which flew obligingly off of the coffee table and onto the carpet. "Dammit!" Gabe said, clenching his teeth. His eyes went from the glass and raced to Brigid's face. He was such an idiot. Had he scared her again? He found she was laughing. Indignation automatically swelled up in his body. He couldn't stand to be laughed at. Usually he was in such control of these things, what was happening to him tonight?

"What is going on?" Brigid said, still laughing. Gabe shook his head, lifting his hand in the tangle of lace.

"I have no idea, honestly. I'm apparently a moron who is ruining the evening."

Brigid sat up, careful not to pull the lace throw and thus his hand. She leaned forward and pecked his cheek.

"Here," she said. Standing, she untangled and bunched the mantle up into a ball and sat back on the couch cushion. He shook his hand out and tried to recover his composure.

"Now I should probably clean up the rug," he said ruefully. But Brigid had already risen and was striding confidently into the kitchen. Over her shoulder, she called "Don't worry! I'm sure it's not the first whiskey that has spilled in this room." She returned with a roll of paper towels and a fresh glass. Raising her eyebrows playfully at him, she set the new glass on a side table with melodramatic caution. "Let's not kiss near this, yes?"

Gabe grinned back at her. "Yes," he said. "Now hand me those." He took the roll of paper towel from her. When they had finished blotting, she reached up and took the mantle in her arms. Spreading it on the floor before them, she winked. "To prevent further accidents." Gabe nodded ruefully and reached back for his fresh drink. He downed it quickly, expecting her to sit back up on the couch. But she sat on the middle of the mantle, gazing out at the lake. The storm had dissipated and the darkness was stifling. He settled himself on the floor next to her.

"Do you have any candles?" Gabe asked, "Can I light a few for us?"

"If we light any candles, you might burn the place down," Brigid answered pertly. To ease the sting of the tease, she leaned forward and kissed him. He cradled her face in his hands.

"But what if I want to see you?" he asked. A bolt of lightning hit the lake, sending light into the air, illuminating the room. She grinned at him. "There you go," she said.

The rain pounded against the big picture windows and the rumble of thunder drowned out the sound of their own ragged breathing. Lightning flew across the sky and struck the lake, lighting up the entire landscape with a brief flash of color. The shock of it made them both tremble and jump.

Looking up at her, Gabe did not see the meek young woman he was falling in love with. Rising before him was a goddess.

CHAPTER 26

The July sun bathed her face in heat. Brigid climbed languidly out of her car and walked across the parking lot to the main doors of the nursing home. The ache that usually formed in her stomach when she came to visit her grandfather was absent. Floating through the checkpoint, she ignored the pervasive floral room spray trying to mask the sting of urine. Smiling at the elderly people assembled around the living area television, she waltzed to her grandfather's room. A soft chorus of voices brought her back to reality. The door to his room was flung open. Her buoyant step slowed to a nervous tip toe. Peeking her head around the doorway, she saw Graham, Emma, and David surrounding her grandfather's bed. David stood as soon as he saw her enter, his old knees creaking with the gallantry.

"Brigid! We were just talking about you. Come in, take my chair." As David motioned her forward, the facets of his polished granite bracelet grabbed the sunlight and scattered it around the small room.

As she approached, Graham nodded toward Morgan. "We came to tell your grandpa that we think you could be our Diviner. That we want to begin our work again. The hot summers have been just awful for the crops; we feel that we could help these people. And my God – the poison that's been pervading the Bay – surely we can help with that!"

Brigid turned to her grandfather, lying helpless on the bed, skin stretched across his cheekbones. His hair was wild across the pillow, tubes snaking out from his body. Morgan looked back at her, a cavern of feeling in his eyes.

She turned back to the group and asked, "Has he communicated... I don't know – anything?"

"Honey, you know he can't speak," said Emma gently. "But we've told him of the other night. He knows you were able to send away the storm. We believe he wants this for us. For you. We truly believe he agrees. You are the Diviner."

Morgan's eyes were now shining, even though the muscles in his desiccated hand clenched in desperation. Brigid watched hopelessly, trying to discern anything from his movements. She felt the pain, the frustration coursing through his veins until finally she could not stand it. Reaching out to grab his hand, she squeezed gently and looked up to the others.

"I'm sorry if I seem rude, but... What is all of this?" She sat up and twirled a loose curl around her fingers. Trying to find a sympathetic eye, she turned to Emma. "I mean, I never knew anything about this at all and it seems... I don't know..." Graham's eyes narrowed at her. Brigid met his gaze and straightened her shouldered. "It seems crazy."

Everyone in the room stiffened. Brigid looked down at her grandfather's hand, patting it gently. She took a deep breath. "What is it, exactly, that you believe you are doing? How can I possibly help? And I'm sorry, what is a Diviner?"

Graham smacked the armrest of his chair. "It's your damn mother. She kept you from your grandparents and now you don't know anything. Had to bring you up in that fancy idiotic neighborhood in town, starched and spotless." He shook his head, snorting breath out of his nose. Turning to Brigid, he said, "What is this, you ask? It's your heritage for God's sake."

"Graham." David shot a warning glance to his friend. "Brigid has asked a question. Several questions. If we believe she is meant for this, she deserves answers." He strode quietly across the room and shut the door.

Moving to the other side of Morgan's bed, he lifted the wrinkled hand into his own. "The Stone Society was formed out of love," David said gently. "Out of the desire to help. Your ancestors saw need in their community, and they knew they had the means to fill that need. We believe the Earth has much to tell us, and we have forgotten to how to listen. We know that the stones resting in the waters have been there for thousands of years, watching, observing, gathering knowledge of the world and its workings. We also know that stones have meanings, properties and powers, that have been used since time immemorial. Most people think that healing stones come only from the ocean or mines. The truth is, we have agates and jasper and granite and coral in our freshwater lakes too. These stones were formed by the union of elements: water, fire, air, sand. When a stone is lifted from the lake and examined, a Diviner can see pictures, meanings in the markings in the stone. A question can be asked, and the stone gives the answer. Markings, flaws, indentations that have been created into the stone by the Earth are interpreted by the Diviner."

Brigid dropped her gaze to the agate resting on her wrist. It looked banal, just another piece of jewelry. Yet when she put it on each morning, she felt a strange rush through her veins.

"We can answer questions, Brigid," David said. "We can help those who are confused, who are in pain. We can connect with the Earth and help to heal people. We can bring the joy from the Earth and pass it along. Just by looking into the stones."

"But can't anyone with a little imagination do this?" Brigid swallowed hard as she watched the hope melt from David's face. "I mean, I always stop to look at the rocks at the beach, or in Cairn Cottage – they're all over the house." The others nodded knowingly. Brigid ran a hand through her hair. "I can see that they may have pictures or stripes may seem like letters, but... I'm sorry, but isn't this kind of woo-woo? Like reading tea leaves? Or a horoscope?" Graham's eyes flashed, but Emma placed a calming hand on his knee.

"Yes," Emma said. "You're right. You said it perfectly: Anyone with imagination can see pictures in the stones and create meanings from them. But a Diviner isn't simply imagining. A Diviner is connecting deeply with the Earth. Hearing Her pain. Her Joy. Her messages. Taking the joy and the pain of others to the Earth. To the Divine. Reaching beyond the veil. We think you can do that."

"How do you know?" Brigid asked.

"Because you brought out the sun."

"That is what happened two nights ago, Brigid," Emma said calmly. "You weren't even trying; you didn't have all the knowledge, and yet you did it. I don't know what your thoughts were, but your happiness, your innate ability to connect with the Earth; with the Divine was shown to us. You pushed away the storm."

Under her breath, Brigid said "I was thinking of..." She stopped suddenly. The word "love" was on the tip of her tongue and it shocked her senses. Of course she loved Gabe. She just simply loved him. There were no more excuses and no more hesitation. Looking around the room, she realized she didn't want to confess that here. She wanted to trust these friends, this adopted family, but did they really think she could control the weather? It made no sense. "So..." Brigid looked down at her grandfather, who was now squeezing her hand. "The Diviner's happiness makes the sun come out? And I suppose sadness makes it rain? Anger is what – a thunderstorm? A tornado?"

Graham chuckled. "Depends on the anger," he said softly. "No, Brigid. It isn't that simple. Life isn't simple. The Diviner doesn't control the Earth and the Earth doesn't control the Diviner. It's a mutual understanding, an equality. They are a team. The Diviner learns to tap into the Divine within themselves."

"The Divine within themselves," echoed Brigid, wrinkling her brow. She brought her knees up into the chair.

"We know how it can sound," said Emma. "But nearly every spiritual practice, every religion speaks of the holy within. Look it up if you feel unsure."

"There are scores of quotes," Graham said, palms slapping the armrests of his chair. "From dust to dust, you are made of stardust, the earth and humans are made of the same percentage of water. Rumi, Sagan, the Bible! The great poets, the writers... they all say this truth. It's hard to deny."

"I mean, those are beautiful quotes and I suppose in some way I believe them, but you are suggesting I can affect the weather. The <u>weather</u>," Brigid said. "We're talking about science. Air pressure, atmosphere, clouds. I'm an education major who minored in poetry, but science... I don't know. Science is based on facts. And you can't change facts."

"Literal and tunnel-visioned. That's Lynn's influence," said Graham, nodding to Emma.

"My mother is not tunnel-visioned," Brigid said. The venom that laced this defense surprised her. "She's brilliant. In fact, she minored in physics."

"We know," said Graham ruefully.

"Sweet girl, your mother is brilliant," David said. "And you know our Graham is passionate." Brigid looked up at David, her shoulders pulled back tight. She didn't know anything about Graham, not really. Throughout her childhood she maybe saw these people once, twice a year. They had doted on her, clearly loved her without question although she had done nothing to earn their affection. She looked down at her grandfather's taut face, emotions straining against his powerless body. She loved him too, without any real reason except that he was her blood. Brigid swallowed her nerves. Forced herself to speak calmly.

"I asked before what you wanted of me. No one really answered," she said.

The machines that kept Morgan's body tethered to the world beeped and buzzed. The hacking cough of a stranger could be heard down the hall.

David broke the silence. "Brigid, we want you to be our Diviner. You have an uncanny sense of people's truth. It's clear just by your body language that you anticipate other people's needs, take their feelings on as your own. All of us feel lighter after we've spoken with you, simply being in a room with you makes a person feel free. Do you ever find that people spill their thoughts to you, tell you their secrets and their hardships?" Brigid's thoughts turned inward. People did this all the time; her friends always unloading their problems onto her, needing her to listen and help them work it out. Most of her friendships were rooted in her role as the listener, the helper. Even strangers would sit down next to her and begin to talk, invading her comfort and her space to chat and unload some issue. It was exhausting, reaching out for the emotions of others and carrying them in your body. David could see the recognition in her eyes and continued.

"So you do know what I'm talking about. And in your profession as a teacher, you must be very kind, patient, and caring. You must be aware at all times of the moods and desires of your students, how your own mood and desires are affecting everything. The core tenet of teaching is the desire to help others, correct?" Brigid nodded. "Furthermore, you have a degree in literature, poetry. You have actually spent your schooling analyzing the deeper meaning of great written art. And whether or not you believe it, we witnessed you sending the storm away." He held up his hand to stop her protest. "The week of Morgan's stroke, when your mother came to Cairn Cottage for dinner. There was a big ruckus. I could hear it from my porch." Brigid blushed and averted her eyes. "No no, there's no need to be embarrassed. You didn't do anything wrong. But you were upset, weren't you?" Brigid looked at him, not willing to answer. "Confused, angry, sad, torn? Did you not notice the sudden rain that drove you all inside? Were you not wading in the lake the next morning, gathering chairs that the wind blew down? A large branch was even felled I believe."

"Evening storms are typical in the summer," Brigid said quickly. "It was a risk we took having happy hour on the dock."

"Evening storms are typical in late August, early September. This was May." David looked hard at her. Did she want to fight, to protest? The woman was smart, very educated and while quiet, clearly knew what she was about. He decided it was best not to push it.

"Well, let's put the weather aside for now. We believe you can interpret the stones that we give you. How about this... take problems presented to you and just look inward. Connect with Earth wherever you can, on a hike, on a sail, on a swim. Take the stones with you. Look at them. See what you see and report back. Let us know. Could you do that?"

Brigid squirmed in the seat. Was this a religion, a cult? As if he heard her thoughts, David answered, "We're only asking you to use your skills as an interpreter, as a feeler. You're not making magic," he chuckled softly, looking around in affirmation to Emma and Graham. "If anything, you can think of yourself as a mystic."

"Brigid, there are people who need help in this community. People whose farms are failing, whose lakeshores are rotting with this new pestilence. And beyond that, people who are being abused." Rose shot into Brigid's mind. She saw the little girl's brutally thin arms and angry thick bruises.

"With your skills, we can help them. You can help them."

Brigid swallowed hard. "What if I'm wrong?" she asked quietly. "What if I try and my interpretations are wrong?"

This time when Emma spoke, her voice was sure and true. "There is no wrong here. If you put all of yourself into the thoughts, the intentions, the good wishes, the only thing you will do is help. There is no way to harm."

What they were asking wasn't much, Brigid thought. It seemed so important to them. She studied their wrinkled faces, felt her grandfather's papery palm in her own. Life was so brief. It might be a kindness to give them this gift in the autumn of their lives. Her mother would be furious. Then again, her mother wasn't speaking to her. Her mother wouldn't even deign to meet this man she had fallen in love with, dismissing yet again something Brigid cared about. Well, it was enough. Brigid was tired of being thought of as incapable. These people believed in her and approval was a nice feeling. She took a deep breath and looked down at her grandfather.

His eyes were bright, his muscles shaking. Morgan seemed to be desperately wanting to speak to his granddaughter. Brigid recalled the night of her first date with Gabe, when her grandfather placed her grandmother's bracelet on her wrist.

The Divining bracelet. He must have thought she was capable; must have wanted her to know. He loved her, with an affection and abundance never expressed by her own mother.

She bent and kissed Morgan's forehead, brushing his white locks away. She would do this for her grandfather. For these adults who had watched over her like aunts and uncles, written her letters, asked after her all her life. And she would allow herself to love Gabe. There would be no more worrying and weighing the worth of her feelings for him. No more eyes peeled for red flags and analyzing every possibility. She had never felt this free in her life, and she was going to live in it. If they wanted her to gaze at stones, think about love, there was nothing wrong in that. She could do that.

Placing Morgan's hand back onto the bedsheet, she stood.

"I can do this. I will. If this is what you want from me, I will be your Diviner."

Emma clapped her hands in delight, and Graham reached forward, clutching Brigid's hands in his own. He kissed her on both cheeks. She embraced him and turned to David, who had tears shining in his eyes.

"You'll have to teach me," Brigid said smiling. "I know you all think I can do this, but I really have no idea how to go about it."

"We'll meet every week, just like before," said Graham, putting arm around Emma. "Now Brigid, you'll have to spend some time collecting the stones, walking the beach. None of us are in the best shape to be hiking up that long two-track road. I recommend you go two, three times per week and spend several hours each day looking at the stones and recording what they tell you. That's what your grandmother did."

"Now wait just a minute," David said, putting his palm up to slow Graham's rambling. "We need to be patient with her, take time to teach her, wait a bit…"

Graham cut him off, "Teach her? She is an educator, she understands, she doesn't need us to teach her. No, David. No more waiting, no more patience. It's been too long already."

Brigid stepped gingerly between the men. "I can go on hikes every week to collect the stones. And I'll spend time looking at them. I'll write down my thoughts so you all can see, is that alright?"

"We'll meet one evening a week at our cabin," Emma said. "I'll make pie and we can go over everything over dessert."

"And whiskey!" Graham exclaimed.

Emma laughed at him. "Yes, and whiskey. David, perhaps you can give Brigid a few of the problems community members have presented to us in the past year? She can contemplate them while she spends time with the stones."

"I certainly can. Brigid, would you mind dropping by when we all return to the lake? I have some index cards."

"Let's see, today is Sunday. Shall we meet tomorrow?" Graham asked.

"Sweetheart, let's give her a little time," Emma said. "Brigid, do you think you'll be able to hike back to Big Omann Lake tomorrow and collect some stones?" Brigid nodded. "Well, why don't you do that, spend some time with them, write down your interpretations, and we'll have our gathering on Tuesday. Shall we say dusk?"

"Dusk it is," Brigid said.

"Now we won't be interfering with a date, will we?" Emma asked, straining for seriousness.

"How did you know I was seeing someone?" Brigid asked, playing at being incredulous.

"Oh, we know," winked Graham. "He's a handsome fella. Make sure he treats you properly, or he'll have me to deal with!" Graham raised his fists like a boxer, laughing until a hacking cough came from deep in his throat. Emma quietly handed her husband the bottle of water from her purse and he took a sip. One by one, they bid goodbye to Morgan, who lay on the bed, his hands relaxed now. As Brigid closed the door, she failed to see the tear that trickled down his cheek.

CHAPTER 27

The scar between her shoulder blades glistened in the sunlight. Instinct told Gabe not to ask about the scar, but a morbid curiosity made him want to run his fingers along its twisted path. He had noticed it that first night on the beach. Running his hand up her back, he felt the unnaturally smooth line that cut through her perfect skin. Brigid had stiffened under his hand that first time, and he had been careful to avoid touching that part of her since. He wanted to tell her that she was beautiful in spite of the scar. Beautiful because of it. But it didn't seem like talking about it would get him anywhere. Better to love her and say nothing.

Today was the first time he saw her in a tank top. The low neckline was intoxicating. When she had answered the door, it was all he could do to keep his eyes up, keep from wrapping her lithe body in his arms and throwing her down on the couch. When she walked out of Cairn Cottage as he held the door, he saw that the low back revealed the scar snaking between her shoulders. He had assumed she dressed conservatively because she was a teacher. Even her sundresses had necklines that began at the collarbone. For some reason, today was different...

Gabe shook his head. Thinking of her body wasn't going to get him anywhere right now. There had been people on the two-track path back to the Big Lake, surely there would be more on the beach. He caught up to her and placed his broad hand lightly on her lower back.

"Do you have more rocks for me?" he asked, jingling the pail.

She grinned up at him. "You are such a cute errand boy," she said playfully. "Yes, I do. I think this one is granite, what do you think?"

Gabe examined the rock she held in her palm. He had absolutely no idea. Each day they spent together she became more adorable in his eyes. As she became comfortable with him, her clever wit came out, she flirted shamelessly, disarming his usual suave confidence. And the other night, lightening flashing through the windows as they lay on the living room rug...

"Hello?" Brigid's voice interrupted his thoughts. "What do we think? Granite or basalt?"

"I have no clue," he said. In this case, he figured, the truth was safe enough. "It's really pretty though with that stripe through it. Would you like to put it in the bucket, madam?" he asked with an exaggerated bow.

They walked along, hand in hand. The air on the Peninsula was known for being sweet. Soft. Even in the heat of July, the northern winds always had a refreshing hint of coolness to them. People surmised that it was the latitude, the untouched and protected lands that gave the air here such a pure quality. But today, a noxious scent seemed to be lurking, getting more forceful as they walked toward the big sand bluffs. Soon the scent was so overpowering that it broke their reverie. Their hands fell apart as they covered their noses. Big nasty horseflies flew around them.

Hundreds of dead fish lay on top of the stony sand. Carcasses had broken open to the sun and their organs oozed into the summer air. The swarming horseflies bit Gabe and Brigid relentlessly as they backed up and flailed their arms in the air. Unsatisfied with the gruesome banquet, the flies craved the taste of living flesh.

"Alewives," said Gabe, his face wrinkling in disgust. Brigid looked at him in confusion. "The fish," he said. "They're alewives. It's an invasive species in the lake. They wash up a bit every few years, but it's never been anything like this." Brigid waved her hand in front of her face, a losing battle with the insects and the stench.

"They don't all look the same though. Look at those." Brigid pointed to larger spotted fish with a pink stripe along its side. Gabe saw with surprise that she was right.

"Whoa," he said. "Those are trout, I think. That's a big problem if the trout are washing up. The restaurants are going to freak." He yelped and pointed, "Brigid, do you see those with the black stripes and the orange fins? I think those are perch. Every restaurant on the Peninsula has perch baskets on Fridays. The populations in the inland lakes have been so over-fished, they're almost gone."

Brigid wasn't listening. She was bent over a white and silver fish as long as her arm. Its black tail and fins were flapping hopelessly on the sand. She lifted it up awkwardly and waded into the water, submerging the fish's gills. Waving away the flies with one hand, she walked slowly back the way they had come, away from the throng of death. Still holding the fish underwater, she walked deeper into the lake until the scent of decay lay behind her. After taking a few pictures of the pesca-tarian annihilation, Gabe jogged along the shoreline to catch up with Brigid. He saw with alarm that she was wading out into the waters in her clothes. The waves licked her waist and her auburn curls were getting soaked as she hunched forward. Splashing out to meet her, he called out.

"Brigid! Brigid, are you ok? What are you doing?" She didn't turn or answer. It was as if she didn't hear him. Ripping his phone and wallet out of the pocket of his shorts before they were submerged, he swore under his breath and waded further. "Brigid!" He was close to her now, close enough to see that she was holding tight to something. She still did not answer him. A seraphic tune reached his ears and he realized she was humming. Gabe looked askance at her and noticed the muscles in her arms were taut. Was she trying to pull a big rock out of the bottom of the lake? The waves calmed and he saw something wriggling below the surface. She was holding a gigantic whitefish in her arms. The animal seemed to get stronger by the second. When the next big swell came, Brigid released her arms and the whitefish swam away. Confidently, it swished its fins, gaining speed until it moved beyond their sight into the depths of Big Omann Lake. Brigid straightened, realizing she was soaked. She gathered her hair in front of one shoulder and squeezed the moisture out. Her head trembled lightly, involuntarily, as if shaking off a spell. With a start, she noticed Gabe standing beside her, phone and wallet held awkwardly above the waves. He was staring at her.

"I'm...I'm sorry," she stuttered. "I just wanted to save one."

"Come on," he said. "Let's get dried off." Gabe led them down the beach, away from the rotting fish and merciless flies. He took her crumpled towel and stood downwind, shaking the sand from it. His own was already laid meticulously on the sand. He spread hers out next to his, facing the lake. "Do you want to stay here or walk back?" he asked.

"Let's stay here," Brigid said, still absently squeezing water out of her hair. "I'm soaked. I don't want to walk back through the woods like this. Too many mosquitoes."

"Fair enough," said Gabe, settling down on his towel and stretching out his legs. He glanced over at her. She really was completely wet. He couldn't think of one other girl he knew who would march out, fully clothed, into chilly water of Big Omann Lake. Most girls squealed and pranced around at the prospect of a dip in Big Omann Lake. It was cute, but he always thought it was just a little bit stupid. Were they really that cold or was it just a ploy to bring the attention back to themselves? That, or they'd strip into bra and panties and give a show, throwing back their heads and laughing at their ability to tease and deny him. He knew how to act in those situations, stroke their egos with words, strip off his own shirt and flex some muscles. Gauge to a moment whether the girls actually wanted him to participate, or just wanted to revel in the glory of their beautiful selves. Either way, Gabe had always been a happy participant.

But this one, this dripping, fully-clothed woman lifting her face to the sun, what had she just done? Take a giant fish, a fish that probably weighed fifty pounds, and carry it from the rotting carcasses of its fellows and back into the lake. She had saved it. Gabe had witnessed many animal deaths on the farm; he had become practical about the inevitable end of life. The years and his schooling had honed his ability to detect the signs of death. He had worked mostly with mammals and birds, but he knew enough to know that the whitefish Brigid had hauled back into the lake was minutes from death. The dull glaze in the eyes, the near lack of movement. And yet it swam strongly away when Brigid released it from her hands.

Brigid felt exhausted. The fish hadn't been that heavy, but she figured the stress of trying to save it wore her out. And the tinge of embarrassment. Gabe had looked at her strangely as he led her back onto the shore. Had he been next to her that whole time? She hadn't heard a thing except for the wind blowing by her ear and the waves crashing onto the shoreline. It was beautiful, feeling the limp creature right itself in her arms. She felt it begin breathing stronger and stronger. It was if she could feel the fish tell her it was ready to be released. Ready to swim home. The tune she hummed as she walked out into the water, she couldn't place it. It seemed as if she knew it from long ago.

In any case, she had saved the fish. One less death to add to that pile of carcasses. She had seen alewives wash up from time to time, but the prevalence of the other species was worrying. Releasing a sigh, she lowered herself down onto the towel. It would be good to take a minute to breathe.

A sharp, stinging pain shot from between her shoulders down through all of her limbs. She scrambled up, anguish crossing her face.

"Ouch!" She yelped. Gabe immediately sprang to action. "What happened?" He placed his hand protectively where she reached her own, touching the scar on her upper back gingerly. She leapt away from his touch. A mixture of mortification and physical pain flew across her face. On a normal day, her scar felt like zipping, stinging numbness if touched. The feeling was like nails on a chalkboard. It had clearly healed wrong; the nerve endings were broken and acerbic. She hated how it looked, hated that people could see it, stare at it and at her from behind without her knowledge. Why the hell had she worn a tank top today? Furious at herself, at her false confidence, at the pep talk she had given herself this morning. He's clearly seen it, she told herself. God knows he's seen everything else and he's ok with all of it. It was going to be hot today, it was alright for her to be comfortable. Comfortable, and a little sexy, just like other women her age would try to be.

How fucking stupid. The minute she exposed the scar, she got hurt. As always. Right now though, the pain was not only to her pride. The actual scar ached. She lifted the towel off of the sand. A large, jagged stone lurked in the sand. Lifting it up, she wanted to smash it, throw it. Tears threatened behind her eyes.

"Granite?"

Brigid looked at Gabe. The look that met hers was one of feeble desperation. The joke was bad, he knew. He had no idea how to deal with this. She swallowed and visibly tried to soften her expression.

"It stabbed me," she said, voice clenched. "I'm sorry."

Gabe lifted the stone from her hand. Placing it on the ground, he enveloped his hand in hers.

"Why are you sorry?" Gabe met her gaze and kept it. "You're always sorry and as far as I've seen, you hardly do anything wrong. It's the rock's fault, if anything." She let out a small smile and he was relieved.

"Are you bleeding?" he asked softly. "Can I look?" She swallowed hard. What did it matter at this point? He'd obviously seen her scar from her low-cut top. She hadn't been able to cover up the ugly rage on her face when the rock pierced her. At her nod, he shifted his position to sit behind her. He gazed at the jagged keloid pathway.

There was a valley marking the original slash, and the place where the skin had been stitched together were clearly visible.

The skin had grown over the stitches perhaps, or had never lost the feeling of the threads of steel. On either side of the thin valley, the skin grew raised, and unnaturally smooth, like dunes rising up from a river. The color was off too, slightly more blushed than the rest of her milky skin. So far, in the heat of their nights together, he avoided touching the scar. Not from any disgust on his own part, but because it was clear that it was a touch Brigid did not welcome. Seeing it now, in the harsh unforgiving daylight, he found he was simply curious. How did a woman of twenty-five get a scar like this one? Did it hurt? Was she hurt now? She didn't seem to be bleeding, but a thought occurred to him — could scars bleed? Gabe had an overpowering desire to touch her scar. It would be a good idea to touch it, he rationalized. He may be able to determine where she was truly hurt. He reached out, tracing the pathway of the scar with his forefinger.

Pain and overwhelming irritation shot through Brigid's blood vessels. Zinging sensations emanated from her scar making her see black behind her eyes. She hunched forward away from his touch and suppressed an animal urge to turn and strike him. "Stop," she choked out. "Please."

"I'm so sorry," said Gabe, pulling his hand away. "You <u>are</u> hurt. I can't see where though."

"No, that's just how it always feels," Brigid said, turning to face him, guarding her back from his touch.

"Wow, just... all the time?" A wave of disgust washed over her. The anger she could feel for him at this moment was like a warm cave for the shame and hatred with which she chastised herself. She gazed at him, seeing only sincerity, and worry in his eyes. She sighed. This was Gabe. The man she was falling in love with, this man who looked at her as if she held the moon in her fingertips.

"No," She said. "Not all the time. Just when people touch it. It's... I dunno. It's like if your leg goes numb, right? Like when you have a charlie horse. Or you sleep funny on your arm and your arm and hand are numb. You know what that feels like?

Like static or zinging, or something?" Gabe nodded. "Well imagine if that happened and then someone scratched your skin. Or ran a nail over it." Gabe's face wrinkled at the thought. "Now multiply that by a thousand. That's what it feels like when someone touches my scar. I think the nerve endings healed wrong. Now they're broken, or something." Brigid swallowed hard. "I hate it."

"I'm so sorry," Gabe said.

"Now you just told me I don't have to be sorry. Why are you sorry now? It's not your fault I have a scar," Brigid retorted, eager to pass the feeling of insecurity onto him.

"Well, I'm sorry because I hurt you," Gabe said, meeting her gaze firmly. "Certainly unintentionally, but I actually physically hurt you. That's a good reason to be sorry. And I am sorry. You, on the other hand, do not need to be sorry. For lying on a jagged rock, or anything else. And you don't need to be sorry for having a scar."

Brigid looked out at the lake, squinting her eyes to push back the tears. God, she hoped his next words wouldn't pierce her heart. She'd heard so much bullshit over the years. "Your scar is so beautiful," intoned the guy she had slept with after Matt, his expression dripping with schmaltz. It was insincere, and so cheesy. She had wanted to get up, gather her clothes and her pride and leave. But she had stayed. Slept with him, ashamed at herself for needing to hear those words.

And Matt. Her stomach clenched just thinking about that night. Matt had flipped her over, examining her ass, her shoulders, her tiny waist, and eventually, her scar. "It's ok," he had said. "I think you're hot. In spite of the scar." His possession, his approval. It was crucial to be acceptable in his eyes, in his world. And she had been so happy, so relieved to hear that he would forgive this flaw that she had done nothing to earn. Now, with the sunlight beating down on her face, and the distant stench of rotting fish down the lake, she clenched her jaw, anticipating what Gabe would say next. Maybe, mercifully, he would say nothing.

A warm hand covered her own. She turned to face him, realizing he had been looking at her this whole time.

"You're beautiful, Brigid. If you don't know that, if you don't believe that, please do." He squeezed her hand, fumbling for his next words. "I want to tell you — I've never met a woman like you. I mean, you're smart, you care about things - you saved a fish today..." He smiled nervously. Despite herself, she laughed. The sparkle in it calmed his nerves. "You're really different, Brigid. In the best ways. And... and I want to tell you, I'm falling in love with you."

The words that had been buried in her mind since their third date exploded to the surface. She loved him too. Against all prudence, against all sanity, she had loved him. She knew, in the very pit of her being, that Gabe was the man she was going to be with for the rest of her life. The knowledge had been sudden and all consuming. She felt so peaceful when the knowledge came upon her. It had been the oddest thing because of course staying with him for the rest of her life was not something within her control. He could easily not feel the same way, she could change her mind. And yet the certainty, the same certainty that told her that the sky was blue and the up north air was clean and pure, filled her with serenity.

And now, here he was, saying he felt the same way. Brigid leaned forward into his arms, hugging him hard. "I love you too." Her breath was warm against his neck.

Gabe held her close, a firm grip as if he was afraid she would change her mind and float away. Leaning back, Brigid meant to break away, sit alone, to grill him. But he grasped her harder, gently placing his hand behind her head so that she stayed nestled in his shoulder. She smiled into the warm softness of his tee-shirt. He always smelled so good, the bergamot and cedar notes of his cologne emanated from his skin. Inhaling the scent of him, she felt at peace.

"So you love me, huh?" she asked. "Even though I'm a little crazy?" Gabe laughed. "Saving fish? Collecting rocks? Needing time to myself every once in awhile? You don't even know the depth of crazy we're talking about here. I'm not even sure that I do," she said.

"You're not crazy," he answered, kissing her hair. His voice was husky, an intensity and gratitude that bravado couldn't hide. "And I'm sure I'm not your parent's ideal guy. A Peninsula farmer who hauls sailboats on the side? Still lives with his mother. Paying off college debt. Kind of a loser in their book I bet." She felt him swallow.

"I don't care what my mother thinks," said Brigid. She pulled back fiercely and looked in his eyes. "You are a man who takes care of his family, who runs his family farm, and who went to college to do it." He made a face and shifted his grip on her, accidentally brushing her scar which shot a cruel bolt of pain through her.

"I am so sorry!" Gabe said. "Goddamn it," he muttered under his breath. Burying her face in his shoulder again to hide her expression, she summoned her courage. She had never really asked anyone, and now she could hardly bear to risk it. Intellectually she knew it was silly, narcissistic even. But she had to ask. What did love mean to him? Was it strong enough to love even the wounds she carried, wounds she never asked for and didn't inflict on herself? These deep and abiding wounds that trampled across her very existence, baring their gnarled truth to the world? She took a breath. Asked the question.

"You don't mind about my scar?"

Gabe went very still. He leaned back and held her by the shoulders. Looking into her eyes, he said,

"Brigid, it's part of you. To me, it's not really a big deal. To you though, it seems like a big deal. I probably don't understand why, but if you want to tell me, I'll listen. If you don't want to, that's fine too." He wiped a tear from her cheek with a calloused thumb. "I love you, so I love your scar."

The wind fluttered the leaves of the nearby trees.

"But I will tell you one thing: I promise never ever to touch it again. I am very tired of hurting you," he said, gritting his teeth. She smiled through her tears and sniffed loudly. Looking down at herself, she realized as if for the first time, that she was soaking wet.

"Oh my God, I'm a mess!" she said, shaking her hands out and standing up. `

"You sort of are," he said. "And I am starving. What do you say we go grab lunch?"

"After I change!" Brigid shook sand from her bottom and from her legs.

"Obviously." Gabe gave her an exaggerated up and down glance. "Sandy, but beautiful," he proclaimed. She slapped his arm. "Shall I carry these pebbles for you, ma'am?" he said, bowing dramatically.

"Yes please," she laughed, gathering the beach towels and stepping downwind to shake them out.

He held out his arm for her and wrapped it around her shoulders. He bent and kissed the top of her head, and they walked away from the bright lakeside beach into the shadowy light of the forest path.

CHAPTER 28

The enamel sink was gritty. An old plastic spaghetti strainer dripped from the dish rack, small clumps of sand still clinging to its holes. The north wind rattled the screen door. Brigid glanced back, wondering if she should close the big wooden door. No one ever shut the doors at Little Owrawn Lake.

After the hike, she had run in to change and then they went to a little restaurant for lunch. As predicted, the popular perch and whitefish baskets were off the menu. It was obvious that afterwards, Gabe had wanted to come into Cairn Cottage with her, but she was too mentally drained. He gave her a quick hard hug, a searching glance, and then pecked her cheek and drove away.

The stones she had chosen were not necessarily beautiful, but intriguing. There were seven in total. It had occurred to Brigid that she should place them in a thoughtful vessel for the meeting, rather than toss them in her pocket. Searching the cupboards, she found a small porcelain dish, celadon green with hand-painted chickadees soaring around its circumference. To protect the antique ceramic from the rough stones, she rummaged around the drawers of the china cabinet and found an old handkerchief. She placed that in the bottom of the bowl, set the stones on top, and walked down to the Websters'.

The sky began to glow with the distinctive punch-colored sunset of the north woods. Graham paced the kitchen of their cottage. Emma set out platters of cheese, crackers, and home-made chocolate chip cookies. She rinsed the tender raspberries under a gentle stream of water and tipped them into a bowl. David immediately loped over to the counter and began popping the fragile berries into his mouth.

"Save some for Brigid," said Emma, smiling. The screen door creaked open.

"Ah!" said Graham, clapping his hands together. "The sun is setting, so let's not waste another moment nattering. Did you bring the stones, my dear?" Brigid proffered her dish. Graham took it and nodded appreciatively. "Beautiful." As he picked through the selection examining each stone, David elbowed Brigid and offered a glass of whiskey and water, on top of which were stacked two chocolate chip cookies. She grinned at him.

"Now, these are interesting," Graham said. "I'm just fascinated by what you've chosen." Graham held up a small speckled granite and dipped it in the wooden bowl of water set on the coffee table. The shape of an arrowhead and about the size of a serving spoon, the stone was burnt orange and rose colored, with flecks of pearlescent gray.

"Oh, I couldn't stop staring at that one." Brigid stepped forward. "Do you see how the indentation makes it look as if countless tiny stones were glued together to make this larger rock? If you look closer, even the flecking in the granite has its own markings, flaws. Do you see?" Brigid reached up to take the stone, then dropped her arm awkwardly when it became clear that Graham was unwilling to hand it back to her. "It made me think of how people are connected. We're our own tiny pieces, with flaws and minuscule beauty, but it takes all of us to make a whole." Brigid looked around, encouraged by the sparkle in Emma's eyes, and David's knowing smile. "I think I understand what you wanted me to see." Stepping past Graham, she reached into the bowl and lifted the midnight blue stone. She dipped it in the wooden dish and held it to the light. "I thought the color of this stone was beautiful. At first glance it seems plain, dark gray or even black. If you look closely though, it's the color of the sky just past midnight. At that time of the month where there is no moon. And this band, circling around it..."

"Quartz," Emma said softly.

"Yes," Brigid continued. "The band, splits it down the middle. Or encircles it, I don't know. At first it made me think of good and evil. You know, like the lighter color was good and the darker color was evil. But I didn't like that, you know?" Graham stared at her.

Brigid continued. "Darkness at midnight isn't evil. It can be peaceful. My main impression is that the stone itself represents completeness. The dark color is comforting in a way. It's real. True. And the quartz band... it is beautiful, and maybe it represents purity or love or goodness. But it could represent anger, or fear. I know I've seen white-hot anger..." She trailed off. Looking at the fading light from the window, a bolt of uncertainly rushed through her. "I'm sorry, it's getting late — should I continue? I feel like I'm rambling."

"Oh no, dear, you're doing beautifully." Emma placed a soft hand on Brigid's shoulder.

"You are rambling a bit." David turned a disapproving glance at the sound of Graham's voice. "I'm sorry," said Graham. "I don't mean to be so blunt, but the sun is setting and you know we need to create the cairn in the dusk. Brigid dear, your interpretations are getting there. In time you will learn to become more concise."

Brigid pursed her lips and gave a tight smile. She felt like she had been verbally slapped. Graham made his face into a mask of contrition. "Perhaps you could write down your thoughts?" He set paper and pencil down on the table near the stones. Brigid found the only comfortable way to reach the writing utensils was to kneel in front of the table. As she did, Graham leaned over a shoulder. "A gentle reminder, if I may quote Shakespeare, brevity is the soul of wit." Brigid gave him a submissive smile and resented herself for doing it.

She quickly dotted down some thoughts while the group shuffled toward the lake. Graham carried the bowl of stones.

Emma carried a stack of towels and Brigid wondered if they were going swimming. She hoped not; she'd been in enough lake water for today. Emma rolled up her pants and stepped into the clear, shallow water. Walking out on the steep drop-off until the water reached her calves, she beckoned for the rest to follow. Graham and David strode the few feet in their shorts. Brigid followed and slipped off her sandals. She waded into the water. She was glad she had thrown on a sweater. The chill in the air combined with nerves were making her shiver. The three elders glanced out, searching to see if the neighboring docks were within their sightline. David quietly pointed out the end of a dock three cabins down. "There," he said. Collectively, they moved inward until they were behind a small grove of trees that leaned out over the water's edge. Once the neighboring dock was no longer in sight, David lifted the bowl from Graham's hands. Bending down to touch the bottom of the bowl to the surface of the water, he lifted it, dripping, to the setting sun.

"May these stones, formed in the fiery heart of the Earth, smoothed by the eternal waters of our glacial lake, and lifted from the sand by one of your children, receive your blessing." Emma and Graham closed their eyes and bowed their heads briefly, muttering something unintelligible. Brigid followed suit, breathing "Amen," into the silence. This seemed like a prayer; and it was the only response she knew.

David continued. "May your blessings fall down on us like leaves, and brush our hearts like the breeze. May you be with our Diviner," David smiled meaningfully at Brigid as he paused. "Be with her as she hones her skills, and uses her divine kindness, creativity, and intelligence to pass the messages of the Earth onto us, her children." Another pause. Brigid soaked up David's words, feeling warm and important. "May you be with our departed, Shannon Ayers, and my sweet Nieve..." he paused, swallowing hard. "And our brother Morgan, who is bound in the confines of a broken body, but is surely here with us in spirit this evening." Brigid ached at the thought of her grandfather. He should be here, beside her as she uncovered this new side to her heart, the secrets of her family.

"Please bless our Society," David was saying. "Let us help our fellow children of the Earth. Let the work of our minds, hearts, and hands benefit the struggling, and the downtrodden. This we ask of You." More muttering. Everyone looked up, smiling, relaxing their shoulders and necks. Was this it? Brigid thought. She itched with curiosity. What religion was this? Whose blessing were they asking for? Her spiraling thoughts were broken by the calling of her name. As she snapped to attention, she realized they were all laughing softly. "Brigid," said David, smiling. "We appreciate your concentration. But as Diviner, we need you to stack the cairn." She stepped forward, puzzled. "Simply stack these stones in a tower, in the manner that you see fit."

Brigid reached forward and stopped. "But, where should I put them?"

Graham rolled his eyes and huffed. Brigid tensed at his reaction. How was she supposed to automatically know these things? They were standing in the middle of the lake for God's sake, several yards from the dock or the shore. Emma said sternly, "Graham, we discussed this. We're not going to place them as we had. It's not safe anymore."

"It's ridiculous," Graham muttered darkly.

David said quickly, "Brigid, just stack them in the bowl. Don't worry too much about biggest to smallest. If you look closely at their shapes, you'll figure it out. Use your instinct." Brigid stepped forward and stacked them. At the top, she placed the midnight blue stone, its quartz band glimmering in the last vestiges of sunlight.

When the tower was complete, solace washed over David's face. "Very good, Brigid. Very good." The other three adults stepped forward to look at her handiwork.

"In lieu of placing the cairn in our lake, could we scoop a handful of water over the stones?" asked Emma. David nodded enthusiastically. "Wonderful idea! You start, Emma." Emma reverently cupped her hands and lifted water. Holding her hands over the bowl of stones, she watched as the drips fell quickly and gently over the tower. David carefully handed the bowl to her and did the same. He nodded to Brigid who imitated the movement. David nodded to Graham, sending him a look of warning. Graham lowered his tense shoulders, and, looking David in the eye, scooped up some water and let it fall over the stones. Emma began to carry the bowl toward the shore. As the rest followed, the mood broke into a sense of ease and familiarity. Emma set the bowl down carefully on a wooden table they kept on the beach, and handed out towels. Everyone automatically rubbed the towels on their bare legs and arms, scrubbing the invisible parasite away.

"I'd like to suggest we all wash off with soap," said Emma. "I keep hearing more terrible things about the swimmers' curse this year. A young girl has been taken seriously ill and is in intensive care."

"From this lake?" David asked with alarm.

"No, from Bear Lake," Emma said.

"Just south of here. It's getting closer," said David gravely. "It's on the Peninsula." Emma drew a sharp breath. Brigid set her towel on the chair and looked at them.

"I'm sorry, but I have so many questions," she said. "You — we — were praying. Who were we praying to? Is this based on a religion of some kind?" Just as Emma began to answer, they heard a splash in the lake.

"Graham!" shouted Emma, scrambling to the shore. "What are you doing?"

Graham was nearly up to his knees already. He had the bowl in his hand. Facing the horizon, he lifted the cairn and tipped it into his palm, destroying it shape. Ignoring the shouts from the shoreline, Graham methodically dropped each of the seven stones into the lake. He began with the bottom stone of Brigid's cairn and ascended. When he lifted the basalt stone with the quartz band, he turned to Emma and David, who had reached him and were yelling. Holding the final stone in his fist, he lifted his arm up to stop the protest. "If we're going to do this, we need to follow the procedures." The stone splashed gently into the water.

"But Graham, there is a warning against putting any materials from the Big Omann Lake into our inland waters!" Emma shouted. "A firm warning! You've read it and I've read it. It was issued by the Health Department and backed up by the hospital!"

"I realize this," Graham said, calmly walking back to shore. "But we're talking about seven small stones. I'm sure Brigid rinsed them off; I saw no sand or particles clinging to them. I understand the precautions, but I highly doubt the bacteria could be carried on rocks. Rocks that have been washed. If we want our blessings to work, we need to follow procedure."

"Graham, our first contract is to respect the land. To love the land," David said angrily. "Your action now is breaking that contract."

"I do love the land," Graham said. "I understand the land, David. I've studied it for decades. This will not harm us. And regardless, it's done now."

The water rippled gently as Brigid's stones sank into its murky depth.

CHAPTER 29

The mouthwatering scent of the pizza bread wafted from the paper bag. Brigid lifted the fluffy, fresh-baked roll out and stopped to inhale the combination of poppyseeds, garlic, and yeast. Reaching into the grocery bag, she lifted the can of frozen lemonade and she felt the panic rise. Did nine-year-olds even like lemonade? She knew her students did, but should she have picked up pop for an older kid? Cursing herself for not asking Gabe what Mikey liked, she bent to find the old wooden salad bowl among the jumble of serving dishes in the cupboard below the island.

She rinsed the glass pitcher and began to mix the lemonade. As she reached for the tap, she caught sight of the lake between the branches of the birch trees. Taking a deep breath of the fresh air, Brigid willed herself to be calm. This was Gabe. Gabe who knew every part of her. Gabe who loved her. And this was Mikey, his adorable little brother who looked at her as if she hung the moon. No one was going to judge her here.

She heard the truck door slam. She smiled. Mikey's reedy voice rang out through the air. "Can we go in the lake? Right now? Please?" She opened the screen door and Mikey threw his bony arms around her waist.

"Hi buddy!" Brigid said, as she hugged him back. "Come on in the house. Let's eat first and then yes, we can go in the lake." Ushering him over the threshold, she turned to Gabe who bent down and kissed her.

"Hi," he said. His lips brushed her bare neck.

"Hi."

"Ewwww!" Mikey popped his head around the corner. "Stop

165

kissing!" Gabe and Brigid laughed and followed Mikey into the house.

She gave Mikey a tour of Cairn Cottage, and he picked up every little thing he could find.

"Mikey, knock it off," Gabe warned, as his little brother tossed a glass doo-dad into the air. "These are not your things." Brigid dramatically rolled her eyes at him, making Mikey collapse into laughter.

"He's fine — he's not going to hurt anything," she said. "Sit down and have some lemonade." When Mikey turned back to the shiny object at hand, Brigid threw Gabe a wink. His body relaxed into the old wooden chair.

Having found every conceivable treasure inside, Mikey barreled out toward the lakefront, nodding at a stern command from Gabe not to go in the water. Gabe and Brigid stood behind the old island together and made sandwiches, quietly happy. Gabe reached for a butter knife, placing his hand on hers. Brigid placed a hand on his waist to gently push him aside so she could take a bowl from the cupboard he blocked. Out of respect for Mikey's presence, they did not kiss again, but took every excuse to touch. Brigid's skin was electrified by the brush of his fingers.

When lunch was prepared, they called Mikey. He raced in, plopped in a chair, and promptly knocked over his lemonade. His face fell as he watched it splash from the yellowed plastic tablecloth onto the antique rug, inexplicably placed underneath the long wooden table. Gabe's face was like thunder, as he rose to scold his younger brother for his carelessness. Brigid put her hand out.

"Mikey, don't even worry. You are not the first person to spill something in this house." Her comforting smile twinkled into a smirk. "In fact, your brother knocked his drink over last time he was here."

"I bet he didn't ruin a rug," Mikey said mournfully, although a hint of relief shone through his eyes.

"Oh, he did some damage to the rug," Brigid said.

Now it was Gabe's turn to be embarrassed.

Brigid gathered the napkins and passed them to Mikey, who obediently began sopping up the lemonade on the table. The adults knelt on the plush crimson rug and cleared up the rest of the spill.

"We've been here before," said Brigid, winking at Gabe. "Blot."

"I'm sorry," said Gabe. "I don't want us to ruin your fancy things."

"Oh my God, nobody's ruining anything. It's lemonade! Don't worry."

Gabe took the mess of soaked towels and napkins to the kitchen trash and began rummaging under the sink.

"What are you doing?" asked Brigid

"Looking for carpet cleaner," said Gabe. Brigid looked at Mikey, who looked guilty.

"Mikey, eat," she said. "Please. I promise you, it's not a big deal." When he didn't meet her eyes, she patted the table to get his attention. When he looked up, Brigid lifted a fresh strawberry out of her salad with her fingers. The fruit dripping with oily dressing, she dropped it onto the carpet. Using the tip of her toe, she squished it into the soft fibers.

"Now we've all spilled something." Mikey looked at her askance. "The rug is just a thing, buddy. An inanimate object. It doesn't matter." She turned to the kitchen. "Gabe! Enough with the cleaning. Let's enjoy our lunch!" Smiling at both of them, she sat and beckoned Gabe back to the table. The rest of the meal passed with ease. Gabe gazed at Brigid. She was a rapt audience for Mikey's soliloquy on every little thing he had seen outside. She answered his questions and asked even better ones of him. Gabe winced as he watched tiny particles of food fly through the air as Mikey refused to stop talking to chew. Chomping his potato chips with vigor, Mikey's dejection from spilling the lemonade quickly transformed into enthusiasm under Brigid's encouraging attention. Gabe wanted to correct his brother's poor manners, but something stopped him.

The eager rapport between the two of them was too precious to break.

Gabe never knew family could be this way: simple, easy. Meals at his home centered around their mother's litany of woes. Life was against them, she claimed. Nothing Gabe did or accomplished could relieve them, according to his mother. Their family was ruined and trampled upon by those born to a better life, and always would be. It was how the world was scripted. Occasionally, Gabe went toe to toe with her, debating, refuting. He could handle all of her negativity, but he worried for Mikey. When he argued with his mother though, she inevitably either cried or punished all of them with silence. Most days, he didn't bother. Ann was free to proselytize her gospel of injustice on a nightly basis. Mikey consumed it along with the casserole, and Gabe hated himself for allowing it to happen.

After the dishes were cleared, Mikey bounced up and down, begging to go in the lake. Brigid directed him to the bathroom to change into his bathing suit, and pointed sheepishly to her grandfather's room for Gabe. She was unwilling to let Mikey know that she and his brother were comfortable seeing each other naked.

Towels in hand, they walked toward the dock. Gabe suddenly stopped them in the middle of the slate path. "Brigid, I just thought of this. Are we sure the water is safe? I read that the DNR thinks the bacteria may be spreading in the inland lakes."

"How?" Brigid asked, furrowing her brow.

"Well, something about the inland lakes being over-fished. And the minerals being imbalanced, and people removing soil and big stones as they build those new houses."

Brigid thought guiltily of the rocks she had brought from the Big Lake. She had rinsed them, but Graham's tossing them into the water seemed to horrify David and Emma. For a moment, she thought of explaining it to Gabe. But how could she possibly describe what the Stone Society was, what a Diviner was? She wasn't even sure what, if anything, she was doing.

She decided it was all too complicated to deal with and besides, Mikey so badly wanted to swim.

Brigid tossed her hand breezily and said, "It's fine."

CHAPTER 30

Lynn had been calling the nursing home each day. She knew Brigid had been visiting, almost on a daily basis. Annoyance at her daughter for spending her time in a place like that conflicted with the pride that threatened to open her heart. Brigid wouldn't answer Lynn's phone calls these days, only texting back polite answers to Lynn's litany of questions. The ability to communicate with well-bred detachment was a point of pride for Lynn; but it tasted sour when others applied it.

Lynn had been urging Brigid to act more independently for decades. She hoped her only child would find a profitable, admirable job in a big city; and then go explore her life. If she had, Lynn believed she could cut the fear out of her heart once and for all. She and Kelsey had worked and strove to give their wounded daughter every chance to succeed in life. Instead, she had settled for an uninspired career and living in a drab apartment on the outskirts of town. Far enough away to rob Lynn of the comfort of her daughter living in Domhnall Hills, but close enough to be a constant reminder of her daughter's mediocrity. Brigid could never manage to rise to her potential, nor did she have the courage to cut completely loose from the apron strings.

Now her daughter was staying out in the countryside and refusing to communicate with Lynn. She was dividing her time between a nursing home, those charlatans that had called themselves her mother's friends, and a goddamn Sherland. It was infuriating. The life her daughter was leading was not what Lynn had planned for her.

Kelsey would have to be dispatched. He'd offered to accompany Lynn to visit Morgan, but she refused. The doctors were indeterminate as to whether Morgan knew what was happening around him, so she didn't much see the point in taking the time. They had, however, made it quite clear that any stress could worsen his condition. It seemed to Lynn that her absence from his bedside was the best action she could take to help maintain his health. Perhaps Kelsey could visit Morgan by himself and thereby run into Brigid. It was an excellent idea. If she asked, Lynn knew her husband would stay there for hours, especially for the chance to visit with their daughter. He wasn't much of a "phone man," as he liked to say, so Lynn had been unable to enlist him to track their daughter. If Kelsey texted while he was with Brigid, she'd be sure to discover her mother's fingers in the pie and take off.

After dinner that evening, she posed the plan to him. Kelsey had rolled his eyes and admonished her to simply call their daughter. He offered to call, even to drive out to Cairn Cottage. But something in Lynn made her want her daughter and her husband to meet at the nursing home. Perhaps she just wanted to know her daughter was nearby. As she knew he would, Kelsey acquiesced. The next morning, with a novel and a stack of newspapers, Kelsey set off for the nursing home.

Brigid breezed in the lobby of the nursing home right after lunch and made the familiar path to her grandfather's room. When she saw her father sitting on the settee, her face brightened into an expansive grin. Kelsey rose to embrace her and then pulled her back for a good look.

"Wow, young lady! You are tan. And you look so...relaxed." In truth, Kelsey was taken aback by her easy confidence. His daughter strode into the room, shoulders calm, head held high. None of the usual lines of tension marred her pretty forehead. Bracelets on her left hand tinkled as she reached for the metal railing of her grandfather's hospital bed. As she leaned down to plant a kiss on his wrinkled brow, Kelsey saw the old man's eyes sparkle with happiness.

"Dad, what are you doing here?" she asked.

"Visiting!" he answered with false brightness. Brigid looked at him in gentle accusation.

"Mmm hmm," she said. "And is my mother here?"

"She had to work, unfortunately." Brigid sighed, but he continued, "Well, kiddo, I sure am glad to see you." Kelsey looked closely at his pretty daughter. Never did she allow herself to sit so close. Usually, Brigid was like a rare bird, perching on the edge of whatever was furthest from the people in the room. Like prey ready for flight. "What have you been up to? I hear you're dating a farmer." Kelsey clapped his hands with enthusiasm. "Way to go! Are you mucking hay? Driving the tractor?"

Her father's tone set Brigid at ease and she laughed, the sound brightening the room. "I don't think you muck hay, Dad. You bale it. And no, Gabe does not let me drive the tractor."

"Well, that's probably a good thing, considering the way you drive a car. Please tell me you're actually staying between the yellow lines these days when you drive on the curvy roads up here?"

"The lines are really more of a suggestion, Dad." Brigid grinned. "No one really slows down to thirty-five miles per hour to make the hairpin turns. If there's no one else on the road, you just drive whereever you want."

Kelsey guffawed and put his bearlike arm around Brigid's shoulders. Feeling her muscles at ease and seeing the soft lines in her face, he felt that she was sufficiently trusting enough to get to the meat of his investigation.

"Well, you be careful," he said. "So tell me about this man of yours. Gabe, you said?"

"Oh God, did Mom put you up to this?" Brigid pulled immediately away. "She hates him. And without cause. She has some problem with his family, or that they're farmers or something."

"I'm not interested in what your mother thinks." Brigid cut him off with an incredulous look. "Alright," Kelsey said. "I have to be a tiny bit interested in what your mother thinks. For my own survival." Brigid broke into an involuntary smile. Kelsey felt relief wash over him. Her defenses were down once again. "But I want to know what you think. Tell me about this guy, this hard-working man who has earned my daughter's heart."

Brigid sank back into the settee. "Well, he is hard-working, let's start there. He runs his family's farm. It's a cherry orchard, actually. Much of the land is untended now; they just don't have the workers to keep up with the demand." Brigid searched her father's face as she revealed this small truth. Kelsey kept his expression pleasantly neutral. "They also have a barn with a few animals, his younger brother Mikey takes care of them."

"Sounds good," Kelsey said.

Brigid continued. "He went to college, you know. He graduated at the top of his class and has a degree in agriculture."

"Very good." Kelsey nodded approvingly. "Your mother said you met him when he was delivering a sailboat?"

Brigid grinned. "On the weekends he works at Sunset Marina. My friend Chris knows him. Chris, you know, the guy who teaches at my school? He delivered a new sailboat to Emma and Graham Webster."

"Emma and Graham!" Kelsey broke in enthusiastically. "I haven't seen them in so long! How are they — do you know? Have you seen them at all since you've been at Cairn Cottage?"

Brigid hedged. It was obvious that Kelsey was sent as an emissary by her mother. She was certainly not going to confide a word about the Stone Society or her role as Diviner. If her mother caught wind of that, she might burn Cairn Cottage down over their heads.

"I've seen them a bit," Brigid said. "They're doing well. They've invited me over for drinks and dinner a few times."

"Oh, that's nice of them," Kelsey said. "They knew you when you were a baby — just doted on you. I'm glad to hear they're doing well. Tell them hello from me, will you?" Brigid nodded.

Kelsey sighed and a shadow passed over his face that puzzled Brigid. He quickly recovered. "Let's get back to the boyfriend," he said brightly. "He runs the family farm, you said? What about his father?"

Here we go, thought Brigid. "His father left the family when Gabe was younger." She saw the mask of neutrality descend upon her father's face again.

"Hmm," said Kelsey.

"This happens in families all across the socio-economic scale," said Brigid coldly. "Parents leave, or disengage. Gabe took on the responsibility as head of the household."

Kelsey chose his next words very carefully. "Gabe sounds like an upstanding man. Runs a cherry orchard, works at a marina, takes care of his mother and siblings."

"One sibling," Brigid corrected. "Mikey."

"Takes care of his family," Kelsey said. "He sounds like a man with a lot of responsibilities. Where does that leave time for you?"

"He makes plenty of time for me," said Brigid firmly.

Father and daughter stared at each other for a moment. The air-conditioner and oxygen tank hummed a low, discordant duet into the silence.

Finally, Brigid said, "Would you like to meet him?"

Kelsey heard the hope behind the challenge. He smiled at his daughter. Maybe this man was a good influence in Brigid's life. She certainly looked more content, more joyful than he had seen her look in years. This grudge Lynn was fussing about, he felt sure it was nothing. "I'd love to," he said. "Maybe we can grab lunch, or dinner next week. The three of us."

Brigid jumped up and impulsively hugged her father. His heart swelled with warmth.

"How should we schedule this? Shall I text you?" Brigid asked playfully. Kelsey gave a mock exaggerated sigh.

"I suppose," he said. Checking his watch, he realized that three hours had passed since he arrived that morning. Surely he had done his duty, he thought. He began gathering his papers, pouring the vestiges of his cold coffee into the sink. Turning, he saw Brigid settling comfortably into the chair beside the bed. It occurred to him that she had brought no distractions, no ways to pass the time. No books of poetry, magazines, nothing. Ah well, he thought, perhaps she would fiddle on her phone.

"How long do you stay usually?" Kelsey asked her.

"A few hours," said Brigid pleasantly. Kelsey's face scrunched up. "What do you do?"

"Oh, I don't know. I talk to him. Open the curtains, wheel the bed into the sunlight. Mostly I just sit and keep him company. The time passes pretty quickly." Kelsey shook his head and walked over to plant a kiss on the top of his daughter's auburn curls. Almost as an afterthought, he reached beyond the metal barrier and patted Morgan's hand.

"Well, I'd better be off. Love you, kiddo."

"I love you too, Dad."

Kelsey stood up and got ready stride out the door and the newspaper that he had left on the table caught his eye. "Oh," he said, wheeling back around. "I almost forgot! Brigid, this is crucial; look at this." He handed her the paper. It was the *Domhnall Hill Express*. The headline seemed to scream at them.

Bacteria Found in Inland Lakes: Bear, Owrann, and Little Keoel Lakes Affected

"You should not swim in the lake right now," said Kelsey gravely. "I'm sorry honey, but I really don't think it's safe."

CHAPTER 31

Mikey rolled over on the couch; his face contorted in pain. Gabe brought a cold washcloth, folded it and placed it on his brother's head. The fever was high, soaring to one hundred and four degrees. He hoped that between the Advil Mikey had swallowed and the cool washcloth, it would begin to go down.

Ann sat at the kitchen table, forehead in her hand, studying the printout from the doctor's office.

"This is going to cost a fortune," she said, running a hand through her hair. "I wish you had taken him to the emergency room, like I asked. They see people who have bad insurance for free."

"They see people with no insurance for free," corrected Gabe, gritting his teeth. "We have insurance. It's shitty, but it's insurance."

"Language, Gabe!"

Gabe gave a shuddering sigh. The shrill tone of his mother's panic provoked his desire to yell. Yelling would stop the nagging; it's what his father used to do. But he could be better than that. He had to be. The problem was, acquiescing created so much buried frustration that he wanted to punch a hole in the wall.

Remembering Brigid's wish, he urged himself to be kinder to his mother. He moved over to the table and looked at the paper, placing a hand on her shoulder. She immediately reached back and grasped his hand in her own, turning her chestnut eyes up to her eldest son. He saw the gratitude in them and softened.

"It's okay, Mom," he said. "I'll take care of it." He gently

176

released her hand and sat down next to her, sliding the papers over so he could see. Unconsciously mirroring his mother's gesture, he put his forehead in his palm and read through the documents.

"The doctor says he has a bacterial infection. It says it's consistent with what they've been seeing from people who have been swimming in Big Omann Lake." Gabe looked up at his mother. "Did the doctor say anything to you about this?"

Ann had tears in her eyes. "I don't know, Gabey. I was just so worried. He said something about the bacteria in Big Omann Lake and how it was making people sick, but I told Mikey not to swim in Big Omann Lake! I don't know how he could've gotten this." Ann began to cry in earnest. Gabe's heart sank at the sight of his mother's tears. The feeling of helplessness was overwhelming. He felt like shit. Moreover, he knew exactly how Mikey had contracted this dangerous illness. The paper delivered to the lounge of Sunset Marina that morning had the news plastered across the front page:

Bacteria Found: Little Owrann Lake.

Mikey had swallowed half the lake on Saturday. After lunch, they had spent hours playing in the water, watching Mikey jump off the raft, play on the giant inflatable giraffe that Brigid had unearthed from the dusty garage. He remembered the feeling of admiration that rose in his chest when she matter-of-factly told him she had used an old air compressor to fill the toy up with air. Brigid had taken his brother sailing, allowing him to man the tiller. They even pushed the old, rusty canoe out from the shore and paddled down the lake. When Mikey stood up and pretended to surf, the canoe flipped and they all fell overboard. Laughing, Gabe had held the boat steady while the two of them climbed in. He pulled the canoe back, wading in the lake. After the canoe adventure, Brigid had insisted that they all soap off with the bar of harsh Irish Spring that she kept in a plastic basket underneath the table on the dock. He remembered glancing over at Mikey's legs, scraped and bruised like any active, outdoor-loving nine-year-olds might be. After they had finished scrubbing their legs and hosing down with a garden hose, she handed out towels and taught them how to rub their limbs hard with a towel to rid themselves of any trace of the minor bacteria that caused swimmers' curse.

It seemed, though, that there was a much stronger bacteria that no bar of soap could scrub away.

Gabe looked over at Mikey, agony in his eyes. Ann knew immediately that there was something her son wasn't saying. She pulled back, wiping her tears brusquely.

"Gabe." She peeked low, trying to catch his gaze from his bowed head. He knew she needed to know, but found he couldn't bring himself to look his mother in the eyes. Rising from his chair, he went to grab his duffel bag that he brought to the marina every day. It contained a change of clothes, a towel, and his phone charger. Today, he had slipped the *Bear Paw Press* into the outside pocket, intending to show it to Brigid. He pulled the paper out and walked back to the table. His mother's eyes were wide with anxiety. Without saying a word, he let the paper fall open to the headline and placed it in front of her.

Ann let out a moan.

"Oh Gabe," she said. "I told you. I told you not to trust that woman."

"Brigid didn't know anything about this, Mom. This paper came out today; we were there on Saturday."

"Yes, but she should have known. It's her property, her lake."

"That doesn't even make any sense, Mom. How could she have known before the DNR discovered it? And anyway, it's not her property; she's staying at her grandfather's lake house."

Ann sniffed knowingly.

"What?" asked Gabe.

"Her grandfather's lake house. Listen to you. It must be nice to have several homes at your disposal." Gabe shook his head at

Ann's twisted path of thoughts.

"Mom, her grandpa has one home. Her parents live at their home in Domhnall Hills. Before this summer, Brigid lived in a little apartment behind the grocery store in town."

"Domhnall Hills," Ann broke in. "Domhnall Hills where all of those new subdivisions are destroying the land!" Ann swept her arm in the air, wrapping every newly built home in the city into her accusation. "They are destroying the land and the runoff from all the construction is poisoning the lakes."

Gabe sighed. "That hasn't been proven."

"Gabe, honey, what proof do you need? These people, they do what they want. Exactly what they want without regard to how it affects others. They have the money, so they assume they have the power. They build perfect lives and then barricade themselves in that life so they don't have to see the reality of everyone else's hardship. It's not just Domhnall Hills, either. It's all of these big homes going up around our inland lakes on the Peninsula. Haven't you noticed that the big houses that people build — you know, the ones that look like they were plucked from the suburbs?" She waited for Gabe to nod. He did. His mother had a point. Most of the fancy new boats he delivered to were to places like these. Properties where the new owners had demolished the modest, charming cabin, built a brick-encased, multi-peaked showcase home and stripped the trees. The cutting down of the lakefront trees was ostensibly to create a view of the water from the home. Gabe thought that the trees were sacrificed so that everyone on the lake could jealously admire the shiny new McMansion.

Seeing bitterness cross her son's face, Ann continued eagerly. "These big new homes, don't you notice so many of them suddenly have murky lake bottoms with reeds and cattails growing around the docks?" Gabe looked away. "They do, don't they?" Ann crowed. "It's from the construction. Materials and waste seep into the lake. Now, I may not have a fancy college education, but I do understand that." Gabe suppressed the urge to roll his eyes. "And then what do you think the homeowners do?" Ann continued. "They pour more chemicals in the lake to kill the reeds and the wildlife and to restore their precious clear waters and sandy bottoms."

"You're right," Gabe admitted. "That happens a lot."

"Mmm hmm." Ann sat back, crossing her arms in satisfaction. She looked at her son. This boy of hers was so like his father in the best ways. Strong, handsome, bull-headed. However, she could see the ravages of temper and passion that roiled under the surface. Ann thanked Whoever was listening up there that so far, Gabe could control it. His shouting was much more subdued than her husband's had been, and thus-far could always be stopped with her tears. And he had never raised a hand to anyone. Unlike his father. Her right wrist still gave her pain from the day her husband had snapped it. After he had brought her home from the emergency room, he had tucked her gently into bed, apology and agony on his face. When she awoke, he was gone.

Clenching her jaw to push away the heartbreak, she willed herself to forget the last ten years. The best work she could do now would be to save Gabe from a life of frustration. This woman may be infatuated with him, and what woman wouldn't be? He was handsome and smart, and she had watched his way with women. Her eldest son knew exactly what he was doing. But this girl was wrong for him. Brigid would wake up to reality sooner or later, and it would break Gabe's heart. Ann wasn't fooled by quaint cottages on the lake. She knew that once Brigid's family understood that her son was a farmer on the Peninsula, supporting an uneducated mother and a younger brother, they'd step in to whisk her away. Or worse, she'd defy them, marry Gabe, and realize years in that the hard life was not one she could contend with. In either case, her son would be destroyed. And Gabe could choose from so many girls out here who understood what life was really like. Women who understood what sacrifice was about, who accepted and embraced it as part of life.

Ann had seen the men in her life destroyed by yearning.

Wreaked by the idea of upward mobility, of any way to make life easier for them and theirs. No, it was better to accept life as it was and move forward. Her job, as a mother, was to see what her son couldn't see. She hadn't been able to give him much, but she could at least spare him this heartbreak.

"Gabe." Her eldest son turned to her. "I'm not going to say anything else against Brigid. I know you like her. But as an adult, as the caretaker of the property, she has a responsibility to make sure that it is safe for others who visit. It's not only courtesy, but a legal issue."

"What, so you're going to sue her because Mikey got sick?" Gabe spat.

Ann suppressed a smile. "No. I'm just saying that she's a grown up. And a college graduate. If she was ignorant about this, it's something to think about. If she just disregarded the danger, thinking that because of her education and her up-bringing, she knew better, you need to think about that even harder. Mother Nature is bigger and stronger than us. No amount of money or education can change that."

Gabe grasped the papers from the doctor in his fist and stood up. "I'll go pick up Mikey's prescription," he said. "Keep giving him something to drink and please take his tempera-ture. The Advil should have brought it down a bit by now."

"Gabe, I'm his mother," Ann said. "Yours too. Even if you're a big man now, even if I don't have a good education and my pretty hair and pretty face has faded away. I'm the mother. I know how to take care of my kids."

CHAPTER 32

The dawn cast her gentle rays over the hillsides. The sun found Graham wading up to his knees in Little Owrawn Lake, back bent, peering into the water. He plucked the stones out one by one, tucking them into the pockets of his bathing trunks. When the final stone was brought up from the sandy bottom, he shook the water off of his hands and wrapped his arms around his chest, shielding his body from the chilly north wind. After toweling off his legs and hands, he wrapped up the stones with it and made for the house. It was time for a hot, soapy shower. He glanced to the heavens, saying a little prayer that his wife was still asleep.

It had been a long time since the people of the Peninsula wanted to buy cairns. That business with Ruby had pretty much obliterated the Society's ability to sell these blessed stones. With the loss of the cairn revenue came the loss of consultation fees, prayers, placement fees. Even the sale of jewelry had slowed considerably. So many shops made cheap imitations of his wife's beautiful artwork, selling Petoskey and granite rings that wriggled in their settings and left green film on the fingers of unwitting buyers.

The profits had never been enough to make a living, but it kept them in supplies and left a nice little pot of cash left for everyone. A good "side hustle," in the words of his grandson. But it was more than that to Graham. Working together with his friends, watching his wife craft her beautiful pieces, holding the stones after they had been blessed — it meant something. It made him feel like he was contributing something more to the world, filling a hole in the hearts of his neighbors.

It made Graham feel worthy. When he passed, people would remember him as someone who had given to the greater good. He would be remembered as something more than just another man who paid the mortgage for his family. When the Society stopped selling the cairns, Graham became invisible.

Ruby's death had crushed the women. And when Nieve succumbed to cancer so early in life, David crumbled as well. His friends became content with memories of the Stone Society and their camaraderie. They nursed carefully buried pride in their past accomplishments and tried to forget the haunting consequences of their actions. Privately, they all still collected stones, held them, prayed over them. But the true magic, the power, was sacrificed to their guilt.

Now that Brigid had unearthed the Book and proven her abilities as a Diviner, even if she didn't believe them herself, David and Emma were eager to reopen the Society. The three elders had argued interminably about the idea of selling anything again. David and Emma were dead set against it. They maintained that it was enough to practice together, to interpret the stones and send blessings out into the world. Emma even refused to sell her jewelry again, despite agreement between David and Graham that this could be done in the most secular, businesslike ways. Citing arthritis in her hands, Emma stalwartly shook her head.

Well, Graham would prove them all wrong. There was a stash of unsold jewelry deep in Emma's dresser drawer, truly beautiful pieces. And this first cairn Brigid had made, Graham was sure the blessings it carried were strong. Many people on the Peninsula were still struggling. They needed these stones, even if they didn't know it yet. Graham had spent his whole life as a businessman; he knew how to sell, how to market. And he knew his target. This was a good risk, he thought. After a nice, hot shower, he would package the cairn and take the box of jewelry. There was a certain farm that was in trouble, one he was sure could use the blessings of the Stone Society.

CHAPTER 33

The white screen door was grimy with age. Graham raised his fist to knock gently, pulling down his cable knit sweater with his other hand. It was a chilly morning for July, a sure harbinger for a summer storm. After several moments, a young boy opened the door, his face flushed and his hair damp with sweat. Graham took a step back as memory pounded his senses. The boy's dark locks and high cheekbones were like an apparition. A miniature Theodore Sherland this lad was. A little Teddy. Graham struggled to maintain his sensibility.

"Well hello, young lad!" Graham said, a little louder than he meant. "Is your mother at home?"

"I'm sick," announced the boy. "My mom is doing my chores. I'm supposed to feed the chickens but I'm not supposed to go outside." Graham and the young boy stared at each other. "I don't think I'm supposed to let you in."

"I understand that," said Graham in a friendly tone. "Stranger danger. My grandsons have learned that too. Do you mind if I wait on the porch until your mother is finished with her chores?" The boy shook his head. Graham wasn't sure whether that was an invitation to sit or a warning to leave. He decided to take charge.

"Well, young man, if you're sick you'd better go back inside. I'll sit on this bench and wait for Mother. Does that sound ok?" At this, the boy nodded. Graham was relieved. "May I ask your name?" Graham asked.

"Mikey," said the boy.

"Mikey," Graham echoed. "Well now Mikey, my name's

Graham. You just go back inside and lie down. And lock the door behind you, just to be safe. If Mother wants to let me in, I'll see you soon. If not, I hope you feel better."

Mikey wrinkled his nose at the false buoyancy that swam underneath the old man's friendly tone. Without taking his eyes off the visitor, Mikey stepped backwards into the house. Graham heard the bolt slide into the latch.

Graham placed the velvet boxes on the bench and stepped off the porch to survey the farm. The barn's faded crimson paint could not conceal its sturdy frame. It had been repaired by patient hands since the last time he had stood on this land. The few horses roamed contently in the pasture and the chickens pecked the ground in their pen below the hill. He knew the dairy cows had been sold long ago for rock-bottom prices to avoid the bank coming and driving them away. The few rows of trees left in the orchard were swaying gently in the wind. Neat boxes of harvested cherries were stacked on the side of the barn opposite the pasture. Clearly, the Sherland farm was under careful care. They may not need the cairns and prayers that Graham carried with him. His shoulders began to slump.

Turning again to the house, the grime on the door caught his eye. He brightened. The house cried out for help. Someone here was unable to keep up with everything. After all, Graham thought, there had been a time when the Sherland farm flourished; thirty acres of cherry trees bursting into bloom each spring, yielding prosperous crops that built the barn and the second wing of the white farmhouse. He remembered the days when Shannon and Morgan were here every week, stacking cairns freshly collected from the lake, wandering under the canopy of trees with prayers on their lips. In those days, the Sherlands would even pay for the Society to bring buckets of fresh lake water to sprinkle on the ground beneath the trees. Melanie Sherland, the denizen of the farm, had worn bracelets and necklaces purchased from the Society, some of the first ever made by Emma. Morgan remembered how they shone on Melanie Sherland's wrist as she happily handed over the payment for all of the Society's blessings. The Sherlands were not tight with their bounty either, always ready with an open purse to help the community. Of course, that all changed when old man Sherland was felled by a heart attack out in the fields. His son Teddy took over and promptly set about to spending all the money his father had earned, buying new cars and shiny farm equipment. By the time Teddy met and ruined their Ruby, the farm was run into the ground.

Graham shook his head. So much greed turned into so much waste. Bile rose in his throat. This farm could be turned around. Row by row, tree by tree even, they would bring it back. The Sherlands could partner with the Society once again, and together they would restore the land to its rightful glory. The name of Graham Webster would be remembered, not as another old man who passed a life paying his bills on time, but as the person responsible for restoring the most formidable farm in the area. Graham Webster would reopen the Society, and begin the integral work of making peace with the Land once more.

The air held the spice of wild grasses that grew among the gardens. Taking a deep breath, Graham began to feel better. In the distance, he spotted a head of dark hair rising up the hill. As the person moved closer, Graham could see it was a woman. Her face was tired and her body worn. In her arms, she carried a basket and an empty plastic bucket. Graham cleared his throat and pulled assertively on his lapels. Plastering a smile, he waited for the woman's approach.

Ann looked down as she climbed the hill. Grateful that their brace of hens had yielded eggs, she was still exhausted from the work. Never well herself, she had risen early as she did every morning. Made the coffee, set out the bread and margarine. Waited at the table in her robe to see Gabe off. This morning she had fixed warm honey water for poor Mikey, taken his temperature and recorded his persistent fever as the doctor ordered. When she saw the number, one hundred and three, fear seized her body, making her vision blur. She took several huffing breaths, leaning on the counter with eyes shut, until she could force herself to move. She poured the medicine into the measuring cup and handed it to her younger son, but the tidal wave of anxiety was hard to fight through. Gabe had already put a cold compress on his brother's head before he left for Sunset Marina. Ann had shaken her head, avoided the mercurial pull to the arm chair, and gathered the pail of chicken feed from the hall. She would not disappoint both of her sons by failing to do the simple chores imposed upon them since they were little. Worse than the worry was the nagging feeling that Gabe was beginning to shut down around her. She was the mother who was supposed to fix and nurture everything. Clearly, Gabe was doing that. It was bad enough that the responsibility of the farm kept Gabe tied to her apron strings, the anxiety that seemed to paralyze her more and more these days made her unable to help in the most basic ways. Breathing shallowly, she remembered all the times Gabe had stepped in between his father... and Gabe had really been so young then... Shaking her head against the thought, she raised her face to the house.

Graham bounced down the steps toward her, hand extended before she could react.

"Good morning!" he said. "Please forgive the intrusion. My name is Graham and I'd like to talk to you about your farm, if I may." Ann squinted at him. She had seen this man before and a feeling of danger filled her belly. Before she could place him, his voice broke into the air between them.

"May I be so bold as to ask your name?" The flowery speech grated on her nerves. She rolled her eyes.

"I'm the owner of this farm. My name is Mrs. Ann Sherland. I'd like to know what you are doing on my property." The man called Graham grinned like a Cheshire cat and gazed at her up and down. Ann ignored his impropriety and looked him square in the eye. "I've answered your question. Now answer mine." Her tone was hard. "What are you doing here?"

Graham gestured grandly, welcoming Ann onto her own

porch. "If you have a moment, I'd love to sit and chat. Here, let me relieve you of your burden." Graham reached for the basket of eggs and Ann instinctively pulled her arm away. A few still-warm eggs bounced out of the pile and smashed onto the ground. "Well, that's breakfast," Ann said in disgust. For a brief moment, Graham looked terrified, like an actor who had forgotten his lines.

"I'm dreadfully sorry about the eggs. Excuse my impertinence, but you seem weary. Shall we sit?"

Now Ann looked her uninvited visitor up and down. He didn't seem to pose any physical danger. He was as old as her father, and although her body ached, she knew she was strong enough to knock him down with the back of her arm. I may as well sit with him, she thought. Grasping the rail, she hauled herself up the rickety steps and fell back on the bench with a thud. The basket of eggs she set down gently. She noted the boxes stacked neatly on the bench, and looked suspiciously up at Graham.

"Did you bring those?" she asked. She did appreciate the soft beauty of the caramel-colored velvet embroidered with rich ebony thread. Graham grinned and sat down, lifting the boxes into his lap. As he prepared to open them, Ann pointed. "Did you come here to sell me something?" she asked, guarding her curiosity with gruff defensiveness.

"I came to offer help," Graham said smoothly. "A partnership, if you will." He knew to offer the jewelry first to a woman like this. A hint of exquisite beauty would melt her resolve for the rest of the proposition. It wasn't the way they used to do it; after all, this Mrs. Sherland hadn't even been through the Ceremony. How was he to know what her spirit stone was? Graham told himself that this didn't matter. Once she agreed to purchase the whole package, they could arrange a Ceremony. For now, it was enough that she choose for herself. Graham lifted a wide, shallow box and placed it between them. Pulling up on the lid, he turned it toward her, his face a mask of benevolence.

Ann stared down at the collection of bracelets, unable to

mask the sheer joy she felt at their beauty. She recognized them as local lake stones, but they were set so uniquely, so carefully wrought.

"I feel that one of these beautiful pieces belongs to you," Graham said softly. "Would you choose one?" Ann did not want to smile at this man, but she couldn't help it. She'd never seen beach stones polished this perfectly. The deep blue stone with flecks of white reminded her of the night sky in winter. The Petoskey was huge and gorgeous. She appreciated it, but immediately dismissed it as too expensive. Giant Petoskeys were the stones that the rich people in Domhnall Hills draped across the necks of their linen shifts, making a show of connection with the land while they plowed over it. The pink and speckled stone looked almost like an opal she had seen once, polished to the point where it seemed to be glowing with an internal light. The ivory stone looked surprisingly plain at first, but when she bent to see it more closely, she could see every shade of golden shoreline making waves across its surface. The last bracelet held a slate black stone with a straight white streak falling diagonally through it. It was striking and unique — a stone Ann felt she had seen countless times before. Without thinking, she lifted it out of the case.

Graham let out a sigh of relief. He took Ann's free hand reverently, as if she was princess of the realm. Taking the bracelet she had selected, he slipped it onto her wrist.

"Beautiful," Graham whispered. Ann was mesmerized by the way the silver shone in the bright sunshine. And the stone felt cool and calming on her skin. Letting her arm stretch into the warming air, she caught sight of her chipped fingernails. Her smile collapsed as she yanked the bracelet off. Setting it on top of the box, she shook her head.

"Too expensive for me." Ann said.

"On the contrary," Graham said. "I've been looking around your beautiful farm. You can't afford not to have this." Ann looked at him with skepticism. Graham cleared his throat and waved his hand expansively over the horizon. "Your cherry orchard, Mrs. Sherland. It is stunning. So many acres. How many, if I may ask?"

"About fifty," Ann said haltingly. "Well, it used to be fifty. I mean, we own fifty acres. But now we can only farm five or six each year." Graham looked at her with sympathy. "My son, my older boy, Gabe. He does the farming. But it's only him and me these days, and as you can see, I can't do too much."

"It must be so difficult." Graham's caramel tone soothed.

"Well, it is! Thank you for saying that." Ann looked at her uninvited guest begrudgingly. "It really is. My Gabe, he's a good boy. He went to college and got his degree in Agriculture." A prideful smile lit up her face. "I was so proud of him. And he came home and brought the farm back. We were going to lose it, you know." Ann pursed her lips together with the memory. "The bank, they were going to take it. My husband..." Ann shook her head, rocking back and forth subtly, as if to gather strength for her next admission. "My husband... he ran off. Just left us when Gabe was young. Mikey, my younger son, was a baby. I tried to keep the farm up myself, but with two little boys... well, we weren't doing that great before he left. Down to only three farmable acres. Money just wasn't coming in, the economy was bad."

"I'm so sorry." Graham dropped his voice to a rich baritone. "I can tell you're a hard-working woman. A hard-working woman whom Life has handed a tricky hand. It's not fair."

Ann looked at him hard. "It certainly isn't. But I've got two good boys to take care of me. And my husband..." Tears sprang to her eyes and she hated herself for the weakness in them. "My husband can rot in Hell."

Graham nodded knowingly. Hoping his impatience didn't show, he forced himself to lift the box carefully. He had heard enough of her life story and it was time to get to the point.

"Mrs. Sherland, I've come to help you. This farm deserves to be restored to its former glory. You deserve it and frankly, the county needs it."

"Oh, Gabe doesn't approve of me taking out a line of credit.

We've talked about this a lot and agreed not to do it. I don't know what bank would send out a man with bracelets, but I can't."

"No, no Mrs. Sherland. This has nothing to do with that. I've come to offer a plan, a procedure if you will. A contract from the Land, with the Land."

Now it was Ann's turn to be impatient and she didn't feel the need to hide it. "I don't understand you." She glanced at her cheap, fake leather watch, the red filaments breaking apart. Whatever he had, however much she may want it, she couldn't have it. "Speak plainly and get to the point," she said sharply. "I have work to do."

Graham took a deep breath. It had been over thirty years since he had made this pitch. Everything was riding on what he said right now. "I belong to a Society. The Stone Society." The name resonated in the air. It felt so good to say those words aloud. When he said them, Graham knew he was part of something. Something hundreds of years old that blended science and spirituality. His great-great-grandparents had discovered a Truth before it was ever published in papers and preached from pulpits. Their knowledge had almost been obliterated at the hands of a fool. But Graham was the only one brave enough to carry it through. If he succeeded now, he would be remembered. And what better place to succeed than with the Sherland Farm?

"The Stone Society believes we need to harness the powers of the whole landscape," Graham intoned. "We believe that the farmlands and the waters are symbiotic. They work together. The stones that lie on the lake beds and make the beaches of sand beneath our feet are the very same stones that enrich the soil with minerals. When the land was farmed so many years ago, the Stone Society discovered that the rocks and minerals in the soil were disturbed. Removed even further with the advent of modern farming and chemicals. Crops suffered as a result. We have a formula, a scientific formula to bring the soil back to its original genetic makeup. If we do this, the crops will flourish."

Graham glanced at his subject. The science was always the easy sell. And through the science, it was easy to move into the prescription of prayers and rituals that followed. Mrs. Sherland leaned forward, eyes wide. She was buying this. He would continue.

"There is another part to this formula. We believe that more power lies in the stones than just their chemical compounds. In the Stone Society, we know that the rocks in the waters have spiritual powers." Immediately Ann's expression changed, she pulled away as if she was in danger. And just as quickly, Graham continued. "This too, is proven by science. You know uranium radiates tremendous energy and power; quartz crystals can collect and disperse energy."

"There's no uranium in the lakes," Ann protested, eyebrows furrowed. "And no quartz crystals."

Graham chuckled. "Of course there is no uranium. But there is quartz. The white band in the bracelet you chose is actually quartz. And we believe that contains a certain energy. One energy contained in quartz is cleansing. Heart cleansing. Soul cleansing. Does that speak to you?"

Ann just stared at him.

"I can tell that it does. That means you feel it too. You can feel the deeper spiritual powers at work in this land." He waited for her assent. There was only silence.

"I know you are from this land, Ann Sherland. I know the history of your family. You are a true custodian." Graham opened the box to reveal a carefully stacked cairn. "This is a blessing cairn. A cairn is a stack of rocks. This one has been carefully chosen and blessed. Just for you." Ann's tight jaw twitched.

"A cairn is a spiritual symbol," Graham continued in a patronizing tone. "Each of these stones was lifted from Big Omann Lake by the hands of one of our spiritual women. We call her our Diviner. She chose the stones and used her intuition to interpret the pictures and signs that lie within them.

These interpretations are written down; I have them here." Graham pulled out a small stack of paper. Ann glanced at it. "After the stones are interpreted for you, they are blessed in the Dedication Ceremony. Finally, they are stacked and presented to you."

In a flat voice, Ann asked. "How much?"

Graham breathed a sigh of relief. He'd passed the first two hurdles. Now all that remained was to convince the woman that the investment was worth it. "Well, we offer a sliding scale. At the Stone Society, we believe that you receive what you give to the Land. And we certainly don't believe in taking food out of anyone's mouth. Traditionally, houses of worship ask for a tithe. Ten percent of the household income. We realize that this may be too dear. And, we also realize that many of our land custodians may belong and contribute to a house of worship. We therefore ask for only seven percent of your declared household income."

Ann's face was expressionless. "And for my seven percent, what would you give?" Graham smiled. Now it was his turn to sell.

"Well, first, we would give you a bracelet, one we hope you might wear every day to declare your membership into the Society. And, oh, of course you would be an official member. We would give you a Ceremony." Graham was stumbling. He glanced at the cairn sitting between them. The bundle of lies he had told in the last few minutes caught in his throat. These stones had been picked by Brigid, that was true. But not for this particular purpose. Nor had she been meditating on this particular land when she made her interpretations. And the blessing had not been... official. No matter, he told himself. There would be time to amend all of that.

"The cairn would be yours, and we would have the members of our Society come out and walk your land. Our Diviner would walk along every acre you wish to plant, and make a blessing cairn for each acre. We would write up a program of soil enhancement made from same minerals as the stones she has chosen. You could, for best results, add these mineral compounds to your soil. Further, our Society would bring water from Big Omann Lake on a weekly basis to bless each tree. And anything else you needed, personal blessings, problems to be solved, holistic cures for illnesses, you could consult with the Society and that would be made available to you." Ann stared into the distance.

"So for seven percent of my money, you would give me rocks and prayers?"

Graham tensed, grasping for any thought that might turn this conversation back in his favor. She had spoken proudly of her son. He imagined this Gabe was about Brigid's age. Maybe their reluctant Diviner could be of some use after all. "You know Mrs. Sherland, not all of our Society members are as elderly as me. Our Diviner is young. She is perhaps the same age as your son Gabe." Ann turned to him at the mention of her son's name. "Her connection with the earth is very powerful. Of course, she's still learning how to truly use her intuition, her creativity. She's still discovering her power. But I think she will be a true asset to us. To everyone. Even to you." Ann still had not responded. Graham floundered. He could not fail here. He would not lose this chance. "Perhaps you would like to meet her. Her name is Brigid."

Ann cocked her head at him. "What did you say?"

"You could meet her. I'm sure she'd be willing."

"No," said Ann. "What is her name?"

"Brigid," Graham said brightly. "Lovely name, isn't it? Brigid Firth. She's from Domhnall Hills but she's staying at her grandfather's cabin on Little Owrawn Lake."

"And did Brigid know you were coming here today?" Graham didn't hesitate. "Yes, yes of course she did." Another lie he was going to have to smooth over, but once they began their work, he was sure he could wheedle approval out of Brigid. "She... in fact, she recommended it."

"I'm going to stop you right here." Ann's voice was heavy with anger. "I don't have the money to buy snake oil. And standing on this porch, telling you I don't have the money, is not making my life any easier."

Graham stammered. "Snake oil? It's not..."

Ann held up her hand. "One of your people came to this farm years ago. I wasn't here then, but I know the stories. My husband's grandfather bought your bullshit. His wife convinced him. She got involved with the women, asked them for some prayer or spell or something. Convinced Theodore to buy the rocks, buy the water. Used all of their savings. Crops had been bad, too cold in the winter, too many spring frosts that killed the buds before they could blossom into fruit. Theodore had held that savings so that his sons could go to college. Instead, you people convinced him to give the money for your 'program' and then it was the year the gypsy moths came. Decimated the trees. They had almost zero crop yield. And they went broke. The boys couldn't go to college. Almost had to sell the farm, but out of the unbelievable hard work by Theodore, they held onto it. Leased the land for several years, sold off equipment. Two years later, Theodore had a heart attack. Died. And then his son Teddy Jr. took up with your friend Ruby. I think we all know what happened there."

Graham's face was ashen. He had hoped that the story had died out.

"Ann..."

"Mrs. Sherland." Her voice had turned regal.

"I apologize. Mrs. Sherland. Of course, that was tragic. A horrible situation. But surely you agree, we had nothing to do with gypsy moths. And I think you would like our Brigid."

"I know your Brigid," Ann broke in. She fairly spat the name. "She's dating my son. My Gabe."

Graham closed his eyes. Of course. Emma had mentioned this a week ago. She had even said his name. Graham had just rolled his eyes, annoyed that their young Diviner had a distraction. Emma had even gone over to Cairn Cottage, saying she had to prepare it for Brigid and her new beau.

"I see now," Ann said, chin in the air. "I understand. Your

girl from Domhnall Hills thought she would hook herself a dumb farmer for your Society. And you all, you college-educated elitists, would fleece my family for everything we've worked to bring back since you fleeced us years ago."

"No, no that's not it at all! I — I'm not even sure Brigid knew I was coming here today." Graham stood shakily, knocking over the cairn.

"That is it," said Ann, standing too. "You said yourself that it was her idea. On top of all of this, she's gotten my younger son, my Mikey, sick. She invited my boys to lunch at Little Owrawn Lake and let them swim, even though she knew it was polluted with bacteria. Now Mikey is sick." Crimson rose through her neck as a realization flooded over her. "And now here you are, selling me hokey crap for illnesses!" Her voice rose to a shriek.

"Mom?" Mikey poked his head out of the door, fear at the commotion written on his young face.

Ann turned to him, felt his head. It was burning up. She kissed his hair, the boyish scent of him filling her nostrils. "Go inside, sweetheart. I'll be right there."

"You were yelling," Mikey said. "Do you need help?" Ann took a shuddering breath. What was wrong with her, what was wrong with the world that her thin, feverish child felt the need to protect her?

"Go in and lie down," she said firmly. Mikey backed in and shut the door behind him. Ann turned to Graham.

"Get off my porch and get off my land."

CHAPTER 34

The hike up to Omann Point was gorgeous. The trees made a canopy overhead and rustled as Gabe and Brigid walked. His hands were in his pockets and his brow was furrowed. He didn't reach for her. He had canceled their lunch, saying he needed to take extra hours at the marina. She had convinced him to take a walk with her before he returned back home.

Mikey's illness tore at her conscience. She was horrified that it had happened at Little Owrawn Lake, but there was a small part of her that felt the blame shouldn't be on her shoulders. She had no way of knowing that the bacteria had spread into their lake. It hadn't even come out in the papers. And the cuts that Mikey got climbing all over everything, running around without really any permission, had she not bandaged them up? How was she to know he could get infected so quickly? She'd apologized to Gabe countless times, even calling his mother. Mrs. Sherland had been icy on the phone. Strong antibiotics had made loud noises painful, made his stomach upset. But the fever had finally gone down. Gabe told her that Ann was obsessed with feeding Mikey enough that his spine wasn't visible. Her proposed diet of corn chips and ice cream wasn't going to do much for his health, Brigid was sure. When she was ill, her mother always made homemade chicken-noodle soup, boiling the carcass of the bird to make a broth. Orange juice and fresh bread from the bakery, loaded with cinnamon and sugar. Lynn would set the food down on the coffee table firmly, her brusqueness disguising the worry she always felt when her family was ill. But there was no hiding her tenderness. You could taste it.

Brigid didn't know quite how to make her mother's soup, and she didn't feel like she could call and ask. Instead, she had brought over ointment for the rash and a basket of fresh fruit. Gabe's mother had lifted it and set it aside as if it was a basket of dead mice. Brigid shook her head at the memory.

The past week, she hadn't seen much of Gabe. It was easy to understand that he had to help out at home, taking extra shifts to pay the doctor's bills. It boggled her mind that they didn't have decent health insurance. Why wouldn't his mother take care of that? Her mother had always carried the insurance for the family, a fact that Kelsey joked about to no end.

Brigid missed Gabe in her bed, missed his arms around her. She had spent her time wandering the beaches, picking up stones and writing down her thoughts. July was galloping across the calendar; she would have to think about school before she knew it. The apartment complex had been calling her to see if she wanted to renew her lease. She didn't really have permission to live at Cairn Cottage past the summer. The only person who could logically grant permission was her mother, and that would never happen. She wasn't even speaking to Lynn. Maybe it was necessary to bridge the divide, if only to gain permission to stay. Her own brow furrowed at the thought.

"What?" Gabe's voice broke the silence.

"Nothing," she said.

Gabe gazed at her. "That look is not nothing," he said.

"I was just thinking about the future." Brigid saw his shoulders tense. "No, not like that. I just meant, where I would live. After the summer."

The path twisted right and a field of wild sweet peas came into view. They only bloomed in the third week of July and were considered endangered. So many people picked and transplanted them that now they only existed in these protected areas.

Brigid smiled at Gabe. "Should we walk over there? I can

smell them from here. The petals are so soft."

"The park service says to stay on the pathway." She started at his tone. "It was on the sign at the trailhead. Didn't you see it?" Quelled, Brigid fell silent and walked on, a few paces ahead of Gabe. She let out an audible sigh. He rolled his eyes at this passive-aggressive gesture. God, he had hoped she wouldn't be a carbon copy of other women he had known. He had told his mother how Brigid was different, how she was innocent, and smart. Ann had countered with her own words. Privileged. Naive. Advantaged.

Gabe didn't quite understand what Ann had told him. Surely Brigid couldn't be involved in some religious scam. He thought back to walking the beach with her, collecting the stones, how serious she had been. But everyone combed the beaches for stones around here, especially tourists. His mother had always been scornful of this practice. Then again, she was scornful of anything tourists did that smacked of robbing the land.

Gabe took a few long strides to catch up with Brigid. The sadness in her face softened him. His mother had to be wrong. Reaching over, he gently pulled her hand out of her pocket and squeezed it.

"Let's just have some fun today," he said. A smile broke over her face as she leaned her cheek on his arm. They stepped politely to the side of the trail as a group of tourists marched past. Clad in fancy hiking gear and pristine backpacks, their ergonomic steel walking sticks pierced the soft earth. Music blared from wireless headphones and they talked loudly over their devices. Sensing danger in the clamor, the birds in the forest fell silent. As they passed, Gabe shook his head.

"What is in those backpacks?" Brigid said when they were out of earshot. "I mean, you can't camp here. And this is essentially a hill, not Mount Everest." Her laugh sparkled through the air.

"Tourists," Gabe muttered. "We pay the taxes while they have the fun."

Brigid looked at him askance. "Are we not having fun?"

"No, we're having fun," Gabe said. "But you know what I mean. They come here with their expensive stuff and make like they know what it's all about. Like they're in charge. But it's our home."

Another older couple marched back down the trail. These two carried shiny shellacked walking sticks and waved to the younger couple. Brigid and Gabe waved back.

"You're going to love it up there! It's amazing," the woman said.

As they passed, Gabe turned to Brigid. "You know, I've never been up to Moher Point. It's on all the postcards, but I've never seen it."

Brigid grinned. "They're right then. You are going to love it. It's been years since I've been there. I'm too lazy to drive over here. I always just hike to the beach by Cairn Cottage. It has better stones."

Gabe swallowed. It was the perfect intro. He had to ask her. It wouldn't stop bothering him until he got it out.

"Brigid?"

Hearing the tone in his voice made her nervous. To her embarrassment, her hands immediately became hot and clammy. She pulled away and tucked her hands back into her pockets. "What's up?"

"I..." The words were stuck in his throat. Even asking made him feel stupid. He hated the feeling, any feeling of vulnerability. Why couldn't this be easier? The relationship was going so well. Brigid was a unique woman and they had been having fun. It had been simple. He liked easy, simple. No drama. Especially the kind of drama he didn't understand. But he knew he wouldn't shake this feeling until he asked. He needed to man up.

"My mom said something to me the other day. Something about your family — your neighbors. I wanted to hear your take on it."

Brigid froze. She had been planning to tell him about the

Stone Society, but she hadn't seen him for a week. The problem was, she didn't know how to begin. She didn't even know what she believed. The feeling of peace, of floating almost, had gotten stronger the more time she spent in the outdoors. The more she concentrated, breathing deep, in and out, letting the air into her lungs, the more serenity she felt. And it was true, she had been spending a few hours every day gazing at the stones and writing down her thoughts. It felt like the swirl of intensity in her mind was released anytime she wrote her thoughts onto the page.

The weather piece had bothered her. Emma continued to insist that Brigid had the power to change the weather. That was the hardest to believe. But then again, the lightning storm the last night they were together... What had truly happened there?

She decided it was best to answer only the questions he asked. There was no advantage in trying to explain the depths of her soul. The point of today was to get back the connection they had enjoyed all summer. She steeled herself.

"What is the question?" she asked, more haughtily than she meant.

Gabe raised his eyebrows at her tone. "Are you involved in some sort of business selling stones?"

"Selling stones?" Brigid knew that in the past Emma's jewelry had been sold, but she didn't think Emma had resumed selling anything. "No," she answered. "I don't think we sell anything. I mean, I think they used to, but not anymore."

"So you are involved in this group?"

"I... I've been working with my grandfather's friends on... something. Honestly, it's really hard to explain."

"Try."

Brigid heard the anger and noticed his shoulders taut up to his ears.

"Ok. Well, remember the day you found me in my bedroom, with all of those papers? The day my grandfather had a stroke?"

The memory of her turning to him, lace over her head and shoulders, cheeks flushed and sunlight making her curls shine like amber would be forever embedded into his heart. It was when he knew this woman held something so different, so unique. He had to explore what she had. He was mesmerized by it. Did he remember that day? He would never forget it.

"Those papers, those rocks," she continued. "It turns out they were a part of this group. The papers were actually a Book. The Book of Stones. The group is called the Stone Society. It was formed several generations ago. My grandparents and their friends kept it up. It was disbanded when I was little."

"What do you do?" Gabe asked.

"Well..." Brigid hesitated. There was really nothing to say but the truth. "We collect rocks on the shore of the Big Omann Lake. Well, I collect them, actually. And then... it's kind of weird, but I spend time with the rocks, looking at them. Seeing if I can see any pictures in them. I write down what the pictures are and what I think they mean. All the types of stones have different properties, real mineral properties and spiritual properties. Like my stone, agate, means peace and power and healing. Which means I have peace and power and healing. Those are the attributes I was born with."

"Time out," said Gabe. He stopped walking and turned to her. "Your stone?"

Another group of hikers, a well-dressed young family with a yellow lab passed them.

Brigid looked down at the bracelet she wore. Gabe's eyes followed her. "Is that it? Your stone?"

"Yes," Brigid said. "We all... I guess mine was when I was a baby, but we all have a Ceremony where we choose the stone. I obviously don't remember my Ceremony, but I guess I picked this stone. Emma kept it for me and made it into this bracelet. She gave it to me after I found the boxes of stones and the Book. Everyone who is a member of the Stone Society wears their stone on a bracelet. Even the men."

Gabe was trying to wrap his head around this entire concept. "So, the stones — they have special powers?"

"No!" Brigid said. "Well, maybe. Sort of. I really don't know. I'm still learning about it myself."

"So why do you have to wear the bracelet?"

"I don't have to. I don't really know. I guess it helps me," Brigid said.

"So, it does have special powers," Gabe said. He scratched the back of his neck. Brigid sighed.

"I don't know if the stone itself has special, magical powers. I learned what the metaphysical meaning of agates are, the metaphors. Mine means peace, healing, love. When I wear my stone, when I see it and feel it against my wrist every time I move my right hand, I am reminded of what I could be. The best of me. It makes me feel peaceful. Like I could use kindness and intuition to heal people. To remember love."

The passion and strength behind Brigid's eyes struck something deep in Gabe. His mother had called her naive, sheltered, and privileged. He saw her tanned shoulders were pulled back and her chin was lifted. The fields of wild sweet pea in the glen behind her seemed like a carpet she was destined to walk on. Love, she had said. Who knew what love meant? He had loved, he had been in love. His heart had been broken. But this feeling, this deep peace, this drive to protect her, this wash of happiness that filled him when she smiled, the ease he felt in her presence, if this wasn't love, what was? And she was smart. What she was talking about now challenged him to reach far into his brain, deep into his knowledge to places he didn't usually explore. It was different. It wasn't simple and easy.

A cloud passed over them as he remembered that one of her people had hassled his mother. Had tried to scam her out of seven percent of their income, for a bracelet of her own and empty promises. Brigid was talking about dreams, but this was a fact.

"Ok," he said. "Here's the thing. Your friend Graham came to the farm the other day."

Brigid looked at him in confusion. "Graham came over?

How does he even know where you live?"

Gabe shrugged. "He showed up on our porch two days ago. Scared Mikey."

Brigid swallowed hard. Her hands had begun to shake inside her pockets.

"He came with jewelry, bracelets like the one you wear," Gabe said. "Tried to sell them to my mom. We don't have the money for that kind of thing, and I think she was embarrassed and really pissed off."

"I'm so sorry," said Brigid. "I know his wife Emma makes bracelets and stone jewelry, but I didn't know he was selling them."

"The thing is, he was trying to sell her more than just the jewelry. I guess he talked to her about some whole program thing that you guys do."

Brigid's confusion deepened. What program could he possibly be talking about? Her mind ran briefly to the ridiculous idea of changing the weather. She thought briefly to the belief that they held that she could change the weather. She reddened to think that Graham could have told Gabe about this. It sounded ludicrous, and if she didn't believe it could occur when she saw it with her own eyes, she had no idea what Gabe would think about it.

"Did he say anything about the weather?" she asked.

"I don't think it was about the weather," Gabe said. "The program you guys do. I guess," he paused, scratching his head and moving slightly away from her. "Can you explain it to me?"

"I have no idea what it is, honestly. We... they, the group believes that if you concentrate, meditate, really, that you can sort of..." She paused. "Interpret the weather."

Gabe shook his head. This whole thing was not something he wanted to deal with. Ann's tears and angst were seared into his memory. Most of the time they were wolf's tears, crying to get his attention, elicit his sympathy and forgiveness. But the other night, after Graham's visit, they were real. Frustration and defeat had washed down her tired cheeks. It made him feel helpless. And when he felt helpless, the easiest balm was fury.

His tone was hard. "It was nothing about the weather. Graham talked about the failure of our farm. Like we aren't aware. He tried to sell my mother a program of rocks and blessings and prayers. I'm asking you to explain what he was talking about. And more than that, I need you to explain why you told this group about my family's farm, and you tried to use us to sell whatever it is that you're selling."

Brigid had heard that tone before. Her face froze and she straightened her own shoulders to mirror his stance.

"I have no idea what he was trying to sell," she said firmly. "I'm sorry he bothered your mom. I certainly didn't send him over there. I would never do that. And the fact that you think that I would, I think, is the bigger problem."

Gabe was not to be cowed. "Do you understand what he asked of her?"

"I really don't," Brigid said.

"He asked for seven percent of our money. He asked us to pay seven percent of our annual income — he compared it to a tithe."

Brigid interrupted him. "But for what? What was he saying this would buy?"

"I told you! I feel like you would know more than me since you are involved in this. My mom didn't really understand." Gabe caught the tiny eyeroll that Brigid was unable to hide. Color rose to his cheeks and he continued, a hair louder than he would have liked. "Yes, Brigid, I'm aware that you think my mother is stupid."

"I've never said..."

"You've never had to," Gabe continued. "Your parents are educated; my parents are not. That means something to you and let's not pretend it doesn't. But in this case, the reason she didn't understand is because what your friend Graham was trying to sell her for our seven percent made no sense."

"What?" Brigid asked, louder than she meant.

"Is there a problem here?" Both of them whipped around to

see a man in expensive running gear. Brigid's first thought was that he looked like the many friends that she had known in college. Handsome. Well-dressed. In control. Lynn's ideal.

Gabe's humiliation washed over him again. With humiliation was anger. He had not shouted at Brigid. Had he?

"We're fine. Thanks," Brigid said, more quietly. The man looked her in the eyes for several beats.

"Are you sure?" At her nod, the runner gave a long, appraising look at Gabe, taking in his worn t-shirt and dirty sandals. It was clear the man thought Gabe was below her level. "Okay," the runner said reluctantly. "Are you guys going up the trail?" At her nod, he added, "Ok, see ya later!" Taking his eyes off of Brigid, he slapped Gabe on the shoulder with a sweaty palm. "Take it easy, guy. No more shouting, ok?"

Words tangled in Gabe's mouth like snakes. He wanted to disappear and at the same time wanted to rip this running fool to shreds. He'd start by tearing the fancy, sweat-wicking clothes and shoving them down his pretentious throat.

Brigid watched the runner turn around the bend and out of sight. She turned to Gabe. Wiping her sweaty palm on her skirt, she took his hand.

"Come on. Let's keep walking." They walked up the trail in a silence that got heavier by the second. As the sound of the lake began to break through the trees, Brigid realized she didn't want to come to the end of the trail in a fight with her boyfriend.

"Gabe, I don't know what Graham was talking about. Truly, I don't. I have absolutely no idea why he went to your house of all places. I haven't told them about you."

Gabe heard the truth in her voice. But that last sentence ... he found that it stung.

"Clearly I need to speak to him," she continued. "I want to understand what happened. And it sounds like he owes your mom an apology. I'll try to make that happen. For the record, here is my apology. I had no idea about any of it, but I am sorry that my people hurt and embarrassed your people." She tucked her hair behind her ear. "And I'm sorry I haven't told you about the Stone Society. It's just... well, it's weird. And I haven't figured it out yet and I thought you would think it was weird. Or that I was weird. And I've had enough experience having people think I was different, and odd, and not enough. And I didn't want that with you."

Gabe sighed deeply. The whole situation was odd, but never had he heard such an honest, vulnerable apology about anything with any woman he'd been with. And that was worth something. For now, the clean, fragrant smell of her curls, her soft arms wrapped around his back, that was enough. He could drop this until they figured it out.

"I get it. Well, I don't get it, but I really appreciate your apology."

"Do you believe me?" she asked.

"Yes," he said. "But I think you need to have a serious conversation with Graham about what is going on in this group. What you guys are really doing. And why he's lying about the fact that you are sending him places. Because in this case, it was offensive."

She nodded. "I will."

"Good. And I would actually like to hear more about what you're getting out of all of this. But not right now, is that ok?" She nodded, relieved. Her head was swirling. "I'd like to just see Moher Point with you for the first time. Could we just do that?"

"Please," she said. Standing on tip-toes, she kissed him. Shyly, pecking his lips, she felt no resistance from him, and stroked his top lip with the tip of her tongue. The salt of his sweat was like a balm. She held the kiss a few moments longer, feeling his hand run up her back and tangle in the nape of her neck. Aware that this trail was busy, and not wanting attract more nosy strangers, she pulled away.

When they came to the end of the trail, Gabe was visibly struck. The cliff face dropped three-hundred feet down to azure waters. South Colm and North Colm Islands were clearly visible, their evergreen forests nearly black in the distance. The curving, bowl-shaped dunes of the Peninsula could be seen for miles, forested at the top, and then falling into a golden, rocky cliff face.

The sunlight lit the waters below and made them sparkle crystalline blue. Pale birch and beech trees stood like sentries to guide their way to the cliff edge, leaves blowing and beckoning them forward.

Many years ago, this hike was only known to the people who lived in Birch Glen. A quiet treasure. People respected their neighbors' needs to walk up this pathway, sit with the earth in her stunning beauty. No one ran or raced, music was not needed. The trail was sacred. Lives began and changed here, it was the site of many marriage proposals, and some secret weddings. There were some residents who could even claim to be conceived on this sandy cliff side.

Today, the cliff face was cluttered with people. Gabe and Brigid slipped beside tourists with selfie-sticks, marathon runners taking the opportunity to train in a beautiful natural area, and families looking to run the energy out of their children. All were forced to contend with the awesome power and beauty of nature that was beyond anything humans could ever create.

When Gabe recovered his senses, he walked over to one of several warning signs posted at the end of the trail.

"Do NOT attempt to scale the cliff face. You risk INJURY OR DEATH."

"Cliff Face is DECEIVING. ROCK is under the sand."

"IF YOU FALL YOU WILL PAY RESCUE FEES."

The signs barely took away from the natural beauty. Gabe and Brigid stepped away from them, closer to the cliff face, joining the rest of the assembled strangers gaping in awe.

Runners breathing deep, hands on hips. Hikers, leaning on their walking sticks, chins jutted forward. Kids climbed the aching birch boughs and parents responded with varying levels of anxiety.

Looking to the right, Brigid remembered a small trail that led to a second, smaller, but no less dramatic cove.

"Come on," she said. A brief jaunt through the sandy woods led them to face the view again. The cliff face here was even steeper, almost a ninety-degree angle. Here there were no fences, no warning signs.

A small child ran happily among the grasses. Brigid spotted him immediately, wondering if this toe-headed boy was one of her first-grade students. She watched as he wandered deeper into the grasses behind the cliff, toward the trees and forest. He called back to his mother, and she heard her voice call out in reassurance. Realizing that he was not a student, she kept one eye on him anyway as she assessed Gabe's mood. He seemed to be calmer now. It would be hard to hold onto the grudges of this world when Big Omann Lake beckoned below. She threaded her hand through his arm.

"What do you think?"

Gabe shook his head. "I have no idea how I lived my entire life on the Peninsula without seeing this."

"My grandpa told me people used to get married up here." Gabe looked down at her and smiled. Brigid blushed at the implication. She felt him squeeze his arm tight around her hand.

"Brigid, I'm sorry for earlier," Gabe said. He gazed out at the shimmering water. "I have a lot of stress. At home, you know."

"I know."

"I... I've had to take care of my family since my dad left."

"Doesn't your mom help?" Brigid asked, unable to hide the indignation in her tone.

"She does. She tries. It really broke her heart when he left. She struggled a lot. Plus, when he first left, her arm was..." He paused, suddenly reluctant to share the family secrets.

"What?" Brigid asked. "What was wrong with her arm?"

Clenching his teeth, Gabe decided to just say it. She'd have to find out sometime. And he just found out that her family was involved in some crazy rock-selling scheme.

"Her arm was broken. My dad broke it when he threw her up against a wall. I tried to get between them and he threw me too."

"Oh my God," Brigid breathed. "Were you ok?"

"Oh, I was fine," Gabe said, his voice hard and fast. "I always got between them — sometimes it worked, sometimes he just whaled on me a little too hard. But if he was hitting me, he left my mom alone."

"But weren't you just a teenager?"

"I was thirteen."

The wind whipped through the trees above their heads. The little boy squealed in delight behind them, using the sturdy tree branches like monkey bars.

"I'm so sorry, Gabe."

"Brigid, it's fine. It isn't about me."

"But you were just a kid and he beat you."

"I was not a kid. Mikey was a kid. I was a tough— I could take it. It's about my mom. She shouldn't have had to deal with that. And after he left... Well, it was good because no one was getting hit, but you know, she was really sad. And we didn't have his income after that. So I had to get the farm going again, take care of some stuff while she took care of Mikey. We didn't always have enough money..." He stopped as his voice caught. Jaw working back and forth, tears pooled at the corner of his eyes.

"Oh Gabe." The pity in her voice was unbearable. He loosened her hand and walked quickly away. She still didn't understand, this girl who thought she could interpret stones, could save dying animals. She was so smart yet she couldn't understand the basic realities of life. It was about his mom. No woman should be treated like that. It had been hard to get the farm going, hard to learn to cook basic meals like grilled cheese and eggs, really hard to hide the pain in his belly and exhaustion in his bones when there hadn't even been enough food, but the hardest part was seeing his mother wallow in sorrow.

How could she miss a man who was so awful? The shame was... Gabe did know how she could miss that man. Because despite everything his father had done, Gabe missed him too.

A high-pitched scream caused Gabe's head to whip in the direction of the sound. A young boy was dangling with one arm gripping a tree branch that sailed in the airy expanse over the drop. Gabe was halfway to the tree before he realized he was running.

Gabe ran to the edge of the cliff and realized to his horror that it was too steep to set his foot down and reach out. The child was dangling three feet over the cliff, too far for even Gabe's strong arms to reach. He would have to climb the tree to reach the child. Gabe quickly scaled the trunk of the tree, reaching for the lowest branch and hauling himself up. The child was on the branch above, five feet higher than Gabe. Gabe swore under his breath as he gingerly balanced his feet on the lower branch. He looked up at the child. "Hang on, buddy. I'm going to get you," Gabe said. "Just hold on tight."

"Sammy!!" Another woman's voice shrieked through the air and made the boy turn violently toward the sound, nearly destroying the tepid grip he had on the branch.

"Mommy!" The sound wrenched the hearts of the three adults. Gabe called up with a light calm that he did not feel. "Buddy. Do not move. Ok? My name is Gabe. I'm going to get you out of here. You're not going to fall. Ok?"

The boy looked at this man inching out on the branch below him with desperate hope that only a child could believe. "Your name is Sam, right?" The boy nodded. "Ok, Sam. Lift your other hand up and grab the branch. Don't wiggle, just grab the branch with both hands." Sam got the branch, but it bent lower, eliciting a sob from mother and child. Brigid had her arms wrapped around the mother, whispering assurances to her as they watched Gabe. "Good job, Sam, great job! The branch is just bending, you're so strong, buddy. Be strong, I'm coming for you." Gabe kept his eyes locked on the boy as he slowly reached up for something to support him as he walked out on the branch over the cliff. He found nothing.

Breathing deep he said, "Look, watch me, I feel like I'm in the circus! Walking a tightrope. It's kind of fun. Don't move, ok? Just hold on with those big strong arms." With each sentence of patter, he tiptoed further out. On the ground, it would have been three easy steps, but over the cliff face, the movement was agonizingly slow. Gabe placed his feet out further onto the branch. Boy and man were suspended over the lake, Gabe refusing to glance at the sheer drop below. He was within reaching distance of Sam now, all he had to do was keep his balance. "Sam!" Gabe called. Tears were streaming down the boy's cheeks, his little belly heaving with sobs. "Sam, I'm right under you. Don't look at the lake, but look down just a tiny bit." Gabe slowly raised his arms skyward, feeling the branch creak under his feet. Sweat poured down his back. A loud cry escaped the boy as he tried to glance at the man on the branch, but the shimmering waters so far below caught his eye. The hand he had raised to the branch slipped down and he swung out wildly.

On the cliff's edge, Brigid and the boy's mother cried out. Brigid's tight grip on the woman could not hold her back from racing to the edge of the tree.

"Sam! Sam, I'm right here. I've got you, do NOT look down." Sam's wild swing caused Gabe to take a few more steps out onto the branch. He felt it bend underneath his feet. Gabe knew if he could just catch the boy, he could heave him close enough to the edge that the women would catch him. Not taking his eyes off of Sam, Gabe called out to Brigid. "Back away from the tree trunk and stand at the edge. When I catch him, we might need help getting back up."

It was now or never. "Sam, listen to me. Don't look down. I'm right under you. I'm going to catch you and we're going to take you back to your mom. I need you to trust me. I'm a strong guy, I work on a farm. I played football. You like football?" Sam's terrified eyes met Gabe's. "Good. Me too. I'm going to catch you like a football. I need you to just drop. Just let go."

The boy shook his head. Gabe reached up and gingerly touched the sole of the boy's shoe. It was the highest he could reach. Thin lines began to form within the branch, making it crack. "Can you feel my hand on your foot? I've got you. Sam. Buddy. You're not going for a swim in this lake today. I promise. Just drop. I've got you."

"Sammy, baby!" The woman's voice sliced through the air and Sam moved his head in her direction. "He's gonna catch you, sweetheart. Do what he says. Let go of the branch." The mother's body was extended almost farther than humanly possible over the cliff face. Arms outstretched, every vein in her neck rigid, skin tight to the bones in her face. Her life hung by a plump little hand on a branch of a tree. If he fell, she would die as well.

She watched as her baby boy's fingers slipped one by one from the branch. It was a horror in slow motion, each finger she had kissed, stroked, had patted her hair, had been baptized with markers and playdoh and the sandbox.

The boy dropped the few short inches into Gabe's arms. Gabe gripped him tight, bending his knees to offset the new weight on the branch. One arm tight around the boy's stomach, he lurched forward the few feet toward the trunk of the tree as a section of the branch behind him broke and fell into the water below. He hurled the boy forward with all of his strength. Brigid was there, right at the edge, and she grabbed Sam by his t-shirt, anchoring her knees hard in the sandy ground. Gripping the boy, she instinctively leaned backwards, away from the cliff. Sammy rolled on top of her, crying. Immediately his mother lifted him off, sobbing. Sitting upright, Brigid's heart jumped in her throat. Gabe should have landed at her side.

Only the blue horizon of sky and water remained.

CHAPTER 35

"Mommy, the man!!" Sam cried out and dug his arm out from his mother's fierce embrace, pointing toward the tree. Brigid had rushed over and seeing Gabe's arm gripping the rocks at the cliff face, she fell to her stomach and grabbed his wrists. He was looking down, feet scrambling for a toehold in the sand. Finding none, they flailed helplessly in the wind. The branch that had held Sam and Gabe floated lazily along the shoreline, far below.

Gabe felt her sweaty palms on his wrists, her nails piercing his skin. Adrenaline coursed through him. He calculated the drop. The water would be like a sheet of concrete that far down, not to mention the rocks that pierced up from the shoreline. There would be no chance of survival. Desperately, he kicked his feet toward the cliff face. He could feel the sand under his toes. He kicked off his sandals, blocking his ears from hearing the splash below.

"Gabe!"

Her voice called to him. It sounded like she was a world away, in a faraway tunnel.

"Gabe, I've got you, climb up!"

Swinging in, his bare feet reached, toes flexing and bending to find something, anything to hold onto. There was nothing. With each swing, his grip on the rocks above loosened. He was getting tired. All the muscles in his body that had tensed to hold the boy, to catch him, to steady them both on the branch were giving out. He looked up and saw her face.

Gabe loved her. The thought crystalized in this moment. He loved her. It was simple, an indisputable fact. He knew he loved her the same way he knew the sun would rise over the hill by the farm in the morning, knew the blossoms of May would turn to ripe, sweet cherries in July. His love for Brigid was simply a part of his world.

With this realization came another, as clear as the last. He knew that he would not pull her down with him.

Digging his fingers into the sandy hilltop, trying to find the rocks underneath, he tensed his torso and lifted his head.

"Brigid."

"Gabe! Gabe, I'm right here! Try to climb up, I will help you, I've got you."

"Brigid, let go." He locked eyes with her. "I've got a good grip, really. Let go." She shook her head, curls flying.

"You need to hear me, Brigid. I promise I'll be fine. Let. Go."

Her hands squeezed harder. "No," she said, her voice was commanding. "Find a foothold. You're only holding onto sand. If I let go, you'll fall!" Gabe clenched his teeth and kicked forward again. Nothing.

"Brigid," he said, voice beginning to give way. "You can't see it, but I've got something. I've got a good stone under my foot, I can climb up from here. Brigid, I love you. Please let go."

Her only answer was to push his hand down further into the sand, leaning back on her haunches and flexing her arms. He knew he could whip his hands out, throw hers away. He still had that strength. If he did this, she would be flung backwards. But she would not fall.

But then, under the pressure of Brigid's hands, he felt something press hard against the palm of his right hand. A stone. Gripping it, he attempted to pull himself up, but his arms were robbed of their strength. He lifted just enough for Brigid to shift and put her hand underneath his bicep, giving him leverage. Together, they lifted and pulled until half of his upper torso was lying on the cliff face. Brigid reached back and grabbed the waistband of his shorts, giving a big lurch of energy and hauling as hard as she could.

Gabe laid on his side, completely exhausted. Any composure he may have had was drained from him and he sobbed. He buried his face in his hands. The need, the will to live washed over him like a brutal truth.

For a moment, Brigid was afraid to touch him. In her family, outbursts of emotion were treated as private matters. It was best to leave the person to their grief, turn away and shield your eyes to spare them the shame. She watched his broad shoulders shake as she sat in the sand, her own breath heaving. Instinctively, she wanted to wrap her arms around him, but she was paralyzed.

The boy Sam came from behind with his mother gripping his hand. He patted Gabe on the shoulder. "Are you ok?" he asked in his reedy voice.

The mother stood near. "I cannot thank you enough," she said, voice raw with tears and belayed fear. "I truly — you have no idea. I will do anything, what can I do to pay you back?"

Gabe raised his head, swiping the back of his shaking hand across his eyes. He cleared his throat.

"Nothing." His voice was rough. He coughed. "Nothing," he repeated, his voice restored to its baritone timbre. "Your son was in danger — I did what anyone would do." The mother shook her head, tears streaming down her face.

"But I didn't." She began to sob. "I wasn't paying attention and I couldn't have gotten to him fast enough. I was trying to give him some freedom. I wasn't paying attention..." Dropping his little jaw open, Sam's bottom lip stuck out and he began to wail as well. "I was scared, Mama! Why didn't you get me?" Every vowel in the boy's sentence was excruciatingly drawn out, and the tone snapped Brigid out of her daze. Brigid stood and stroked the mother's back. "We had him. He's ok," she said. "He's going to be okay." She continued murmuring comforting platitudes to mother and child until the wracking sobs stopped. The mother finally recovered herself and stood, lifting the boy onto her hip.

"Please tell me your names. I need to know how to get in contact with you,"

Brigid turned to Gabe, who had risen and sturdied his legs, standing behind her, well away from the cliff. He gave his hands a quick swipe on his shorts and extended his right palm. Taking the woman's hand gently, he said, "I'm Gabe. This is Brigid. And please, don't worry about it. It was scary for a second there, but we got him and everything's alright."

"No, you don't understand," the woman continued.

Brigid interrupted. A few years of dealing with high-strung parents kicked in. "We do understand," she said. "I promise. I'm a teacher — I know how quickly kids can get themselves into fixes."

"You're a teacher?" the woman asked, aghast. "You must think I'm a terrible parent." Her lip quivered, a perfect imitation of her son.

"No, no," Brigid and Gabe protested in unison. "You were just giving him a little bit of freedom," Brigid said. "All kids need some freedom."

Gabe smiled down at the boy. "Right, buddy?" Sammy smiled up at him. He leaned in, obviously wanting to hug this big man, but unwilling to let go of his mother. Gabe understood and knelt down, giving the boy a quick, hard hug. "Freedom is good, but stay away from cliffs, ok?" He gave a laugh to erase any harshness of the direction. Sammy smiled up at him. "Thanks for getting me out of that scary tree."

"Anytime," said Gabe.

"Mommy?" Sammy looked up at the woman. "I have to pee." She let out a small sigh and closed her eyes. "Just a minute, sweet love. I just need to get these people's numbers."

"Ma'am, really," Gabe put his hand out. The woman smiled despite herself at the designation 'Ma'am.' "Sammy's safe, you thanked us more than enough. It's fine. And he's gotta go." Gabe winked at him.

"Thank you." She said, and embraced them hard. Turning with her son, she made her way back down the hill.

Brigid turned to Gabe. She saw him once again, gripping the slipping sand, kicking out for a toehold, the lake below waiting to swallow him and she eased herself into his arms. She felt the strong beat of his heart through his hard chest, smelled the sweat of fear emanating through his body. Wetness soaked her cheek and she realized it was her own tears. She was filled with a deep gratitude for life. Life that still was theirs, here in this moment. Life that was not guaranteed, that could be stolen, that was so unjustly short. Life was theirs for the taking.

CHAPTER 36

They had had time to recover with a quick lunch, neither saying nor eating much. They sat at Edgewood Cafe holding hands and looking out at the lake. Words were unnecessary. Falling into each other's arms was not possible that afternoon. Gabe had an afternoon shift at the marina, after which he was obligated to go home and work at the farm.

After Gabe dropped her off at Cairn Cottage, Brigid texted Emma. Tonight would be for settling this score once and for all. What the hell had Graham been doing — what had he been thinking? And why the Sherlands? She had almost lost Gabe, emotionally and literally. Propriety, politeness; none of that mattered. Brigid felt a new clarity that invigorated her.

Her phone vibrated on the counter.
Emma.

"Hi Honey.
I think I understand what happened.
We would like to invite you over for dinner.
Please come at 6:00 pm.
Don't worry about bringing anything."

The message felt like she was being summoned. Brigid snorted in disgust. She would go. But how to fill the remaining hours? Her body was physically drained, yet her mind would not allow her to relax. She glanced at the old bank calendar on the fridge. July was hurtling to an end. School would start before she knew it. It wouldn't hurt to go over lesson plans, plan out how to decorate her classroom. She thought of her little Rose. There had been a meeting to determine whether Rose should stay in Brigid's classroom one more year. Being held back wasn't great, but Brigid was sure it would be good for Rose's learning. And good for her heart as well. Brigid wanted the chance to watch over her again. Perhaps she would send an email to her principal, to see what had been decided.

Yes. An afternoon on the dock in the sun planning the future was just what she needed.

It was unusually warm that day, the lapping lake tantalizing while the sun seemed determined to burn.

CHAPTER 37

In a few minutes, the clock would chime six. Emma pulled the casserole out of the oven. Graham had offered to grill, but she had declined. After what happened at the Sherlands, Emma wanted complete control over this dinner. And she wanted it ready on the dot. More eating meant less talking.

Graham came in, contrition and rebellion warring on his face. He turned to his wife. "I cannot believe you insisted on having the oven on today. It's such a scorcher! You couldn't buy a breeze."

Emma turned the dial off on the corn on the cob boiling on the stove. "I know. I could feel her anger all day."

"What?" Graham looked at his wife like she had grown a second nose. "Don't be ridiculous."

"You don't be dismissive," Emma said firmly. "We have no idea what this woman is capable of. We watched her send away the rain. She may not believe she did, but we witnessed it. No one has been able to summon or banish water from the sky since before our time. Even her grandmother couldn't do it."

"Emma..."

But Emma was not to be cajoled or pacified. Not today. "You made a big mistake going over to the Sherlands. Especially without consulting us." She looked her husband straight in the eye. "I don't know if you knew she was dating the son or not. Frankly, I'm not sure that I even want to know if you knew she was connected to the family before you tried to go sell them whatever it was. The appropriate thing to do would be to use this dinner to apologize. To her. To all of us."

Graham was unused to hearing this strong tone out of his sweet wife. He didn't quite know what to do next.

"Go change into a fresh shirt," Emma directed. "Brigid and David will be here any minute." Without a retort at hand, he turned on his heel and did what he was told.

A knock at the screen door made Emma drop the forks she was placing on the table. Brigid stood there; hands folded formally around a plastic tumbler. Why was she knocking? It was common knowledge that folks simply came in and out of houses around here, calling out if it was too early or too late to be conventionally polite. She walked around the table, holding the door open.

"Come on in, honey," Emma said. Not knowing whether to reach in for a hug, she stood awkwardly. Brigid seemed taller to her. A quick glance at her flip flops told her it wasn't the shoes. The bones in her cheekbones seemed to absorb the summer sunshine. The softness in her arms had hardened slightly into muscle. Her chin, usually bowed in blushes, was held high.

"Brigid!" Graham bounded into the room, fresh-shirted and scented with minty cologne. Her expression broke his stride. Being astute enough to read that she would not welcome his embrace, he turned to something he could do.

"I see you brought a roadie — you're getting the hang of lake living! May I freshen your drink?"

"No."

Graham faltered. Women did not usually speak to him so coldly. He was used to charming everyone with vivaciousness. Men and women alike admired his ability to take all the air in the room and turn it into party confetti. Finding the silence stifling, he decided to take his wife's advice.

"Brigid, I want to apologize…"

"You should apologize," Brigid said, not moving from the doorway. "You owe several apologizes. To me, to Gabe, to his family. I cannot believe that you would use our Society to extract money from people who don't have any."

So it's *our* Society now, thought Graham. Lovely.

A red-hot current of anger flowed freely through Brigid's veins and she began to lose a grip on what she was saying.

"I have no idea what this scam is with the rock cairns or the jewelry, but if this is a scam that you all are perpetuating, I want nothing to do with it."

Emma broke in, "It's not a scam, honey, the package that Graham was trying to put together was sincere. Sincere, but misinformed."

Brigid raised her hand to stop the older woman. "From my understanding, it was sold as a scam. Graham actually asked for a tithe, like a church. Now. I'm young, but I've been through some stuff and today... today I experienced something that changed me." She stopped, thinking of the stone that had appeared under Gabe's palm as it slipped off the cliff. It did not make sense that it had been there, any more did it make sense that Gabe was able to balance out on that limb. She saw Emma and Graham staring, questions in their eyes. Shaking her head of the memory, she continued. "Never mind. I need you to understand that I will not be involved in a scheme or a cult. I thought the Stone Society was something greater, something noble. A chance to connect to our true selves and nature. Now, if I'm wrong, if the Stone Society is simply a way to sell things, I'm out. I'm happy to continue our friendship, as you are such old friends with my grandfather. But that's it."

A gentle knock at the screen door split the air. David had been standing on the porch, waiting to enter. Hearing Brigid's speech, he was more convinced than ever that this young woman had the power to be the Diviner. He opened the door and took a giant step in next to Brigid.

"Brigid," he said softly, not wanting to spook the power that emanated through her. "Your intuition that the Stone Society is a noble, mystical pathway is completely correct. Not something to sell or market." It took every ounce of David's self-control not to send a furious glance at Graham. "Since we are all gathered, perhaps you would allow me to explain what the Stone Society is truly about. After that, I think it is only fair to allow Graham time to explain his actions. I, for one, am very interested in what he has to say for himself."

Brigid nodded. David's words were wrapped in respect and it calmed her racing heart. Emma let out an audible sigh of relief. David pulled out Brigid's chair and filled her waiting wine glass.

Once they had bowed heads for a moment in silent, private prayers, the fragrant food was scooped onto plates. Emma had made chicken and rice in a butter-based orange sauce, spiced with nutmeg and ginger. It was really a winter dish, but she had felt that the sweet, creamy comfort would lend itself well to reconciliation. Ears of corn were painted with butter and dusted with salt and pepper, fresh country bread and a deep green salad with dried cherries, tiny, jeweled strawberries, and poppyseed dressing rounded out the meal. Everyone took quiet enjoyment of Emma's skilled cooking. A cool evening breeze swept across the lake, brushing through the screen door carrying the sweet, spicy scent of wild grass. Graham began shuffling in his seat, clearing his throat in preparation to speak. He was silenced by a glance from David.

David took a long, graceful pull from his water glass, and dabbed his lips with the napkin resting in his lap.

"I would like to tell the history of the Stone Society." The other three adults looked up from their plates, each waiting for another's ascent. Taking their silence for approval, David began.

"Several generations before ours, a few families emigrated from Scotland onto the Peninsula. They purchased property on Little Owrawn Lake. The men cut the driveways and used the lumber to build cabins. Brigid, a small part of Cairn Cottage is the original structure: your grandfathers' bedroom, as well as the loft and small kitchen. Of course, in those days, the kitchen was a fireplace oven."

Brigid nodded. This information was not news.

"The families were friends; the husbands had studied geology in the rocky cliffs and hills of Scotland. They were hoping to mine the Peninsula for precious stones, and perhaps gold and silver. The women were trained healers. They practiced a religion that didn't have any codes or creeds or pictures of divinity. They believed simply that God was love. Meditation, serving people, and respecting the land; these were their core beliefs."

Brigid stared, fork suspended in the air. "Did they have a church?" she asked.

David shook his head. "It wasn't defined. They had no church or organizational system. They simply believed what they believed. Soon the more established houses of worship in the area squelched any curiosity that blossomed in the community. The families still practiced, just more quietly. But this curiosity led to a partnership between the original families and the farmers. While the men didn't find traditional gemstones, they did discover that the stones from the freshwater lakes were not only beautiful; they contained minerals that could enhance the soil. They began grinding the stones to dust and mixing them into new seedlings in their gardens. When the farmers saw the prosperous vegetable plots of the three families, they gave way and asked for help. Together, by trial and error, it was discovered that the stones as well as the lake water contained minerals that were beneficial to the crops. After the head of one of the families — yours, Brigid, died..."

Brigid cut him off "How did he die?"

David smiled. "It was your great-great-great grandfather. He took in a cold dip into Big Omann Lake hunting for stones and cut himself on the way down. Medicine was much different then, and penicillin wasn't available. He succumbed to a bacterial infection. In any case, after his death, the families began to record everyone's collected knowledge. Of healing, of geology, of farming, of spirituality. This became a central system of beliefs and practices. Eventually, they named themselves: Uisdeen Fireen. The Society of Stone Seekers. For generations, the families and the farmers worked together. The farmers received scientific help with their crops, and the families received a share of the yield."

"This is incredible," Brigid said. "How did they have the science to discover all of this? Did they have instruments?"

"Some they brought with them, along with their education. But mostly it was just trial and error." David chuckled. "And a lot of goodwill."

Brigid's eyes were bright as she gazed across the table at David. "And it worked?"

David smiled. "It did. For a very long time. It worked well enough that it gained the attention of the people on Domhnall Hills. They were struggling with their crop yields, but of course that was because their land was so hilly and they were stripping so much of it to build the city. But they sent officials up to study what was happening on the Peninsula and stole the mixture of chemicals that were being extracted from the rocks. The original families had never thought to put a patent on anything. They were simply living in harmony with their neighbors, giving help and taking it. Soon, industrial-grade fertilizer was being produced and ordered to mimic and enhance the results being gained from the rocks and powder made by the Stone Society. They sold it to the Peninsula farmers at a low price, and well... there you have it. The Stone Society went out of business"

"So what happened? Did the Society dissolve?"

"No," David said. "Not yet. By this point, the Stone Society had gathered many artisans and spiritual people. We were creating beautiful pieces of jewelry that were sold to tourists and locals alike. Most of our spiritual leaders and healers were female and these women made and sold holistic tonics. They held small workshops where deep breathing, stretching, and prayer were taught. They also gave blessings for free — they only asked that in return for the blessing, the person performed a selfless act of service to the community."

"This is amazing," said Brigid. "This is the same thing that so many people are discovering now."

Emma and David smiled knowingly. Graham gave a huff.

"These women were well ahead of their time." said Emma. "But they used techniques that are as old as time."

"Unfortunately," said David. "The wider community here at the time was not ready to accept that sort of spiritual thought. We had members of several formal religions among our ranks, many Christians, some Jewish people, some agnostic. And the rituals, like the Ceremony, and the blessings of the cairns; those were universal. I don't know how any person believing in divinity could protest. But... we did begin to receive a lot of pushback"

"And the jewelers, don't forget the jewelers," Graham spat.

"Yes. Several area shops and jewelers adopted the techniques."

"Stole the techniques," Graham butt in.

"Perhaps. In any case, many shops in Birch Glen and Domhnall Hills began to use the same stone-polishing and jewelry-making techniques used by the Stone Society artisans. They had the money to build and market the business so well that we were pushed out."

"The Stone Society didn't have capital for store fronts, which was what was needed in those times," explained Emma. "No tourist wanted to take a backroad to a cabin and buy their jewelry in someone's living room. They wanted the experience, the name brand."

"Yes, and once the name brand was slapped on," Graham said, "It was the brand and status rather than the meaning that people wanted. Even the locals. They claimed to hold themselves apart from the materialism of Domhnall Hills. The lure of prestige is an unrelenting mistress. Eventually, the jewelers in the towns had so many customers that they were able to lower their prices. When that happened, the Stone Society artisans had a choice — to sell nothing, or to work for the competitor."

"The rifts that happened effectively broke many bonds and severed many relationships. Between the fertilizer taking over usage of minerals for crops and the loss of the stone jewelry businesses, the Stone Society began to fade away."

Brigid looked at the agate sparkling on her wrist. Although it was unfaceted, the evening light washed over it. This was more than beautiful. This was pure art. She looked at Emma. "Did this happen to you?"

Emma shook her head. "My mother. Both of my parents were true artisans. They passed the techniques down to me. Sadly, by the time I learned them, there wasn't much business left. I could have found a job at one of the in-town shops, but I was loathe to sell my secrets. I married Graham, raised our children, and continued to practice my craft in my own time."

"Was that enough for you?" Brigid knew her question was cruel. Emma looked at her firmly.

"No," Emma answered. "But that was life."

Brigid looked down, a blush rising in her cheeks. "So that was it? The unmooring of the Stone Society?"

More truth hung heavy in the air. Brigid did not know about Ruby and the tragedy with Teddy Sherland. The elder three did not dare even exchange a glance. Brigid was becoming too sharp and they could not risk breaking her trust again. Most of the afternoon had been spent in a whispered, furious debate whether to tell her that truth. In the end, it had been decided that tonight's dinner should be about apology. And history. And perhaps, if they could get through that, what a true Diviner was capable of.

The story of Ruby had been sunk at the bottom of the waters for decades; she could wait awhile longer.

"That was it," said Graham. "And now, if I may speak?" He glanced at David for approval. The tall man nodded.

"Brigid," Graham stood and raised his glass. "I want to apologize to you. I truly had no idea you were dating Gabe Sherland. I imagine the fallout was embarrassing."

"It was," said Brigid coldly.

Determined not to be shaken, Graham continued. "My heart was in the right place with my actions. I truly believe we have something to offer here. Both scientifically and spiritually. And that farm is suffering."

"That farm is fine." Brigid's voice sent chills through them all.

"The farm is fine, it's fine," said Graham. "But the truth is, and I'm sorry, but you were not born yet, so you cannot know. The truth is, the Sherland Farm used to be glorious. The best in the county. Now it's left to an older woman, who frankly, cannot muster the self-respect to clean her home, much less run a farm."

Brigid hated herself for agreeing with him on that score. But still, she felt she had to defend Gabe.

"Gabe is running the farm to the best of his ability. While working a second job at Sunset Marina, while caring for his family."

"Brigid, you make my point for me," Graham said, not unkindly. "He is overworked. She is exhausted. So much potential is just being wasted. I went to help."

Brigid wanted to be furious, but despite herself, she saw the sense in his intention. "But why the tithing? Why did you want to charge them so much money?"

"I never understood why we didn't charge for blessings," Graham said, taking his seat again. "Or the time it took for the Diviners and the Blessers to find and work with the stones. Or why placement and water carrying was free. It's simple business sense; our time is valuable. Mine, yours, David's. Valuable in ways that can be monetized. I worked out what I thought was a fair price for our time, on an hourly basis. And I translated it to a sliding scale, based on the income of each property. I was as ethical and mathematical as my business background taught me to be."

"Yes, but you miss the point, Graham," said David. "The blessings and spiritual work are above monetization. We do that for the benefit of the community, for the love of each other and the love of the land. You attempted to charge for Brigid's time and talents without her consent."

Graham looked down and slumped his shoulders. Crickets

began to sing, heralding the dusk. After a few moments, Graham raised his head. "I know that what I did does not have the consensus of the group. I apologize to all of you. It was a grave mistake"

"We accept," said David and Emma in unison. All three hesitantly looked at Brigid.

"I also accept," she said. "On one condition."

"Name it."

"That if I can get Gabe to come here, you apologize to him as well."

"I certainly will," said Graham gratefully.

The tension cleared out of the air and bodies crumpled in relief back into their seats.

"Tea and pie?" Emma asked cheerfully. She was met with resounding approval. The rest of the evening passed in light conversation and ease. Brigid asked for more stories about the work of the Stone Society and the elders happily obliged. When the moon began to rise over the summer sky, David and Brigid began to gather their things. Emma suggested that she walk Brigid home.

"Thank you," Brigid demurred. "But you've worked really hard on this dinner. I'm sure you need some rest."

Emma shook her head. "I'm a night owl. Besides, there's one more part of Stone Society that I'd like to show you. Something that's best to learn without the menfolk." David and Graham smiled at her. Everyone knew that the best teacher of this particular practice would have been Brigid's grandmother Shannon. But Emma was present and willing and knew the ceremony and rituals. She would have to stand in.

CHAPTER 38

Emma linked Brigid's arm in hers, and they walked down the narrow sandy pathway toward Cairn Cottage. When David was anxious or sad, he would rake the pathways around the cabins, twisting parallel lines showcasing the traverses of his mind. When Nieve had died, he had raked the path down to mud.

Tonight, birch leaves and bits of white cedar sprigs littered the path, and pebbles found the soles of their flip flops. Brigid was slightly uncomfortable with the touch, but tried to embrace it the way she embraced hugs from her students.

Emma's gray shining bob was lifted in the night breezes. She welcomed the coolness. Brigid's palm, which she had placed on her arm, was warm and ever so slightly damp. That bit of vulnerability, that sign of youth, was so welcome to Emma's heart. Brigid was a true Diviner, she knew. It was up to her to convince the younger woman to harness her destiny.

Brigid turned on the fork of the path that led to the door, but felt that she was gently halted by Emma's arm.

"Shall we go sit on the dock?" Emma asked. "It's a beautiful night." Brigid obliged. It was obvious that the older woman had something more to tell, perhaps a secret. Once they had reached the end of the dock, Brigid slipped her arm away.

"Emma." Assurity laced her voice. "Tell me what you think I need to know."

Emma took a deep breath. "Brigid, in the Stone Society — in almost every culture that has been lost, really, women have a connection. A unique connection with the Divine. We are the sources of life, we are the first contact with love. Often, we are the last contact with human love before a person passes over. Many societies knew this, and many still do. But sadly, in ours, the men..."

"Hold the power." Brigid finished the sentence.

"Yes," answered Emma. "But there's a reason that our planet is called Mother Earth. A reason that Wisdom has a female name. We are the ones who hold love, who hold empathy, who hold sacrifice. And sometimes, if we are able to drop all the mundanities and cares and sorrows and anger of the human experience, we can connect with the Divine. You've felt those moments?" It wasn't a question. Brigid nodded.

"In addition to interpreting the stones, a Diviner learns to harness and extend those moments. To be with the Divine. The way to do this is to eliminate all thoughts. Acknowledge them, yes, but let them go. Practice this until the only thought in your heart, the only element running through your veins, is Love. Pure Love. This has been done by wise people since the beginning of time. It is still being practiced today in religions around the world. By far fewer people than you might think, but still..."

"Emma, tell me exactly what you want me to do."

"I want you to be this Diviner for us. For our community. I want you to spend time, outside, under a tree, over the water. Breathing in. Breathing deep. When you are able to do this, you may feel a spark, a glowing inside of you. That is communion. I've only felt it a few times, but it is the most beautiful, peaceful feeling in existence. If you practice this for months, maybe years, you may be able to develop a communication with the Divine that allows you to ask, on all of our behalf, for intervention. For rain. For sun. For warmth. For forgiveness. We could bring back the true purpose of Uisdean Firinn, your ancestors. Forget what Graham did. Forget the money. You could help us heal."

Emma reached up on tiptoes and kissed the younger woman on the forehead. She turned and left the dock.

Brigid stood there, feeling the waves and wind lap around her. She had felt that feeling. Many times. Always, there was a persistent longing for escape. She never had a name for it. Hence all the wandering, all the searching. Perhaps, if she gained nothing else, her experience with the Stone Society would allow her to deepen this practice of connecting with something larger than herself. A chill forced her back into reality. She padded off the dock and into the cottage. She found herself standing in the dining room, with no idea why she had come in. Oh yes…she was cold. Her eyes were blurry from staring into the night sky and the shock of the bright light of the dining room fixture. Her mind was muddled at all the new information.

Finding the lace mantle folded across the dining chair, she threw it over her arm and walked back out onto the dock.

Pulling a chair out so she faced the lake, she placed the mantle in her lap. A note fell onto the wooden boards. Holding it to the moonlight, Brigid squinted to make out the careful, slanted script.

"This mantle has seen the coming and going of the Ayers Family back to recorded memory. Children have been wrapped in this cloth at birth — it is the first object of this world to touch their physical bodies. When an Ayers is close to death, she is covered with the mantle, like a blanket. She passes onto the shining world wrapped in the love of all of her ancestors.

In all the important moments of life in between birth and death, this mantle has been with each member of the Ayers family. It has been used as a veil at weddings, as a carpet for the Spirit Stone Ceremony, and worn under graduation robes.

After each marking of life, death, and experience, the veil has been lovingly cleaned with water gathered from Little Owrawn Lake. Every crevice has been scrubbed of the stains of life, every tear has been patched by the loving fingers of a family member. Until you came, it has been folded and put in the cedar chest, covering the sacred stones.

I encourage you now to use it, wrap yourself in it as you medi-tate on the traditions of the Stone Society. Use it when you medi-

tate on pure Love. Imagine what the world could be like if only we loved.

Because the tragedy is that your grandmother has passed over, your grandfather cannot speak, and your mother has rejected the Stone Society. I have taken it upon myself to bestow this knowledge to you. I hope that you know this comes from a place of hope and respect, and that you forgive my boldness.

With all of my love and affection,

Emma Webster

P.S. — I assume this mantle had been thoroughly cleaned, but just in case, I have taken the liberty of giving it a full ceremonial cleaning and patching."

Brigid folded the note and put it in her pocket. She shook out the mantle. Light from the starry sky made it seem at once transparent and opaque. Delicate lace covered silk. She hesitated. Her mother would certainly think this was all foolishness. In some secret part of her, Brigid agreed. A swift north wind blew across the lake and Brigid shivered in her cotton shift dress. Oh well. She was holding a blanket and it was cold. Carefully, she wrapped it around her shoulders, reaching behind her neck to sweep loose her long auburn curls. She was surprised at the warmth it offered.

The night sky was so bright in the northern part of the peninsula. Without the light pollution from the city, she could see the wash of the Milky Way galaxy. It was strange to think that her grandfather and grandmother had stood on this very dock and looked up at these very stars. And their parents before them, and theirs. All the way back.

The stars and the night sky were the same.

Brigid felt the familiar pang in her chest she had grown to associate with thoughts of her grandfather. It was not fair that his life was ending this way. It was cruel that just as she began to reconnect with him, he was slowly being taken. And her grandmother. How would Brigid's life have been different if she had had the chance to know a woman who seemed so much like her?

She felt robbed. A tightness squeezed in Brigid's chest and the air suddenly felt cold and damp. Brigid shivered and pulled the blanket closer. Her grandfather's eyes held such a twinkle when he looked at her, his expression filled with admiration and pride. How could this be, when he truly barely knew her? Brigid supposed that's what the love of a grandparent meant. She didn't understand it, or perhaps she didn't deserve it, but it was palpable.

The love she held for her grandfather was wrapped in tenderness and respect. Of course there had been some shyness as they got to know each other in those short few weeks before his collapse. There was an unspoken need in both of them to care for the other. Domesticity had never been her style, but she found herself eager to bring the old man a cup of tea, a warm breakfast. And he had wanted to see her smile burst onto her face, provide her with a safe home, one that was comfortable, one where she could be herself. He wanted to have the power to bring her happiness and joy, and then let her loose out into the world.

Brigid found that she was breathing evenly with each thought. It was calming. Warming. Exhaling deliberately now, she thought again of little Rosie. A child who needed so much love. Grubby soft fingers always reaching out to touch Brigid. Rosie's smile of joy when Brigid would share her lunch, shocked with a sweet gullibility into believing that her teacher ate peanut-butter-and-jelly sandwiches, goldfish crackers, juice boxes, and sandwich cookies. Brigid bought the largest slices of bread she could find, finishing her half and protesting that Rose had to eat the rest of the lunch — teacher was too full.

And Gabe. How was it that in such a short time, Gabe had come to feel like her missing piece? She knew it was illogical, but it seemed like she had known him forever. That they truly knew each other's secrets.

Brigid gazed up at the stars, eyes focusing and blurring at

intervals. Her body felt welded to the plastic chair. Inside her core there was a vibration. A sparkling, a crackling flowed through her veins and made her sway. It scared her and she shook her hands, landing with a thud back into reality. Around her was wind and chill. What was this feeling? She closed her eyes and breathed deep. Willed it to come back.

Let go.

The words seemed to come to her and through her.

Love.

Eyes closed, her heartbeat seemed to pulse with those words. Love. Let go. Love. Let go. Love. Let go. The sparkling flew through her now. Down to her fingers, racing up her spine and cradling the back of her head. Her body anchored heavily to the chair, her limbs felt like lead. Daring to open her eyes, she saw the stars melt together and explode. Sparkling fire filled her body and she felt lifted, carried. It was the most beautiful, peaceful sensation. Opening her eyes to the sky, she could see the reality of clouds forming in the distant horizon. She wanted to see the clouds. Wanted to know what they were made of.

Closing her eyes slightly, she opened them again, focused hard on the clouds. Beckoned them in closer. They swept across the sky and Brigid could see, feel their dampness, feel their molecules. A cloud sank down around her and she saw it was not a solid thing, but something that blocked the light when the air became too burdened. Understanding, she tilted her head back and with closed eyes, sent it away.

Stars were next. What were the stars? Brigid wanted to see one, to be one. A shower of shooting stars raced across the sky. Life, and all the triumphs, sadness, love, hatred of one person could be encased in a star. If it was opened, death. It would explode — a million beams of energy and light of every moment of a person's life burst into being.

What was the wind? Breeze rustled up and swirled around her, lifting the ends of the mantle and wisps of her curls. Messages, the wind was a message.

Brigid wanted to feel the heat of the sun; the wind had chilled her. It was the climax of night but she wanted the day. Banish the darkness, let me live only in light. It was a thought and a scream. As her gaze whipped to the West, she felt the world bend. A dissonant chord on a tight string rang in her ears.

This is not Love. This is Power.

Snapping back to reality, Brigid gave a tiny shudder. There were tears behind her eyes. The stars were clear and still. Wind blew gently across the waves. The cloud cover loped staidly over the horizon. What had really happened? Had she done it?

A warm sensation seemed to curl around her, relaxing her.

I am here. I am Love. You are Love. But you are human. And you must rest.

Rising, Brigid stood quietly. Catching herself, she walked, blinded, off of the dock and into the cottage. She climbed the stairs without knowing and fell into her bed.

Sleep.

Immediately, Brigid fell deep into unconsciousness and a dreamless sleep.

Three docks away, Emma stood, watching the weather, the tiny strand of sunlight that had been lifted and sent back down, glowing eerily over the western horizon. Reverently, she held her palm to her mouth and wept.

CHAPTER 39

Lynn held the tiles under the light in the bathroom, scrutinizing each one with squinted eyes. A whistled showtune waltzing down the hall broke her concentration. She set the tiles down carefully and stepped out of the doorway.

"Kelsey?" she called. "Could you come in here for a minute?" He popped his head in.

"What's up, buttercup?" He wrapped his arm around her waist and kissed the top of her head. "Ooh, what is going on in here? Are we redecorating?"

"Well, I don't think Brigid will go back to that apartment. And my father..."

"I know, sweetheart." Kelsey wrapped her up in a hug. She stiffened. He smiled ruefully. "I'm sorry."

"Thank you," she said, swallowing hard. Kelsey was the only person on earth with whom she allowed herself to be vulnerable. But even with him, she had to hold back. "I spoke to the doctors yesterday and he continues to decline. It's inevitable, Kelsey." Kelsey nodded calmly, knowing that pity was the last thing she would tolerate. "When it happens, the only logical thing is to sell that house."

"You're going to sell Cairn Cottage?" Kelsey's eyes widened.

Lynn rolled her own icy blue eyes. "Please don't call it by that ridiculous name. And yes, what else is there to do with it?"

Kelsey considered the moment carefully. "Well, honestly..."

Lynn's eyes narrowed. "What?"

"Honestly, I thought maybe it could be Brigid's inheritance. She needs a place to live, and as you say, that apartment is entirely unsuitable."

"Absolutely not, Kelsey! That cottage is falling down. It would take an army to clean the grime from the place and beyond that, I'm sure my father hasn't spent a dime on the structure. Did you not see the roof when we were over there? I could see the rot all the way from the dock!"

Her temper began to seep upwards in a pink flush from her pretty neck through her face. Kelsey felt helpless; he wanted to touch her, attempt to send the anger back down before it exploded.

"These are fixable problems. Your father has money in the bank, we could get a new roof for the place. Brigid's always been..." He looked past the pristine bathroom into his daughter's childhood bedroom, books of poetry stacked haphazardly on the dresser, a collection of potted plants on the windowsill. "... a little lost." He sighed. "It might be nice for her to have this. In a way, she's earned it. Taking care of your father and visiting him almost every day." Lynn felt her husband's rebuke. Silk-clad shoulders melted and she sighed, visibly deflating from the fight.

"You're right, Kelsey. Honestly, you're right about all of it. Brigid does need an extra boost, and she has been wonderful with my dad. We should find a way to help her. But I don't think a cottage on the Peninsula that hasn't seen a repairman in sixty years is going to help her find her way. I'm sorry, Kelsey, but he's my father, not yours. I'm going to make the decision here. At the end of the summer, we will sell that cottage and put the proceeds in a trust for Brigid. I've already spoken to a realtor. With the fall colors in bloom, priced right, it should sell quickly."

Kelsey shook his head quietly. "And what's your endgame, my dear? What is your plan for our only kid?"

Winning the argument always made Lynn relax. She gave him a sly smile and turned to the sink. "I'm going to fix up her bedroom and bathroom. It's no wonder why she won't stay here — look at this baby blue color. So immature. She needs a home that is elegant. Serious. I figure after the summer is over, she can move back here and consider her options."

"She picked out those tiles herself," Kelsey said.

"Oh Kelsey, she was thirteen years old! What did she know about style? This is going to be beautiful," Lynn smiled with satisfaction.

"And it's an awfully long commute from here out to her school." Kelsey knew whatever he said at this point may be useless.

"Well." The look on Lynn's face made Kelsey realize she meant to fix that as well.

Kelsey looked at his wife. "Lynn, it may be worthwhile to consider letting Brigid be who she wants to be."

Lynn slammed a palm on the counter. "We did not sacrifice and work and toil to have our only daughter live her life in a falling down cottage, teaching grimy children, and quietly starving to death in the arms of a farmer."

"Lynn, come on. You are being cruel."

"Kelsey." Her tone was final. "It's not happening." Lynn took a deep breath and turned back to the tile squares. She didn't see Kelsey glaring at her, or the blood that began to rise in his face.

Kelsey stood there, unable as usual to find the words to combat his wife's arguments. He thought of the expression on his daughter's face when she talked about her students, the blush that rose to her cheeks when she told him about Gabe. The new, confident set of her shoulders when he saw her at the nursing home, and the tender way she held her grand-father's hand. He looked at his wife and felt his blood begin to boil. Kelsey couldn't tell if he was angrier at his wife for her endless steamrolling or at himself for his inability to shield Brigid from the relentlessness that was Lynn. "Fine," he said finally. His icy tone made Lynn turn in surprise. "That's fine. You continue to control every little detail. Sell the cottage. Find her a job she doesn't want. Rip out the damn tiles. *Fine.*" He took a deep, shuddering breath and picked up one of the bland, creamy sample tiles. "You know, Lynn," he said. "This summer is the first time I've seen our daughter genuinely happy. The first time in a really long time." He swallowed hard. "Maybe, for once, you should just leave her alone." He slammed the tile onto the counter and strode out of the room.

Lynn was speechless. She caught a glimpse of her face in the mirror; it was the same pale shade as the tile Kelsey had been holding. She picked it up and saw it was cracked.

CHAPTER 40

The *Peninsula Press* was folded on the seat beside him as he drove over to Brigid's. They were supposed to go to dinner tonight. Gabe didn't know if she had seen this yet. If she had, she'd be devastated. But if she hadn't heard, he'd have to break it to her himself.

After the incident on Moher Point, Gabe started looking at rings. It was illogical, his mother would flip out, he hadn't even met her parents yet, and he didn't really have the money to buy one. But the look on her face that day, her strong hands pulling him up, the wet of her tears on his chest... there was something inevitable with them. He had had to go home later that night, after they spent the afternoon in her bed. When he arrived, Mikey's fever had broken, and his mother was simmering soup on the stove. Mikey gulped three bowls of the nourishing soup, and wolfed down half a loaf of bread slathered with butter.

They had talked on the phone that evening, for hours. Brigid told Gabe that she had marched through Graham's door and with strength she didn't know she had, ripped him to shreds. And then, Emma had come over later bearing both apologies. Apparently, Graham had been mortified, both in the failure of the sale and the upbraiding from Brigid. Gabe had wanted to come over, Brigid had insisted he stay at home with his mother and Mikey. When they finally hung up, Gabe had checked on his mother and brother. Both were sleeping peacefully in their beds. After quietly cleaning up the dishes, he walked out into the fields. Stretching in the summer air, he looked up. The sky was clear, billions of stars shone and sparkled. A sweet scent came off of the wild grasses and hit his nose. It was all going to be ok. He didn't know how, but he knew if he had Brigid, life would work out.

The next day when he walked into his shift at the marina, he saw the paper lying on the table. The story made Gabe sick to his stomach. The girl had been swimming in Domhnall Bay, sure. But it could have been Mikey.

Now, pulling up to Cairn Cottage, Gabe was unsure as to whether Brigid knew or not. And something in him wanted to rehearse the proposal; plan what he might do. But, isn't this how people proposed, over nice dinners?

He parked the truck and found her at the long kitchen table, facing the lake. Her curls were neatly arranged, and a pretty blue sundress hung from her shoulders. The cap sleeves hung limp, and her head was cradled in her hand. The gentle sound of waves blew through the windows.

Placing his hand on her shoulders, careful to avoid the slice of the scar beneath her dress, Gabe glanced over her shoulder. The paper was open to the story. Her skin seemed to leap toward his touch most days, but now she was as still as stone. Brigid sat like a statue in the rigid Windsor chair.

"She died."

Gabe stroked her back, squeezing her shoulder gently to get her to turn toward him. Getting no response, he bent and kissed the carefully arranged auburn curls. Still, she did not move.

Wrinkling his brow, Gabe lifted his hand from her back. He knelt beside her, looking up into her face. Expecting tears.

Her cheeks were dry and she stared out into the lake, yearning, wishing the waters there could release the pressure she felt in her head. Or, flood the house and swallow her whole.

"Did you know her?" He asked softly. Without taking her eyes off of the lake, she answered.

"Yes."

Gabe let out a sympathetic groan.

"Rosie was my student." At this, Gabe took her hand and wrapped it in both of his.

"I'm so sorry," he said.

They both looked at the paper. "I knew she had a heart condition, but I didn't know it was this severe." Brigid said.

"Kids have heart conditions?" asked Gabe.

"Anyone can be born with a congenital condition," Brigid snapped. When she looked at him, she saw confusion. "Congenital means born with. She had a heart condition she was born with." Irritation enveloped her. It was so much easier to feel angry than sad. Anger gave her armor. Sorrow left her raw. Right now, Gabe was the only person in the room. Without realizing it, she focused the barrel of her bottled emotions onto him.

"Did you read that in the paper?" Gabe asked.

"No, we got an email from the principal. The family reported that she contracted the bacteria in Domhnall Bay three weeks ago. The antibiotics couldn't fight it and it made its way into her heart. And it killed her."

The spite in her voice was unmistakable. Gabe didn't understand it. He would understand crying or crumpling. He wished she would just tumble into his arms. He understood his role as comforter, as the strong one. He had played it all of his life. But this stony woman who sat in the chair, hands deliberately limp, unwilling to accept his comfort. He didn't know what to do with her. His knees were screaming at this point. The old rug was worn and the wooden floor was hard. A persistent drip echoed from the big open living room. Not knowing what else to do, he patted her hand and stood up.

He saw a discoloring along the wooden frame of the big picture windows. A persistent trail of droplets marched down the frame and fell onto the carpet.

"Brigid?" He called back to the dining table. "Did you know this window is leaking?" She turned her head and looked, rolling her eyes.

"I'm sorry," he said, holding up his hands to defend himself from her angry glance. "I thought you would want to know. It's dripping all over the carpet."

"Yes," she said coldly. "I know." Brigid was aching inside, and the ache turned to irritation and anger at every little thing. How was she supposed to address a leaking window frame? And why, in God's name, would it choose to leak at this, of all times?

"Well, I could try to fix it. If you want."

She looked at him. Didn't he know that all she wanted was for him to wrap her up in his arms, cradle her head against his shoulder? Why was he suddenly so intent on home repairs?

"Sure," she said, dejectedly. The knowledge that she was being difficult gnawed at her, but the spite covered the sadness so well.

Gabe shook his head. "Do you have a ladder?" he asked, grateful for something to do, something to physically fix.

"Everything is in the garage," Brigid said, waving her arm in the direction of the outdoors.

Gabe gave her an appraising look. Who was this woman? He wanted so badly to hold her, carry her out of this big, lonely cottage and see her smile. But with her expression like a thundercloud, he was afraid to go near.

An hour and a half later, Gabe climbed down from the ladder and walked into the kitchen to wash his hands. He put away the bathroom grout and wood glue, and carried the ladder out to the garage. Giving a glance to Brigid, he found her curled up on the couch, buried in an old wool throw and the lace mantle. She had watched him the whole time and he was baffled at her lack of offer to help, or ability to make conversation. It was sad that the child had died; of course it was. But honestly, he felt she was overreacting. It wasn't as if this girl were a family member.

He found himself growing bitter, perhaps the whole dinner plan was ruined. What had changed so suddenly? Had he done something?

After a time, he finished the repair and gathered up the supplies. She still lay mute on the couch. "Ready to grab some dinner?" he said, unwilling to hide the irritation in his own voice.

"Sure," she said, pushing aside the blankets.

"I mean, we don't have to go if you don't want to," Gabe said.

"No, it's..." she met his eyes for the first time all evening. "I feel so guilty going to dinner knowing this news. You know?"

Well, he thought. It wasn't him. "I think that's the reason we should go. Because life is short, you know?" She looked stricken.

"I didn't mean that — I'm sorry. But it's for us to enjoy our time here. Let's try. Can we?"

"But am I being heartless? Enjoying my life, enjoying you?"

Gabe couldn't resist. "You're never heartless when you're enjoying me." She stared at him and the wind howling outside blew relentless in the silence. Finally, despite herself, she smiled. Walking up to him, she shyly threaded her hand through his arm. "I'm sad," she said. "And I'm sorry."

"I know." Gabe pulled her close and kissed her hair. It smelled like fresh peaches and mint. This woman... she was not simple. But she was worth it. "How about I go grab take-out and bring it back here?" When she nodded up at him, he saw her jaw clenching to prevent the tears from spilling out of her eyes. "Ok," he said. "Be back in twenty."

"Thank you," she said softly.

He kissed the top of her head and walked out of the door. The rain had stirred up the soil, and a fresh, pine scent pervaded the air.

CHAPTER 41

"Brigid, I would like to see you.
Would you come to dinner on Sunday?
It would be nice to get together."

The text from her mother came just as she was leaving the nursing home. Her heart felt literally pulled. A sudden, desperate desire to go home filled her. She could see herself falling into her mother's soft, plush, cream colored couch, gazing around a room where everything was shining and pristine. It felt easy. Calming. And she actually missed her mother. Missed sparring with her biting wit, even if she always lost. And her jovial father, with his compliments and big bear hugs. Although she found she couldn't quite forgive him for abandoning her at Cairn Cottage when her mother decided they were no longer speaking. She shook her head as she drove back to Cairn Cottage. It had been raining most of the week, but the drips had abated. And Gabe had repaired the leak.

Brigid sighed heavily and returned to the text message. She had plans with Gabe on Sunday — they were vague, but they mattered more. In a rush of defiance, she texted back.

"Would like to see you too.
I have plans with Gabe on Sunday.
Maybe another night?"

She slammed the phone charger into the bottom of the phone and tossed it onto the passenger seat. Rejection or rebuke was not something she had emotional space for today.

Throwing the car into drive, she skidded out of the parking lot and drove north, headed toward the mall. She needed to buy black. Black is what one wore to a funeral. Rosie's funeral. The thought made her nauseous.

A buzzing on the seat snapped her out of her swirling mood. Noting the empty road ahead of her, she reached over and picked up the phone.

"Gabe is welcome to join us."

What?! This was a shock. What trick did her mother have up her sleeve? She thought instantly of Gabe — what would he think? Would he want to? Would he hate her family?

Another, darker thought crept from in the recesses of her mind. Would he fit in?

* * *

She waited for Gabe that Saturday morning. He never turned up. She had not slept the night before. A child's funeral should not be a thing that exists. Brigid found that she hated everyone and everything and every blade of grass. Sitting in the pew, alone, she had raised her hand to her mouth to keep her tears from pouring out. The dreaded walk to the tiny coffin made her entire body get soaked with a cold sweat. Once there, she saw the deflated little body, devoid of color except for the lips, which some beleaguered mortician attempted to paint. No child's lips were orange. Unless they were painted with popsicle. The orange lipstick was a mockery of what could have been.

Without realizing it, she had held her body stiff throughout the service to keep her composure. When she embraced Rosie's devastated family in the receiving line, Brigid felt wooden and heavy with grief. By the time she made it back to Cairn Cottage, a migraine raged behind her left eye.

Gabe called and texted apologies. He had promised to go with her, and she had given him a weak acceptance. She told him it was going to be awful; he didn't need to go through that. And she didn't want him to think about how close Mikey had come to a similar fate. Nevertheless, he *had* promised to come. *She shouldn't go through this alone.* That's what he had said.

The morning of the funeral, Gabe said there had been an emergency on the farm. His mother needed help, Mikey couldn't do it. One of the horses had gotten loose, something. She didn't register it in her brain. Logically, Brigid knew that Gabe's hands were tied. Things happened in life. It was a true emergency.

A horse emergency.

As she walked into the funeral home alone, Brigid had felt her knees buckle. She had cherished a desperate hope that someone in her family would show up. Surely, her father. Granted, she hadn't been speaking much to them, certainly hadn't told them. But it was in the paper. They had to have known...

Even Emma, maybe David, would show up and sit beside her to bear witness. Things in the Stone Society had cooled down considerably since Brigid had confronted Graham about selling stones to the Sherlands, but she was still hunting the beaches, writing down interpretations, bringing dishes full of stones to the Websters for blessings. When she brought an entire bowl of black basalt to them, Emma raised her eyebrows and asked about it. Brigid had mentioned the death and her role in Rosie's life.

Surely, one of them would come. Brigid turned toward the double doors. Nothing.

She stood vigil alone.

That night, after confirming with Gabe that she had made it home and they were still planning to go to her parents' place for dinner, she silenced the device and plugged it in in her grandfather's empty bedroom, shutting the door. Her grief had turned to something ugly and pointed.

Methodically, she toppled every cairn in the house. Slammed the ceramic bowl on the counter, hoping it would break. Not quite daring enough to force it. Hating herself for her cowardice.

She lifted the lid on the box of the store-bought apple pie and stared at it. There was a perverse pleasure in refusing to eat it. It would never be as good as the one she remembered her mother making each July to bring to Cairn Cottage. Apple pie was one of the only things she ever baked, but it was incredible. Brigid stood in front of the open refrigerator, cherishing the growing ache in her belly until the light went off.

She was thirsty. It occurred to her to go out into the rain, kneel on the edge of the dock and scoop a glass of lake water. Swallow it in one gulp.

She poured a glass of whiskey instead. Downed the whole thing, had another and another... She went to lie on top of her bed with her face unwashed and her contact lenses burning through her eyes. It would be worse in the morning, she knew. She'd have to work to peel them out.

The cold wind blew through the open window and Brigid kicked the folded wool throw onto the floor. She felt the whiskey fire through her veins. She waited until the amber liquor flooded her head, making her feel like drowning. Brigid sank down. Gave in.

Gave up.

Morning came, harsh and cold. Brigid's mouth tasted like cotton soaked and dried in bile. A relentless pounding in her head sent a gunshot to her guts. She reeled up from the bed and down the stairs. Kneeling over the toilet, she retched, nothing more solid than anguish coming out.

When she had recovered her breath, she took stock. She was still here and the bathroom floor was dirty. Dirty with her sick and dirty from her laziness. Cleaning was another thing she would have to do. She sat on the grey linoleum tile. Little Rosie was still underground and she was still above it. It was still true that no one had come to sit with her at the funeral yesterday. Not her family, those people for whom blood was supposed to be thicker than water. Not her friends from the Stone Society who told her she was valid, who said they cherished and honored her. Not the man she loved. The man who said he loved her.

She wrapped her robe around her shivering limbs and stalked slowly through the cottage. She found Excedrin and forced herself to wash down two pills with a glass of orange juice. Struggling to find the will to make a pot of coffee, she had to stop and lean on the counter three times. When it finally was brewing, she sunk to the floor and leaned on the cupboards. The hard wood was no comfort.

Head in her hands, she thought of the looming dinner. It could easily be canceled, but then they would miss seeing her pain. Well, they would see her strength too. They would see that she didn't need them.

CHAPTER 42

They stepped into the towering foyer. Gabe gazed up at the silver, curving chandelier. It looked like an octopus dressed up for the prom.

Three pairs of cognac-colored leather shoes fit neatly on the shoe tray. Kelsey's loafers, sandals for the women. Gabe laid his sun-bleached canvas shoes beside them.

Hearing the door, Kelsey bounded into the hallway. A big friendly smile stretched across his face at the sight of his daughter. Manners made him pause before embracing Brigid, first shaking the younger man's hand with gusto.

"You must be Gabe! Welcome, welcome. We're so glad you're here."

Brigid doubted that, but she appreciated the platitude all the same.

She was enveloped in one of her father's bear hugs. Her arms were limp, refusing to return the embrace.

Kelsey pulled back and gave his daughter a quick appraisal. There was a storm hiding behind her usual vulnerable demeanor.

"Well!" He clapped his hands, attempting to erase the tension. "Let's go into the kitchen, shall we?" Striding through the hall ahead of the couple, Kelsey called over his shoulder, "What will you have to drink, son?"

"Just water, thanks," said Gabe. He surveyed the marble and polished wood kitchen. It sparkled aggressively. "I'm driving."

"Oh nonsense!" Kelsey's voice echoed loudly in the space. "You can certainly have one drink. What'll it be? We have beer, wine, any kind of liquor you'd like."

"Well," Gabe hesitated. He had a feeling he would need all of his wits about him tonight. Then again, a drink would take the edge off. "I'll take a beer please."

"Great! Sure, sure. I've got some Modelo right here or would you like an IPA?" Kelsey opened the fridge and rustled around.

"Modelo is fine, thank you."

Kelsey poured the beer into a tall glass. "Now Gabe. The rule in this house is that as your host, I pour you your first drink. After that, you're a friend, not a guest, so anything else you want, you get it yourself." Kelsey slapped him on the back as he handed him the glass.

It was good to know the rules, Gabe thought, trying not to roll his eyes. Maybe next he'd get a manual.

"Where is my mother?"

The men turned to Brigid. In her hand was a tumbler filled to the brim with scotch. Kelsey raised his eyebrows.

"She's finishing up getting dressed." Turning to Gabe he said, "I'm sorry. My wife will be down in a moment."

"Your wife is down now." All three turned toward the staircase. Lynn wore a white silk shirt and linen pants. They hung on her razor thin frame like armor.

Gabe looked at this woman, an older version of the girl he wanted to make his wife. Lynn looked so much like Brigid, but with all the softness chiseled out.

He stepped forward and stuck out his hand.

"It's nice to meet you, Mrs. Firth. Thanks for inviting me." Her skin was cool and dry, her fingers delicate. She gave a quick squeeze and pulled away.

"It's our pleasure, Gabe." Her smile did not reach her eyes.

Lynn forced herself to look at her daughter. She shouldn't have let Brigid pull away so much. Lynn had put so much pressure on her daughter that there was now a Sherland standing in her kitchen.

"Hello, Brigid," she said.

"Hi." The ice in Brigid's glass tinkled as she took a sip of the scotch.

Kelsey heard the terseness in Brigid's voice as the accusation that it was. These women, he thought, suppressing a deep sigh. He wished desperately that they would just embrace and they could go on to have a relaxing evening.

Gabe cleared his throat. "You have a great house, Mrs. Firth."

"Thank you. Yes, we enjoy it. Shall we eat?" Lynn asked. "The meat must be ready by now. I see you've gotten yourself a drink, Gabe."

Brigid wasn't quite sure what to do with herself. Normally, her job would be to pour water from the big crystal pitcher on the table. It had been her job since childhood. Now though, she felt like a guest. Like a stranger. And the whiskey was making her lightheaded. She decided just to sit down.

Lynn spooned the beef Bourguignon into bowls and fresh bread from the bakery was passed. Green salad with toasted pecans and dried cherries rested on chilled China plates.

Gabe waited politely, hands folded, for any prayers that might occur. None did.

Brigid picked at her roll, grateful for the simple comfort to her stomach, still queasy from her liquid dinner the night before.

Kelsey looked at his daughter. Something was definitely wrong. Deciding to step in, he said a little too loudly, "So Gabe — you run your family's farm?"

Gabe picked up his napkin from beside his plate and wiped his mouth. He cleared his throat. "I do, yes. We have a cherry tree orchard. And some animals."

"Do you have pigs on your farm?" Lynn asked, her expression neutral. Gabe looked up. He didn't understand where she was trying to lure him, but he understood the bait.

"No," he said. "Pigs are notoriously hard to care for. There's a difference between a crop farm and a livestock farm. We do have chickens for eggs though, and a few horses."

Lynn lifted her napkin from her lap slowly, deliberately.

Dabbed her lips. Lowered it to her lap again and looked directly at Gabe.

"The farm has been in your family for generations, am I correct?"

He nodded, his mouth full of salad. The tension in the room was strangling his ability to swallow. Deciding silence was worse than ill manners, Gabe answered through a mouthful.

"Yes." He coughed as a piece of food went down the wrong pipe. He glanced at Brigid for help. She didn't meet his eye. Gulping a mouthful of beer, he finally cleared the blockage from his throat.

Lynn was staring at him, eyebrow raised.

"I'm sorry," he said. "Yes. It's been in my family for several generations. We farm less of it now, about three acres."

"And why is that?" Lynn asked. "Did you make that decision when you took over the farm?"

"Ummm..." Gabe stammered as his thoughts swirled in his head. He really didn't want to tell this family the story of his father. He looked at Brigid for courage, but she was staring out the window, shredding her dinner roll. Why would she not look at him? Of course he felt horrible for missing the funeral; he had really fucked that one up. But she had invited him to her family's house and here he was, drowning. Was it too much to ask that she give him something, an acknowledgment of his existence? Screw it, he thought. This evening can't get much worse. Her family would just get to know the truth.

"My father left us when I was young," Gabe said without emotion. "I took over the farming with my mom. We had to sell a lot of acreage."

Kelsey ignored the glint of triumph in his wife's eyes. "I'm sorry, son," he said. "But good on you for keeping it going."

The older man's words were like a life raft. Gabe took another swig of beer. "Well. You do what you can. I work at Sunset Marina too. It helps make ends meet."

"Wow! You are a busy man," Kelsey said. "I'm impressed you have time for our Brigid here."

At this, Brigid gave a bitter snort that made everyone turn. Gabe blushed.

"Everything alright there, kiddo?" This time, Kelsey did not bother to hide a disapproving look.

"Life sure is busy busy," Brigid said. Even Lynn looked askance at her tone. "Those of us that still have life, that is."

Kelsey had no idea what was going on with his daughter, but he wasn't about to indulge this passive-aggressive behavior. Regardless of what his wife thought of this young man's family, Gabe was a guest in their home and deserved to be treated with kindness and respect. The rest of the evening passed in relative ease as Kelsey peppered Gabe with easy questions about farming, drawing him out and acknowledging his expertise. When Gabe offered to help with the dishes, Lynn asked a few more odd questions about his grandfather. Truthfully, Gabe didn't know too much about the man. He had died before Gabe was born. Ann certainly didn't talk too much about her father-in-law. Gabe answered the questions the best that he could.

At last, the evening was over. Brigid was pale and silent on the drive back to the Peninsula. Gabe was too drained from the evening to try.

She allowed a quick peck on her lips before she opened the car door. "Thank you for coming tonight," she said formally. He could see the hurt in her eyes, but there was too much angst in his own heart to reach out to her.

CHAPTER 43

He didn't stay over. Brigid didn't seem to protest or react when he broached his plan of heading home, so he kissed her on the cheek and left.

Rain was pouring when he pulled up to the farm. When he felt the sharpness of the droplets, he looked out at the orchard. A storm like this could rip the branches right off the trees.

He would have to check the damage in the morning, he thought, swearing under his breath. Ducking his head, he ran up the sagging steps of the porch. He'd check in with his mom before heading to his own small place across the fields.

Ann was sitting on the couch, glass of flat Coke at her side. She looked up in surprise.

"You came home, honey?" His mother's warm smile was unexpectedly comforting. Gabe nodded and moved to join her as she happily patted the cushion next to her on the couch. A box the size of a large novel laid on the coffee table, covered in lake stones. "What is that?" he asked. Picking it up, he saw cherry blossoms and bunches of fruit intertwined in an intricate pattern. It looked like a smaller version of the chest at the foot of Brigid's bed. He looked at his mother.

"You need to know about her family," Ann said without malice. Gabe set the box down on the table. Ann took his silence as an invitation.

"Gabe, she's a nice girl," Ann began. "A beautiful girl." He smiled. "I'm sure she's educated and I can understand why you say you love her."

"I do love her."

Ann held up her hand as a gesture of peace. "I get it. But

Gabe, you need to know what her family did to ours."

Gabe sighed heavily and collapsed into the couch cushions.

"The thing with the stones. What that Webster man was trying to sell me?" Ann took a long pull of her Coke, swallowing noisily. "Brigid's family and their friends have been doing this work with the stones for a very long time."

"She explained to me that it's not magic or anything," Gabe interrupted.

"I have no idea about that." Ann waved the notion away. "But it is a scam. You wonder why this house is falling apart? You wonder why your father became so angry that he left?" Tears brimmed at the corners of her eyes. Gabe instinctively pulled his shoulders back, preparing to shut a tantrum down with firm words. Ann took a deep, shuddering breath, gripping for calm.

"When your father was young, the Stone Society came to the farm. The farm was doing well — We were the most profitable farm on the Peninsula."

Gabe kept himself from rolling his eyes at her misplaced pride. She hadn't even known his father when the farm was successful. He forced himself to lower his shoulders. To listen.

"The most profitable," she was saying. "But three years of cold snaps and drought was causing a problem. Not just for us, but for everyone. The head of the Stone Society came to meet with your grandfather." Ann paused, giving her eldest a meaningful look. "The head of the Stone Society," Ann said, "Was Brigid's grandfather."

A memory of cradling the man's bleeding head shot into Gabe's mind. He shook it away and turned to his mother. "So what did he do? What happened?"

"The Stone Society proposed a program of soil enhancements. They were going to grind up the rocks they found in the lake and plant them under the new trees. They promised to bring the mineral-rich lake water from Big Omann Lake every day to water the orchards. It was a big job they proposed to do and they were asking for big money. And your grandfather..."

She looked out the window at the orchard, whipping in the storm. "Your grandfather paid it."

"Did it work?" Gabe asked.

Ann turned to him. "Your grandmother also paid for a blessing to be said," she said quietly. "Bought jewelry, this box here, all kinds of stone crap from their craftswomen. They wasted so much money." Gabe gazed down at the box, wondering how much it cost the family.

"And your grandpa," Ann said, sitting forward in the arm chair, "He always said when a good crop is yielded to you, you thank the earth by investing in next year's crop. He spent nearly every dollar they made preparing for the next year — that's how the farm grew so prosperous. But that meant he didn't have much put by."

"He didn't save any of it?" Gabe thought of their meager but persistently growing savings. He kept his family in old clothes, encouraging his mom to buy dented cans at the grocery store, bargain-basket produce, all in the name of building their savings account.

"He saved some," Ann said. "When the Stone Society came with their program, he gave every last dime of his savings to those people. And then your grandmother gave thousands more, on credit, buying the jewelry and the knick-knacks."

A sick feeling stirred in Gabe's stomach. This was his nightmare. They were barely scraping by as it was, and he took great pride in the months when all the bills were paid on time. Losing what little safety net they had was unthinkable.

Ann looked at him hard. "It didn't work. All that money your grandfather gave to the Stone Society was for nothing. There were several more blossoms on the trees, sure. But the gypsy moths came that year. Destroyed seventy percent of the crop."

The thought of gypsy moths made Gabe shiver. It was a blight that came upon the northern part of the state every decade or so. Nowadays there were chemicals to prevent the spread, but in years past... One day you would spot a gray silken wrapping covering a few branches, suffocating them. The next day, the entire tree would be engulfed, along with several of its neighbors. In a week, the grove would be consumed, the blossoms wrapped like mummies. Gypsy moths were the mortal fear of every farmer.

"So, what happened?" Gabe wasn't sure he wanted to hear the answer.

"What happened?" Ann's tone was incredulous. "We nearly went bankrupt! That winter, your great-grandfather sold off most of the equipment. He had a heart attack the following spring."

Gabe took that in. He always wondered why they were so under-equipped.

"Your grandfather's younger brother had to take over the farm. He was only twenty. He did his best, hiring local hands, transients. Paid them what he could. But he was a fiery guy. A lot like your dad." Gabe turned away at her smile.

"So he hit people?" Gabe asked, scorn dripping from his tone. Ann looked as if she'd been slapped.

"I don't know, Gabe," she said. "What I do know is that he got involved with Ruby Ayers. She was the girl tasked with bringing water to the farm, and she strutted her little self around seducing anyone in sight."

"Mom, how do you know anything about this Ruby Ayers?"

"Gabe, everyone knew. It was common knowledge. The Peninsula is a small community now, imagine how much smaller it was back then! This Ruby, she seduced your great Uncle Teddy, made him crazy. The families by this point really couldn't stand each other, but everyone hoped they'd just get married before she got knocked up."

"Mom." Her blatant language embarrassed him.

"Well, it's true. Everyone figured either the passion would burn out or they'd just kill each other, but in any case, it didn't happen."

"They didn't get married?" Gabe asked.

"Ruby died," Ann said flatly.

"What?"

"There was an accident..." Ann looked away.

"He hit her, I bet. Jesus." Gabe got up from the couch and paced. God, he hated the men of his blood.

"Teddy did not hit Ruby Ayers," Ann said firmly. "The spring after Teddy took over the farm, there was a bonfire out at the beach. They were drinking. She was drinking a lot. She fell into the fire."

Gabe stopped pacing and stared at his mother.

"Teddy pulled her out. Burned his arm doing it! But her face... her face was ruined. Melted, people said. Plastic surgery wasn't what it is now, obviously. And it really was sad. She was a beautiful girl. Anyway, two weeks later, she went sailing in a rainstorm with her pockets full of stones. Got out into the middle of the lake, tied the main sheet line around her neck and capsized the boat."

Shock pulled Gabe back down onto the couch. He put his head in his hands. Tonight had been stressful enough, he didn't know if he had the energy to digest his mother's story.

Ann bided her time, watching her son take in the truth. When he finally lifted his head, she reached over and cupped his strong jaw in her hand.

"There's something wrong with her family, Gabe," she said quietly. "Whether they believe they're helping or not, they scammed hard-working people out of their livelihood. Ruby was sick in the head. Taking your own life... that's unnatural. I sure hope I'm wrong, but who can tell if that sort of sickness doesn't run downstream? Who knows if your Brigid is like that, or will be at the first sign of trauma?" Gabe glared at his mother, but Brigid's cold, desolate depression shone fresh in his mind.

"And my sweet boy..." Ann took a breath for bravery, for this was the hardest truth of all. "You are a good man. You deserve an easy, simple life. All my prayers for you have been answered. But I want you to stay away from drama in your life. Stay away from people who are going to make you angry, who make you feel helpless. You are a good man; you're not like your father or like Teddy." Gabe looked up at his mother, tears in his eyes.

"Still," she said. "I want you to be careful. Their blood runs in you too."

CHAPTER 44

Lynn steered her beige Lexus onto the brick driveway. A sigh of satisfaction escaped her lips and the muscles around her eyes melted slightly. Plans to attend this party had been made in early June, and Lynn was frankly surprised that Brigid had agreed to go. Her daughter had arrived at the house in Domnhall Hills properly dressed, with tan shoulders and an unfamiliar cool demeanor.

"Have you been to Lighthouse Point lately, Brigid?"

Brigid turned to her mother. "No, I haven't had the chance."

"You look nice in your white," Lynn said.

Brigid blushed. "I had to go buy it. I didn't have any."

"Well, that's what money is for. Presenting yourself as well as you can." Lynn turned off the car. "Taking pride in yourself." She longed to brush an errant curl from Brigid's cheek. Instead, she stepped out of the car briskly and marched into the house. Over her shoulder, Lynn said, "I thought it would be nice for you to see the DeGroots. I believe several of your college friends will be here." Brigid was silent.

Diane DeGroot stood at the counter, pouring vodka tonics from a hand-blown glass pitcher. Delicate gold bracelets clinked gracefully on her slender wrist. Seeing the Firth women, she set the bulbous pitcher down with the grace of a ballerina.

"Lynn!" She embraced her friend delicately. "And Brigid!" Diane hugged the younger woman harder and then stepped back for an appraisal, holding onto her shoulders. "My goodness, you are so slender!" Approval dripped from her voice. Lynn took a second look at her daughter and found she agreed.

Her daughter did look very svelte these days. The softness that had always rounded her figure had disappeared. In fact, her cheekbones sliced the air with a prominence that made Lynn very proud.

"Well ladies," Diane said, "Let me get you a drink."

"Oh, just water for me, thanks," said Lynn.

Diane pulled a bottle of Perrier out of the stainless-steel refrigerator. She turned to Brigid.

"Easier on the waistline." Diane winked at Lynn as she handed her the glass. Turning to Brigid, she asked, "And for you, honey?"

"I'll take the harder stuff, please."

Lynn clenched her teeth at her daughter's choice.

"Oh, to be young and full of metabolism," Diane said. "The kids are outside, Brigid. Why don't you go say hello? I'm sure Isolde will be thrilled to see you."

Brigid was sure Isolde would not be thrilled. But she smiled past the "kids" comment and waltzed across the marble-encased kitchen, drink in hand. She suppressed an eye roll as she took note of the catered spread that no one would eat. Its crowning glory was a five-story cake made of caramelized spun sugar in the shape of a sand castle.

She threw open the French doors. The sun's heat felt like a slap in the face after the chill of the air conditioning. Young men and women in white littered the immaculate emerald grounds. False and flirtatious laughter floated on the breeze to her ears. Lowering her sunglasses from their perch in her hair and placing them on her face, Brigid indulged in the eye roll. The DeGroots claimed they could trace their family tree back to the Dutch settlers. They were the only people here who truly belonged in this life they had created for themselves. The rest were just cosplaying.

Brigid smelled citronella candles, lit to drive the mosquitoes away. She assumed it was also a ploy to mask the rancid scent of decay coming off of the lake. Even the air was perfumed in falsehood.

As she glowered into the horizon, she noticed a darkening of the sky out to the north. A sudden chill in the air wafted over the lake.

CHAPTER 45

Chelsea noticed Brigid standing on the olive-stained deck. She was surprised to see her at this party. After Matt dumped her, Brigid had slunk away from their group. And Chelsea had briefly dated Matt. He had been fun, but clearly still hung up on that girl. Honestly, Chelsea didn't understand the appeal. For some reason, Matt wanted that girl-next-door wide-eyed doe look.

Chelsea decided to investigate. The party was staid and she was aching for some fresh amusement. "Hey lady," Chelsea called out in sing-song voice. "What have you been up to?"

"Not much," Brigid said. Her stomach felt like lead. A northern wind blew over the deck and Chelsea crossed her arms over her chest protectively. Brigid wracked her mind for something interesting to say to this woman, but intimidation plundered her mind until it was a barren shell. Chelsea waited, eyebrows raised.

"I love your outfit," Chelsea finally said. "Jeans are not ideal for bocce," she gave a once-over, laughing, "But your ass looks great." Brigid tried to smile. It came out like a grimace. "Seriously, you look thinner since college!" Chelsea exclaimed, bestowing her highest compliment. "What have you been doing?"

Brigid shrugged. "Relaxing. Living out at my grandpa's cottage. Drinking whiskey."

"Whiskey?" Chelsea raised her eyebrows. "Bad ass."

Brigid took a slug of the drink.

"So tell me about where you're staying! I had no idea your grandparents had a lake home! What lake is it on?"

The fact that Chelsea's entire demeanor changed when she assumed that Brigid had something valuable made Brigid want to slap her.

"It's on Little Owrawn Lake. It's not a big place, just a small cottage. We call it Cairn Cottage."

"Oh my God, like Care Bears? That's hilarious!" Chelsea lightly touched Brigid's arm with a practiced gesture. They were best friends now, apparently.

Brigid suddenly realized Chelsea and her ilk were pretty, but vapid. If Lynn had been standing here listening, she would've given one of her trademark eyebrow raises, quickly and silently dismissing Chelsea as a worthless twit.

"No," Brigid explained. "Cairn. C-a-i-r-n. It's Gaelic. It means pillar."

"Oh wow, does the cottage have pillars? The wineries always do — I think they look amazing."

Brigid turned back to the house. Maybe her mother would make one of her legendary Irish exits, leaving far before the end of the party without a fuss, and take Brigid with her. She could see Lynn standing, water in hand, chatting happily with Mrs. DeGroot. No such luck.

"Unfortunately there are no pillars on the cottage," Brigid said. "My grandfather and his friends used to collect stones and stack them. The stones have different symbols. They interpreted the symbols and stacked the tower, saving it as a blessing for whoever might need one." Chelsea narrowed her carefully-made-up eyes in confusion.

"Wow. That's...a lot." Chelsea said.

Brigid nodded. "It is."

Why had she ever been scared of this person? She was dumb. Beautiful, but dumb. And mean. And grasping. She contemplated going further, telling Chelsea that her grandfather and his friends believed that she, Brigid, had special powers. That she could possibly communicate with the Divine and influence the weather. That their Stone Society could actually find and sell Chelsea a stone that would shine through her personality. In fact, there were stones in her pocket. They could conduct a Ceremony right here.

Glancing back at Lynn, Brigid thought the better of this idea. It was unnecessary to make a scene. A smirk crossed Brigid's face. Chelsea's spirit stone would probably be a slab of concrete.

"Chelsea, it's been nice talking to you."

Chelsea stepped back. She could usually read her fellow women like a book, and clearly, this one had a secret she was unwilling to tell. She plastered on a smile. "You too, girl!"

Brigid swallowed the rest of her drink, set the glass on the teak table, and stepped onto the lawn.

God, hours of small talk was ahead of her. These people had nothing to say except sharp-tongued observations of popular culture. She had read more books than all of them, studied harder than any of them, and yet she had been terrified to talk to any of them because they would cut her down to size. They were like well-groomed, cruel giraffes. She climbed the gentle incline of the dune, wrapping her arms around her body to shield herself from the relentless north wind.

"Same old gang, huh?" The familiar voice froze her insides. Brigid found she couldn't move. "Do you own this dune, ma'am, or can I come up?" She forced herself to turn to him. Despite herself, she smiled at his neat blonde curls.

"Matt," she said. The word was full of all of her doubts, all of her insecurities. "How are you?"

"I'm doing great. You look gorgeous. I know I'm probably not allowed to say that, but hey. I'm a lawyer now. I'm duty-bound to speak the truth."

"Isn't that exactly what lawyers don't do?" Brigid responded tartly.

Matt gave an approving glance at her wit. Five years had changed her. Where had this confidence, this little sexy body been in college? He went in for a hug. "It's so good to see you," he said. His tanned face oozed charm.

Ignoring the red flag of discomfort in her stomach, Brigid allowed herself to be folded into his arms. The scent of expensive cologne emanated from his polo shirt. She felt his carefully sculpted frame under the light material. There was no softness there, all hard muscle.

Stepping out of the hug, she said, "It's good to see you too." He caught a blush rising in her cheeks and instantly remembered why he had dated her for so long. His friends had teased him and certainly some of the ladies in their group had given him the opportunity to make different decisions, but this vulnerability was her charm. This woman had no idea the effect she had on people. When she was comfortable, her massive intelligence came out to play, but it was her honesty that made him want to capture her.

Gazing at her in the sunlight, he couldn't quite remember why he had given her up. She crossed her arms against a gust of wind and he remembered. That vulnerability, that honesty; she had needed too much from him. The deep conversations she insisted on having all the time were exhausting. She had a hard time relaxing, making small talk in a crowd.

Well, let's see if any of that has changed, he thought. Looking the way she did, it might be worth seeing if she deserved a second chance. The trick was to keep her on her toes, keep her intimidated, so she leaned into him for approval.

"So, what are you doing alone up on this dune?" Matt asked. "Contemplating life?" She gave him a wry glance. "Or maybe death. Because you looked like a tragic heroine — waiting to jump into the water. I felt like I had to come save you before you did anything drastic."

Brigid heard the flirt and recognized his savior complex. She decided to string him on a little.

"The conversation out there is a little..."

"Vapid?" he asked, smiling knowingly. She nodded. "Well, let me make you a deal. You don't swim into the middle of Big Bay and drown, and I will save you by getting you another drink."

She laughed. The sound sparkled in the air. Matt was momentarily stunned by the shimmering of the sunlight on the water.

"Come on, let's go," he said. "I'll rustle you up a whiskey."

They walked together back down the dune and across the lawn, Matt with his hands in his pockets, Brigid's auburn curls escaping their confinement and swirling in the breeze.

CHAPTER 46

Matt gave a smug nod and a tight wave to the assemblage on the bocce court. Brigid remembered how it felt to be recognized next to him. Instant approval from a crowd whose most sacred value was status. Men who had only briefly registered her arrival now waved to her with well-mannered lust in their eyes. Women assessed, registered her as a threat, and plastered on fake, friendly smiles. She shook her head. The sham was exhausting.

Having procured a whiskey for Brigid and charmed her mother, Matt decided to sweeten the chase. He would convince Brigid to join the bocce playing. See if she had gotten any better at having fun.

Brigid took a long pull of her drink and decided to join Matt on the bocce field when he asked her. There was subsequent hair tucking and twirling from the single women as the two of them approached the court. Those women who had won the race to the altar and married right out of college sat apart, grasping at their well-dressed children. For a brief, stomach-sinking moment, Brigid saw what might have been her fate. She turned to Matt. His hand was resting warmly on her lower back. She flinched slightly and he pulled an apologetic face.

"Sorry. Old habit."

"Brigid!" A deep voice echoed, with a little too much excitement behind it to be authentic. "Oh my God — it's been so long since we've seen you!" Matt's old roommate Cal had her in a tight embrace, his tanned arms flexing out of habit. She pulled back quickly and smiled up at him.

"You look great," he exclaimed. "What have you been up to? "A tastefully manicured hand slid through Cal's arm. Brigid saw a tiny, beautifully sculpted figure with bottled-blond hair pulled into a pert ponytail.

"Hi Brie." Brigid modified her tone higher and brighter to address Cal's longtime girlfriend. She noticed the whopper sparking on her hand. "Oh wow, are you guys engaged?"

Realizing that Brigid was no threat to the handsome, chiseled-jaw man who was hers by right, Brie softened and smiled. "Yes!" she squealed." Cal proposed this spring — it's going to be a Christmas wedding."

Of course they would steal a holiday for their personal celebration. Brigid turned an eye roll into a tight, fake grin. It was amazing to be able to see through all of this now. When she wasn't seeking Matt's approval, Brigid found she didn't really care how these people felt about her. It was incredibly freeing. She decided in that moment to play a little game.

She would play the part to the edge of ridicule. She wanted to see if Matt could tell the real Brigid from the fake Brigid. If anyone could. Echoing Brie's vocal fry, she exclaimed "Oh my god, Brie! That's so exciting! Tell me all about the wedding!!" Brie heard none of the sarcasm behind Brigid's tone, and Brigid soon found herself pulled into a lawn chair, listening with false rapture to Brie's wedding planning soliloquy.

Sometime between bespoke bridesmaid dresses and gluten-free wedding cakes, Matt emerged and handed her another whiskey with a wink on the side.

"Thank you," she said. She sipped the drink gratefully and then coughed. It was significantly stronger. She threw a rueful look up at Matt, who shrugged unapologetically.

"Want to play bocce, ladies? We need a few more people on the team." Brigid stiffened. She was not eager to embarrass herself on the playing field. Athletics had never been her strong suit. "Come on, it'll be fun," Matt urged. "I'll help you."

Brigid was amused at his gallantry. When they were dating, she was simply expected to entertain herself at these types of gatherings, only appearing at his side to cheer him on or look pretty.

My God, Brigid thought. All I ever needed was not to care. Not to care what other people thought or what they thought they saw in me.

As they approached the court, Brigid turned to Matt. "You know I have no idea how to play bocce, right?"

"I figured," he said, laughing. "Let's have some practice lessons."

Matt smiled and picked up a spare ball on the pitch. Handing it to Brigid, he demonstrated how to swing the arm back and slide it across the grass. She imitated his movement and he watched her appraisingly, in complete control of his own reaction. He gave only athletic commentary, but Brigid could feel him judging the whole of her body. His hands were circling hers to teach her the exact way to toss the ball when Brie trotted back toward them, phone in hand.

"You guys, I'm taking pictures for the party! Candace came up with the cutest hashtags: #boccebabes and #boccebros!" Matt's hand immediately slid up Brigid's arm and draped across her shoulders. The casual intrusion surprised her so much that she turned her face up to his as a blush flew across her cheeks. He looked down at her, grinning from ear to ear.

"So cute!" Brie squealed. "That's totally going on the socials!" Brigid felt the weight of Matt's arm across her shoulders, his tanned fingers pressing possessively into her skin. Her mind, foggy with grief and too much whiskey, suddenly cleared. She was winning this game of fraudulence, but at what cost? The relationships she could build with Matt, or with anyone on this lawn were as worthless to her now as her true self was to them. It was time to go.

She broke away from Matt and set the ball back on the soft green grass. "I've got to leave," she said, voice like lead.

"Oh, hon, really?" he asked, aware that several people were watching. "We were having fun."

"This isn't fun," Brigid said. "Not to me. And besides, I'm

seeing someone —I really don't think this is appropriate."

"Appropriate, no fun, come on," Matt said, twisting his face into a cajoling grin. He wrapped his arm around her again, intending to turn her from what was becoming a rapt audience. This time, she stepped away forcefully.

"This is not what I want." Brigid was aware of how loud she sounded and forced herself to keep his gaze. Matt could sense eyes on him from across the field, hear the whispers that were already starting.

"I really thought you'd changed," he hissed at her from behind a smiling facade. "How stupid of me. I thought maybe you could be chill for once. Relax. Be fun. But clearly you're no different."

"That's where you're wrong," Brigid said as storm clouds began to gather over the water. "I am different."

CHAPTER 47

His eyes blurred with anger and he felt a familiar tightness in his chest. He felt his breathing get shallow and quick. He wanted so badly to just smash something, anything. Was it all a damn lie? Slamming the phone down on the table, he shook his head, teeth clenched, fighting through the desire for violence. He hated this part of himself, this unwanted legacy from his father and his great uncle. Pacing the small living room of the tiny house he had built for himself a few years ago on the edge of the property, he let out a yell that started from the base of his throat and squeezed through his vocal cords, emitting through the wall. It didn't release the tension.

There was a knock at the door and he looked up to see Mikey peeping in through the screen door.

"Gabe?" he asked. The fear in his little brother's voice humiliated him and he sat heavily on the couch, rubbing his eyes. The anger that coursed through his veins sunk into a sullen weight.

"Mikey, buddy come in. Do you need something right now?" Gabe asked, forcing himself to sound calm.

"Naw," Mikey said, kicking the stray sock that lay on the floor. "I just wanted to come see you. I heard you yell."

"I've got a lot going on in my head right now, Mikey," said Gabe. "I'm ok, I just need some privacy. Ok?"

Mikey met his brother's eyes for a brave moment, and quickly lowered his own again.

"Ok."

Gabe stared at his clenched fists, waiting to hear Mikey's light footsteps step out of the door and down the porch stairs.

Mikey just stood there.

"What?" said Gabe, to the floor.

"I'm going," said Mikey. "Umm... how is Brigid?" The boy's voice brightened as he said her name. Gabe sighed heavily and met his brother's eyes.

"She's fine. She's going to be fine." Gabe heaved himself up from the couch. There was no point in any of this. It would be easier just to get it over with and shove the pain down. He stood up and patted Mikey gently on the back, guiding him back toward the main house.

CHAPTER 48

Phone in hand, Gabe willed himself to be calm as he entered Cairn Cottage. His stomach was in knots. When he saw the picture that afternoon, he felt like he had been shot. Anger and fury, those familiar friends, swiftly covered his heartbreak until it became encased in steel.

Brigid flew down the stairs to meet him, all smiles and innocence. His resolve stuttered. How could she do this? How could she act like everything was normal? She bounced into his arms and he wanted to hold her, to kiss her, but the anger made him stand stiff. She pulled back, setting her glass of water on the counter.

"What's wrong?" she asked, worry marking her face. Her naked concern made him ache, but anger massaged that away too.

"How is your ex?" he asked.

"My ex?"

Shit, Gabe thought. He meant to let her explain first, but you know what? Screw it. Truth was truth. He had the picture right here, there was no need for this charade.

"Gabe, what are you talking about?" Brigid took a step back, scanning his face and folding her arms protectively over her chest.

"I saw you were at this party with your ex yesterday. Every-one in white, playing cricket or something."

"Bocce," she said flatly.

Gabe raised his eyebrows. "So you do know what I'm talking about."

"I have no idea what you're talking about regarding my ex," Brigid said icily. Jesus, Gabe thought. She's a perfect imitation of her mother and she doesn't even know it. "I did get dragged to a party the other day and I haven't had the chance to tell you about it."

"Dragged?" asked Gabe. "You look like you were having an okay time in this picture."

He opened his phone and swiped to the post in question. Brigid looked at it and her neck grew flushed. This wasn't great. Matt had his arm thrown around her and she was looking up at him, all rosy-cheeked. She had seen Brie's post and had declined to untag herself. Her grief over Rosie was still raw and the despair she had felt when Gabe left her alone at the funeral two days ago made her want to hurt him back. Looking into Gabe's face, she realized she'd succeeded. She could see now how ridiculous it was and his anger couldn't hide the dismay and fear in his eyes.

She took a breath and looked up at Gabe and sighed. "My mother dragged me to this party at Mrs. DeGroot's house."

Gabe wrinkled his nose and nodded. "I must have missed my invitation." He knew he sounded childish, but somehow the words massaged his hurt.

"You don't even know them, why would they have invited you?" Her words echoed in the silent air. The wind over the lake blew a damp wind through the open windows. Everything Gabe feared hung in those words. Swallowing hard, he finally spoke. "No, no, I get it. The party was definitely too fancy for the likes of me."

"Gabe, that is not what I meant." Brigid wanted to reach out to him, but was afraid to give in. She wasn't ready to acquiesce.

"It's ok, Brigid." A finality snuck into his tone. "Your mom made it pretty clear at that dinner that I'm not quite the type she wants you to associate with."

"Gabe, *I'm* not the type my mom wants to associate with."

The vulnerability on her face softened him for a moment, but something else took over. "No, she brought you — I'm sorry, 'dragged' you to this party where you clearly had a miserable time." He looked pointedly at the picture. Hurting her made his own hurt disappear and for once, he needed that relief. It was like a war: if the enemy was wounded, he would be protected. He continued. "So what happened with this ex – what's his name? Brock?"

"His name is Matt. Matt Opher."

"Ahhh, of course, of the Opher family. They own half of Domhnall Hills. Your mother must be thrilled."

"What is wrong with you?" Brigid was shouting now. "This is ridiculous. Nothing happened. He brought me a couple of drinks and we all played bocce. It was no big deal." At the drink part, Gabe snorted and began pacing the kitchen. "Oh my God, Gabe, it's a drink! Anyone would bring anyone else a drink at the party. We didn't kiss!"

"Oh well thank God for that!" He threw his hands up in mock relief. "Thank you for condescending not to kiss your wonderful ex. Just drinking with him, hugging him, grinning and posing with him and all the fancy people of Domhnall Hills, at some party that your purported boyfriend was too trashy to attend." His voice was raised now and his arms were flexed. When he had argued with girlfriends past, they had cowed at this point, batted their eyes, cried. It was the crying that always snapped him out of it. That's what made him different from his father. When his father got angry, tears fueled his fists.

Brigid stood tall, shoulders back. There was no way she was going to let him speak to her like this. The picture was bad, and she should have called Gabe and told him, untagged herself, anything, but he had left her alone at the funeral. Broken his own promises. "I don't know what the hell your problem is right now, but I'm telling you that nothing happened," she said. Her dry eyes flashed. "I've told you that I love you and I do. My mom invited me to a party with family friends and I didn't think to invite you because you weren't invited. Are you so insecure that you need to be at my side every second?" The words were cruel and untrue, but they tasted delicious on her tongue. He wheeled around to face her, shock and fury on his face. "Oh, you know what? I'm wrong," she escalated. "You don't need to be at my side every second. At the funeral of a child, of my <u>student</u>, when I needed you most, you were more than happy to leave me alone. It's amazing I didn't pick up a guy there! I could have had a sordid affair, right under your nose." She was taking it way too far, but there was no point in stopping now.

Gabe felt like he had been stabbed. "Brigid, I told you, we had an emergency on the farm."

"Oh, and how do I know you weren't just making out with one of your high school girlfriends?" Brigid heard her voice echo through the cottage.

"Brigid, grow up!" Gabe yelled, his voice overpowering hers, trying to make her stop. He couldn't take it, the guilt of what he had failed to do, who he failed to be for her was making his heart split in two. "We had a real emergency in my real life at the real farm. You're acting like a spoiled brat."

"Excuse me? A spoiled brat? I work and pay my own bills and take care of this house."

"You were given everything you needed to start your career and had your education paid for and you live in your grandfather's house." At the last sentence she looked as if she had been slapped. He knew he should stop but he had to twist the knife one more time. "And, even if I'm not good enough for your family, for the stupid bocce party, you've been more than happy to let me take you out for dinners and lunches and give you gifts. Even the sail on your damn boat is a gift from me. You've been living off of my largesse for most of the summer." Embarrassment flooded her face and the look calmed his anger. He took a deep, shuddering breath. He needed her to stop — stop yelling, stop talking, stop naming his failures. He looked at her face and couldn't read it. "Brigid, I love you, but you have no idea what reality is."

Color drained from her face and her eyes went dark. "I have no idea about reality?" Her voice rose above the claps of thunder on the lake. "I grew up in a household with astronomical expectations and met them all. I teach kids who don't have enough at home, who don't have the resources they need at school. I care for all of them and get them to learn too, every student that comes in my door. I got thrown into taking care of my grandfather who I barely knew before this summer. I loved and grieved a little kid who was beaten..." Brigid stopped and swallowed hard to stop the tears from flowing. "I had to count the bruises when she was alive and I saw them under the makeup they put on her when she died. I did all of this alone." Accusation bored into him and he found he couldn't meet her eyes. "I'm adult enough to trust the man I love when he says he's taking care of some goddamn horse emergency and not accuse him of having an affair. And I know the difference between having a stupid picture posted and cheating on my boyfriend. You obviously do not. You come in here, accusing me of some childish idiocy out of your own sense of insecurity!" Gabe flinched and turned away from her. "I didn't call you insecure, I didn't call you not enough — you did! Maybe my start was easier than yours. Maybe that's true. But I love you for all that you are, good and bad and I thought you loved me for everything I am, good and bad. I'm walking through my life trying to do the best I can with what I have and who I am. And you dare to come in here and tell me what I don't know? That I have no idea what reality is? Fuck you!"

Gabe hadn't been spoken to like that in years. In fact, only one other person in his life had raised his voice to him, cussed him, screamed a tirade. He suddenly became that young kid in the farmhouse kitchen, trying to deflect the string of profanity and blows that were about to rain down on him and those he loved. "What did you say to me?" Gabe's voice was white hot; his face beat red.

Brigid's was icy pale. Throwing her shoulders back, she said, "I said. Fuck. YOU."

CHAPTER 49

It happened really fast. The explosion of shattered glass deflated them both. Brigid felt a wetness on her cheeks and reached up gingerly, wiping away water that had splashed onto her face. She was frozen, and something deep in her gut made her search silently for the nearest exit. She could probably make it out the back door and scream loud enough for the neighbors to hear. She couldn't believe he had done something like that. Had she really fallen in love with a man who would do this? He had accused her of being unfaithful, but when the glass shattered onto the floor, she was the one who felt betrayed.

Gabe felt his hand hang limp at his side. What in the hell just happened? Instinct kicked in and he just wanted to deflect, to distract, to stop the screaming. Without a thought, he had yelled "STOP" and slammed the counter with his fists. Her water glass had tumbled to the floor and smashed into pieces. Broken glass was everywhere. Forcing himself to raise his eyes to hers, Gabe nearly wept in relief to see that none of the broken shards had hit her. Then he saw a sparkle on her collarbone. A sizeable shard lay flat on her bare skin. She stood stock still, looking past him. Looking at the lake. If he moved carefully, he could lift it off before the sharp edge cut her. He took a tentative step forward, reaching out his hand.

She jumped backwards and pulled her arms up protectively, scrunching her shoulders. Instantly, a tiny crimson river snaked down her neck and between her breasts, sinking underneath her shirt.

"Brigid." His voice was choked.

Keeping her wide eyes on him, she reached up and felt the cut, lifted the glass off her skin. The garbage can was behind him. She didn't want to go any nearer, so she held the shard in her hand.

Realizing what she was doing, that she was afraid, he stepped back, ceding the space. Slowly, he reached out his hand, trying to show her that he was no threat. "I'll throw it away."

Not taking her eyes off of his movements, she placed the piece of broken glass in his palm. Her blood was warm on his skin. His chest seized up. Looking up at her still bleeding neck, he wished the glass had pierced him directly in his throat, and that he was already dead.

The truth was, he was very much alive. And in that life, reality had spoken truth. The truth was that he had shown the famous Sherland temper. The temper that had inspired his father to make Gabe's own skin bleed. The temper that had broken his mother's arm while she held his little brother. The temper that surged through his great uncle so fiercely that it led to the death of Brigid's great aunt. The temper made him storm into this house, yelling at this woman he loved, accusing her of something much more than the action that annoyed him. The temper that urged him to slam his fists and cause the glass to smash all over the floor. The temper that resulted in the woman he loved to be standing in front of him, bleeding. The truth tore him apart. The sob that had lodged in his throat escaped him and he swiped the tears from his eyes.

Brigid stared at him in stunned silence. She didn't know how to deal with any of this. All her life she had shouldered harsh expectations, cruel words, passive-aggressive arguments that she always lost. Matt had objectified her, belittled her in subtle, insidious ways. She had come out to Cairn Cottage to escape all of that, but she had no idea how to deal with this passionate outburst of truth.

Gabe's...or her own.

She needed to leave before the dramatic apology came. She couldn't bear that. The feelings that coursed through her were too much to handle and now the familiar shooting pain from her shoulder brought her back to reality. She forced herself to concentrate on facts. The first aid kit was underneath the bathroom sink and she backed up slowly, still facing him. Once she reached the bathroom, she locked the door. The harsh electric light illuminated her pale face. Lack of sleep and appetite had painted dark circles under her eyes. She lifted the towel, still wet from lake water, and dabbed at her bleeding skin. The cool dampness felt good against the cut. There was a faint stench from the towel, but she was sure it was from her laziness in leaving it hanging. Gingerly, she examined the wound. It was very shallow and it was clear even to her untrained eye that no stitches would be needed. She reached under the sink and lifted out the first aid kit. The tube of antibiotic ointment was empty, but Brigid shrugged. The glass hadn't been dirty. Placing a bandage over the gash, Brigid realized there was nothing left to do but return to the kitchen.

Every muscle in her body was tense as she walked back into the kitchen. Gabe was nowhere to be found, but every shard of glass was removed from the floor. She saw the old broom leaning up against the pantry.

Gabe stepped out of the tiny alcove where the garbage was kept. He shook the last remnants out of the dustpan and wiped it thoroughly with a wet paper towel. He felt completely broken, but strangely calm. At least now he could stop wondering. The question of whether he carried the legendary Sherland temper had been answered, but there was one more thing he could control. There was no part of him that wanted to go through with it, but when he turned to see her standing there, he knew it was the only good choice. The bloody bandage on her throat sealed his fate.

He shoved his strong hands in his pockets and took a deep, shuddering breath. When he spoke, his voice was low and calm. "Brigid, you have no idea how sorry I am. Are you ok?"

"I'm fine." Her icy tone was meant to protect the fear she still felt by what he had done, but it didn't fool him. Hearing that sliver of fear in her voice broke his heart when he didn't think it could break any further.

"Ok," he continued. "I... I completely lost my temper."

"Yes, you did." Her voice trembled, "And so did I."

"Brigid, I know I have no right to ask you for anything right now, but I'm going to. Please just let me speak." In response, she folded her arms across her chest. The movement made the small cut sting and she flinched. But it was important that he finish this. For her sake.

"We clearly have a lot of differences," he began, forcing the emotion from his voice. "Our families are different; we were raised very differently. It's pretty obvious to me that I'm not the man your family dreamed of for you."

She moved to speak and he put his hands up to stop her words. "That's okay. It's really okay. I can understand their perspective. And I think if you're very honest with yourself, life on the farm is not what you always dreamed of."

Brigid felt her throat seize up. She had, in fact, been dreaming frequently of life on the farm. In her imagination, she saw them making a very happy life between the lake and the farm, or perhaps on a little piece of land of their very own. She could teach, he could run the farm. They could make a life. Maybe not the life her mother dreamed for her, full of money and prestige, but a life that was simple. A life that was happy. A life where she could breathe, where she could be content. She had been afraid to hope that he felt the same way. That he had wanted a life that was so simple, so calm. She knew she wasn't as cute and bouncy and flirty as the many women he usually dated. She didn't allow herself to imagine that he would actually choose her. A reticent woman. A complicated woman.

She wasn't naive; she had played the battles out in her head, convincing her mother and drawing boundaries with his. But she felt sure they could get through it all if they stuck together. To hear him imply that he had been dreaming this same dream made her want to weep with happiness.

Gabe paused and looked at her for a response. He saw her turn her face away, swallowing the tears that pooled behind her eyes. He took that for an unspoken agreement to his words. Before last night, he had allowed himself to hope that her love for him was strong enough to break through the conventions of society and the angst it would create with their families. Judging from her reaction, it was not. He swallowed again.

"Brigid," he said, very gently. "I think it's best if we take a break."

She turned to him. She had been trying to find a way to tell him that she did dream of life on the farm, life together, but the lump in her throat was preventing her from speaking. She wanted to tell him that she loved him, more than she imagined possible. But, then, what had he just said? A break? She was unable to stop the tears as they flowed down her face.

"Honestly, I love you, Brigid," Gabe said. "I'm in love with you. But we haven't really known each other that long, if you think about it. Right?" he asked. She wiped away the tears. He wanted so badly to take the two steps closer to her, wipe the tender, tired skin under her eyes, wrap her shivering, hurt body up in his arms and tell her he was lying. Tell her he was so sorry and he loved her more than anything. Tell her he had a velvet box with a diamond ring tucked inside the glovebox of his truck. He looked down at the floor and saw one small piece of glass. It lay on the floor between them.

No, he thought. He wouldn't risk it. He would not ever risk her safety against even the most remote possibility of his temper. Not ever again.

"Our whole relationship has been unusual, if you think about it." His body relaxed as he made his case. He could convince her to let him go. "The boy on the cliff, Graham trying to sell your stuff to my mom, the day where you sang to the fish and saved it?"

He forced a laugh about the fish, attempting to add humor to this horrible situation. The sound of his laughter broke her heart. That day at the lake, when she talked about her scar, it was one of the most affirming days of her life. For the first time in her life, she did not feel grotesque. She had felt whole. To hear him say it had been trivial, just another silly thing to laugh at, made her world turn upside down. In that moment, Brigid realized she could either collapse into sobs under the weight of her sorrow, or build a fortress of anger and pride around herself. Lynn had always told her to save her pride above all else. Tears and begging were things she just couldn't do. The best thing would be to let him finish saying his piece, pretend he was not killing her inside, and let him leave. If he would laugh at her, he didn't understand her. Maybe her family was right. Maybe everything she had felt, once again, was wrong.

He watched her stand tall, longing for her sweet voice to tell him to stop talking. He ached to hear her call him out on his lies, say that she loved him too.

She held his stare in silence.

He sighed. It was better this way. He would hurt, but she wouldn't. She would live the life she was meant to live and find some happiness. It was time to finish the job. "Brigid, I've read that relationships that start really dramatically are hard to keep going when the real world steps in. I feel like maybe that's us. I think it would be best if we stop seeing each other."

Brigid felt empty. Gabe waited, unnerved by her silence. He began to babble, anything to fill the cavern between them. "You can call or text me anytime," he said. "We can still be friends, and I can still help you with the cottage or boats or whatever." He could still help her with boats? He sounded like an idiot. The best thing to do was leave, before he made a fool of himself.

Without another glance at Brigid, he turned and walked out the front door, toward the lake. There was no possible way he could have crossed near her, toward the back door, wrapped her in a goodbye hug. If he touched her, he could never bear to say goodbye. If he stayed with her, his touch might draw blood.

And that could never happen.

The screen doors slammed shut. Brigid stood as still as a statue. She listened to his quick footsteps across the sandy path, heard the door of the truck slam shut, heard the engine turn on. When the sound of the tires rolling down the driveway reached her ears, Brigid collapsed to the floor. Her tired body was wracked in sobs.

The wind blew around Gabe, and he heard the groaning of the masts of the sailboats and the call of the birds. He sped down the driveway, leaving before he lost his courage. As he turned down the road, it started to rain.

CHAPTER 50

The Stone Society was supposed to meet that evening, but Brigid did not arrive at the Websters as planned. When the clock passed eight and she still hadn't appeared, Emma walked down the path to check on their Diviner. Phone calls and texts had gone unanswered for days. Graham blamed her youth, her flightiness, but David and Emma had concern behind their eyes. Opening an umbrella into the biting rain, Emma hurried to Cairn Cottage. Emma could hear Shannon's old Edith Piaf record on the stereo, mournful and moaning through the air. Somebody must be home.

Emma knocked and called out, with no answer. It occurred to her that the young man's truck might be in the driveway. A small part of her hoped that Brigid had simply forgotten about their meeting in favor of a date. Emma walked around to check, but knew that she would find no truck, no man. The beating rain told her so.

Emma eased the screen door open, removing her shoes. She was taken aback by the mess. Plates full of untouched toast were scattered on the counter along with cups of cold coffee and empty tumblers with a tiny pool of brown liquid at the bottom. Emma lifted one to her nose. Whiskey.

"Brigid," she said, firmly. The young woman turned slowly from her perch in the big arm chair facing the lake. Emma saw stones on the table, stones in Brigid's hand. She crossed the room and waited for Brigid to rise, hug her, invite her to sit. Brigid merely glanced at her, and turned back to the rain.

"Did I miss our meeting?"

"You did," Emma said, disarmed by Brigid's flat and dusty

289

voice. "Dinner was at six. It is now nearly eight."

"I apologize." There was no remorse in Brigid's words.

"Brigid, I accept your apology, but it's important that we have these meetings once a week. If we're going to do this properly."

"What are we doing?" Brigid said, watching the rain fall down the window panes.

Emma let out an exasperated sigh. "Brigid, we have explained this to you several times now."

"Don't condescend to me. I'm not a child."

Emma stared at her. What had happened to the sweet, pliable young woman? Morgan's pixie granddaughter, this softer version of Emma's best friend?

Brigid turned in her chair to face the older woman. "I mean, what are we doing? Coming together with happy thoughts, with prayers? Trying to heal our community by stacking stones just the right way?"

"Well, yes," Emma stammered. "That's exactly it. There's much more behind it, but that's the essence."

"Doesn't seem to be working," Brigid said, turning back to the rain.

Emma felt a drip on her cheek and looked up in alarm. The rain was leaking between the window pane and the roof. She noticed an odd patch on one side, but the rain was still getting in. In fact, droplets were falling inside the window.

"Brigid," she said. "What is going on?"

Brigid ached to cry, but there didn't seem to be any tears left. No strength. And so, there was no release. Brigid felt anchored down. Hollow. She looked at Emma. It was amazing that no one could see this, no one understand that she was breaking apart. No one had come to Rosie's funeral with her. No one acknowledged her pain. Gabe had dropped her like there had been nothing between them. Like it was easy. Maybe he would get pleasure at the memory of dating a Domhnall Hills girl. Maybe that's all she was. Through her haze, a thought began to form.

Maybe she just didn't matter very much at all.

Now this old woman, this shyster priestess, came to admonish her in her own home. Brigid stopped and corrected at herself. Cairn Cottage wasn't her home. It belonged to her grandfather. Another mark of her uselessness. Brigid, who had only ever done what everyone asked her to do. She followed the rules. She toed the line. And now, after missing one meeting, this woman saw her as worthless. Emma, who pretended to be the long-lost mother figure, who had no idea what was really going on in Brigid's life. Brigid didn't even feel angry. She just felt tired and empty.

Emma's voice pulled her back into the room. "This leak is a problem," she was saying. "Brigid, are you listening to me? Can you hear me?" Emma reached out and touched the younger woman's arm. Brigid's skin was freezing under her hand.

Startled at the touch, Brigid yanked her arm away, and Emma saw the bandage.

"Gabe fixed it," Brigid said.

"Gabe — your boyfriend?" asked Emma, trying to get a better look at the wound.

"No," answered Brigid.

"What Gabe then? Did you call a repairman or something?"

"Gabe isn't my boyfriend. We broke up."

"Oh honey, I'm sorry." Emma leaned down to embrace Brigid, but was stopped when Brigid pushed her hands out.

"Don't," she said in a strangled voice. "Emma. Please don't."

Emma sat down, startled by the scent of the younger woman's hair. It had clearly not been washed in days. She took another look around the cottage. The whole situation seemed painfully familiar. "Brigid, I'm very worried about you," she said. "You've every right to keep house how you want to, but it's a mess in here. Honey, you look like you haven't eaten or slept in days." Brigid raised her eyebrows in response. Emma continued. "I had a glance at that roof line when I was walking over here. That roof is badly in need of repair. And now I see the rain is leaking inside the house?"

Brigid couldn't believe she could feel crushed further, but Emma was managing to do it. Why couldn't she deal with this? These responsibilities would be easy for anyone else — what was wrong with her that she couldn't tackle them? Some small remaining part of her knew it would be a simple thing to call a repair person, but she found she didn't have the energy to walk to the phone.

Yesterday, she had walked to the Big Lake as soon as she arose, walking along the shoreline, eyes blurry, gathering every stone that struck her fancy. Until she reached the cliff face. Looking up, Brigid realized she must have walked at least eight miles. Her body felt wasted, but there was no other choice but to turn back. She couldn't even call anyone for a ride. She had deliberately isolated herself by leaving her phone at home. Determined to punish herself further, she had not lightened her burden by leaving even one stone behind on the trip back. When she returned to Cairn Cottage, she had placed the stones on the side table and lay down on the couch. The thought of a soft blanket easing her sunburnt, starved body was repulsive. Before she collapsed into sleep, she took the soft lace mantle and tossed it onto the floor behind the couch.

She had awoken midmorning, disoriented and shivering. Unable to face the prospect of making coffee, she poured a whiskey and water, and sipped gently, until the pain faded into a gentle ache that she could curl herself around.

"I may have missed the meeting, but I collected the stones." She gestured to the cairns stacked on the table. There must have been twenty of them. Next to the cairns was a pad of legal paper scrawled with writing. She gestured to Emma. "I'm not completely useless," she said.

Emma looked at the younger woman for a long moment. There was something truly amiss here. She looked at the piles of stones, all stacked so carefully. "There are many beautiful basalts here"" she said, noting the endless towers of midnight black and ochre blue stones. It was rare to find a basalt along the big lake shoreline that did have not a shimmering pearl quartz band, but Brigid had found a score of them. It was incredible, really. She assessed the towers for the usual pink and coral stones that Brigid favored, and the banded silky agates. In Brigid's collections, there was always a rainbow-colored speckled granite or two, and of course the requisite spotted corals that were unique to the area. She found none of these. Alongside the dark basalts there were only misshapen, flat gray stones.

"What are those?" Emma asked.

"The stones I found," Brigid said. "Basalt. A lot of basalt. And the gray ones. I'm not sure what they are."

"Those are limestone. Not exactly what we use in the Stone Society, Brigid. They are not a precious mineral."

"These are the stones I wanted to collect."

Emma let out a sigh. "So, what did you interpret from them?"

"Nothing."

"Brigid..."

"I mean, my interpretation was literally nothing. The stones are plain and flat. No detail, no sparkle, no uniqueness except for their shape. A pile of different shapes compiled of nothing meaningful. They do nothing. They are, for the purposes of what the Stone Society does, nothing."

"I see." Emma pursed her lips "And how does it help us?"

"It doesn't matter."

Emma clenched her jaw. Memories of Morgan's "sinking spells," as his late wife called them, washed over her. Shannon would rush over to Emma's in tears. Morgan was not responding, she'd say. He had been sleeping for days. Morgan wouldn't speak unless it was dripping with sarcasm. Morgan had been cruel to the baby. Back then, his attitude had seemed selfish, unnecessary. Emma was of the generation who still considered this type of moping to be an indulgence. The attitude Brigid was displaying made her furious, but she felt sorry for the unkempt, heartbroken young woman all the same.

"Brigid, honey," she began again, in a cajoling tone. "I think you need to get up. Get something to eat — I can bring you a plate. Take a shower maybe. It would feel good. We can worry about our meeting another day. Besides, I don't believe we're going to get much out of your piles of limestone."

Brigid turned to her coldly. "I didn't ask for advice. Or instructions." Emma stared back. "Emma, I'm sorry to say this, but I don't know you that well. And you don't really know me."

"Of course I know you!" Emma sputtered.

"No, you don't," Brigid said, holding up her hand. The pain of searing off another relationship was delicious. If she was truly alone, at least she couldn't be hurt. "You may have known me as a baby, but we've known each other for adults for only a season. I appreciate you telling me about your society, and including me."

"Including you? Brigid, you're our Diviner. You were born to be part of this Society!"

The young woman shook her matted head. "I don't really know what that is."

"Brigid, this is nonsense," Emma said, no longer afraid to let her anger show. "You have immense intuition. Creativity. You can see what others can't see. You can feel what others feel in a way that is deeply comforting, deeply important. You sent the rain away — you have the ability to connect with the spiritual and natural world — with the Great Beyond! I saw it the night of the Ceremony and I watched you the night on the dock. You thought you were alone, but I saw you. You have a gift. A gift that I would kill for — that all of us would die for!"

"What happened with the rain is a coincidence." Brigid sat straight in the chair. "And as for the other night, I don't know what that was. It was nothing." It was less complicated to deny the voice she had heard, the cradle of love and peace she had felt, the dialogue with Something so much greater than herself, Something that felt like the essence of everything.

"It was not nothing," Emma said firmly.

Brigid stood. "Emma, I've asked this before and I'll ask it again. What do you want from me?"

"I want you to believe in this." Emma gestured to the air, the stones, the rain pounding on the windows and dripping down from the frame. Brigid only gazed at her. "If you refuse to believe in the stones, you must understand reality when you see it right in your face. With Gabe." At his name, Brigid flinched. Emma saw she had struck a chord. Continuing, she said, "The lakes are being poisoned by bacteria. And the weather is unsuitable for the season. Unsuitable for the farmers. You believe these facts, yes?"

"Yes," said Brigid. "What do you want me to do about it?"

"We'd like you to change it." Emma said this like it was the most logical thing in the world. "You have the power, if you would only use it."

Brigid shook her head. "No."

"You are making a mistake, young lady. You are throwing away something extremely important."

"It doesn't matter."

Emma could not stand this. If she stayed one more second, she would let loose everything she had always wanted to say to Morgan, and to Lynn. The words of truth that she wanted so badly to say to Brigid. If she said another word, she wasn't sure she would be able to stop. She walked toward the door and picked up her umbrella.

"Emma?" Standing with her hand on the screen door, she turned to Brigid. "What you do, what I do — it doesn't matter," the younger woman said. "Nothing matters."

Emma felt an awful chill come over her body as the wind whipped through the house. Looking at the disheveled, pale younger woman, she could feel only anger. Opening the umbrella, she stepped out into the rain.

CHAPTER 51

Graham had never heard his wife exclaim in such high-handed tones. Emma ranted about the unkempt house, the ugly gray stones, the smell. She only quieted when Graham poured her a large glass of wine. David also talked her down, counseled patience. As always.

Patience, it was always patience with that man. As if patience had gotten them anywhere. Finally, exhausted with effort that accomplished nothing, Emma cursed the cold and climbed the stairs to bed.

Graham poured a whiskey and considered. He felt this display of backbone on Brigid's part was encouraging. Diviners needed to have independence and confidence. Perhaps taking on his wife was Brigid's first step to leading. What that girl needed was nature, he thought. More time connected with the natural world. If that farmer had left her, so much the better — she would have more time to concentrate on her work with the Stone Society. He knew from watching Morgan and Shannon that heartbreak often led to the most meaningful interpretations of the stones. Brigid could work through this. She could use it. Love, Graham felt, was overrated. Sometimes pain was the path that people needed to walk.

He picked up the newspaper. Clean-up of the waters had begun in earnest. The pollution was hammering tourism, which was having a detrimental effect on the local economy. As he suspected, as soon as the pocketbooks of Domhnall Hills were threatened, the problem found a solution.

The creak of the masts groaned through the closed windows. How he longed to go sailing. Alas, Emma forbade him. It was ridiculous, really. The pollution level in Little Owrawn Lake was low — as long as he didn't swallow water or go into the lake with a gaping wound, a person would be fine. The DNR was beginning to dump the neutralizing chemicals into their lake already. He wondered when the last time was that Brigid had gone for a sail. The feel and rush of harnessing the wind, steering the craft so that it cut through the waves — it was one of Graham's greatest pleasures.

Finishing his whiskey, he set the glass down. In the morning, he would make a pot of coffee, make up a plate of food and walk it over to Cairn Cottage.

CHAPTER 52

The morning dawned cold and rainy. A look at the lake level caused Graham to raise his eyebrows sharply. If this precipitation did not abate, there would be a bigger problem. Carrying the tray up the stairs, he gently opened the door to the master bedroom. Placing the coffee on the bedside table beside his wife, he kissed her wrinkled brow and set the tray on the bed. She smiled at the unexpected treat. He had made a hearty omelet, with buttered toast and fruit on the side. Graham set the newspaper down beside her, folded to the page explaining the steps that were being taken to address the pollution in the lake. Before she could rope him into a conversation, he excused himself, pleading the need to tidy up the kitchen.

Once downstairs, he wrapped the second plate in foil and poured the coffee into a mug. Thinking again, he set everything down, put on his rain slicker, and took the entire pot and the wrapped plate quietly out of the door.

The faint putrid smell hit him first. Since the young woman had been here, Cairn Cottage looked the best it had looked in decades. She had done much work those first few weeks cleaning grime from surfaces. Since then, she kept things mostly tidy, sand off the floor, stains wiped up. Today, there were dishes everywhere and the smell of mildew hit his nose. He could smell something else too, and it shocked him to identify it: the feral smell of unwashed body. Morgan used to get like this. Shannon called them his sinking spells. After she died, Graham found Cairn Cottage in a similar state; he and Emma had taken charge, cleaning the place. Emma had brought food every night and Graham...well, Graham had thrown his friend in the lake. He had challenged Morgan to a sailing match, and proceeded to compete so aggressively that the boats capsized and both men ended up soaked. The shock of the cold water and the adrenaline release of the competition seemed to knock Morgan out of his sunken mood enough that he began to care for himself again.

Graham had no doubt that was what was needed here as well. Determined not to react to the sights and smells of Cairn Cottage, he scanned the room and found Brigid lying on the sofa in her clothes, uncovered by a blanket, eyes to the rain. He marched over to the couch with the plate and set it on the coffee table.

Seeing the older man in the room conjured up the smallest hint of embarrassment and modesty from her flattened soul. She grabbed a few pillows to cover her bare legs. Graham picked up a wool blanket that hung folded on a chair and tossed it to her.

"Sit up, young lady," he said, not unkindly. "Eat." She slowly sat up and stared at him.

"I'm not really ready for company," she said in an empty voice.

"I'm not company," Graham said. "I am your grandfather's best friend. I'm family."

"I'm not really ready for that either," muttered Brigid, uncovering the plate. The scent of the warm, filling food went straight to her belly. A visceral hunger shot through her body, and despite herself, she wanted to eat.

Graham returned with the pot of coffee and a mug. "Drink that up." Ruffling through the detritus on the table, he found an old magazine to use as a coaster and set the coffee pot down. "Drink as much as you can. You need some strength."

Brigid found she was ravenous, but forced herself to eat slowly. It had been several days since she ate much of anything and each morsel of food met an uncertain fate when it hit her stomach. The coffee tasted rich and delicious. She sipped slowly, the warmth slipping down her throat.

"Cream or sugar?" Graham called from the kitchen. Brigid shook her head, mouth full. She listened to him whistle as he scrubbed the counter and set her numerous glasses and plates in the dishwasher. She began to feel a little warmer.

Returning to Brigid's side, he was pleased to see that the plate was clean and the coffee pot was half empty.

"May I?" he asked. She nodded and he lifted the plate to the kitchen.

"Thank you," she said softly.

"You are quite welcome!" Graham answered brightly, happy that his plan was working. The next part would be a bit trickier. All those years ago, Graham was able to tell Morgan flat out that he stunk, and needed to throw his dirty body into the lake. The sentiment, however, would be a bit tricker to convey to a young woman. Best stick to sailing.

Graham sat across from her in the big arm chair. "Now then," he said, slapping his knees. "I understand you've had a bit of a rough week. Emma tells me your young man has ahhhh... that you are no longer seeing the Sherland gentleman." Brigid nodded almost imperceptibly. He held up his palm to the ice that began to frost her expression to mask her tears. "No no. Affairs of the heart are not my business. I didn't come to discuss that. Nor did I come to discuss the Stone Society."

"Graham, I need to tell you what I told Emma," Brigid began.

Graham shook his head firmly. "Talk is not what is needed right now. I didn't come to discuss these things with you. I came because you are the beloved granddaughter of my best friend. And you need a little help." Brigid blushed. "Your grandfather," he continued, "Felt much the same way when your grandmother died. Had a bit of a sinking spell. Emma and I popped over, brought him some food, some nourishing things to drink." At this, he eyed the bottle of Jameson meaningfully. Brigid looked away. "But one of the most important things Morgan did to rise from his sinking spell was to get some exercise. Blow off some steam in the fresh cleansing air."

The subtle hint had been taken. Brigid brushed her limp oily locks from her face. "I went on a long hike the other day," she said.

"That's good, that's good," said Graham. "What used to help your grandpa though, is a good sail."

"Yes, but we can't go sailing right now with the bacteria level the way it is," Brigid said, sinking back into the couch.

"Oh no! They're cleaning it up!" Graham pushed a copy of the newspaper across the table and folded it to the front page.

Efforts Have Begun to Clear Up Lakes

Graham tapped his thumb against the chair as she read the article. Finishing, she looked up at him. "Yes, but have they measured the bacteria levels? Done any tests?"

Graham ruffled. "I'm sure they have; I'm quite sure they have. In fact, I saw the DNR out in their boat the other day."

"On this lake?" Brigid asked.

"Certainly! They were testing the water. I could see them from my dock. I'm sure it's fine. I mean, you don't want to go swimming perhaps, but you'll be in the boat! You're a good enough of a seaman, I presume?"

A faint smile played at the corner of her mouth. "Seawoman."

Graham clapped his meaty hands. "There it is then. Trust me, Brigid. Go out for a nice sail! Bring a towel to dry off your legs if it makes you feel better. And when you've felt the wind in your hair, felt the freedom of the waves, come in, take a nice long hot shower, and give us a shout. I'm sure Emma will bring something delicious down for you."

"I think I've made Emma angry," Brigid said.

"Oh no," Graham said, sweeping his arms out to erase the very idea. "She might have been a bit tiffed for a moment, but she completely understands."

"It was kind of her to make me breakfast," Brigid said softly.

"It really was delicious."

"Well," Graham said, who couldn't help puffing up just a bit. "If I'm being completely truthful, that was me."

Brigid's surprised smile made him glow from the inside out. He rose, gathered the coffee pot and glanced out of the window.

"Look at that," he said. "It's already clearing up a little bit! I'd check the radar, but if you have a break in the rain, I think you should go."

"It's a little dangerous without a spotter," Brigid said, her voice cracking on the last word.

"I'll watch out for you!" said Graham. "I don't have much on the docket today — I'll look for that sunrise sail." That smile again. So arresting. That young man must be a fool to have let her go, Graham thought. With a crisp nod, he headed out of the screen door and down the sandy path.

Brigid sighed deeply. The good food and strong coffee were warming her from the inside. It might feel good to go for a sail. She looked out the window. The landscape was encased in fog, and she could feel the chill in the air. The rain, however, had stopped. She might as well go.

CHAPTER 53

Brigid walked onto the dock, walking determinedly past the life jacket resting on the chair. The water was too cold for summer, but she waded out to the sailboat. The hull bucked and strained at the old line that clipped it to the anchor. It would be difficult to even raise the sail. Brigid yanked on the line and the boat swung wildly as the rising sail gave it power. Brigid had to leap out of the way, her sinews tight with the effort of holding the line. Wrapping it around one wrist, she waded closer to the little vessel and twisted it around the cleat. Releasing the boat from the anchor, she pushed the boat into the wind and leapt onto the stern.

The lake water felt pure as it splashed her aching skin. She sailed straight into the middle of the lake. The other side of the lake was clear as a mirror, but Brigid knew if she made it there and saw her reflection, she would be becalmed. Trapped. She'd have to jump out of the boat, grab it by the bow, and swim across the lake to the cottage.

Brigid wrenched the rudder to the right. The boat whipped around, obeying Brigid's direction. The heavy metal boom that held the sail parallel to the hull of the boat came swinging around, ready to catch the wind and take Brigid where she wanted to go. A thunderclap snapped her eyes skyward and before she could duck under the swinging boom, a shooting pain slammed through her forehead. Tumbling off of the hull, her leg scraped sharply against the boat and she let go of the line holding the sail.

Brigid heard the tipping of the boat first. On instinct, she began to swim away, but found she was stuck.

The loose line had snagged on her bracelet.

Brigid dove down to avoid the mast as it slammed into the lake. Her lungs screamed for air as she shook her wrist to try and free it from the line. It wouldn't budge. She tried to see the snag through the murky water, trying to save the bracelet. Her vision became hazy and she realized she was losing consciousness. She yanked hard. Nothing. Her mouth opened against her will. She swallowed water.

A violent pull brought daylight into her vision as the movement of the boat took her above the surface of the water. Choking, she gulped oxygen before being pulled under again by a swell.

Naked fear of survival was beginning to take over. Brigid knew if she did not free herself soon, she would meet a brutal end. She kicked as hard as she could, propelling herself above the surface. Gulping one giant breath, she swam under the hull. Eyes wide open, the water stung her pupils as she located the cleat. Unwound the line. The rope that bound her to the ship tumbled out long and loose underneath the waves. Brigid resurfaced and grasped the slimy underside of the hull with both arms. Sucking oxygen desperately, she lay still for several moments, indifferent to the moldy grime on her skin.

Something was flowing from her leg; she could feel it pulsing into the water. She looked down and her eyes rested on the deep gash. The pain was sudden and incredible. By the sinking sensation in her body, she knew she was losing blood at an alarming rate. Squirming out of her sweatshirt, she gingerly tied it around her leg. God, it hurt. The bleeding seemed to subside slightly now that there was a barrier between it and the open arms of the water.

Panic began to set in. She was at least half a mile from shore and a fresh thunderstorm was pelting the lake with rain. She knew there was no way she could swim back with her leg bleeding, but perhaps she had enough strength to right the sailboat. Throwing her arms over the hull, she planted her feet on the centerboard and bore down, but her injured leg could no longer hold any weight. With a cry of pain, she fell off of the hull and back into the water. She felt her body begin to shiver. The water in the middle of the lake was cold, but Brigid knew this was the beginnings of shock. She had to get back.

She began to perform slow frog strokes, kicking with her uninjured leg. The wounded limb she let hang, suspended in the water. She breathed deep, steadily, in and out of her nose. Bolts of terror shot up her chest, and she used every ounce of self-control to simply keep moving forward.

In.

Out.

Swim.

In.

Out.

Swim.

Mortality was making itself felt in the exhaustion of her chest and arms, and the consistent pulsing of the wound. Her concentration was broken by a low anguished wail, and screams from the shoreline. Shifting her eyes toward the sound, she saw Emma out on the end of the dock, hands at her face. Graham stood next to her, hands cupped around his mouth, calling into the storm.

Looking again, she saw David lope out onto the dock, and begin to strip off his sweatshirt. She wanted to call out but knew she couldn't afford the exertion. As she swam, she was slightly aware of tears streaming down her face. She had danced with death, challenged it. Her anger had flowed out.

Now it just seemed useless. Brigid found her arms weakening as the life she knew she wanted faded into a haziness and soft light.

CHAPTER 54

Emma collapsed in anguish, keening on the dock. "Not again," she wailed. "Not again."

"I should never have encouraged her to go — she's a good sailor but the wind is too strong," Graham wrung his hands and called out again. "Brigid! Brigid!"

Her husband's words snapped Emma out of her stupor. "YOU told her to sail in this? You BASTARD!!" Never in his life had his wife spoken to him like this. It brought Graham to tears.

"You fool," said David muttered. Scanning the horizon for any sign of life, he splashed into the water, pulling his own canoe from its perch on the shoreline. The rain obscured his vision, but there didn't seem to be any figure near the overturned sailboat. He leapt into the boat and began to paddle out, knowing that if she was underwater, it was already too late.

A movement near the Ayers raft caught his eye. Something flopped onto the wooden planks and at first, he thought it was a diving bird. Turning his canoe toward the raft, he saw another movement.

Paddling hard through the rain, David saw that the figure lying prone on the raft began to take shape of a woman.

A splash near the canoe startled David. Graham was swimming toward the raft with a sure, strong breast stroke. Together, they lifted Brigid into the canoe and paddled fiercely toward the shore.

"I hurt my leg," she said, in a small voice.

David and Graham looked, appalled. Blood was seeping through the sweatshirt bound around her leg.

"I'll get her in the house — you call an ambulance," said Graham. David hustled off of the dock, not stopping to wipe down his legs.

"Can you walk, my girl?" asked Graham. Brigid nodded, and hopped in, leaning heavily onto Graham's arms. Emma met them at the pathway. Ducking under Brigid's other shoulder, she helped Graham drag her into the house.

"The EMTs say to bind her leg. Use a sheet or something." called David over his shoulder. "They'll be here in 10 minutes."

Graham carefully set Brigid in the chair at the head of the table.

"I'm kind of dizzy," said Brigid. Her voice sounded faint in her ears.

Emma looked at her in alarm. "I know, honey," she said. "Try to stay awake for us, ok?" Brigid nodded.

Graham grabbed the lace mantle from the chair and stared at Emma who was gingerly examining the wounded leg. "I couldn't find a sheet," he said.

Emma raised her eyebrows at the object hanging from Graham's dripping arm. "This is perfect." Emma hoped desperately that this mantle would keep the girl's blood from pouring out of her body. An image of wrapping it around Brigid's lifeless face burst into her mind and made her stomach jump into her throat.

Emma quickly folded the mantle into a thin strip and wrapped it tightly around the gash. Looking up at Brigid, she saw the young woman's eyes trying to focus.

"Talk to her, Graham," Emma said urgently, under her breath. "Keep her talking." Graham immediately began chattering with Brigid, asking her innocuous questions about the boat, sailing, Gabe. When he saw that a question irritated her enough to get a response, he redoubled that line of inquiry.

The ambulance actually arrived in seven minutes, but it seemed like an eternity. Graham was whipped into a frenzy by the time the EMTs arrived, and had to be sternly reprimanded and told to stand aside. They bound Brigid to the stretcher, their soothing, proficient voices surrounding her. One of the EMTs unwrapped her leg and placed the mantle into Emma's outstretched hand. Gazing at the wound, he said, "This isn't great — she'll need stitches and maybe a blood transfusion. We'll get her fixed up." The doctor raised his eyebrows at Emma. "Are you her grandmother?"

"My grandmother is dead," answered Brigid. "My grandfather is trapped."

"Trapped?" asked the EMT. "Was he with you on the sailboat?"

"No, she's confused," Graham cut in. "Her grandfather is suffering from a stroke and paralysis in a nursing home." The EMT looked hard at Brigid. "We need to get her to the ER." He turned again to the crowd of elderly people.

"We'll get her all fixed up," the EMT repeated. "You folks should shower with lye soap — the lakes have a bad bacterium these days. Watch for symptoms if any of you have any cuts."

"We know," said David. "Thank you."

"Take care of our girl," called Emma. The EMTs nodded and shut the doors.

As they drove away, Emma turned to the men.

"We need to call Lynn."

CHAPTER 55

Brigid awoke encased in a creamy summer duvet. The mattress under her body was firm but supple, molding to her frame in delicious luxury. An air conditioner hummed in background. Brigid shook the cobwebs from her tired mind.

Why was she at her parents' house? She reached up to rub her eyes and a deep pain wrenched through her right leg. Bile rose in her throat as the memories washed over her. The sailing accident. The hospital.

The stitches.

Brigid groaned. Those were going to be ugly. A mix of fury and despair flooded her heart. Another scar. But then, Gabe didn't mind the scar on her back. Maybe he would love this one too. A wave of tenderness was quickly replaced with sinking feelings and the drowning wave of loss as Brigid remembered that Gabe was gone.

Tears, sudden and cruel as a summer storm, washed down her cheeks as she counted her losses. Her leg was mauled by a scar of her own making. Little Rosie was dead. Her grandfather was unreachable. And Gabe, the man she loved beyond logic, had said he loved her too. Just not quite enough.

A firm tap was heard at the door.

"Brigid?" Lynn asked, opening the door. Her voice was gentler than her daughter was used to and it made her tears flow even freer. Lynn bucked back.

"Brigid, please don't cry. Tears are not necessary." Lynn set the tray down on the dresser and stood at the edge of the bed. Her jaw clenched at the disconsolate expression on her daughter's face. She looked away. Passing tissue, she said, "Wipe your face, Brigid. Your eyes will swell." Brigid's baleful look made Lynn wince with guilt. She cleared her throat. "Brigid, it's been a bad summer. I understand that. But you're going to be okay. Your leg will heal." She reached out carefully and gave three firm pats on her daughter's good leg. "And everything else..."

Brigid looked up at her mother. Lynn sighed. "Everything else will fade away with time. I know it's hard to see that now, but it will." Brigid clamped her jaw hard to prevent another flood of tears. The ingrained pattern to please Lynn kicked in, and Brigid knew her own sorrow would cause Lynn to feel awkward. Awkwardness was a feeling that her mother would quickly turn to rancor.

Lynn rose and brought the ebony tray to the bed. "Sit up, honey." Brigid hauled herself up heavily, babying her leg as Lynn balanced the tray on one palm while she reached around her daughter's back to adjust the pillows. Once she had settled her daughter, Lynn pulled a chair to the side of the bed.

"I've loved... people." Lynn brushed her hands on her trousers, pushing away invisible dust. "My love wasn't appreciated, or returned. I do know how that is. How you must be feeling. The best thing is to just... put up a wall. A fortress. Protect yourself from people who don't value you. And when you love them, yes, that's hard."

Brigid looked at the curtains, lifeless against the closed window. Lynn kept talking. "Don't let those feelings of rejection or inadequacy take root. They are not who you are. Find something to do, something to be. The world will value you for what you do, Brigid. Not the love you pour into people who don't deserve it."

Lynn cleared her throat again. That was enough. Her daughter was hurt, she needed to rest. To recover.

"Eat, Brigid." Lynn stood up and walked to the door. Brigid was too tired to be cowed anymore. She threw her mother a smirk and gave a sarcastic salute. The quick movement hurt her leg again and she winced. Lynn's heart ached at the sight of her daughter's pain. God damn that lake and those fools who encouraged this nonsense.

"Brigid, you're due for another pain pill in a half hour. I'll bring it up. But if it gets too bad, I've brought this bell. Just ring it and I'll bring some ibuprofen."

"Can't I just text you?" Lynn thought of the text messages that kept flashing across her daughter's phone. Kelsey had exploded when she revealed her plan to keep Brigid's phone hidden for now. Lynn felt there was no reason for her daughter to be upset and confused further. The best thing for recovery was a clean break. In a rare fit of rebellion and temper, Kelsey had accused Lynn of being a dictator. He refused to deny Brigid's status as an independent adult, saying they may break her trust in a way that might never be repaired. Lynn had backed down, promising to bring Brigid her phone as soon as she was awake. But Kelsey was at work, at least until dinner. It would do no harm for Brigid to rest peacefully for one more day.

"Your phone ran out of battery at the hospital," Lynn lied. "When it's charged, I'll bring it to you."

Brigid nodded.

"You need to rest," Lynn said firmly. "Finish that breakfast. Ring the bell when you're done and I'll come get it, help you to the bathroom, and you can get some sleep."

Lynn shut the door softly. Brigid forced herself to relax her shoulders. Her heart was broken, but despite herself, she sank back gratefully into the plush pillows.

CHAPTER 56

Contentment glowed on Lynn's face. Brigid was home, recovering. Away from that rotting cottage with its interminable piles of stones. With any luck, the unacceptable romance with the Sherland man would fade away. Lynn knew of an administrative position opening up in the Domhnall Hills school district in January. It would come with a significant pay-raise and more importantly, get her heart-strong daughter out of the fatigue and strain of the classroom. Several Domhnall Hills School Board members were on the Neighborhood Association with Lynn and she had been subtly lobbying for Brigid all summer. All Brigid had to do was pass the interview. Lynn was already imagining taking her shopping for a proper suit.

Sun peaked through the big bay windows as Lynn stepped into the kitchen. She was so happy that she considered pouring herself a celebratory glass of chardonnay. It wasn't quite noon yet, but it was a Saturday. A small indulgence wouldn't hurt.

Kelsey lifted his head from his hands and rose to greet his wife. Lynn beamed at him, a smile that shattered when she saw the expression on his face.

"Lynn... sweetheart," he began. He crossed the spotless floor and placed gentle hands on her shoulders. "The nursing home just called." Lynn's jaw clenched as she fought against the tears behind her eyes. "Your dad..." Kelsey swallowed hard, chastising himself for his weakness. Lynn was the pillar for them all, he needed to be strong enough at least to deliver this news. "Your dad has passed. I'm so sorry." He waited, hands warm against her uncovered arms. Lynn's jaw worked back and forth. With deliberate calm, she broke away from his grasp and walked toward the window. The beautiful, sunlit view seemed to mock her. She wrapped her arms around her body and stood tall.

Kelsey knew this posture. Every muscle in her body was rigid and she would reject his comfort. Punish herself by isolation. He had also learned to comfort her anyway. If left to herself, she would sink so low she may not be reached. Doctors called it depression, but Lynn refused to acknowledge the term. It was Kelsey's job to comfort her, feed her, nourish her in times like this. Ever so gently, he walked behind her and wrapped his arms around hers, touching her stiff hands with fingers light as feathers. He knew not to say much. With a whisper, he said simply, "I'm here."

A tear or two flew out of Lynn's blue eyes and the droplets felt like sweet relief. She allowed herself to feel her husband's presence. After several moments, she reigned in her tears and stiffened her jaw. Turning to Kelsey, she said, "We need to let people know."

"Brigid first?" Kelsey asked. "I can tell her."

"Brigid last," Lynn said. There was no room for debate left in her tone. "She's been through enough."

CHAPTER 57

The funeral was set for Friday. Brigid was nearly catatonic in response to this third tragedy, refusing to speak except for brief responses to the hundreds of condolences. Lynn admired her stoicism, feeling that Brigid had finally shed her last touch of flightiness.

Everyone else who walked through the funeral home was shocked at the change in the Firth daughter. Brigid stood silent, an emaciated stone monument. Over the long hours of the visitation, Brigid took several breaks to sit in a somber wing chair at Kelsey's insistence. It was still hard to stand on her injured leg.

Lynn arranged for the funeral to take place three days after Morgan's passing. In his will, he had specified cremation and for his ashes to be scattered at Cairn Cottage as well as on the path to Big Omann Lake. This was how his wife, Lynn's mother, had been laid to rest. Their final wish was to become part of the Earth, part of the water, part of the stones they loved so much.

Lynn found as always, the best way to keep the grief and regret away was to work. The funeral was arranged in less than a week, and in that same time, she found a realtor experienced in the Peninsula area. Despite Kelsey's pleading that she wait until her head was clear, Cairn Cottage was listed for sale the same day that the family formally mourned their patriarch.

After the funeral, the days went by as normal, Lynn quietly fielding phone calls from the real estate agent. Lynn decided to tell Brigid once the deal was finished. Less fuss, less sentimentality. It was merely a fact, and a reasonable decision.

Kelsey was worried about Brigid's reaction, but Lynn felt that she had that under control as well. She seemed open to the idea of this new job in Domhnall Hills. Brigid had mentioned under her breath at dinner one evening that she couldn't abide returning to her school in the fall. She also didn't speak at all about Gabe. Lynn felt a twinge of guilt for deleting the man's texts and voice mails from the phone before giving it back to her daughter. Kelsey did have a valid point that Brigid was a full-grown adult who deserved autonomy. The protective instinct of motherhood had won, however, and in this instance, Lynn believed that she had been right in her actions. It was unsuitable in every way for her daughter to be tied to a Sherland man. Whatever grief she felt for her father's death, there was a sense of relief that the mistakes and pain of the past were well and truly banished from this lifetime.

CHAPTER 58

Nearly a month. Four weeks, thirty days. Hours that felt endless. Brigid could not believe it had been so long since the sailing accident. It was late August already, leaning into fall. Her leg felt much stronger, but she couldn't bear to look at the scar. Raised and ripped, it was another ugly mark on her being.

Her heart was still raw. How could so much be lost so quickly? Anything that remained, she pushed away. Stark reality was the only thing she was capable of dealing with.

Reality told her that the love she felt for Gabe was useless. Moreover, it was not returned. She had checked her phone obsessively for the first few weeks, wanting more than anything to hear his voice. She ached to tell him what had happened in her glorious, stupid error. Feel his embrace. As much as every fiber of her being longed to reach out, she found she couldn't. Pride ran too swiftly in her blood.

He had only contacted her once, after her grandfather's obituary was printed in the paper. "I'm so sorry for your loss," he had texted. "I hope you are well." The formality of his words was worse than if he had said nothing at all.

The morning dawned foggy and still. She gazed out of the window and sighed. There was really nothing to do but get up. She would dress and sip some coffee. Force herself to update her resume. The interview was in two days.

She pulled on the linen shift that her mother left in her closet and descended the stairs. The kitchen was unusually quiet. She looked around for any sign of her parents. On the table near Kelsey's usual chair, she saw the note.

"*Kelsey,*
At the closing — meet me there. They agreed to take possession on Monday. Please bring extra set of cottage keys hanging in the hall.
Love,
Lynn"

Brigid's stomach rose into her chest and she thought for a moment she would throw up all over the kitchen floor. She hobbled up to her room, eyes blurry and fogged. Ignoring the pain in her leg, she began packing her suitcase. There was no plan, no thought, but leaving. She was thinking clearly for the first time in months. There were opportunities everywhere. Friends from college had moved to different, exciting parts of the country. Surely they had a couch she could crash on for a week or two. Seattle was enticing; Courtney lived there. Nashville was where Laura wrote songs and played as a session artist. Maybe someone, a musician, could use her poetry. In any case, she had a teaching degree — she would find a job. Zipping the bag closed, she took a breath. Reaching for her purse on the dresser, her naked wrist caught her eye. Something was missing.

Maybe there was no Diviner, no Voice. Maybe there was only this breath in this moment, and the broken body that stared back at her in the mirror. Whatever the Truth was, her past was part of her. The people who loved and mourned and strived and worked were part of her blood. That bracelet was the only connection Brigid had left, and it was at Cairn Cottage.

It was time to go.

CHAPTER 59

Brigid navigated the car slowly through the driving rain, wincing at the thunder that crashed through the sky. After what seemed like an eternity, she turned into the driveway. Unlocking the door, she paced through Cairn Cottage, gaping at the view. This was no ordinary storm. A snowy cloud capped the horizon, turning down at the corners like a frown. The storm surge obliterated the sun, but the gangrene interior pulsed with its own monstrous glow. The front edge of the storm dripped like a giant tattered curtain in front of the putrid abyss. Thunder cracked and the sound bounced off the water like an echo chamber. The old brass chandelier shook. The storm cloud had not even crossed the far side of the lake, yet the wind was so strong that the open windows were straining from their hinges.

Brigid hurried into what was her grandfather's bedroom, using all of her strength to crank the windows closed. Slamming the locks into place, she scrambled up the steep stairs to what was once her loft. The power cut out as she reached the landing and she stumbled, banging her good knee on the wooden floorboards. Swearing and stumbling to the windows that faced the lake, she pulled and twisted until those too were closed.

Brigid stood up. Securing the bedrooms had only taken a few minutes, but the wind was screaming. Taking the stairs two at a time, ignoring the pain pulsing through her kneecap, she heard a wrenching metallic sound followed by a shattering crash. She rounded the kitchen island to see the second dining room window peel off from the frame and get sucked outside. It slammed into a nearby tree and shattered. The screens blew into the cottage and rain surged into the dining room. Brigid's hands flew to her mouth as she realized the antique furniture, the wood floors, the carpets, and every fiber of the beloved home would soon be ruined.

Cairn Cottage would be in the hands of a stranger any moment, but Brigid wanted to save what she could. She stepped carefully through the rainwater to bolt the heavy wooden door.

What she saw through the screen door froze the very blood in her veins.

The heart of the storm had made its way to the lake. Brigid was mesmerized by the aquamarine curtain that blew relentlessly forward. The winds were so strong that the smaller boats were being lifted in the air and propelled across the lake. Some sailboats were already marooned on their masts, hulls spinning in the air. The newer metal dock sections were riding the crashing waves, having been ripped from their moorings. Her own dock, the precious, splintering, curving hulk of waterlogged wood, was swaying, almost dancing in the storm.

Brigid's eyes blurred with panic, but she forced herself to keep moving. Kicking aside the heavy iron doorstop, she put all her strength, all of her love, all of her fury behind the door. Bracing against the howling wind with her good knee, all weight on her bad, pushing until her muscles in her arms, the veins in her neck strained. With one scream of determination, Brigid slammed the heavy door into the frame.

The storm pushed back.

CHAPTER 60

A heinous gust blew the unbolted door back open, slamming Brigid against the kitchen counter. The edge hit her right on her scar line, sending rockets of pain up her back, through her skull. She was trapped between the door and the counter, the pain in her scar and the pain of her knee almost unbearable. She turned, pressing her chest against the Formica surface, and gave a mighty kick. The door moved just enough to allow her to wriggle free.

Rainwater was flooding into the cottage. Brigid stood in the middle of the great room, water flowing around her bare feet, stunned. There was something, something to do next, but she couldn't make her mind or her body work. A light flashed in the side windows of the living room, illuminated something glinting on the coffee table near the picture windows.

Her grandmother's bracelet. The Diviner bracelet. Brigid's bracelet. This mysterious object of power, of love. Where did the truth lie? What did her grandmother know of love that she would abandon Brigid for her entire childhood? What did Brigid know of love that she could love so deeply and it was never returned? And where was the power in this circlet of stones? This bracelet wasn't strong enough to save her grandfather, or Rosie, or David's wife. It didn't have the power to make Brigid into the woman she was meant to be.

She turned to the tempest howling across the lake. Her humiliation, her impuissance, every summer sickness would be washed away in this ungodly storm. But by hell she would take that bracelet. She would take it and walk away. Turn her back on all of this, on everyone. Brigid limped to the hand-hewn table. As she scooped the bracelet into her palm, the back door slammed.

"Brigid!"

His voice was muffled by the roaring wind and an unfamiliar creaking.

"Brigid, where are you?"

Her heart clenched, ducking in on itself. Tears stung her eyes.

It didn't matter. Nothing mattered. She heard his voice and knew that she loved him, would always love him. What she felt for him was eternal, and would stay with her whether he walked away or not.

He was across the room in a second.

"Brigid, I'm so sorry." He hugged her, hard. "I was so worried you were here. We need to get somewhere safe, a closet, a bathroom. Come on!" Gabe tugged her arm, trying to make her move. She was frozen, staring over his shoulder. His mouth fell open as he turned around. A massive gray form was hurtling toward the cottage. The circular dock slammed into the old maple tree. The wooden dock splintered into pieces.

A guttural creak from the depths of the earth took the breath from their lungs. Gabe saw it first, and pulled Brigid down with all of his might. The old, gnarled tree fell slowly, taking its final bow. It slammed onto the main beam of the roof. The walls around them began to shake.

The giant windows broke loose from their frames as the beam of Cairn Cottage collapsed. They floated for a moment before falling forward into the room.

Brigid felt a huge push, a dark confused warmth, and then sheer terror. The shards of glass sliced into Brigid's back, making her writhe in agony. Tiny vicious shrapnel rained onto her head. She could do nothing, not even raise her bleeding arms in protection. The pain began to reach foggy tentacles into her consciousness. Where was Gabe? Blood seeped out of her wounds and she became aware of a heaviness on the side of her body, a warm faint pulsing on the crown of her head. She forced herself to turn.

Gabe lay on the carpet where he had slumped off her back. He had pushed her down, bracing his body against the relentless fatality of the storm. Raising her head over the fragments of glass and tree bark, she saw it. A single shard of glass rose into the air, splattered with his blood, encased in his skin.

CHAPTER 61

Everything was so cruelly clear. She heard David yelling, watched him rush through the rubble. She listened as he called the ambulance, sobbing. Gabe lay next to her, eyes open and unseeing. His blood pooled on the wet carpet. The blare of the siren screeched through the wind, and the EMTs ran into the cottage with gurneys.

Brigid watched as they put an oxygen mask over Gabe's face. He was pale, too pale. Gauze was shoved in Brigid's deepest cuts and she heard the muttered apologizes for her pain. "Are you ok?" they asked. "We need to help your friend." Brigid nodded. The ambulance raced to the hospital and skidded in front of the emergency doors. Brigid watched from her gurney as Gabe was transferred onto the stretcher and raced down the hallway. Out of sight. Away.

She was next, and she landed hard on a cut on her back, yelping as little as possible as they wheeled her into a room. The room had a beautiful view of the city, but Brigid couldn't see it. Pounding rain shook Domhnall Hills. Nurses bustled in and out. Brigid was held down gently as a doctor numbed her interminable wounds, bandaging what was shallow. Stitching what was deep.

When they were done, a nurse sat down in a chair. The woman typed on her phone, looking up at Brigid every few minutes.

"I'm sorry I'm on my phone," the nurse said. "I'm staying later than my shift and I just texted my husband to let him know."

"I'm sorry," Brigid said.

"Oh no, honey, it's okay." The nurse rose and tucked a curl back behind Brigid's ear. "I couldn't leave without seeing if you were going to be okay."

Brigid wanted to smile, but strangely felt that she didn't have the strength. The nurse felt Brigid's eyes on her. "Can I get you anything, sweetheart? Something to drink maybe?"

"Maybe," said Brigid. The room began to haze. "I'm feeling a little faint," she said quietly. The nurse jumped up and placed her phone on the table. As she did, she saw the deep crimson pool out from underneath the blanket. "Oh honey," she said, her eyes wide.

The nurse rushed over to push a button on the wall. Brigid watched as several doctors ran into the room. Naked worry shone on their faces. Doctors shouldn't show their emotions, Brigid thought. They shouldn't show the truth. This can't be that bad — the EMTs attended Gabe before me. Why are they looking like that?

"This is not great," she heard someone say. "We're going to have to intubate."

"I'm not sure that's the best idea..."

A firm voice drowned out all of the other voices in the room.

Stay awake.

Brigid looked around the room to see which doctor was making this command.

Brigid.

The voice sounded like her own, but stronger, ethereal. No one was looking at her. No one else in the room had heard.

Stay. Awake.

Brigid understood immediately that to allow herself to sink

down in the simple bliss of unconsciousness would mean the end. If she let herself leave this terrifying pain, she would not come back.

Fighting the deep haze pulling her down, Brigid searched for something to concentrate on. The doctors and nurses moved too fast, their swiftness confused her mind. A warmth began to circle her and something heavy urged her into sleep. Brigid heard the voice that sounded so much like her own float through the air.

I know it hurts. You can be done if you want to be done. If you want to be done, just close your eyes. I will wrap you in love and peace. But there is so much love left here. And the love here, if you are brave enough to take it, to give it, is the same as the love I give. It is the same. If you want to stay awhile longer, you'll have to fight through the pain. Find something real.

She looked at her left hand, lying limp against the white hospital blanket. The light blue pallor of the skin scared her.

"She's going under," Brigid heard someone say.

"No." Her voice came out choked and weak. The nurse turned to her. "Sorry," Brigid said, struggling through a wave of dizziness. "No, I'm awake. I'm ok." The nurse nodded to a doctor holding a gas mask. The doctor shrugged and left the room.

Above her hand were a set of arrows. It took her a minute to understand what this was, but in a moment the answer came to her foggy brain. They were the controls for the bed, to push the head and feet up and down. The arrows were real.

"Up," she thought. "That is the up arrow. Down. This is the down arrow." If she could keep these things straight, just these two mundane little pieces of life on this earth, maybe she could stay awake. Keep herself from sinking into an abyss from which there was no return.

"Up. Up arrow. Makes the bed rise. Down. Down arrow. It makes the bed sink." She said this to herself over and over, calmly, not allowing herself to think of another thing. It seemed to be working. The intubation tray in the corner, waiting to extinguish her reality, was unmanned.

"Up. Down."

"Does this hurt, honey?" A nurse pushed on her abdomen, her toes lifting off of the ground. "We're trying to get this bleeding to stop."

The pain was excruciating, but Brigid knew now that she preferred the pain to the nothingness. She gazed back at her arrows. Up, Down. "No," Brigid answered through clenched teeth. "I'm fine. I can take it." The nurse looked at her with pity.

Brigid gave a cautious glance at the door. It was open, but there was no one there. Where were her parents? Where was her mother?

Where was Gabe?

The thought of him began to make her heart race and she panicked a little. Pain flowed in and out as the nurse continued to bear down.

"Look at her face!" Brigid heard one of the doctors shout. "She should not be feeling that much pain!"

"She's lost too much blood, we cannot put her under."

"We need to sew this up and get antibiotics in immediately."

Swallowing hard, Brigid spoke hoarsely. "I'm okay, I'm okay," she said. "Please don't take me to the operating room."

"You will be fine in the operating room," A doctor leaned over her. "Many patients are frightened, but there's no need for fear." He simpered at her. "We are professionals. We'll get you fixed up and with no pain at all."

Brigid shook her head.

"Doctor, we've got three patients lined up for the operating room already." An older female doctor stepped forward. "Let's just see if we can get her patched up here. We can order a blood transfusion."

"I'm not in the practice of taking orders from patients," the male doctor growled.

"It's not an order from her, it's an order from me." Dr. Hú

smiled at Brigid. "I know this young lady. She's going to pull through."

CHAPTER 62

Ann sat at her son's bedside trying to control her sobs. The doctors had firmly advised her that she would have to leave unless she got her emotions under control. She couldn't leave him alone now. She just couldn't. The things she hadn't done for him could fill a cavern.

It had been easier to let him take over when his father left them. The arrangement seemed to soothe him. Ann hoped that if she ceded control, the nasty temper that ran through his father's veins would be subdued in Gabe. If she could do it all again...Ann sighed and wiped her eyes. There was no going back. Not in this life.

She remembered the look on his face the night he ended things with Brigid. It was beyond the usual frustration he tried to mask. He had looked, she realized, the way he looked now. Pale, pinched. As if he was fighting a mortal wound. Late that night, Ann was awakened by heaving, muffled sobs. She threw off her covers and hustled down the hallway, fearing for Mikey. But the younger boy was sound asleep in his room. She had realized the sound was coming from Gabe.

Tiptoeing down the hall, she called to him softly. Hearing no answer, she had hesitated. Her son was a man. She wasn't sure she had the right to intrude on his privacy. The sobs continued and Ann found she couldn't stand it. Mother's instinct took over and she quietly walked into the living room.

Ann found her son sitting on the edge of the couch with his head in his hands. When did her baby grow so big? Tears gathered in her own throat, but his desperation left no room for her feelings. She walked over and gently rubbed his back.

Gabe lifted reddened eyes and ran his hand through his hair. Unable to look at his mother, he gazed out at the fields.

"Oh Gabriel." Ann said softly.

The sound of his full name made him lose the tenuous control he had on his emotions and began to sob again in earnest.

"Did Brigid break up with you?" Ann asked, an edge in her voice. Her son shook his hanging head.

"Is everything ok with your job?" Fear gripped Ann's heart and she was ashamed. "You didn't lose your job, did you honey?"

"No," said Gabe. He rubbed his forehead and Ann saw several small cuts on his hand.

"What happened to your hand?" she asked, pulling back from him.

Gabe's face pinched as he fought back more tears. "Broken glass."

"What kind of glass?" Ann asked. Gabe shook his head again.

She glanced back at her son's wounded hand. "Gabe," she said gently. "This isn't like you. What is going on?"

"I'm a mess, Mom," His shoulders slumped and he stared at the floor.

"Well that's clear."

He looked at his mother, a thousand apologies in her smile. Maybe she would understand.

"Mom." He swallowed back a sob and forced the words out. "I hurt her." Ann felt the old fear like ice in her veins. Not her son. Not her kind, hardworking son who held up the family, who worked for them all, who carried burdens far too heavy, far too young.

In a voice sunk with grief, she asked, "Gabe, what did you do?"

"We...we got in a fight." He swiped at his eyes with the back of his hand. "She went to some party with her ex-boyfriend. Somebody posted a picture of the two of them." He looked at her in despair. "Mom, she looked so happy, so right in that world. And I don't know...I got mad."

Ann was afraid to breathe. She stared at him, willing him to continue, terrified to hear.

"I went over to talk to her about it and she — she started yelling at me. Screaming, swearing. I don't know — I haven't been yelled at like that since..."

Now it was Ann's turn to look away. "Anyway, I tried to be calm. Tried to calm her down. But she said these things that were so... true. I yelled back I guess and then..." Gabe swallowed hard. His mother's face was white in the moonlight. "Then I don't know. I just wanted it to stop, you know? I just wanted the yelling to stop. She had her water glass on the counter and suddenly it was broken all over the floor."

"You threw it at her?" asked Ann.

"No!" Gabe looked up with wide eyes and she could see the little boy he once was. "I didn't throw it at her. I would never do that. I just... slammed my hands on the counter... my fists. I didn't plan to, I just hoped the sound would stop her from yelling. It fell down. It was an old glass, you know – an antique or something. Glass went everywhere. She had glass in her hair." The tears escaped his eyes at the memory. "A big piece landed on her throat. I went to take it off before it cut her and she jumped. She was afraid of me, Mom." The tousled head fell back into the big hands. "She made me promise, I promised," he said through tears.

"Promised what, Gabe?" Ann tried to digest this, tried to push back the flood of memories, of so many broken promises, vows made with tears in a strong man's eyes and liquor on his breath. "Have you hurt her before?"

"No, never!" he said. "It's just — her mom is...hard on her. I promised not to yell at her and instead — she got cut because of me." Ann reached out to touch his bowed back. He flinched away.

"I'm just like Dad."

A great well of indignation rose in Ann's heart.

"No you're not," she said. She moved herself heavily off of

the couch and knelt beside her son. She knelt before him the way she used to do when he was a child, when she would zip his little coat against the winter cold, or take him onto her shoulder for comfort after his father's drunken outbursts. Bending her head so she met his eyes, she lifted his chin with her hand.

"You are not one bit like your father," she said. "You are a good man, Gabe. You didn't hurt Brigid."

"She bled because of me."

"Did you throw the glass at her?"

Gabe shook his head. "I would never throw something at her."

"Did you hit her with anything? Your hands? Your belt?" Gabe gave an involuntary cower at the memory of a sharp belt buckle against his young skin. He shook his head.

"Did you grab her hair and scream in her face?" Ann's face twisted with the memories of her husband's hands in her own hair, dragging her through the kitchen by the scalp. "Did you slam her against the wall?"

"No," Gabe fighting back memories too. "Mom, please stop." He looked at her with pleading in his eyes.

"Son, you are not like your father. Nothing like him. Your outburst should serve as a warning to you, but it is not abuse."

"I made her bleed."

"It was an accident, Gabe. You did not use your hands or your words to hurt her." Ann asked. She looked hard at her son. "Do you love this woman?"

"Yes," came the husky reply. "Before all this, I was planning..." The ache of a dream deferred rendered him speechless.

"I saw the ring," Ann said quietly. "I'll say it to you, I don't think you two would have an easy time of it. Your backgrounds are so different. She might have expectations that you could never meet, as hard as you work." Tears ran down Gabe's cheeks. "You love her, though. That's very clear. And it's the most important thing. You can get past this. Apologize to her."

"I left her," he said. He moved away from his mother's incredulous look. "She's not safe with me."

"Gabe, that's the most ridiculous thing I've ever heard."

"Really Mom? Don't you wish Dad had left you the first time he hurt you? And what about Uncle Teddy? I found the letters – he basically killed Ruby Ayers. This kind of stuff is hereditary —"

"Hitting is not hereditary." Ann's voice was firm. "Hurting the ones you love, on purpose, is a choice. It's not going to happen to you, Gabe. You are not that kind of man. The violence, this curse? It stops with you."

CHAPTER 63

Lynn sat at Brigid's bedside, unable to understand the events of this summer. How was she here again, in this hospital? Needles stuck into her daughter's pale, bony hands. Lynn wondered if Brigid felt the pain of their invasion. Stickers pasted wires all over the young woman's chest underneath the flimsy hospital gown. The infection which had bloomed in her body was now threatening her heart. Brigid had woken only once, eyes unfocused. "I'm cold," she had whispered. Lynn had bent over to hear and could feel the fever radiating off of Brigid's skin before she even stroked her forehead. She shouted "We need assistance in here, immediately!"

A nurse meandered in, rolling her eyes at Lynn's sharp words. When she took Brigid's temperature, she ran out of the room. Lynn had heard a shout: "One hundred and six point three."

"Seizure" and "stroke" floated in the air between the doctors and Lynn's entire body froze. Healthy young women don't have strokes. She wanted to scream at the doctors, demand that they fix this, repair her daughter, save her from a fate that could not possibly be true. But when Lynn tried to speak, she realized she was powerless.

Brigid woke up several days later, and her first sensation was the intense dryness in her mouth, as if she had swallowed cotton balls. She tried to focus her eyes. The view from her sixth story room should have been lush and expansive. Instead, the world was veiled in gray fog. Brigid turned her head away from the window. Her hair, sprawled along the pillow, felt tangled and dirty. She ached for a shower, but she was tied to the bed by a jungle of wires.

"Would you like something to drink?" The voice seemed to come from a distance, but Brigid could see that the door was closed. Lynn rose from a chair in the corner. Her mother. Her mother was here. Lynn still was speaking, but Brigid found she couldn't quite comprehend what she was saying. Something about juice and ice chips being less caloric. Brigid took a deep breath and formed one word.

"Gabe."

Lynn's body tightened. It was a question and she didn't have any answers. Brigid had asked for him every time she had opened her eyes. Until now, she had fallen back into a fitful sleep before she could muster the strength to demand an answer.

Lynn walked over to her daughter, heart wrenching at the sight of greasy curls matted on the pillow and the dark blue circles under her daughter's eyes. "Gabe is fine," she said. It was a lie. Lynn had no idea how Gabe was doing. She didn't dare ask. Whatever the answer was, it wasn't going to help her daughter get any better. Proffering a Styrofoam cup, she gently tucked the straw into her daughter's chapped lips. "Drink," she said.

Brigid obeyed. The juice felt soothing on her dry tongue. A few sips of the sugary drink made her head ache enormously and she winced and turned away.

Frowning, Lynn walked over and placed the cup back on the table. Brigid heard a voice echoing in the room again. It sounded like her mother's, but her head was muddled. A ringing sound invaded, Brigid guessed from one of the many machines. She gingerly reached up one hand to rub her ear.

Lynn stepped closer to the bedside and pulled up a chair. "I understand if you're too tired to talk," she said to Brigid. Was her daughter blocking her ears like a child throwing a tantrum? Lynn told herself to be patient. "And I do understand if you'd rather not talk to me."

"I can't hear you," said Brigid, still rubbing her ears.

Lynn looked at her daughter. "I'm right here."

"No, I know, it's just like an echo chamber in here. Is it because there's no carpet or curtains?"

"It sounds fine to me. What do you mean an echo chamber?"

"Everything sounds like an echo," said Brigid, her voice hoarse with under-use. "It sounds like you're speaking underwater. And what is that ringing?"

"It's a side effect of the antibiotics." Both women looked up at the male voice. Brigid took in the handsome doctor's features and reddened in embarrassment of her grimy state. "I'm sorry that you're dealing with this," the doctor said. He bent down to the other side of the bed so that Brigid could hear him clearly. "We have you on a very strong antibiotic. It's called Gentamicin and unfortunately, one of the side effects is tinnitus."

"What is tinnitus?" asked Lynn sharply.

"It's a ringing in the ears, which often causes a disruption in normal hearing," explained the doctor.

"So none of the machines are ringing or buzzing or whatever?" asked Brigid.

"No, Miss Firth," answered the doctor. "It's the medication. The sound is in your head. The effects should wear off when we are able to lower the dosage. And that," he said, clapping Brigid's chart closed, "is what we are here to determine this afternoon."

Lynn discreetly stepped out of the room while the doctor examined her daughter. He met her in the hall with a grim face. "Mrs. Firth?"

"How is she?" Lynn asked.

"Well, as you know, there is a doctor-patient privilege situation. Fortunately, Miss Firth has asked that I give my report to you as well as her. She mentioned she may be too tired to speak to you if you come back in."

"And?" Lynn asked, trying to mask her terror with an imperious tone.

The doctor coughed. "Well, she's not where we'd like her to

be. The infection isn't getting any worse, but it's not getting any better either. I don't think we can increase her dosage of Gentamicin without risking some permanent hearing loss. She also needs to eat something. If she's unable or unwilling to eat some food in the next day or so, we're going to have to give her nutrition via IV."

"Another IV?" asked Lynn.

"Two, unfortunately," said the doctor.

"You can't do that — you've seen her hands! They're black and blue as it is!"

"That isn't my preferred treatment method either," said the doctor. "She's physically able to eat and drink. I think she just needs some convincing. Maybe the persuasion of her mother? Maybe you could go home and fix her favorite home-cooked meal?" He smiled at her and Lynn wanted to slap him for his assumption.

"This is not 1952. I work as a lawyer which has provided your patient with a beautiful home to grow up in and a college education. I did not and do not sit in my kitchen baking cookies."

"I was not suggesting that you did," he said, unfazed. "I'm going to be frank with you, Mrs. Firth. Your daughter is very ill. If the infection gets any worse, we are going to have to put her on dialysis. Possibly a ventilator. Additionally, Brigid needs to eat and drink something. Today." He paused and let the truth sink in. "Oftentimes, loved ones are one of our greatest allies in treating patients. I assumed, as her mother, that you would know her better than anyone."

"We're not close," Lynn said, choking on the words.

"Well," said the doctor. "Maybe you can think of a comfort food that would tempt her appetite. Something she loved as a child, maybe? If she is able to eat and drink, her body will be just that much stronger. Perhaps then she will be able to fight this infection without more severe interventions." He checked his watch. He was already well behind on his rounds. Looking at the young woman's mother, he saw a woman scared half to death. Good, he thought. She should be.

"If you have a moment, I suggest you return to her room. See how you might make her comfortable."

Without waiting for her reply, the doctor strode down the hallway.

Lynn stood frozen to the tiles, no thoughts in her head except that she had to force her child to eat. She straightened her shoulders and flung the door open. She would make her eat and drink, make Brigid hear her, tinnitus or not. The sight of tears rolling down that pale, pinched face made Lynn panic more. The doctor said she needed fluid, and there was precious fluid, rolling down her cheeks. Before she could demand for her to stop crying, Brigid turned her bare face to her mother.

"I hate this," she said. Sobs began to wrack her body as she struggled against the EKG lines to sit up. "I hate this." Lynn put a manicured hand behind her back and helped her sit up. For a moment she turned to her mother for comfort and saw no friendly arms welcoming an embrace. She doesn't care, thought Brigid. She looked out of the window and cried. Rain poured down in sheets, smudging the landscape.

Lynn was struck mute. No commands, no declarations could escape her lips as she watched her daughter's bony back rise and fall. She too looked out at the rain, hands in her lap, wringing them. If she gave into these hysterics, who would be there steady when her daughter finally calmed down? Who would be the rock?

A dark droplet fell on her pristine hand and Lynn looked at it in confusion. A thin black river ran through the tiny lines in her skin and down between her fingers. She felt a wetness on her face and realized she was crying too. Mascara melted down her cheeks, but the tissues were on the other table, across from Brigid. Not wanting to disturb Brigid by asking her to pass a tissue, she reached around her daughter. Brigid felt her mother's arm wrap around her, and every ounce of pride fled. She turned and fell into her mother's arms. Lynn let her strong body curl around her daughter's shivering weak one, and she wrapped her other arm around her. She leaned her head on her daughter's neck and wept.

After a time, the shaking of both bodies abated. Lynn whispered softly, "I hate this too."

Lynn gave her daughter one more squeeze, and feeling Brigid relax her grip, she leaned back and straightened her blouse. Rising, she gathered the tissue box and set it between them. She looked up to see a smile on her daughter's face, a sight she had not seen in far too long.

"Mom, you are a mess." Brigid looked up at her shyly. Lynn wiped the mascara from her cheeks and raised a rueful eyebrow at her daughter. "You're not in such great shape yourself," she said.

"I need a shower," said Brigid.

"We can make that happen," said Lynn. "I'll call the nurse." Having pressed the button, she turned back to her daughter. "Sweetheart." The endearment hung in the air. Lynn coughed. "I spoke to the doctor. Your body is extremely weak and the infection is...bad. You need to drink something."

"The juice tasted really good, but it gave me a headache," Brigid said.

"It's because of the sugar," said Lynn. Brigid rolled her eyes. "No, I don't mean you shouldn't drink it," Lynn said quickly. "I'm not talking about calories. It's that your body has been so long with nourishment, that even the sweetness gave you pain. You need to eat very slowly, but you need to eat. The doctor said you need to eat today." Lynn stood, smoothing down her slacks. "Now. What sounds good? I'll make a deal with you: while you have your shower, I'll run out and get you anything you want. Name a food and a drink."

"Whiskey and apple pie," Brigid said, a smirk lifting her chapped lips.

"That's a no on the whiskey."

"Apple pie?"

Lynn looked at her daughter. Her aquamarine eyes looked enormous in her pale, thin face. Lynn had done everything in her power to keep her safe, worked day and night to give her a life that was easy and fulfilling. Tenderness had been sacrificed to protection.

"Yes," she said firmly. "Apple pie. Once the nurse arrives and I see you settled in the bath, I'll run out and pick up a pie and a fork. But you need to promise me to eat every bite." The gratitude on her daughter's face filled her with shame. She should have done this long ago. "I can make that chicken noodle soup. I don't know if you remember, but when you were little..."

"I remember," Brigid cut in. "But that takes a really long time, right?" Lynn nodded. "Maybe you could just get a pie and come back soon?"

"How can I help?" A gray-haired nurse stood in the doorway. Lynn straightened herself into her most imperious state.

"My daughter would like to get into the shower."

"She's got several IVs," said the nurse, staring at the tubes that snaked from Brigid's hands. "A sponge bath would be better."

Before the cutting words left Lynn's mouth, she heard her daughter's hoarse voice.

"I'd really prefer a shower. I'm very uncomfortable. I promise to make it quick if you'll help me." she said, smiling politely at the older woman. "Please?"

The nurse's face softened at Brigid's gentle smile. "Ok, honey," she said. "I'll get the water warmed up for you and then we'll get you in. Let's be quick though. The medicine in the IVs need to be in your body."

Lynn sucked in a breath and picked up her purse. As she walked out of the room, she heard the nurse say, "If you feel ok by yourself, honey, I'll go change those sheets for you."

The door closed slowly enough for Lynn to hear her daughter's polite, "Thank you."

CHAPTER 64

The pie was delicious. Cinnamon-soaked apples melted on Brigid's dry tongue as she took bite after tiny bite. Lynn smiled, as she watched her daughter eat the entire pie over the course of the day. Brigid took catnaps between slices and Lynn was amazed at the change in her features. Her daughter seemed comfortable for the first time in days. The worrisome pallor remained, but the pinched expression vanished; the wrinkles on her forehead disappeared. Along with the pie, Lynn had brought a half gallon of milk and a bottle of chocolate sauce. Procuring a Styrofoam cup from the nurse, she mixed chocolate milk the exactly the way Brigid had liked it as a child.

The sun was setting and the women watched the glow from the window. It occurred to Lynn that she had not seen the sun in several days. Assured by the doctor that Brigid would pass a peaceful, comfortable night, Lynn resolved to return home. She would shower, sleep in her own bed. Report Brigid's improvement to Kelsey. She rose and straightened her blouse.

"Go home, Mom," Brigid said, smiling at her. "I feel a lot better. I just need to sleep."

Lynn nodded. She wanted to reach out, hug her daughter, kiss her forehead, lift her up and carry her home in her arms. Instead, she patted her hand, mindful of the IV tubes draping over it.

"Have a good rest. I'll see you in the morning."

Closing the door gently, Lynn stepped into the hall, relief evident on her face.

"Mrs. Firth?"

Lynn turned to see a stout woman with red circles under her eyes and a cheap perm fluffing a head of dark hair. Lynn had the feeling she knew this woman, but judging from the clothes and old boots she wore, Lynn couldn't fathom how she fit into her tidy life.

"Yes?" Lynn said. "I apologize, I can't seem to remember your name."

"We haven't met. I'm Ann Sherland. Gabe's mother." The color drained from Lynn's face. "I'd like to talk to you."

CHAPTER 65

A ticker tape of disasters ran through Lynn's mind. The young man was dead. Her daughter might not get over this heartbreak. Or, perhaps worse, he was injured irreparably and the Firths were somehow to blame. Ann would sue, they could lose their home, their savings. She scrambled to think of her next steps. Should she contact a lawyer? Call Kelsey? What if this woman's son was dead? What if Ann had lost her son so that Lynn could keep her daughter?

"The cafeteria, maybe?" Lynn snapped back into reality. The woman was still speaking. "I could sure use some coffee."

Lynn nodded. "Yes. Yes, let's chat in the cafeteria." The two women walked side by side, in silence. There was no point in small talk. After getting coffees, they found an empty table in the corner and sat facing each other. Lynn sipped hers gingerly, the bitterness of the black brew igniting her senses. Ann poured cream and sugar into hers, stirring it with the red straw. Lynn watched her, realizing there was no escaping the question. Clearing her throat and throwing back her shoulders, she asked,

"How is your son?"

"He's recovering," Ann said. "They're sending him home tomorrow."

A tidal wave of relief shocked Lynn as it washed over her body. She was ashamed of the tears that sprang to her eyes.

Ann feared to ask the obvious follow-up question. "How is Brigid?"

Lynn quickly scrunched up a paper napkin, dabbing at her eyes. When she had gained control of her body, she set down

342

the napkin and looked at Ann.

"She's recovering too. Unfortunately, she sustained an infection that does not seem to be abating. She made the mistake of sailing in the lake and got a cut on her leg. The doctors believe the infection stemmed from that."

"I'm so sorry," said Ann. She had been planning to berate this woman about the apathy she seemed to possess about Brigid's guests swimming in the bacteria-laden water. The trembling at Lynn's mouth stayed Ann's anger. Gently, she said, "My son — my younger one, Mikey. He had a bad infection too after he went over there with Gabe."

Lynn looked alarmed. "I didn't know," she said. "Is he alright?"

"He's just fine now," Ann said. "It was a bad infection though. He was on some strong antibiotics. You know how young boys are — always running around scraping themselves one way or another. I'm sure he had a bunch of little cuts and he was swimming in that lake all day."

"I had no idea," Lynn said.

A stern comment was about to escape Ann's lips when she felt Lynn's hand briefly cover her own.

"I'm sorry, Mrs. Sherland." Lynn drew her hand away quickly, a small part of her worried that the apology was an admission of guilt. She knew for legal reasons she should hold back, but she was too tired. "I'm so sorry about both of your sons."

"There's nothing you could have done," said Ann, falling back into the chair with a deep sigh. "Brigid didn't know how bad the bacteria was that day. And Gabe...well, the storm was worse than anyone has ever seen in these parts. I read in the paper it was called a bow arrow. Just a straight shot of wind. Have you been out to the Peninsula?"

Lynn shook her head. The real estate agent had reported back. The cottage had been completely destroyed. The buyers had pulled out of the deal. Kelsey said he would drive out when the roads were clear, but Lynn could not imagine there was anything to salvage.

"The trees along the lakeshore were flattened," Ann continued. "So many homes were destroyed. It's awful."

"Did your home survive?" Lynn wondered about the fate of the cherry farm.

Ann nodded. "We got lucky. We're just about smack in the middle of the Peninsula, so our home and our farm were spared." Ann set her coffee down and looked hard at Lynn. "Now that we've figured out the kids are ok, I want to talk with you about something else."

Here it comes, thought Lynn. She's going to broach the idea of restitution. They had the finances to pay Gabe's medical bills, she could agree to that, but nothing more. She should never have admitted fault.

"Our families have a history," said Ann. Lynn snapped her head up in alarm. "Ahh, I can see that you know. There has been a lot of swindling." Lynn moved to speak and Ann held up her hand. "And violence. And just...bad blood in general. It kind of all went away in our generation when you moved to Domhnall Hills. I was glad to see that you didn't continue the Stone Society."

Lynn chose her words carefully. "The Stone Society was never something I was interested in being involved with."

"I know," said Ann. "I remember thinking that was smart. It couldn't continue because you didn't pay attention to it. Look, Lynn, I know we didn't know each other well in school and we definitely don't know each other now. Here's the thing, though: our kids are in love."

Lynn's face wrinkled up automatically and Ann folded her arms across her chest watching her.

"Is there something wrong?" Ann's words were a challenge.

Lynn swallowed hard. The image of Ann's son, face down on the gurney with a slice of glass sticking through his back shot through Lynn's mind. "Your son saved my daughter's life. I can never repay what Gabe did for Brigid during the storm. Never. But Mrs. Sherland..."

"Call me Ann."

"Ann." Lynn took a deep breath. "Brigid and Gabe were raised very differently. With different ideas of what to expect from life. I don't know that Brigid would be happy or useful on a farm. Or that Gabe would enjoy spending time with us in Domhnall Hills."

"I have no idea about any of that either." Ann said. "I just know how much my son loves your daughter. And from watching her with him, it's clear she loves him too."

Lynn stared ruefully into her coffee. Could she admit that Ann was right? Lynn had tried to steer the path of Brigid's life for a quarter of a century, but everything she had done to ensure her daughter's safety had been in vain. She had almost lost Brigid this week. It might be time to give up control. Lynn found all she really wanted was to have her happy daughter back. If loving this man made her happy, maybe that was enough.

"I suppose we can give them permission," Lynn said.

Ann burst out laughing, a throaty cackle that elicited smiles from the other people in the cafeteria. "Permission?" Ann leaned back heartily in her chair, hand at her chest. "Lynn, they're grown adults! They don't need our permission."

Lynn shifted uncomfortably in her chair.

"Look, you're right." Ann patted Lynn's arm. "Life is going to be harder for them than it needs to be. But the past?" Ann brushed the air, sweeping the idea away. "The people who hurt each other in our families are dead and gone. Gabe and Brigid have a chance to make a new start. Do we want to make it harder for them by holding onto the bad blood? Or do we want to let it go? Let these two make the life that they want to live?"

"Can they?"

"Can they what?"

"Make the life that they want?"

"I don't think we can know that, Lynn. We just have to let life be what it is."

CHAPTER 66

Kelsey folded the newspaper and took the reading glasses from his face. "This is incredible," he said. Lynn perched in the dining room chair, one leg tucked underneath, scrolling on her phone. "I know," she said. "It says here that it was a simple issue of overfishing the smaller lakes. And something about overbuilding on Big Omann Lake between the Peninsula and Domhnall Hills. The soil and stone removal at the building sites made the lake bottom murkier. An imbalance of bacteria, they say."

Kelsey rose and wrapped his arms around his wife's shoulders. "The Farmers Collective presented a plan to the City Council meeting last night," he said. "They plan to reintroduce the fish to the smaller lakes, and rebuild the lake bottom on the shores of Big Omann Lake where it's been disturbed with stones and soil from all the surrounding lakes. They are amending the mineral content in the smaller lakes; taking stones from Big Omann and grinding them up. The DNR says that it wasn't the bacteria alone; lakes need some bacteria. It had just become imbalanced due to all the overuse. The City of Domhnall Hills has agreed to fund the project to restore the correct bacteria levels in the lakes. There will be a millage, of course, but I can't imagine people will vote it down. The waters are our most important economic resource. There's enough in the budget to begin the project immediately."

A hint of a smile glowed in Lynn's eyes. "The smaller lakes feed into Big Omann. If this can be fixed, we may avoid bacteria being spread into the big lake."

Suddenly, the doorbell chimed down the cavernous hallway. Lynn frowned again. "I have to go to the hospital soon. I can't imagine who this could be."

"I'll go with you," Kelsey called after his wife before picking up the paper to reread the wonderful headline. Two sets of footsteps sounded their way into the kitchen. He looked up. Lynn was standing beside Gabe.

Kelsey looked at this man. Gabe was taller than he was, and stronger, but he stood with obvious pain from the wound in his back. The wound created by a shard of glass from that falling-down cottage. The place Kelsey should have never allowed his daughter to live. He should have heeded his wife's many warnings. That shard of glass that could have killed this young man. It could have killed his daughter. Kelsey face went deathly pale as he walked forward. Gabe found himself enveloped in the older man's embrace.

Kelsey let the tears flow freely. "You saved my little girl," he said, looking up into Gabe's eyes. "You saved her life." Gabe pulled back uncomfortably.

"It was the only thing I could do," he said.

Lynn heard the depth in his words. She turned to him, unable to speak.

Gabe looked from one to the other. Finally, he cleared his throat.

"I would like to do more," he began.

"Son, we owe *you*."

"Mr. Firth, I'm in love with your daughter. There was nothing I could possibly do except save her," Gabe said. His firm tone struck a chord in Lynn and she was snapped out of her silence.

"What do you want?" The words came out harsher than she meant, but he didn't seem to notice.

"First, I would like to know how she is." Gabe's voice cracked. "I've heard lots of stories." Lynn watched him swallow back tears.

"She's recovering, thank God," said Kelsey. "Thanks to you. It's been horrible though." Lynn handed her husband a tissue with a touch of annoyance.

"It has been a slow recovery," Lynn said. "She contracted an infection from the bacteria in the lake. Brigid had gone sailing after..."

Mercy, thought Lynn. This young man needed mercy. No need to mention the fact that he had left her. "She went sailing. The boat capsized and she cut her leg. The bacteria got into her bloodstream from that wound, and apparently she somehow cut her neck that same day or sometime before. I don't quite understand the details."

Gabe remembered the glass shattering. He went white.

"In any case," Lynn continued. "There were several points of entry for the bacteria, and the infection was really quite bad. She is recovering, but as my husband said, slowly."

Gabe pinched the bridge of his nose. He would not cry in front of her parents. Taking a great, shuddering breath, he began the speech he came to give.

"Mrs. Firth, Mr. Firth, I love Brigid. I love her with everything that I am. I would like to ask her to marry me. I came today to ask for your blessing." Kelsey moved to say something, but Gabe held up his hand. "I realize I'm not your ideal son-in-law, but I would work all my life to make her life happy. Our orchard is successful. My degree allows me to manage both the operations and the business aspect of it." He turned to Lynn. "My family and yours have had their share of troubles. I didn't know about all that when I first met Brigid, but I do now. I want to promise you, Mrs. Firth, that I would never, ever do to your daughter what my Uncle Teddy did to your Aunt Ruby."

She narrowed her eyes at him. "I appreciate that. The reality is, however, that that kind of temperament runs in the blood. Your promises are noble, but married life is hard and Brigid is far from perfect. How can you be sure that you wouldn't get carried away when times get tough?"

Gabe met her gaze. "I would do anything to ensure that I never hurt Brigid. In fact, that's why I broke up with her." He took a deep breath and met Lynn's eyes. "My father abused us.

Hit my mother, hit me. It would always start with him yelling. Sometimes the only way to make him stop long enough for one of us to take cover was to throw something. Brigid and I got into an argument. She was yelling. That's ok. It's okay that she was yelling, people are allowed to get angry. But I kept asking her to stop, to please stop yelling. She just got louder. Something triggered up inside of me and I..."

Lynn's eyes flashed, her manicured hands balled in fists. "I knocked a water glass on the floor and a shard of it cut her" he said. Lynn's nose wrinkled in confusion. "I knew then I had to end it. And so I did."

Lynn looked hard at him.

"It was the biggest mistake I've ever made in my life," Gabe said, throat tightening.

"Knocking a water glass onto the floor?" Kelsey said. "That doesn't seem like such a sin."

Lynn rounded on her husband. "This man has just told you he threw something at your daughter."

"No," Kelsey said. "That's not what he said." Kelsey put his hand up to stop Lynn. "You, my dear, have thrown much worse in your time. I remember a glass dish that came flying precariously close to my head."

"That's not the same thing," Lynn said.

"You have just made my point."

"I've been seeing a therapist." Lynn and Kelsey turned toward Gabe. "I want to make sure that I can always control my anger. That I'm not..." Gabe ran a hand through his hair. "That I'm not shaped by other people's decisions."

"We are all shaped by other people's decisions," said Lynn.

"Lynn," Kelsey broke in, wiping his eyes with a napkin. "The past is the past. This young man loves her. And clearly, she loves him."

Gabe looked at Kelsey with such naked hope in his eyes, the older man stumbled back a step. "She does?"

Kelsey patted his arm. "Yes, Gabe. She does. She's hurt. Her body, her spirit, her pride are all hurt. But it's obvious that she loves you."

Gabe took a moment to digest this news. "There is one last thing," he said. "I know you might need to think about giving your blessing. And Brigid might not want to marry me, or even see me. I have no idea. There is one thing I can give her though, no matter what happens." Gabe stood up as straight as his wounded back would allow. "I would like to buy Cairn Cottage and give it to Brigid."

"Son," Kelsey said, looking warily at Lynn. "The cottage is destroyed. Flattened."

"I know," said Gabe. "I also know that your original buyers pulled out of the deal. I've consulted a realtor, and I'm prepared to make you an offer. I believe it is a fair price, considering that there is no structure on the land, and that significant clean-up would be involved." He pulled a folded document out of his back pocket.

Lynn put up her hand. "Stop."

"Lynn," Kelsey broke in. "I've got to put my foot down here. You need to at least listen to him."

"I've heard enough," Lynn said. "Gabe," she said, turning to him. Her eyes were weary and she looked as old as her years. "You saved my daughter. You love her. You do work very hard; I can see that now. And my husband is right. She does love you." Lynn paused for the briefest moment and then looked up at him firmly. "I don't think your life will be easy together. I simply don't." Lynn's shoulders lowered. "I'm exhausted. Nothing I decide can make her happy. She needs to find her own happiness." Kelsey's eyes widened. Lynn continued. "If you can promise us that you will love her, I think my husband and I can give you our blessing." Kelsey, struck dumb for once in his life, merely nodded. "We will leave it to Brigid to choose for herself."

"I promise," Gabe said.

Gabe accepted Kelsey's hand and shook it heartily. Turning to Lynn, he handed her the document with the written offer. It would be a large mortgage, and he would have to sell some his family's land, but it was a fair offer and he was determined to make it.

She took the paper and set it face-down on the counter.

"We should have put the property in Brigid's name the day my father died." Lynn collapsed onto a barstool. "It was in his will, but he never had the document notarized. I thought it best to just be rid of that place altogether. I was mistaken. She belongs there." Lynn folded the paper without glancing at it and handed it back to Gabe.

"I'm afraid I can't accept your offer to purchase Cairn Cottage," she said. "I think the best thing would be to sign the deed over to Brigid." Kelsey put his arm around his wife.

"Then I would like to build on it." asked Gabe. Brigid's parents looked at him in surprise. "I'd like to build her a home. Whether she chooses to share it with me or not. I've saved; I could clean up the debris and build a modest house for her there. Regardless of...whether she wants a future with me, the home would be hers."

"Well, it would have to be, if we deed the property to her," said Lynn.

Gabe nodded. "If she says no, I will walk out of her life and leave you all alone. The house I build can serve as a truce between our families."

Lynn looked at this young man. She had planned everything out, played every move by the book. Managing their lives to perfection, presenting a perfect picture to the world. Over and over again, her world was shattered. But she saw the same sincerity and love in this man's eyes that terrified her in her own daughter's eyes. The same vulnerability, the same quiet determination. She looked at this Sherland boy. She couldn't control him. She couldn't control Brigid. It was time to let go. She reached out, putting a tentative hand on his arm.

"Thank you."

CHAPTER 67

The boats zipped across the lake, their motors clattering in the wind. DNR employees and their volunteers lowered buckets of fish into the water. The heat of September was softened by a cool north wind. The minerals sprayed from the hoses in fine mists, settling gently on the surface. It would take months, but the bacteria would be defeated.

Kelsey turned the car down the driveway slowly, mindful of his daughter's injuries. The pathway was much wider, and the family sat in wide-eyed silence to see the sky open up above the flattened birch trees. Centuries-old pines lay prone on the sandy soil. Lynn couldn't help but notice neat piles of logs stacked beside the road, sawed and cleared by an industrious hand.

The final turn should have brought Cairn Cottage into view. There was a collective gasp from the passengers inside the car when they came upon nothing but emptiness. The slate blue siding and sagging roof, the stone chimney and little wooden front stoop, were all gone. Not even wreckage remained. Instead, the debris was stacked in piles and a metal dumpster was parked discreetly in the woods. All the anxiety that her parents' home had brought to Lynn vanished with the bones of the cottage, and a choking sound was heard in the front seat. Brigid looked in alarm while her father calmly handed her mother a tissue from the box on the dash.

"Remember, it's the future we're concerned with now," said Kelsey. Lynn nodded, sniffing resolutely. Parking the car in front of what would have been the small garden, Kelsey stepped out and opened the door for his wife. Brigid unbuckled her seatbelt, wincing in pain as she shifted toward the door.

"Stay put, we'll help you," said Kelsey, opening the back door. Both parents reached out and Brigid grasped their hands, picking gingerly at her footing.

"Why did you want to come here?" Brigid asked her mother, as she leaned onto her father's arm.

"Because you did," answered Lynn, looking into her daughter's blue eyes. The color struck an arrow into her heart to this day. She watched the teal darken and then lighten as Brigid's eyes adjusted to the sun. Instead of blocking the feeling and turning away, Lynn let that intense love and fear wash over her face.

"And you certainly can't drive yourself," added Kelsey, smiling and planting a kiss on her curls.

"I certainly can't do much myself," muttered Brigid. "My life is suspended."

"Your life is not suspended. You have to keep putting one foot in front of the other, whether you want to or not. Life goes on, kiddo, no matter how painful it is."

Brigid forced a smile. The doctors promised her body would heal in time. Brigid hoped her spirit would too.

"I'd like to see the clean-up effort," Brigid said. "I can hear the boats." She caught the smile her parents exchanged above her head. "What?" she asked.

"Nothing," Lynn said. "Let's go." Taking Brigid's other hand, the three walked slowly over the slate pathway. The clothes line had fallen with the tree on which it was hung, but the thin rope was wound neatly on the ground. Stepping carefully on her wounded leg, she noticed the sand was raked as well. Had David really done all this? She heard his cottage was damaged beyond repair; how would he have time?

"Look up." Lynn's squeezed her daughter's arm. Brigid lifted her chin and saw the lake. Fishing boats zigged and zagged across. The sweet coves and inlets of their shoreline were gone, ripped up by the storm, and she could nearly see the entire perimeter of the lake. The new unguarded landscape shook her senses. She turned away. There was no other place for her eyes to rest but on the grave that once was Cairn Cottage.

A small cobalt structure rose where the picture window towered over the tree branches just a few weeks ago. Large stones surrounded the bottom, and the sound of hammering could be heard over the boats. Mesmerized, she let go of her parents' hands and walked slowly toward the sound.

"Be careful!" Lynn choked, squeezing hard on her arm.

"Let her go," said Kelsey, gently pulling his wife's hand away.

The pieces of slate that had once snaked around the rattle-trap cottage were re-laid in a neat pathway. They led to the front door of the structure. Brigid ran her hand over the railing of the porch. The wood under her palm felt familiar. Gazing at its grayed tint, she realized it was a board from the dock. She pulled herself up the steps, tears in her eyes. She had accepted that this property now belonged to strangers, but seeing how the new owners used the very boards of the Cairn Cottage to build this new home was a pain she didn't know if she could bear. The front door was a work of art, fashioned from the boards of the house. The knots and markings of the old pine made her ache for the home she had grown to love.

Brigid wanted to scramble down the steps, run back, run away. She could see the life she could have lived, the truth of who she was. Something that had been denied her for so long was now gone forever.

She took a deep breath. Walk forward, her father had said. There was no chance she would ever set foot here again, so she might as well say goodbye. This little house broke her heart. It was all anyone would need, nothing more, nothing less. Unwilling to let her mother see her tears, she walked forward through the space. She would gather herself at the back of the house and return to the car. To her parents' life. For awhile. And then she would figure it out. She would find a life she wanted, the life that was true to her. Somehow. With a broken heart and a broken body, she would live her one life on her terms, eking out what little happiness she could find.

Wiping her tears with the back of her hand, she stood at the doorframe of what looked to be a wide front porch. She contemplated sitting down, but knew her injuries would make it difficult.

"Let me help you."

A strong hand reached out from the sunlight into the shadows inside.

Gabe looked up at her. He set the hammer gently by her feet. Taking her hand in his own, he helped her step back down onto the fragrant earth.

Brigid gazed at his tanned face, his warm eyes, and astonishment filled her. Unable to stop herself, she gingerly touched his back. "Are you..."

"I'm ok," he said, taking her hand in his. "It missed all the important parts." He winked at her. "I just have a scar and some pain."

"I'm so sorry," Brigid said.

"I'm so sorry," said Gabe. "I lost control of myself. Brigid, it will never happen again. Not ever. I'm seeing someone now."

Her heart rose to her throat and she looked away quickly, yanking her hand from his.

"No, no. I'm sorry — that's not what I mean. I'm seeing a doctor. A counselor. I will not become the man my father was." He put a hesitant hand on her cheek. "If it's still too much for you, if you don't want to get involved, I understand. This is for you regardless of whether you can still love me or not."

"I don't understand." Brigid found herself unable move away from his touch. "What are you doing here? Are you helping to build a house for the new owners?"

Gabe looked at her for a moment, taking in everything. The bandage on her leg, the pain that sunk her cheekbones and pinched the corners of her eyes. The new set of her shoulders, defiant and determined. He took both of her hands in his.

"This is yours, Brigid. The original buyers stepped away from the sale after the storm. I thought your parents would have told you — your mother put the land in your name. I'm building this house for you." Gabe knelt in the sandy soil.

"I hoped," he said, voice shaking, "To build it for us. If you'll have me. If you'll forgive me." He reached back into his pocket and pulled out a blue velvet box. When he opened it, the sunlight caught a brilliant diamond surrounded by polished stones from the lake.

Brigid stared at the ring and tried to maintain her balance, shifting her weight onto her good leg. She looked up at him. "Gabe, I don't want you to feel like you need to take care of me. I won't be like a burden," said Brigid. "I don't want to be helpless or worthless…"

"Worthless? No." Gabe stood and took her hands in his. "To me, you are worth everything." He stood up and brushed a tear from her cheek. "You call yourself helpless; you're not helpless. You're one of the strongest people I know. But everyone needs help. I need help, you need help. We both have scars. Inside and out. I love you. I love you <u>because</u> you let me see your pain. Of course I want to take care of you, for better or for worse. But what I really want…" He fingered a small curl that blew in the breeze. "What I really want is to walk through this one, short, amazing life with you."

"Gabe, I love you." Brigid swallowed hard and looked out at the shining waters of the lake shining. "What I feel for you is unlike anything I've experienced. It's just… it's right." Relief washed over Gabe's face. Brigid pulled away. "I lost you, though," she said. "Twice. And it nearly broke me. I can't lose you again."

"You won't lose me." Gabe said. "If you say no, I understand. I'll finish this house, hand you the key, and love you from afar for the rest of my life." Gabe smiled. It was such a relief to speak the truth. He looked at her, arrested by those giant blue eyes. "The way I love you is just part of my reality now. It's a part of my being. It's never going to go away, and I'm ok with that. No matter what you decide."

"I never even thought of saying no," Brigid said, looking up into his eyes. "Gabe, I think loved you from the moment we stood in Big Omann Lake, naming the stars. I fell in love with you that night. Nothing can change that, no matter how much it hurts."

"I can't promise that there won't be more hurt, or more hardship in life. I wish I could, but I can't. But what I can promise you Brigid, is that I will never hurt you. And that you can be yourself, your whole self, and I will love every part of you until I draw my last breath. And then maybe more."

"Then there's nothing left to do," said Brigid, reaching up to pull his face to hers. The leaves rustled above them as they kissed. She pulled back and looked him in the eyes. "Let's walk through this life together. My answer is yes."

✳ ✳ ✳

The sun shone through the clouds as Lynn and Kelsey stepped around the small structure. Lynn embraced her daughter and praised the ring with genuine admiration. Kelsey heartily shook hands with his son-in-law to be. Brigid's delicate body was led to a chair by Kelsey and Gabe. They sat in the sunshine, the sharp scent of the cleansing minerals on the late summer air. After a little while, David walked down with a bottle of wine and some glasses. Kelsey shook hands heartily with him and they toasted the young couple. Lynn stepped forward to wrap the older man in a quick gentle embrace, one rebellious tear falling on the soft fabric of his shirt. Graham and Emma tentatively turned around the bend and walked toward the group. Brigid greeted them all with a kindness that obliterated any past discontent. After Brigid and Gabe gave a tour of the new little house, chairs were gathered in a semi-circle in the sandy yard. They spoke confidently of repairs to all the cottages, arborists who would assess the trees, and the science that had saved the waters. More quietly, the names of Shannon, Nieve, and Morgan graced the air. Seven people, carrying scars seen and unseen brokered a fragile peace under the swaying branches of the birch trees as they spoke of the places and people they all had loved. This was what friendship was, they thought, as they sipped the last of David's wine. This is what family meant.

At dusk, Brigid rose and walked to the edge of the shoreline. The boats with their hoses had dispersed and the water was at peace. Gazing at the horizon, she opened herself up to hear whatever needed to be said. That voice, that eternal spirit that she had found on the dock, in the words of poetry, in Gabe's eyes, in Rosie, on that terrible night in the hospital, that voice that sounded so much like her own, whispered through the trees.

You are a conduit of love. This is what I made you for, so that you can share the love and grace that you feel now. But, to feel love, to share love, you also must feel the pain and suffering. How else can you understand? How can you have the courage to shine love into the darkness of the world?

You are divine. You are eternity. You are love.

The voice faded into evening birdsong. Brigid knew that someday she would fade away, slip into the misty peace of the eternal.

She felt herself being filled with a great power, but this time it was not the relief of eternity. Brigid was filled with the exquisite, fleeting joy of life.

THE END

ACKNOWLEDGE-MENTS

I hope this book is a reflection of truth. The truth of pain, the truth of love, the truth of living. I would like to thank the women who walked before me and continue to inspire me with their truths. To my grandma, Carol Young Austin, who taught me to work hard, have a backbone of steel, and love fiercely, this book is for you. To my Mimi, whose name was Grace Marie Rankin, but it was going to be Rose Marie Rankin. You taught me to build fairy houses, hold dragonflies, and embrace the power of my imagination, this book is for you. To my great-grandmother Nellie Young, who dared to walk out of a cruel home with only the clothes on her back and late mother's pearls in search of a life of meaning, this book is for you.

I would like to thank my parents, Sharon and Dan Rankin, for giving me a life filled with kindness, safety, education, and unending support. I thank my Dad for nonchalantly expecting that we would become our best selves and rise to our fullest potential, and giving us every opportunity to do so. Thank you for reading "Little Women" to me, even if you were rolling your eyes the entire time, and taking me to visit Louisa May Alcott's Hill House. Thank you for giving me big fat books to read when I was a little scrawny girl. I thank my Mom for being just the best mom and grandma in the world. Your support, love and selfless giving to everyone around you is simply unparalleled. Thank you for your line edits on the manuscript and all of your advice on the medical side of things. And thank you listening to me describe the story in excruciating detail until two in the morning months before I let you read one word of it, and then getting up four hours later to feed us all a giant Up North breakfast.

I thank my editor, Aimé Merizon, for her beautiful and comprehensive edits on this work. I am so grateful the education I received through her. I adored our hours on the phone, discussing metaphor, themes, truth, debating the true meaning of the word "cherish." A' kept me honest on the workings of nature, encouraged me to lean into the experience of Up North, and truly raised this book to another level.

Thank you to the Plymouth District Library for helping me find and check out every single book about writing and publishing novels. And thank you for your encouragement.

Thank you to Lisa Mesanza of Lisa Mesanza Photography for the wonderful headshots, and for being such a fun and encouraging collaborator and friend.

Thanks to my friend Courtney Rowley for reading an early draft and giving incredible feedback in her precise, kind, and brilliant way. As has been the truth since college, your intelligence and attention to detail has made my work better. Lynn thanks you for the opportunity to become a well-rounded character rooted in truth and tragedy rather than a "Disney Villain."

Thanks to my friend Laura Wilcox-Curll for always immediately answering texts, messages, and phone calls as I agonized over the book and life. Thank you for always giving me your love, understanding, and thoughtfulness, even as you juggled a full-time job and raising a beautiful baby during a pandemic. Your support and love are centerpieces in my life.

To my bestest childhood friend Lauren Kushion; my essential older sister, my Be-Fri, thank you for being by my side since we were tiny. Thank you for seeing me for who I am and for telling me that I could be a Mermaid in a world of Giants, Wizards, and Dwarfs. This book could not have been possible without the years of stories we told and acted out in the basement. Chapter 24 is dedicated to you.

To my brother Bill Rankin, thank you for looking at me askance and saying "Of course you should; you're a singer." "Of course you should; you're a teacher." "Of course you should; you're a writer." Thank you, from… the World, here in writing, for being one of the front-line medical professionals who nursed COVID patients during the global pandemic. You will always be a hero to me.

To my sister-in-law, Louisa Rankin, thank you for your endless enthusiasm, encouragement, and for all the medical advice you gave. I am so lucky to call you my family.

Thank you to my grandpa, Bob Austin, who always provided love, fun, and a giant warm welcome. I wish we had had so much more time with you. To my grandpa Stuart Rankin, thank you for teaching me the names of the trees, reciting poetry to the little blonde girl at your feet, and teaching me how to make pancakes. I wish you could have read this book.

Thank you to Deb and Bill Covington for giving me such a beautiful setting to write and edit many parts of this book over several years. Bill, thank you for schooling me on the finer points of astronomy through the seasons and for letting me know that three full moons could not occur in one month. I will forever be grateful to Deb for raising Adam, and giving him her blessing to marry me. Thank you to Irene, Anne, and Sam Covington for your encouragement. It meant the world.

To my niece and nephews, Rey, Jack, Sean, and Luke, being your Aunt is one of the great joys of my life. You are a gift to the world.

Thank you for all of my tribe here at home who encouraged

me with social media posts, texts, hugs, calling out to me in the neighborhood as we were walking our dogs with "When is that book going to be published?? I want to read it!" We all work so hard to create the world we want our children to live in; this book is for you too.

I thank Dr. Robert Spicer and Dr. Amnon Rosenthal for pioneering medical techniques that could repair a baby's broken heart and thereby giving me health and life.

To my husband Adam, thank you for being my rock. Thank you for believing in me, and being one of the only people in the world to see my tears, my angst, my pain, and my extreme joy. Thank you for putting up with me and caring for me, thank you for all of your "acts of service" throughout our life together and as I took three years to write this book. The calm cup of coffee set down next to my screen and gentle hustling the kids in bed and picking up the house during some of those evenings and weekends when I was scrambling to finish this part or the next did not go unnoticed. Thank you for knowing that it would be a bad idea for our marriage for you to read and critique an early draft. I hope you like this final version. I love you and I am deeply grateful for you.

To my children, Sophie and Henry, thank you for just being you. I could write a million books and have movies, a theme park, and a writing room in a castle. None of that would hold a candle to the joy and pride I have in you. Your kindness, creativity, intelligence, and enthusiasm are what I am most proud of in this life. Keep working hard, learning, and treating others with love and understanding. You are the greatest accomplishment of my life. I love you.

As an educator, I have to thank my own teachers. Dianna Long, Peggy Dunn, Donna Dunlap, thank you for teaching me discipline, focus, how to write, and... how to read. Mary Alice Stollak and Freda Herseth, thank you for teaching me how to sing, the power of lyrics, how to portray true, honest emotions through music. To all of my professors at the University of Michigan School of Music, Theatre & Dance, thank you for never settling for anything less than the best out of us, your students. Go Blue.

To Dr. Eric Nelson, thank you for giving me the opportunity to sing with Atlanta Master Chorale. What I learned about artistry during those wonderful four years will stay with me for the rest of my life. My experience in Atlanta Master Chorale will be a part of every lesson I ever teach and every creation I ever make. To Toni Myers, Jamie Clements, and Jeffrey Clanton, thank you for encouraging me to join the team and allowing me to create and write the blog for Atlanta Master Chorale. Your kindness, intelligence, and innovation created an environment that was truly unique and truly special. I learned so much from being in your presence. Thank you.

Lastly, I would like to thank my students. Your drive, creativity, musicianship, and kindness inspire me each day. I want you to know that this book didn't get written because I am some brilliant person with special abilities. It got written and published because of really hard work. I worked incredibly hard, learned a ton, asked for help from lots of people who know more than me, and put aside distractions like social media and TV. Please let me tell you again that you *can* achieve whatever it is you are dreaming of achieving. You only need to apply the Three Rules of Becoming a Great Musician: Practice, Practice, Practice.

ABOUT THE AUTHOR

Kathryn Rankin Covington

 Kathryn Rankin Covington is a teacher, writer, and singer. A proud graduate of the University of Michigan School of Music, Theatre & Dance, Kathryn has been writing since childhood, and currently teaches music in Michigan. She has lived in Michigan, Denver, and Georgia, where she performed as a chorister with the world-renowned Atlanta Master Chorale, and worked as the blog writer of same.

Kathryn had the great privilege of living briefly on the Leelanau Peninsula in northern Michigan. The beauty of Up North inspires much of her work. Currently, Kathryn resides in metro-Detroit with her husband, two children, their crazy dog, and rotating school of fish.